Ogrefish

Gary Freemantle

This book is for Javier who supported me all the way

Cover illustration by Victoria Stevens

Chapter One

At last the creature could breathe.

It opened its cavernous mouth and savoured the refreshing current. Oxygen surged through its gills and energised its body. Every muscle tingled with life.

It was a blessed relief after the time of suffocation. A time when suddenly it had struggled for every breath. Struggled to gulp the sea like never before, but to no effect.

On the verge of losing consciousness, whether by luck or instinct, it had swum up and up and up, further than it had ever ventured before, into a whole new world.

It was an unfamiliar world. But it felt good. And not just because of the oxygen.

The creature had spent its life in oppressive blackness. Where the only lights came either from prey or other predators. Where the immense body of the ocean gripped you on all sides.

In this new place the creature felt lighter and could move more freely through the thin water. Here, its milky blue eyes could make out blurred new shapes.

Exciting new smells too. So many scent trails. Promises of food.

It caught one now. The scent of something big, and full of fat.

It followed the scent, swaying its black scaly tail back and forth.

But the trail quickly petered out. It was too slow. The big, fat prey was gone. Despite the thinner water and invigorating oxygen the creature seemed lethargic here compared to those around it. Everywhere it looked blurred shapes darted at unfamiliar speeds.

Food had been scarce in the black world, but at least it had been slow and easy to catch when you found it. Pick up a scent, follow it, sense the prey in front of you, and open your mouth. If it was small, suck it in and swallow it whole. If it was big, then bite, and bite, and bite. Nothing was too small and nothing was too big. You couldn't afford to be choosy. You couldn't let anything get away. And nothing did get away once speared on its silvery fangs.

Now it could breathe, but now it might starve.

Something clicked in its resilient primordial brain. A survival instinct to follow a pattern of success. It had swum upwards to escape suffocation. It should swim upwards again to escape hunger.

Its milky eyes surveyed the territory above it. A dazzling bright sheet seared its retinas. But the creature was immune to pain. Or fear. It was a hunter and a survivor. Its kind were as old as the seas. It would always find a way.

It turned up towards the searing brightness.

Perhaps there it would find a slower prey.

Chapter Two

William Sanders savoured the scented humid air of the tropical island as he walked along the newly laid wooden path leading from his temporary office in the staff block to the main hotel building.

The winding path was lined with lush tropical bushes and palm trees. His thick curly brown hair continually brushed against overhanging fronds and branches. This would probably only be a problem for him though as hotel guests would be restricted from this area and the average height of the local staff was well under his own 6 foot 4 frame.

The early morning was warm and thick with the fragrance of tropical flowers. It was mid December but the temperature in The Maldives remained pretty much the same throughout the year, only dipping a little at night. It might rain maybe twice a week but these were usually short heady downpours. The sunshine was never far away.

He smiled to himself. It was all a big contrast from the company's headquarters, and his home, in the Bavarian mountains in southern Germany. There the winter snows had come early, to the delight of the local ski buffs.

A contrast too from his last resort launch just a few weeks ago. The Australian Outback had been hot too, but it was a completely different feeling. The air dry as a bone. No scents, no moisture, no sea. Lots of flies though, which had proved a bugger to control. Not really his scene but the research had shown a huge demand for a super-luxury hotel in the remote Australian desert and it had been proven right. More important, it was a perfect place for the company to realise its goal of turning areas of wasteland into little zones of tourist paradise.

He was on his way to the hotel foyer to meet yet another group of travel journalists. It was not strictly his job, but journalists liked him according to the PR agency. At least, they liked him a lot more than his boss, the company's Head of Marketing.

He took a Staff Only door into the back of the main hotel complex, descended a stairwell to an underground corridor, which allowed staff to avoid disturbing guests, and walked the width of the building to enter the foyer, a huge high-ceilinged room. He paused in the doorway and looked around. It was a beautiful space. Polished hardwood, bamboo features, luxurious white furniture, and brightly coloured artwork.

This was the newest, biggest, most luxurious resort in The Maldives. As with The Life Group's last resort in Australia he had overseen all marketing and publicity, from initial announcement of the chosen site, through the laying of the first foundation stone and recruitment of local staff, to the pre-launch build up to attract the first guests. And in two days, the launch.

He walked in and nodded to the three receptionists behind their long welcome desk on his right. Two of them stood behind shiny new checking-in computer consoles. The third had wires sticking out of a hole in front of him.

Will looked at the guy who held up his hands and smiled. "It's OK Mr Sanders. They promise it's coming this afternoon."

Will shook his head laughing. "Talk about last minute, heh? Good luck with it."

It was always the same, he thought. However carefully you planned there were inevitably going to be last minute problems. The company always intended to have everything finished a week before launch, but it had not happened in the three Life Group hotels Will had worked on so far. It always came good in the end, though. No need to panic.

He gave the guy a hearty thumbs up. A group of four individuals sitting in the lounge area in the far corner of the foyer caught his eye. They all looked very different – a bizarre mix of smart and scruffy, young and old, jolly and miserable – but all carried either a laptop bag or tablet. Journalists, thought Will.

He felt a presence next to him. And a lovely scent. Perhaps jasmine?

"Hi Handsome."

It was Lara from the London PR agency. Middle-aged, short, medium build, with a blond bob. Slightly heavy on the make-up and face powder.

"Hello Beautiful." Will bent down and she planted a smacker on his cheek. He'd need to wipe off the bright red lipstick print surreptitiously later.

He liked her. He'd worked with her before on the Australian launch. She was friendly and bubbly but efficient and professional. Unlike some of the PR air-heads he'd met before.

"So these are the lions you're going to throw me to today huh?" he said smiling cheekily.

She laughed. "You know you're brilliant at this, Will. You should do all the media interviews. And the VIP meetings. And the investor briefings."

Will put his hands together in prayer. "Please no."

"Why not. Anyway you faced a lot worse than this in Oz."

"Don't remind me! Who knew the resort was on a sacred Aboriginal site?"

"Oh really? You didn't know that?"

He smiled. "You still don't believe me do you? Cross my heart," he made the gesture, "I had no idea. I was told after it all blew up and had to face the media storm with practically no facts to defend the company. I was naked out there."

She raised her eyebrows. "Now that I'd like to see."

"Hmmmm".

"But I know, I know." She held up her arms in defeat. "You're taken. She's a lucky girl."

Will was not convinced his firebrand girlfriend of twelve months felt she was lucky, but he let it pass.

"OK, who have we got?"

Lara waved across to the journalists and started walking over to them, Will at her side. "Hi everyone! Let me introduce you to Will Sanders, Marketing Manager for The Life Group. I think some of you know him already..."

He shook hands with each of them as Lara introduced them. Lynda, a tall, slim, stylishly dressed lady from a glossy luxury travel magazine. Sara, her exact opposite, short, dumpy and dressed in charity-shop style – but incongruously freelance writing for a First Class inflight magazine. Bob from an international newspaper, 50's and smiley. And a pimply American youth called Leo whom Will had never heard of but who was "highly influential online" according to Lara.

Introductions over, Will got them all drinks – juices and coffees – and launched into his well practised spiel...

"A quick intro first."

They smiled.

"The Life Group has annual revenues of fifteen billion dollars and over 200,000 employees. That makes us the third biggest travel and leisure company in the world. As you know, we own hotels, residential apartments, shopping malls and commercial property across the globe. But what we are most proud of is our position as world leader in eco tourism and eco development, building and running resorts and commercial property in such a way as to enhance and benefit the local environment, and the global ecosystem as a whole."

The journalists were nodding and jotting the odd note. Except Leo who was frowning.

"You OK Leo?" Will asked.

"Sure. Sure. Carry on, man."

"OK. If anyone wants to ask me anything just shout. I'm here to give you whatever information you need."

They nodded.

"OK. The company's vision, set out by our rather charismatic CEO..." smiles all round, "Is to bring life to the world's barren areas. We select deserts, remote scrubland, wilderness, and any place where little grows and few animals live, and we create Gardens Of Eden, introducing plant and animal life. And then, sympathetic with the location and not disturbing the wildlife, we build a luxury hotel for people to enjoy the new environment."

Leo's frown deepened.

"It's a win-win. Dead or lifeless parts of the planet are revitalised, and people get to enjoy it. Ultimately to the benefit of all life on our planet. Which is why we changed our name from Conglo to The Life Group last year."

Leo finally interrupted. "I don't think the Aborigines would agree with you, Man. They were pissed when you guys stuck a freakin' great building on top of their sacred rock!"

Lara shot the young blogger a look. The two female journalists recoiled slightly, though probably more at the language than the actual accusation, thought Will. Bob just laughed.

Will was a marketing man not a PR man, but he'd been well trained in handling difficult questions from the media. He'd also been through this crisis recently and knew his subject well.

"Leo, you make a fair enough point." Don't be confrontational. Accept the guy is making a point, acknowledge it and answer it as factually as possible. No bullshit.

"Last year, as you know, we built a new luxury resort and commercial complex right in the middle of the Australian Outback. The Gardens Of Uluru. We transformed acres of barren, unused, unusable, fly-infested wasteland not far from Ayers Rock into a beautiful, green, lush paradise. Attracting thousands of guests, visitors, shoppers, even residents. Also attracting hundreds of species of indigenous birds and animals..."

"Yeah, yeah, but that's not what the people living there wanted. You crapped all over their religious site..."

"Leo please!" interjected Lara.

"Well you did." Leo stared at Will defiantly.

"You're not totally correct," said Will calmly. "We consulted fully and in great detail with the Aboriginal elders before building. We would have done anyway. But we had to of course. We'd never have got planning permission from the government otherwise. We did not build on one inch of sacred land. The site was chosen specifically not to interfere with religious sites or rituals. The elders gave one hundred percent approval. There were just two or three trouble-makers who had a vendetta against the tribe and they caused all the trouble. They said we built on sacred ground but we didn't."

Leo shuffled uncomfortably in his seat. "But I read stories online about it, man. Guys I respect."

Will smiled. "I know. But they were lied to. And they repeated those lies because bad news makes a good story. You know that Leo."

Will reached into his pocket and took out a piece of paper with names and numbers on it. He handed it to the blogger. He'd known this was likely to come up.

"Here. Don't take my word for it. These are the contact details of the elders. They'll tell you the truth. They're happy to talk to any journalist that, err, has doubts about the whole thing."

Leo looked at the paper and then at Will.

"You mean I can call them?"

"Yep."

"They're genuine?"

"Check 'em out."

Leo thought for a moment. "You mean it was all made up?"

Will nodded. Bob and Lara nodded too.

Leo smiled for the first time. He handed the paper back.

"That's OK, man. I believe you."

Bob, the newspaper man, laughed. "Great. Now that's cleared up. Enough of Oz. I want to know about this place. Has it really been built out of the empty ocean?"

"Sort of," said Will, relaxing back into his latest story. "Just like we took a desert six months ago and turned it into a paradise, here we've taken empty ocean and created a tropical island. Not quite from nothing though. On this spot there was submerged land just below the surface. The Maldives archipelago consists of around twelve hundred coral islands distributed along a thousand kilometre line and resting on a massive submarine mountain range called the Chagos-Maldives-Laccadive Ridge. The islands are grouped together in twenty-six rings, called atolls. Nirvana Atoll is a man-made island 50 miles below the southernmost tip of archipelago, but still resting on the same ridge, and also within the jurisdiction of The Maldives government."

"So this should be called Nirvana Island not Nirvana Atoll, strictly speaking?" asked Lydia with her polite posh English home counties accent.

"Strictly speaking, yes," Will agreed. "This is one island. We just thought "Atoll" sounded sexier. You're quite right though Lynda. You know your stuff."

Lynda smiled. Lara beamed proudly.

"Anyway," Will continued, "In tune with our policy of bringing new life to barren parts of the globe, we decided – with the full backing of the government and local community..." Will looked at Leo who grinned. "...To build up one of the many submerged islands into new dry land."

"Has this been done before here?" asked Sara from the inflight magazine.

"Yes Sara it has. But only around the capital, Male. For commercial, industrial and residential purposes. But this is the first time a whole new island resort has been created. And in so remote a part of the country. We're the furthest south and west you can get here. Way apart from other islands over there, " Will pointed right, "And with nothing but the open Indian Ocean over there," pointing left.

"The technology is cutting edge too. As you are aware, sea levels globally are rising. Perhaps by a centimetre every year. As 80% of these islands are no more than one meter above sea level, this means they could be submerged in a hundred years. Or less if the sea level rises faster. Some scientists give it just 30 years!"

Lynda looked shocked.

"But we have built for the future. This new island has been built five meters above sea level. But what's really mind-blowing is that all the buildings are resting on hundreds of telescopic pillars. A revolutionary new technology, developed by our associate company Conglo Design.

This means that structures near sea level – like the ocean villas – can be raised as the sea level rises over the decades. But it also means that even if the sea level rises faster than predicted – or if a tsunami strikes - we will still be able to raise the entire resort, up to another five meters higher again."

"Amazing!" said Lynda.

Even Leo looked impressed.

"The unsinkable island," added Bob. "But I have a question."

"Sure."

"You said the company philosophy is to create life in barren regions. I know there was no land here so no land animals. But surely there was sealife?"

"Not so much, no. The Maldives is rich in sealife as you know, but this little patch of ocean was a bit of a dead zone, from what I understand. So not only did we need to plant trees and shrubs on the island, we also created coral reefs all around which have attracted a huge number of marine animals. Plus we have our very own aquarium, the first in the country. Lara I think you're going to show them?"

"That's brilliant," said Lara, taking the hint. "Thank you Will. Now let me show you all around this wonderful paradise!" She stood up to gather her media flock together.

"You were brilliant. They love you," she whispered in his ear as the journalists gathered their belongings.

"You're welcome," said Will. He'd enjoyed it. He always did. It was a great company doing worthy things and he loved to talk about it to people.

"I'll leave you in peace now," said Lara. "I know you have a busy day. Goodbye Handsome!"

"Goodbye, Beautiful!"

They all thanked Will again and Lara bustled them off in the direction of the aquarium, the first stop on her extensive and oft repeated tour of the island.

Chapter Three

R ahul gazed out over the glistening turquoise sea. He was standing on the dark hardwood sun terrace of one of Nirvana Atoll's
luxury over-water villas. He leant against the handrail. In front of him,
the Indian Ocean, as far as the eye could see. A thousand miles over the
horizon was his home and family in India.

"Hey! I'm not paying you to look at the sea, boy! Get back to work!"

The gruff angry voice came from the ugly bearded mouth of his
boss. A South African man, middle-aged, sandy-haired, with a permanent scowl.

"I'll dock your pay, boy. We open in two days and you're standing
here daydreaming? Come on, get on with it!"

"Yes sir. I'm sorry sir." Rahul bowed quickly, grabbed his brush and
tin of varnish and hurried further along the terrace to finish his work.
He was not a boy. He was twenty-nine. But his boss treated him like
was a five year old.

The South African grunted in his direction and disappeared back
inside the villa to shout at more people.

There were thirteen of them working on finishing the villa. Small
last minute labour tasks. Varnishing, painting, polishing, cleaning.

Rahul had only arrived two days before, drafted in as an emergency.
He didn't know anyone at the resort, and had only exchanged a hand-

ful of words with the other migrant workers, even the ones here at the villa. But he guessed, like him, they were all from India. Probably all undocumented, almost anonymous. There were a hundred thousand of them in the Maldives. Attracted by the higher wages. All under the radar. All trying to save money to support their families back home. In Rahul's case his wife and three year old son.

He dipped his brush into the open tin of varnish, wiped off the excess on the lip, and began applying it to the handrail in long even strokes as he had been instructed. The acrid smell of the varnish mingled with the more pleasant fresh saltiness of the ocean. He already hated the smell of the varnish. Even after just two days. He thought even when he grew old it would still remind him of the pain of leaving his home country, his wife, his son.

He missed his wife terribly. He hadn't even had a chance to tell her where he was going, everything had happened so fast. He had heard about a huge international employer in The Maldives suddenly hiring temporary workers. Big money on offer for those willing to drop everything and come immediately. No papers, no questions asked. The ferry was leaving in an hour. Get on board or miss out.

A child was expensive, and there was no work in the village where he lived. Not much either in the nearest town. This was an opportunity to make enough to support his family until things got better. He had heard he could move from one resort to the next in The Maldives and find work easily. And be well paid. He would do it for a year and then go home. He could manage a year. No more though. No more.

His thoughts were interrupted by heavy footsteps coming his way. He sensed his boss behind him, looking over his shoulder. He held his nerve and continued his steady brush strokes. Presumably he was doing well enough as there was a grunt and the man went back inside. There was some loud shouting.

"Hey! Do I pay you to chat to your buddies on the phone all day? Huh? Do I boy? You want to chat all day you can chat all day, when you're out of a job!"

Rahul felt for the man on the receiving end of the tirade. It was probably the short skinny guy. Called Vihaan he thought. He was one of the few with a mobile phone. He would ask Vihaan if he could borrow it tonight to call a friend in his village and get a message to his wife telling her exactly where he was. All she knew was The Maldives as he hadn't himself known which resort he was to work at until he was actually here. And in the past two days the South African had terrified all of them into working head down in silence during the day while at night he had not managed to find anyone with a phone willing to share it. Vihaan would though, he thought. He seemed a nice guy.

Three hours passed, with the sun shining hot in a cloudless blue sky, and the ocean breeze giving occasional light relief from the acrid varnish.

It was now approaching six o'clock he guessed because the sun was sitting just above the ocean horizon. He had finished the handrail, the outer terrace wall and most of the decking. Pretty good, he thought.

They must all have finished inside and done a good job too as he heard the South African dismissing them and for once not shouting, which meant he was happy.

He saw the man step out onto the decked terrace and look around.

Rahul warned him politely, "Careful, boss. All wet here."

The South African grunted and looked up and down the terrace from where he was standing, inspecting the handrail, the wall and finally the decked floor. There was just a semi-circular dry patch at the doorway where they both stood, a little close for comfort.

"Looks OK," said the South African, almost resentfully. "Finish this," he pointed to the spot where they were standing, "And then go.

I'm off now. Be careful when you leave through the villa. Don't touch anything. Don't dirty anything."

"Yes sir."

As his boss for the last two days turned to leave he had a sudden thought. "Boss? What do I do tomorrow?"

The South African half turned his head as he walked away through the living room. "I don't know boy," he said with a dismissive half wave of his hand, "Not my problem. I'm done with you now. The ocean villas are finished. Go report to the office for your next job."

Rahul was about to ask where the office was but the man had gone. Oh well. He'd ask Vihaan. Was that what he was called? Someone would know what he was supposed to do next.

He looked back at the ocean. The sun was now setting. An orange-red disc melting into the blue. It was still bright but you could look at it if you squinted. He loved sunsets, and sun-rises. The only time you could stare at the sun. Beautiful.

He shook himself out of his reverie and set about completing his work.

Ten minutes later and all was done. He had backed himself into the living room, leaving a perfect freshly varnished luxury wooden sun terrace. He smiled at how wonderful it looked.

Then he walked into the middle of the living room and turned slowly full circle to admire the amazing luxury of it all. The high arched wooden beamed ceiling with two hanging fans. Pristine white walls with colourful framed paintings, a huge silver framed mirror, and an absolutely massive flat screen TV. Big white plump sofas with colourful cushions which matched he thought some of the bright colours in the paintings. A million miles away from his village shack.

But what impressed Rahul most was the floor. The edge near the walls was wood, but the huge circular central part was clear glass. He looked down and saw hundreds of brightly coloured fish swimming above and amongst a variety of different shaped corals. Yellow, blue and white striped fish; black, white and yellow fish; black and white striped fish; fish with blue bodies and yellow fins; orange fish; red fish; purple and green fish. Some the size of your finger, some as big as a dinner plate. Some round with pointy mouths; some with hard beak-like mouths; some darting, some stationary; some in groups, some alone. If he lived in this villa, he thought, he wouldn't watch TV. He'd spend all day looking through the floor.

He quickly popped in to the two bedrooms now he had the chance to look around. Again, huge rooms. The same luxury dark woods and white fabrics. So clean and beautiful. Next the bathroom, with its large curvy white bath in the centre and two elegant shower cubicles, one inside and one outside facing the ocean.

He finished his tour of the villa and sighed. It was all another world. Another planet.

The villa he now walked out of was the last in a line of twenty stretching out into the ocean. All looking the same and linked to the main resort island and its beach by a long wooden jetty. Rahul walked slowly towards the island. He had heard it was totally new. Not just the resort, the whole island itself. They said one year ago this spot was nothing but empty ocean.

Rahul wasn't sure he believed them. But it was huge. And it was amazing. There was not only a massive hotel. There were boutique shops, restaurants, a medical centre, private apartments, offices, a residential block for staff, and even an aquarium. He had only seen a small part of the complex as workers were not allowed access to most areas, even though the resort was not yet open and there were only a handful of special guests previewing the site.

Rahul stepped off the ocean villas jetty onto the long sandy beach. He enjoyed the feeling of the sand beneath his bare feet, soft and giving. It was also still warm, the sand and the ocean breeze.

The sun had disappeared now and the sky was still a blend of blue shot through with pinks and reds which changed in hue even as he watched.

He looked up and down the beach. Not a soul.

Could he risk it?

Not many people in his village could swim, but he could. His grandfather had been a fisherman and had taught him to swim at a young age. Since then he had always swum in the sea when visiting his grandparents on the coast. Despite the odd local trying to scare him with stories of poisonous sea snakes.

He looked again up and down. Still empty.

Nobody would see him. Especially not when he was in the sea in this dimming light.

A quick swim, then a shower back at the workers residence, ask around about tomorrow's job, and try and borrow a phone to call his wife.

He took off his T-shirt and dropped it on the sand next to the pot of varnish and brush which he'd taken to return to the office.

What if they were spotted by someone while he was swimming? There were security guards who patrolled the island at night, including the beach he guessed.

He picked up his things and hurried back to the jetty. He hid the pot, brush and T-shirt under the huge wooden structure behind a pillar where nobody would spot it.

Then he waded quickly into the Indian Ocean.

The water was warm, almost body temperature. Like a bath.

He winced twice when he stepped on broken pieces of coral among the sand.

There was coral reef under the sea villas near the jetty, as he knew from the glass floor of the villa. So he headed left away from the jetty and diagonally out to sea along the beachfront. Here he knew there must be sand and deeper water for the tourists to swim safely in.

He was a fairly good swimmer and felt confident enough to head on out to sea so he turned right and swam towards the pink horizon.

There were waves here but the sea was relatively calm considering its depth.

Rahul swam and swam. Breast stroke, the only stroke he knew. But long confident kicks and sweeps of the arms. He breathed deep and enjoyed the expanded feeling in his chest and the slight burning of his shoulder and thigh muscles.

He trod water for a few minutes.

He looked up. The sky was now dark blue and he could see two or three stars appearing.

He looked back at the resort. He was out so far that he could see the entire width of the island now. An island of shimmering pinpricks of light.

Time to head back before he got too tired.

He started swimming again. Long, slow strokes. Savouring the swim. Enjoying the spray in his face. The warm salty smell.

Suddenly he felt his legs bump against something hard. He must have hit a submerged rock. He cursed and stopped abruptly. He'd probably grazed the skin of his calves.

He reached down and felt his calf. He couldn't feel anything unusual. He looked at his hand to check for blood. He couldn't see anything on his palm.

Odd though that there should be a rock this far out. Dangerous too. He would tell the hotel so they could mark it with a buoy to warn off boats. Though this could get him into trouble he thought.

He trod water gingerly, wondering whether he should tell anyone. Strangely he couldn't now feel the rock. He made wider circular movements with his legs, probing the water. No rock. He must have drifted away from it. He looked around. Nothing but dark water. He bobbed gently in the slight swell.

Then suddenly a pain in his right leg like he'd never known.

He cried out in agony and reached down.

His hand closed around a thick long spike impaling his thigh.

He looked down and saw it.

A nightmarish creature.

A wide bony black head. A gaping mouth lined with long translucent javelin teeth. One of which had stabbed clean through his leg.

He gasped and kicked and kicked his free leg against the scaly head.

Suddenly he was yanked downwards by the impaled leg. He screamed but gulped seawater as his head went under. Panic surged through his body. He kicked and thrashed about with his arms but his movements were slow and futile under water.

He was pulled down deeper.

He struggled not to try to take a breath.

The pain in his leg was excruciating.

He could not hold out and involuntarily gasped, filling his lungs with water.

With no oxygen reaching his brain and body he could not struggle anymore.

In the last seconds of his life he looked into the milky staring eyes of his killer.

Then blackness.

Chapter Four

The next day nobody at the resort noticed they were missing one of their migrant workers.

Rahul's colleagues who had been working on the villa with him had all been split up and reassigned to other last-minute tasks. They thought he had been reassigned too, or didn't think about him at all.

The South African boss he'd reported to the previous two days was also now onto a new project with a new team of workers.

And the South African boss's boss, who was in charge of the workers' schedules, didn't notice either. He had too much on his plate with a million manic finishing touches before the next day's grand opening.

For Marketing Manager Will Sanders, though, most of the work had been done. Advertising and PR campaigns were planned over a year in advance. Glossy magazines had been briefed in June to enable them to print their gushing previews and glamorous photographs in time for the December launch. The advertisements too would start to appear shortly, with images of luxury room interiors, bikini-clad beauties lounging by swimming pools, and pristine palm-tree lined beaches.

Will had ten minutes before a meeting with his boss to update him on the campaign.

He walked out of the foyer and stood basking in the morning sun on the front terrace. In front of him were paths leading down to the beach and the ocean villas. They were bustling with activity. Gardeners, people sweeping the walkways, workmen doing last minute adjustments to lights, signs, handrails. It's coming together on time finally, thought Will. Thank God.

The Indian Ocean twinkled in the sunshine.

It felt good to be by the sea after months in locations far away from it - the middle of Europe or the middle of Australia.

He'd grown up by the sea. Born 32 years ago in a small Devon seaside town, raised there, playing on the beaches when it was sunny, walking on the beaches when it was wet.

The sea was familiar. But it was a love hate relationship.

He loved the sea. But he also had good reason to fear it.

He shuddered and changed the chip in his head to stop himself thinking about it.

Instead he thought about The Life Group.

It was a wonderful organisation. He felt lucky.

For years he had worked in marketing departments and agencies promoting cereal, dog food, nappies, cough syrup and other such delights. At first he'd enjoyed the creative challenge of making everyday objects appealing to consumers. Finding the angles and messages that would reach out and grab people's attention among all the noise. But after a few years the fun had worn off and he'd yearned to work on something more meaningful.

Then one day he had attended a marketing conference about businesses helping the environment. He'd been spellbound by the star guest speaker, Penny Crawford. The Life Group CEO.

She had taken over the mega corporation when her father, the founder, died. She had built it into one of the success stories of the

decade. And, already wealthy thanks to inheritances from her aristo-
cratic land-owning Anglo-Austrian family, she had become one of the
world's richest and most influential women.

But her business success had been built recently on a powerful,
driving care for the environment. Not just to protect the planet, but
to enhance it. Creating verdant paradises where once there had been
nothing but barren land. Or empty ocean.

Penny had talked at length in her conference speech about how we
should be more ambitious in our conservationist goals. Not just seek
to protect nature, but to enhance it. Her latest project was a case in
point, thought Will. Not only had she created land from the sea, which
attracted wildlife living in harmony with the guests – fruit bats, birds,
butterflies, plants. But she had also enhanced the existing coral reef,
attracting greater numbers of fish and diverse sealife.

Will remembered talking to Penny after the conference. It had
only been a brief encounter as she was being whisked to her next
appointment. But it had been enough for him to impress her with his
enthusiasm, and she'd interviewed and hired him the following week.
His first task had been to launch the Australian resort, which had
been a massive success, despite the odd attack as Leo had mentioned.
Nirvana was his second task and he was loving it.

He looked at his watch. "Shit!" He'd be a couple of minutes late for
his boss. And you didn't want to be late to a meeting with this man.

Will ran to the office of the Head of Marketing. He didn't have
far to go. Most of the head office employees who had flown in from
Germany to handle the launch were staying and working in the staff
block on the northern part of the island, but John Mackay had set up
his office in a luxury suite in the main hotel itself here on the western
side.

It took Will just a few minutes to cross the hotel and take a flight of stairs to the upper floor and walk the short corridor to the suite.

He knocked.

"Come in!" came a gruff Scottish voice.

Will entered. He was in a hallway with the main part of the suite behind a second closed door to his left. In front of him was the dining room which was now serving as Mackay's temporary office.

The Scot was sitting on the far side of a large oval dining room table which he was using as a work desk, with two laptops and a few files and piles of papers.

He was a man in his early forties, of medium height and medium build but nevertheless his presence was somehow menacing. He wore a navy blue Ralph Lauren polo shirt and smart chinos, which were incongruous with his rough pock-marked face and shaven head. His arms looked like they were made of solid muscle – not the bulging body-builder type, but the hard toughness of a labourer. Or a fighter. Certainly what people called "a bruiser". Part of a tattoo came out under one of the polo shirt sleeves but Will couldn't make out what it was. He looked about as far from the global marketing head of a mega corporation as you could get.

Will disliked his boss intensely but tried never to show it. The man was not only a nasty piece of work but he was also terrible at his job. Will had been continuously surprised since joining the company and working under him how little Mackay knew about marketing. He came across this phenomenon quite a lot of course – useless guys who had risen to high powered positions who knows how. But Mackay took the biscuit.

Mackay hated Will, and often showed it. Will did not know why because he'd always been civil to the man – despite his constant jibes and abuse – and he'd been highly praised by Penny on all his work so far. Maybe Mackay was jealous. Maybe he hated the fact that Penny had hired Will herself. Maybe he just hated everyone.

"Almost on time," said Mackay sardonically. He grinned at Will with slightly stained, slightly crooked teeth. It was not a pretty sight.

Will forced a conciliatory smile. "Sorry I was just taking a quick breather after welcoming the latest batch of journos. Lost track of time. What did you want to see me about?"

"Daydreaming while most of us are working eh?"

"Not quite". Will knew this was a dig not a joke. Mackay didn't banter.

"Should use your generous salary to buy yourself a decent watch."

Change the record, thought Will, hoping the man would get to the point quickly.

"Anyway," said the Scot turning back to his desk and gathering some papers, "I've been talking to the ad agency..."

Will took a sharp intake of breath. "I'm sorry?" Handling the ad campaign for the resort launch was his responsibility. And only he had dealt with the ad agency. Mackay had shown no interest so far.

"I talked to the MD."

"What? To John Badge?"

"Badge, yes. The top man. Well, I had to shout a bit to get to him. You know. Tear a new asshole in a few people...."

"But why? I don't understand. You now this is my agency. I appointed them. With your approval. And Penny's..."

"This is nothing to do with Penny. I'm Head of Marketing. Your boss. My decision." He prodded his own chest with his thumb. "Mine." Then he pointed at Will. "You work for me. Which means they work for me."

Will tried to remain calm. Going direct to the agency without telling him was bad enough. But shouting his way to the agency boss was embarrassing, and an insult to Will.

"John, you should have talked to me first if you'd wanted to amend the ad campaign. Presumably that's what you want to do?"

"Amend it my arse! It's crap! Look at it!" he waved the pictures and scripts in his hand at Will. "I could have done better myself!"

"This is the agency who created the Uluru campaign. It won awards. It created business. Massive bookings beyond expectations. It helped Uluru become the most successful launch ever! "

Neither man spoke for some time. They glared at each other.

Suddenly, like the sun breaking through a thunderous sky, Mackay's face brightened and his body seemed to untense. He held up both palms and smiled.

"OK Will. I could have talked to you first. I know they're your friends..."

"They're not my friends, they're just good..."

"OK. Whatever." Mackay sat down. "But that doesn't change the fact the campaign's no good. You need to change it."

He didn't know whether to continue arguing or to tell his boss he could stick the job up his arse. He forced himself to remain calm. It was business, not personal.

"You need to give me a bit more, John. What exactly don't you like about it? I need specifics."

The Scot looked phased for a moment. "Well...I don't like any of it really."

"Do you like any of the copy?"

"No."

"Any of the images?"

"No."

Will shook his head. It was like dealing with a petulant 3 year old.

"So what sort of images do you want? If not palm trees, sandy beaches and beautiful people?"

"Och, they're all trite, man."

"I don't disagree. But they work. They get bookings. And anyway, the way the agency has shot them they look completely different from the run of the mill tropical paradise images you usually get. They're a cut above. And there's also plenty of new stuff about the eco angle and all the conservation work. Not to mention the tech angle. The hydraulics and so on. So we don't look remotely like any other Maldives resort. We do look different. And better."

Mackay scratched his chin but said nothing.

"So what am I missing, John? What else do you want the ads to say?"

They stared at each other coldly.

"You think you're clever don't you, Sanders?"

"Clever? I don't know. It's all relative isn't it? I think I'm pretty good at my job though. I think I can get bums on seats at our resorts. Which is what it's all about isn't it, John?"

Mackay glared like an animal that's been cornered but is prepared to fight.

"You want to keep the job you're so good at?" he snarled. "Just change the ads."

Will's face hardened. He stopped himself from reaching across the desk and grabbing his boss by the throat. He loved his job but there was only so much of this he was prepared to take. "You're really going to talk to me like that, Mackay? With the launch tomorrow? You think I enjoy working with you?"

Mackay held up his hands. "Och. I didna mean any offence, Will."

Will stared at the man and shook his head. This was one seriously fucked up individual, he thought as he got up and walked to the door.

As he left he heard Mackay calling after him. "Will. Will. We haven't finished…"

He ignored him and walked on.

***

Will rumbled about the exchange with Mackay as he left the hotel building and walked towards the staff block through the lush tropical gardens.

He was naturally an upbeat sort of guy but now he felt dejected.

He knew the campaign was perfectly good, brilliant even. Everyone else he'd shown it to in the company had loved it. Even so, he wouldn't have minded if Mackay had come to him with real concerns about it. Positive criticisms. But it was soul destroying to be savaged by a man he didn't respect for reasons he didn't understand.

Mackay had done this to piss him off. And he'd backed down at the end because he didn't want Will to go. He needed him. He just wanted to bully him. Like he bullied everyone.

Well he can fuck off.

"What?"

Will had not noticed Lara next to him.

"Who can fuck off?"

Will blushed a bit. "Sorry. Did I say that out loud?"

They laughed.

"Good meeting with the Loch Ness Monster?" she said playfully.

"The Loch Ness…? Oh. You mean Mackay."

"He's a hideous man."

Will smiled.

"Every time I meet him he's rude to me. What's his problem?" she said, widening her eyes in exasperation. "All the journalists hate him. They want you." She touched his arm. He knew she was a bit attracted to him, but she was not his type and fifteen years older than he was. Thankfully she knew he already had a girlfriend who was due to come out the very next day to see him.

He smiled again. "It was...you know...one of those business meetings."

"But don't you hate him?" she persisted.

"He's not exactly my best friend. But he is my boss. And Head of Marketing."

"Tactful as ever, Will."

He smiled and shrugged. No matter how much he despised the man it would serve no purpose to slag him off to others. Well, it might make him feel a bit better he conceded to himself, but it would be unprofessional.

"Do you know, I don't think I've heard you say a bad word about anyone," she said, as though reading his mind. "Me, on the other hand, I'm a right bitch!"

Will laughed.

"And Mr Mackay," she went on, "Is what they call a 'see you next Tuesday'!"

Will laughed again.

Suddenly a thought came to her and she grabbed his arm. "Oh! I forgot. We were doing our tour of the resort and got to the aquarium and one of the journos is asking questions about an odd looking fish. Can you help?"

Will was puzzled. He was not aware there were any particularly unusual fish in the hotel's aquarium. But maybe this journalist didn't get out much. "Ok lets pop over now. I'm not a fish expert. But I know a woman who is. Was Fiona not there by the way? She's in charge of getting the aquarium up and running. She's a world-class fish guru!"

"No. There was nobody there."

"Ok. Let's go see."

They took a left hand fork in the path which led to the aquarium.

The aquarium was another unique aspect of Nirvana Atoll. Really just one huge tank and several smaller ones, but still the only aquarium in the country. It had raised quite a few eyebrows when it was announced but CEO Penny Crawford had been adamant that it was needed to help protect endangered species in this part of the Indian Ocean.

They entered the large wooden building and walked across a spacious room lined with the small tanks, some containing brightly coloured corals and fish, some still empty.

At the far end was the 'big tank', five metres high fifteen wide.

Leo, the blogger, was staring into it intently.

"Hey Will," he said excitedly as he saw them.

"Hey Leo," said Will. He'd begun to like this guy. He respected the way he'd challenged him over Uluru and then been prepared to back down once he'd heard the facts. "What you found?"

"A freaky fish, man! Like a monster. Huge teeth! So big it can hardly close its mouth!"

"A shark? We don't have sharks in the tank I don't think."

"No not a shark. Smaller. But scary." Leo measured with his hands a length of about a foot.

Lara laughed.

Leo looked annoyed. "You ever seen teeth like this?" He stretched out a hand to measure around half a foot. "I never saw a fish like it, that's for sure!"

Will stood next to Leo, intrigued. "Where is it?" he said, looking into the tank at sand, rocks and coral.

"Shit! I can't see it now. Where's it gone?" He tapped the glass. "Why you got a fuck off fish tank on an island surrounded by fish anyway?"

Will laughed as the three of them stood motionless, leaning in and scanning the tank with their eyes.

"Yeah. I asked the same myself when I first saw it."

"So?"

"Well, not everyone likes to dive or snorkel in the sea. And even if you do go diving or snorkelling you don't necessarily get to see every kind of fish that lives around here. Some are shy, some are rare, some even endangered. Can anyone see anything?"

Leo and Lara both shook their heads.

"Anyway, we decided we're going to collect together these rarer and endangered species so everyone can be guaranteed to see them. Plus we'll be able to protect them. We'll even have a breeding programme. It's all part of The Life Group philos...."

"There!" interrupted Leo excitedly. "There it is! You can see its head behind that rock at the back there."

Will looked.

He saw it. The fish was lying on the bottom behind a rock with its head sticking out. Leo was right. Will had never seen a fish like it. A huge black head, most of it taken up with a massive gaping mouth full of long translucent needle teeth. The lower jaw jutted out in front, giving the creature an even more belligerent look. Four teeth at the front of the jaw were longer than the others, two at the top, two at the bottom. Staring milky eyes were set high on its domed bony forehead.

Lara gasped.

"My God!" said Will, "You're right, Leo. That's one scary looking bastard!"

"What is it?" asked Lara.

"I have absolutely no idea," said Will, "I'll try and find our fish specialist – leading marine biologist I should say – and I'll get back to you."

But Will could not leave. He was mesmerised by the creature's otherworldly appearance.

"It's not moving at all," said Lara. "Not even its gills."

They stared at it.

The fish stared back.

Chapter Five

A few miles off the new island resort, in the deep ocean, local fishermen were heading for home after a good morning's work.

They had set off in five small wooden boats very early that morning. First they had caught small fish nearer the shore to use as bait. These they kept alive on the boats until they reached deeper water where the predators hunted.

As they did every day and as their forefathers had done for centuries, they had followed the sea birds. The birds led them to where schools of tuna were gathering.

Then they had thrown the live bait fish into the water to start a feeding frenzy among the tuna. That was the moment for each fisherman to grab a fifteen foot bamboo pole and cast their line. A barbless hook with a feather at the end of the line allowed each man to catch and land a massive fish every minute. With at least six men aboard, each boat could catch around three tonnes of tuna in one morning.

For the past few weeks though the boats had been catching nearly twice the usual amount. They had never seen so many tuna. They had never made so much money. They were very happy.

Now they laughed and joked and chatted on each boat as they headed for home – an island a few miles north of Nirvana resort.

The seabirds they had been following earlier were now following them, shrieking for titbits.

The fishermen talked about buying bigger boats, better engines, new clothes for their wives and children.

One boat was out a little way in front. The other four followed in a group, close enough to each other for the men to exchange friendly jibes and jokes.

Suddenly the jovial banter was interrupted by a shout from the lead boat.

The oldest man of the group who was sitting in the front boat of the group of four stood up and shouted for the group to stop. The four boats immediately cut their engines.

He turned his weatherbeaten face towards the lead boat which was 50 meters away. Its engine was groaning and giving off black smoke as it appeared to be straining against some force.

The old man cupped his hands and called to them. What was the problem? Engine trouble?

No, replied the captain of the lead boat. Seaweed. Watch out!

He moved to the prow of the boat and peered at the water, sheltering his eyes with his hands. Just in front of him was a gigantic thick green carpet floating on the ocean surface. It stretched left and right as far as he could see. They had managed to stop just in time.

He had never seen seaweed as thick as this in such a massive quantity. If it was seaweed.

By now his boat had drifted into the mat. He reached over the side and scooped some of it out with his hands. It was thick and gelatinous. Thick enough to clog a propeller.

He called again to the captain of the lead boat. They did not have rope long enough to throw to them and he was wary of more boats getting caught in the tangled weed if they tried to move closer. Perhaps first someone should try to free the propeller and then reverse out on full power.

The captain agreed.

One of the younger men volunteered to brave the gooey mass and stripped off to his underwear.

All the men in the five boats shouted encouragement, then watched hopefully as he dived in and swam to the stern of the boat.

He took a few deep breaths and ducked under.

The old man muttered a brief prayer.

A minute passed.

The fishermen looked at each other.

The old man called to the captain. How was he doing? Could they see anything?

They weren't sure. There was no sign of him. The unbroken green mat undulated gently.

A second minute passed.

The old man prayed again. This time joined by several of the others around him. They all knew the dangers of the sea but it had been years since they had lost anyone to it.

As the third minute approached the men began to get agitated. Three of them were already stripped to the waist and ready to dive in.

Then suddenly two hands broke through the mat, followed by a head. The young man spluttered and coughed. His hair and face was covered in the green weed which he shook off.

He gave a thumbs up. He'd freed the propeller.

A tremendous roar went up from the men.

The captain himself helped the young man on board and patted him heartily on the back. Then he started the engine and gave it full throttle in reverse. The boat strained a little but finally broke free of the strange green carpet.

The old man gave thanks to God as they headed for home, happy once more.

He would warn other fishermen about the green seaweed mat, though who knows where it would drift to. Or what had caused it.

The man who had freed the propeller seemed happy to be the hero of the hour. But his face concealed an unsettling secret.

He wouldn't tell them what he'd seen under the water. He was sure it was the lack of oxygen from holding his breath that had made him imagine things. His friends would only make fun of him and spoil everything if he told them.

Nobody believed in sea monsters.

Chapter Six

Will was just leaving the aquarium when he bumped into the person he was looking for. Fiona Bell.

They had met briefly during an induction session a few days earlier but had not seen each other since.

She was late twenties, pretty, stylish, with a vivacious, confident aura. Her surname was very English but her tanned skin, dark hair and deep brown eyes suggested a Mediterranean family link somewhere.

"Ah! Dr Bell! The very person I was looking for," smiled Will.

"Mr Sanders," she said in mock formality. "How are you? And by the way you can call me Fi now I think – we know each other well enough. But never Fifi." She wagged a finger jokingly.

Will laughed. She had been introduced as Doctor Bell at the induction. On secondment from the world leading Ocean Sciences Department of Plymouth to help set up the unique island aquarium, in exchange for studying the rare and endangered species. Will had expected some middle-aged boffin and so when she was introduced to the group he had grinned widely at her – a bit stupidly he admitted. Some dork had also wolf whistled under his breath. She had been completely unfazed. She radiated self-confidence, he thought.

"In that case you can call me Will," said Will. "But never Willy."

She giggled, in a way which Will found surprising and really quite attractive.

"Anyway," they both said at the same time, a touch self-aware of the childishness of the conversation so far. "How can I help you?" she asked.

"We've spotted a freaky looking fish in your big aquarium tank and my journalist friends are keen on knowing what it is."

"Ok. Let's go see."

They started towards the aquarium.

"A freaky looking fish? Nice scientific description, Will." She inclined her head and smiled at him. A lock of her thick dark brown hair fell across her face and she flicked it away. It was a natural movement, not intentional flirting. Which Will found even more attractive.

"Ok," he said. "How about this. Massive sharp teeth, ugly fat head, scary white eyes, scare the shit out of you if you bumped into it in the sea."

She laughed. "Yes that's pretty thorough. Doesn't sound like anything from around these parts."

"Or this planet."

They arrived at the aquarium and he opened the door for her with a gallant gesture. "After you."

She smiled at him as she walked past. He followed her in and found himself watching her shapely behind. He quickly snapped his eyes back upwards. Don't be a perv, he thought.

They walked over to the large tank. Lara and Leo had gone.

He pointed to the fish. "Take a look at that. Think I was exaggerating?"

The creature had not moved.

She frowned and shook her head slowly.

"Well? What is it?" asked Will. "My blogger friend is dying to know. Me too."

"I don't know."

"Really?"

"I've never seen this species. Except maybe….No it can't be."

"What?"

"Well, it looks a bit like a Fangtooth."

"A Fangtooth? That figures. Great name."

"Anoplogaster Cornuta."

"Ano what now?"

"That's its scientific name. But I don't think that's what this is. It's too big. And the Fangtooth is a deep sea fish. 2,000 metres. Even as deep as 5,000 metres. It's not a fish you see swimming around in aquariums."

Will looked at the motionless black scaly body. "It's not doing much swimming."

"No."

"How did it get in here?"

"One of the assistants must have put it in. We have had the odd fisherman coming in and offering unusual fish they've caught by mistake. We pay them if it's a rare species."

She looked harder into the tank.

"I think we'll ask for our money back on this one though," she said.

"Oh? Why's that?"

"I think it's dead."

She walked to a steep flight of steps running up the side of the tank and climbed up. He made a conscious effort not to stare at her bottom again.

"Hand me one of those nets, would you Will."

He looked around and saw a few long handled fish nets propped up against the back wall.

"You won't reach it with this," he said handing it up to her.

"It's got a telescopic handle, dummy." As she lowered the net into the tank she unscrewed the handle which tripled its length.

"Careful it doesn't grab you and pull you in, Fi." He was enjoying this little adventure.

"I have done this before, you know. Anyway, it's dead. It's not about to pull anyone in."

He smiled and pressed his head against the glass to watch. She aimed the net at the tail of the fish, which was hidden from Will's view behind a rock. As she tried to scoop it she nudged it and he saw the head jerk forward and the mouth gape as though the creature had sprung to life. At that moment his phone vibrated and rang in his pocket.

"Ahhh!" he yelped instinctively.

She let out a cry too and dropped the net into the tank.

Will saw the fish now lying motionless on its side.

"Sorry, sorry," he said raising his hands sheepishly.

"What the...?"

"Just my phone." It was a text from Mackay summoning him urgently.

He felt like a dolt. But then he saw she was giggling.

"It's my boss. I gotta go. Can you manage without me?"

"Ummm...I'll try."

He handed her another of the nets, she blew him a kiss and his heart missed a beat. He turned quickly to conceal the colour rising in his cheeks. What's wrong with me, he thought. I'm not a teenager for God's sake.

He left reluctantly to see what the Scot wanted. How much more annoying could this man get? First he'd interfered with his job, now he was interfering with…well, he'd interrupted a nice little moment. He swore under his breath as he strode towards the hotel building. But somehow he wasn't as angry as he might have been. Deep inside he felt something else.

Chapter Seven

As he walked the short path lined with tropical plants back towards the hotel Will daydreamed about the pretty and feisty marine biologist. Had he seen a spark of interest in those beautiful brown eyes? There had certainly been a wonderful playfulness in her laughter. Her giggling.

He stopped in his tracks. What about his girlfriend? Veronica. A fiery Mexican he'd met 18 months ago. It had been sex at first sight. Rampant, tempestuous. He'd found himself caught up in a whirlwind of passion.

But after a few weeks the whirlwind had subsided. The passion had been gradually replaced by something else. He wasn't sure what. He still found her attractive, but she had become clinging. Like she wanted to own him. To control every aspect of his life. She had opinions on everything – his clothes, his aftershave, his car, the décor of his flat, his friends, his family, his job…Especially his job. She said it took him away from her too much. It exposed him to temptations. Other women would try to take him away from her against his will.

Yes his job took him away from home for long periods, but he had never been unfaithful. Even in thought.

Until now.

As if by some divine influence his phone rang and he saw Veronica's face light up the screen.

What were the chances?

"Hi Ronnie!" He thought he sounded a little too enthusiastic.

"Hello Baby." Her voice was deep and dusky, with a Latino accent he'd once found alluring. "How are things going?"

"Oh good, good. Apart from You Know Who still being a pain. The rest is all going fine. Hot and humid though. How are you doing? I miss you."

"I miss you muchisimo, Baby. Muchisimo. But do you really miss me too?"

"All the time..."

"Or are you oggling all those girls out there? Lots of pretty girls, no?"

"Ogling not oggling. And no I'm not." He felt a tinge of guilt despite himself. Like you feel guilty when you go through the Nothing To Declare channel at the airport even when you really do have nothing to declare.

"But all those chicas guapas in their grass skirts...Have you been good really?" She was persistent.

"They don't wear grass skirts. And no I don't look at girls. You know that. You are my only girl, Ronnie."

"But why you not call me? You never call me." He pictured her pout from her voice.

"I've been busy, Baby. There's so much going on here. Lots of last minute things."

"If you loved me you would find the time."

"But I called you yesterday. And the day before. I call you every day. I can't call you every hour!"

"Maybe you would if you loved me. Maybe you're too busy with the girls. Say you love me."

Two young women in cleaning staff uniform trundled towards him pushing a trolley of linen. He smiled and moved out the way.

"Of course I love you," he said quietly. The women smirked as they walked past.

"I can't hear you."

"I love you," he said loudly but with little feeling. He heard the women giggle. He raised his eyes and set off again down the path.

"Ronnie are you still there?"

"I not sure I believe you."

"Oh God."

"Your voice it's cold."

"Look I'm busy. I'm on my way to a meeting." He was entering the back of the hotel now and heading down the staff corridor. "Can we talk another time."

"No. We talk now."

He was suddenly annoyed. "Veronica stop being stupid. You're being..."

He regretted saying stupid immediately. It was too strong. But as often happened recently in their conversations his annoyance lit a fuse in her to a powderkeg of anger.

"Stupid? You call me stupid?"

"That's not what I meant..."

"Joder! (Fuck!) Stupid?! When you go off and leave me all alone here while you are having fun in the sun and chasing women!"

"Ronnie for Fuck's Sake!" How had this conversation blown up so suddenly?

"Fuck's Sake you!"

"What? That doesn't make sense..."

"You don't love me! You leave me here. I think you go with women."

"Ronnie..."

"I not Ronnie! I Veronica! You no love me!"

"I don't have time for this now. You're being...silly."

"Ah! Now I silly"

"And I'll see you tomorrow. You're flying out tomorrow for the VIP launch right?"

She hesitated. "Maybe." She was suddenly calm, nonchalant.

He was angry again. It was like a see-saw of emotions.

"What do you mean Maybe? We agreed this ages ago! You're coming to the launch. You wanted to be here with me so I fixed the invite!"

"Maybe I come. Maybe I don't. Depend if you love me." She was icy now.

He'd had enough. "Suit yourself. I have to go now."

"No. You not go now..."

"I don't have time to play these games, Veronica. Talk to you later..."

He hung up.

"Christ," he muttered. And then realised he wasn't really that upset. He didn't care if she came to the launch or not. I guess that means I don't love you actually, he thought. And probably she didn't love him either. They should have finished it months ago perhaps.

He thought again about Fiona. And felt a tinge of excited anticipation.

Realising he'd been delayed by the phone call he ran up the steps to the top floor and then on down the corridor to Mackay's room. He knocked at the door and walked in without waiting for an answer.

Mackay was standing in the middle of his office stroking the stubble on his head. Will's eye was drawn to the tattoo on his upper arm. A winged skull holding a dagger in its teeth. As repulsive as the man himself, he thought.

Mackay shot Will an ugly smile.

"Like it?"

"Not to my taste but we're all different aren't we?"

"Aye. We are that."

Mackay sat behind his desk but didn't invite Will to take a seat.

"Good time with your journalists Will?"

"Good briefing yes."

"Well, while you were messing around with your friends I've been progressing our ad campaign."

Will was taken aback. "You what? I thought I was going to amend it..."

Mackay smirked. Again, ugly. "Yeah but you didn't think it needed amending did you?"

"No I didn't. It was pretty brilliant as it was. But I was prepared to ask the agency to change it because you hated it, for some reason only you know."

"Well in the meantime, my friend, I've been talking to Pollards and they've come up with..."

"What?" Pollards was one of the ad agencies which pitched for the launch business and lost. "But their ideas were crap! And they don't have our account – Badge & Granger do. You can't do this!"

Mackay leaned back in his chair and put his hands behind his head. "Oh, I can do what I like. I pay the bills. I've decided to pay Pollards to deliver a decent campaign. Something rather better than you and your friends at Badge & Granger could manage."

Will couldn't believe the man was being so provocative again. He strode to the desk, leaned on it and glared at Mackay. "Look, John. The original campaign was a great one. Nevertheless I was prepared to ask our very good agency to amend it to suit you."

"How very decent of you, Will."

"We are contracted to Badge & Granger and cannot just brief another agency behind their back."

"Really?"

"Really. I have no personal interest in Badge & Granger – they are not my Friends as you call it – you and Penny approved their hire in the first place. Pollards came up with crap ideas for the pitch. I'm meant to be in charge of the ad campaign and you've sidelined me."

Mackay grinned, still leaning back like he hadn't a care in the world. "Have you quite finished?"

"Actually no. I don't think this is working is it John? You want me to go? OK I'll go. I don't need the aggro. I'll stay on to handle the VIP launch event tomorrow as nobody else knows the details. Unless you want me to go right now, which I'd be only too glad to do." It was Will's turn to smile. He'd had enough of this arsehole. He could find another job like a shot, with all his experience. He'd miss it but Mackay had made it impossible for him. Seemingly on purpose.

Mackay hesitated. Will thought he saw a momentary flash of panic in his eyes. But it was quickly replaced by the ugly sneer. "I accept your resignation. And yes do stay to handle tomorrow's event. Not that it's that tough a job of course. Those journos are all a waste of time..."

"So I'll go today and you can handle them...."

The momentary panic returned, just for a split second. Mackay was obviously out of his depth with all this and relied on Will to do almost everything. Especially the PR side which freaked the Scotsman out no end. All those difficult people asking difficult questions. Much easier to buy the space and say what you want to say. So why was Mackay trying to get rid of him? It would just create more work and more angst. Maybe he had a plan. Someone else in mind for the job. Someone whom he could more easily control and who didn't answer back. Or maybe he just couldn't help himself. He just loved rubbing people up the wrong way and never thought about the consequences.

"No no, Will. You know these people. It would be good for you to stay for the event. Penny would expect it too."

"She'll also be a bit surprised to see me leaving afterwards don't you think."

Mackay's eyes flashed in anger and he sprang up. "Yeah but it's not her call. It's mine. So resignation accepted!"

"You're a strange man." Will said. And left.

Chapter Eight

W ill sat at the hotel bar and ordered a cold beer.

He needed a drink.

What a day. Fights with his boss and his girlfriend. He felt drained.

He had been battling with both of them for quite a few months now. In both cases there would be a fiery bust up followed by a making up, and then the cycle would start again.

Who would have thought Veronica and Mackay could be so similar? He smiled at the ridiculousness of it.

The beer was set in front of him. He looked at the cold beads on the outside of the tall glass, and the thick foamy head. Then took a long gulp.

The thought of leaving his job saddened him. He loved it – Mackay apart. He felt he was doing good. Making a difference. Under the inspirational leadership of Penny Crawford the company was really improving life on the planet. It felt trite to say so, he knew – but it was true. Governments and industry either faffed around or passed restrictive laws – you can't do this, you musn't do that. The Life Group took a more pro-active approach. It created life where there was no life, transforming the wastelands of the globe into vibrant habitats. While making money at the same time – but money which was reinvested into transforming more barren areas of the planet. It was a glorious win-win. And he loved being a part of it.

The thought of leaving Veronica also saddened him. Wait. No, he thought, searching his feelings more deeply....it didn't. Why? Because the relationship had run its natural course? Or because there was someone else who had made something click inside him today?

He didn't have a chance to consider the answer. A large hand clapped his shoulder.

"Hey! How're you doing Will?" It was Bob, the newspaper guy. Jolly as ever. Will wondered if he was ever down. He hoped not. A bit of upbeat company was welcome.

"Hi Bob. Join me?"

"Sure. Great"

Bob sat on the next bar stool but one. The stools had been placed along the bar a bit too close together for two hetero men to sit right next to each other unless the place was full.

"Looking forward to it all being over after tomorrow I bet?" said Bob.

Will hesitated. Bob surely couldn't know about his resignation. And he didn't want anyone to know. It would be a distraction and he felt loyal to the company despite Mackay. "All being over?"

"The VIP launch I mean."

"Oh. Yes. But it'll be a good party. You'll enjoy it."

Bob laughed heartily. "Oh I always enjoy a good party! Cheers!"

They clinked glasses and both took a sip of their beers.

Bob wiped the foam from his mouth with satisfaction. "You handled the boy blogger well today Will. He's a cheeky one."

Will smiled and shrugged. "Par for the course Bob. He's entitled to ask whatever questions he wants and I try to give as straight an answer as I can. Anyway, I think I'm warming to the guy."

"Well I couldn't do your job. I'd get wound up I think."

Will laughed. "No use getting wound up. It's business, not personal. I know that. Anyway, we all have the same goal don't we? A good story. You guys only get difficult if you think we're lying and you need to expose the truth, or if you're bored with our version of the story and you need to make one up to sell more papers!"

It was Bob's turn to laugh. "Quite right, my man. Quite right. And I have to say you've got a great story here. I don't want to sound like I'm sucking up but The Life Group are pretty amazing in my book. And Mrs Crawford is one impressive lady. Do you see much of her?"

Will felt a twinge of sadness. He'd miss the company, and he'd miss Penny too. She was an inspirational figure, a natural born leader. And there weren't many of those in the world. "I don't see as much of her as I'd like. She recruited me and I update her now and then. But she's a workaholic. Manic busy. You'll meet her tomorrow though at the launch event."

"I can't wait. She's a hero of mine. Heroine I should say, but somehow hero sounds...er...stronger."

"She's a strong woman Bob – you can be sure of that."

They drained their glasses and Will asked to sign.

"Anyway," Bob continued, leaning towards him. "I just wanted to come and tell you we all think you're a star. We always get the info we need from you. No bullshit."

"Thanks." Will was touched, and suddenly he wanted to tell Bob about the resignation, but stopped himself. It was immaterial whether Bob thought he was a star or not. He would be replaced. Nobody was irreplaceable, whatever people thought. And the great story of The Life Group would continue to be told. By someone else equally as good if not better than him.

As they got up to leave Bob grabbed his arm. "One thing you should know though, Will. And we all think this. That Mackay guy is a complete..." he searched for the right term, "...well I'm too polite to use the C word."

Will shrugged. It was reassuring to hear from others what he felt himself. It meant he wasn't the oddball. But as usual he kept his mouth shut.

"It must drive you mental working for him surely?" Bob persisted. "He has no idea what he's doing as far as I can see. Any journalist who asks him a question he doesn't like gets blackballed. You can't work like that. It makes it look like he's constantly hiding something. If it wasn't for you there'd be a lot of journos writing a lot of ugly stuff about this company you know. Just because they can't stand Mackay and don't trust him."

Will wanted to agree but held back again. "I understand your point Bob. But he's the marketing head and so be it. He can't be that bad or Penny wouldn't put up with him."

Bob looked into Will's eyes. "This is the first time I'm not sure I believe you Will." Then he laughed and slapped Will on the shoulder. "See you tomorrow."

They shook hands warmly. "Goodnight Bob. Sleep well."

Will sat back on his stool. Bob stopped at the door on his way out though, and turned around. Something had just occurred to him. "Oh Will. I forgot. Leo asked me to ask you. Any news on that fish? The weird one? Leo told us about it."

He realised he had completely forgotten. "Sorry Bob. I'll try to find out. Let you know tomorrow."

"Ok my friend. Sleep well."

Bob left. Will took out his phone and called Fiona.

"Hi Fi."

"Will, hi! Sorry I should have called you."

"No worries. The journos are asking about Flipper. I'm intrigued to know too."

She half giggled. It made him feel...something. "Flipper was a dolphin Will. This is a fish. But quite an exciting fish!"

"An exciting fish?"

"I can't identify it as any known species."

"I thought you said it was a...what did you call it...Fangtooth?"

"No I said it looked like a Fangtooth. But the biggest they get is six inches. This one's over twice that size already..."

"Ok."

"I sent a picture of it to Plymouth. The Marine Institute. And my prof doesn't recognise it either. We think it could be a completely new species! One that nobody has ever seen before. It's amazing!"

Will felt her excitement. "Wow. That's pretty big news. There can't be that many new species found every day!"

"Oh...about 20,000 a year."

"What?"

"A lot of beetles though. Not like your amazing freaky fish, Will."

"Yeah, that's right. Not as impressive as our baby."

"Don't say anything to the journalists yet. We need to verify it. It would be terrible if we announced we'd discovered a new species and then we find it's actually a fish that's been identified before."

"But you said you didn't recognise it, nor did your professor..."

"Yes but we could be wrong. And there's a huge difference between a rare fish and a totally new fish. We have to get it right. For the sake of the University's reputation. And mine too. We need to check it hasn't been described before by anyone, and study its DNA if possible. "

"Ok I get it. Mum's the word. I won't tell a sole....or a haddock."

She groaned playfully. "Oh that's awful. But seriously...."

"But seriously, you can trust me. Our secret until you're ready. Then it'll be huge." But not my story to tell, thought Will sadly.

"We also need to name it and publish a detailed description…"

"Name it?"

"Yes."

"After me maybe? Sanderus Toothus?"

"Ha!"

"You don't like the name?"

"Um… actually…We might have to call it something with the word Giganticus in it."

"What do you mean?"

"Well I could be wrong. But looking at the reproductive organs and other factors, there are signs that the fish in the tank is just a youngster. Who knows how big the adults are."

Chapter Nine

After making him swear the umpteenth time to keep quiet, Fi promised to push the University to identify the fish as a new species as soon as possible. They said their goodnights – quite warmly Will thought, which made him feel good despite his underlying sadness at leaving. He would still be able to perhaps pursue her he thought. If he did split with Veronica.

Will then checked with his team that the arrangements for Penny's visit and the VIP launch tomorrow were all on track. Penny was due to arrive by private plane in the small hours of the morning. They were scheduled to meet over breakfast when Will would brief her on the launch events, and the publicity and advertising campaigns. The latter would be an interesting challenge, he thought. Did she know Mackay had forced him out? Did she care? He hoped she did but couldn't be sure. She was a tough cookie.

She would then give a speech at midday to all invited guests and media, before a grand luncheon. In the evening there was to be a cocktail party.

Satisfied the arrangements were sorted, he returned to his small room in the staff quarters and went to bed.

The day's events rumbled in his mind so it took him some time to get to sleep.

Finally though he dozed off.

And dreamed a dream he'd had several times before since he was a child.

The memory of an experience he had managed to forget while awake, but which he could not prevent coming while asleep.

He is a boy again. Ten years old.

He is jumping in the waves off a Cornish beach.

The waves are strong and persistent. They come in series of seven, building in strength, each wave slightly higher and more powerful than the last. Until the seventh wave, the Daddy, lifts him off the seabed for a few seconds before depositing him back down.

He shouts and laughs and revels in the power of the sea.

The sea sometimes holds him, sometimes pushes him, or pulls him.

It sprays in his face and he tastes the salt.

The waves get even stronger and he has fun getting knocked over and tumbling head over heels in the surf.

He laughs loudly and continually. He has no reason to fear the sea yet. It is playing with him and he loves it.

But then suddenly a new sensation. Instead of being pushed and pulled around his body, there's a strange force sweeping against his legs. The surging undertow sweeps his legs from under him. He cannot stand.

And now he is out too deep.

And the current which came from nowhere is carrying him relentlessly out to sea. Further and further away from the beach.

He tries to swim for the shore. He is a good swimmer. He won medals at school. But that was in a swimming pool with no current. This is different. For the first time in his life he experiences the unnerving sensation of swimming hard but going backwards.

He feels a pang of panic.

He calls out but nobody on the beach is watching.

The waves are getting higher too. He loses sight of the beach. He is helpless. A cork tossed about in a suddenly angry sea.

He's exhausted. He can't swim any more.

He treads water, still being swept away from the land.

He feels heavy. The force that was dragging him out to sea now starts to drag him down.

He fights to keep his head above water but can't resist the force. He goes under.

He knows he should not try to breathe. Hold your breath, hold your breath.

He sinks deeper.

He can't hold his breath any longer. He gasps involuntarily and gulps in seawater.

Will woke up with a gasp, drenched in sweat.

He sat up in bed motionless for a full five minutes, trying to control his breathing.

It had all happened to him when he was ten, except of course the final moments of drowning which were purely the stuff of his nightmares.

In reality he had been rescued by a brave and vigilant life guard. But for some reason the rescue never happened in the dream.

It had left him with a permanent fear of the sea.

He made a conscious effort to clear his mind of the nightmare, sprang out of bed and took a shower, focussing his thoughts on what he was going to tell Penny during their meeting.

He towelled off and headed for the breakfast room, the nightmare wiped away, for now.

He had only had one such meeting with his CEO before, at the Uluru launch, and it had been useful not only as a way to brief her but also to hear from her any latest news she might want to announce.

Better enjoy this one, he thought as he strode purposefully into the breakfast room. There won't be a third.

He arrived first and took a table in the corner for privacy.

There were a few VIP guests and media dotted around. He nodded or waved to a few he knew well.

He ordered a flat white coffee and an orange juice, and mused about her. He enjoyed their few meetings. She was a unique woman and had an extraordinary charisma. He'd met quite a few charismatic people in the course of his career – Mandela, Branson, Bill Clinton, five other heads of state... she was a match for any of them.

She also had more cash than most of them. In the world's top 15 richest women, worth $9 billion according to Forbes, which made her 20 times richer than The Queen. Though facts about her wealth were hazy as she hated people talking about it and the Forbes report had made her livid.

The money had only partly come from the company. Most of it was inherited. Her father came from a powerful Austrian dynasty with huge land holdings, besides a wealth of stocks and shares.

When her father died suddenly from unknown causes, she inherited billions. And the company.

She took her name Crawford from her mother who was British. But there too there was sadness. Her mother lost her mind after her husband, Penny's father, died. She now lived in an asylum of some kind in Switzerland. An opulent asylum Will guessed, but an asylum nonetheless.

Will sensed a sudden electricity in the room. He looked up and all eyes had been drawn to her as she swept in.

Penny Crawford. Looking a decade younger than her 50 years. Glamorous, slim, almost sensuous. Blond coiffured hair. Film star make-up. Light pink Chanel power suit. Piercing blue eyes. She owned the room. Owned every room she entered.

"Will!" she said with an engaging smile and outstretched manicured hand. "How are you?"

"Great thanks. Everything's on schedule. We're..."

She waved a hand and sat opposite him. He caught a waft of her perfume. "Yes I know. I didn't expect anything less from you. You're a pro."

He felt her compliment warm him. She only complimented people who had done an outstanding job. A good job got no words. An adequate job got a scalding rebuke. A bad job got you fired. Simple as that. And no second chances.

She unfolded the napkin in front of her and placed it on her lap. Will noticed his own unfolded napkin and quickly followed suit. "I'm famished. What are you having, Will?"

"I just ordered coffee and juice. I haven't ordered food yet."

"What do you recommend?"

"The Eggs Benedict are good. So's the local tropical fruit salad."

A waiter had appeared at their side. He was trying not to look nervous in the presence of one of the world's most powerful women.

"Aaah, Halloom. How are you?"

The waiter relaxed a little, gave a slight bow and smiled.

"Very good thank you, Madam."

"Good. I'll have the fruit salad and the Eggs Benedict. Also black filter coffee, please."

"Same for me," said Will. "Except the coffee."

"Certainly, sir." He bowed again and left for the kitchens.

"How did you know his name?" Will asked.

She tapped her chest. "Name tag. I have good eyesight."

He hadn't noticed. It was as though she actually knew the guy's name. She could have been a magician. "Impressive."

She ignored the compliment and fixed him with her steel-blue eyes.

"I hear you and Mr Mackay are getting along well."

It came out of nowhere and caught him off guard.

He hesitated.

"He's...um...quite challenging to work with," he said at last.

She smiled. "You mean he's a pain in the proverbial."

"Well...he's not making it easy for me to do my job, put it that way."

She leaned towards him slightly and lowered her voice.

"He's a control freak, Will. And a touch abrasive I know. But he's been my right hand man for a long time and he has many great qualities and skills."

Will wondered what they could be but said nothing.

"I know you're thinking of resigning..."

"I am resigning Penny. Sorry. I'll finish...."

She stopped him with a raised finger. "No Will. You're a good operator. A great operator. You're not resigning."

Will couldn't help but feel flattered. But he was unsure. "Well, I don't..."

Again she stopped him with the finger. It was becoming a little playful. They both smiled.

"Will. I've never – ever – asked an employee to stay after resigning. See how special you are to us? You're great at...keeping everyone on side. The media love you. That's very useful. This will blow over. I've spoken with John. He won't trouble you again."

He couldn't help but be flattered. This was a job he loved, and a cause he believed in. Who knew if he'd find another one quite so perfect. If Mackay had been told to leave him alone...And if he was valued so highly by the CEO..."I do like the job. And I love the company. Love what you're doing."

There was a pause in the conversation while the waiter appeared again and placed a bowl of colourful exotic fruit pieces in front of each of them.

Penny nodded her approval at the presentation. She poked at the fruit with her fork.

"You know, Will..." She speared a cube of yellow mango and held it up in front of them. "If people like me don't take action now our grandchildren won't know what fruit is. There will be no fruit. There will be few crops of any kind. Not much will grow. What there will be is famine. Right across the world."

"Because of climate change." He thought she exaggerated for dramatic effect but he was a believer in the threat of global warming and felt the world needed people like her to scare them into action.

Nodding, she took a small bite of the mango cube.

She held up two fingers. "Two degrees. That's all. If the globe heats up by another two degrees we lose a third of all known species. By four degrees and three-quarters are snuffed out."

"Scary." It was.

"And nobody's doing anything about it, Will. Nobody. No governments, no global institutions, no corporations, nobody. They talk. They set targets. They have meetings. But nobody's really tackling the problem on the scale it needs to be tackled." She prodded her chest with her free hand. "Except me."

Will was a bit confused. She was doing great conservation work with her company but was she really tackling climate change on a grand scale? "With your resorts?"

She smiled enigmatically. "No, Will. The resorts only play a very small part. There are much bigger things afoot. You'll see soon."

She clapped her hands suddenly. "So. All good. Let's talk about next year."

He was staying it seemed.

He was glad.

Chapter Ten

"**A**ch, he resigned himself," said Mackay into his office phone. The voice at the other end was brusque.

Mackay snapped the pencil he was holding and swore to himself. "Ok. Ok." He said into the handset before replacing it.

He threw the two halves of the pencil into the bin by his desk and brushed fragments from his palms.

He picked up the phone again and barked, "Get me Carl, now!"

He didn't understand why she had ordered him to reinstate Sanders. She didn't usually interfere with his staff. She liked him too much. The man was an annoyance. Always doing right in everybody's eyes. Repulsively goody goody. But with a habit of disagreeing with his boss far too often. What I really need, he thought, is someone who knows the marketing business but does as he's told and keeps his head down.

He admitted to himself his marketing skills were a bit limited. He'd learned the basics working in the marketing department of HM Prisons – it still amused him that they had a marketing department. But there he had learnt skills far more useful than marketing. In his interactions with various felons he had developed a great talent for bending the rules to meet an objective. Finding the shortest or quickest way to a goal while ignoring – but not alerting – the legal system.

His childhood had prepared him for this way of life, dodging and ducking and working in the shadows. His father had been an aggressive disciplinarian and his mother coldly distant. On top of this miserable homelife he had been relentlessly bullied at school. He'd learnt to survive by lying, cheating, hiding, trickery. He could more than survive in this way, he could prosper. Most people, however bad they seemed or whatever bad stuff they occasionally got up to, had some sense of morality and ethics – to a greater or lesser extent. John Mackay had none. That was his advantage.

So Penny saw some value in Sanders. Maybe she had the hots for him. No she was far too self-controlled for that. Maybe she liked the way his goody goody image reflected on the company. Mackay had little time for Penny's eco philosophy. He didn't give a toss about endangered species, global wastelands or shrinking ice caps. He just liked to do deals and make money.

His thoughts were interrupted by a weak knock at the door.

Well, he'd been humiliated and it had now become his burning desire to get rid of Mr GoodyTwoShoes. Without Penny knowing. He'd make her fire him herself.

A second feeble knock.

"Yeah come in."

The door opened to reveal a dodgy looking, scruffy young man, lanky, long greasy hair, and skin whiter than a sheet of paper. The only colour came from a few red spots and the grey circles around his eyes. The typical look of someone who sleeps during the day and stares at computer screens all night.

"Carl. Come on in."

The youth entered and sat down. "You wanted to see me Mr Mackay?"

"Yes Carl. I have a little job for you."

"Company job or private Mr Mackay?"

Mackay liked this boy. He was direct. He was also untroubled by the ethics of any task he was set. He just loved computer stuff. Mackay had come across the lad during his dealings in the UK underworld and had slotted him into his international marketing team. Carl did company work, but he was loyal solely to Mackay.

"Private job. Not a word to anyone, as usual."

"Got it."

"Look. Can you leak something to the media during this afternoon's launch event and make it look like it came from someone else?"

Carl looked slightly insulted. "You know I can. Easy peasy."

"Some fact or other that would interfere with the story. And which would particularly annoy our leader."

The youth raised his eyebrows. "Mrs Crawford?"

"Yes."

"Wow. What fact?"

"The thing she hates most is people talking about how wealthy she is. I don't get it personally. Perhaps she thinks it doesn't fit with her saving the world, I don't know. Anyway she hates it. You know there is a strict rule that nobody in the company is allowed to talk about how much she's worth."

Carl looked doubtful. "Seems like a small thing. Won't ruin the launch will it?"

Mackay wrinkled his nose. "I don't want to damage the resort, I just want to make her pissed off about someone. Really pissed off."

Carl grinned. "Who's the unlucky guy Mr Mackay?"

The Scot put his finger to his lips.

Chapter Eleven

W ill stood at the back of the restaurant admiring how it had been transformed for the gala luncheon which was about to begin.

Around a hundred people were gathered in groups of 7 or 8 around circular tables bedecked with crisp white linen, fine china and tropical flower arrangements.

A small raised platform had been erected at the far end of the room for Penny's short launch speech.

"Hi Handsome." Fiona had appeared silently at his side.

"Hey. I didn't think you were coming." He gave her a peck on both cheeks, catching a whiff of something like orange blossom.

"Nice perfume."

"Just soap. There's nobody in the aquarium so I thought I'd sneak in here."

"Glad you did."

"Really?" She surreptitiously stroked his hand.

"Yes. She's a great speaker."

He grinned and she nudged him playfully.

The hubbub in the room suddenly died away as the CEO of The Life Group swept into the room. There was a ripple of applause as she stood on the platform behind a lectern and looked out over the guests.

A hush descended as all eyes were fixed upon her. Will observed their awe in the presence of the woman. He felt a surge of pride.

Fiona caught his expression and smiled.

Penny placed her notes on the lectern and took out a pair of blue reading glasses.

"Ladies and gentlemen. My honoured guests. It is a great pleasure to welcome you to the launch of the world's newest island. Nirvana Atoll."

Hearty applause.

"Where once there was empty lifeless ocean. Now we have a thriving habitat on land and sea. A haven for endangered species. And at the same time, and in complete harmony with nature, a paradise for humans."

Equally hearty applause.

They're all hooked from the start, thought Will, scanning the guests. Not a dissenter in sight, thank God. He hadn't spotted any trouble-makers while he'd been on the island, but you could never be sure. He relaxed.

"More than seventy percent of our planet is covered by water, whether oceans, seas, rivers or lakes. Sometimes we can't get enough dry land to set foot on so we create artificial islands for our needs. We have been doing this for millennia. Five thousand years ago the native inhabitants of Scotland and Ireland built small circular islands, called crannogs, to use as dwellings. On Lake Titicaca in Peru there are forty floating reed islands used by the native Uros people even today. More recently of course we have built islands in the sea for other uses – Hong Kong Airport for example, and Tokyo Disneyland. Even the rather less glamorous Thilafushi island here in The Maldives, used as a landfill dump!"

Laughter.

"Today tourism is the driving force behind the creation of man-made islands. Dubai took things to a whole new level with the building of The Palm Islands and World Islands. We are indebted to their spirit of innovation."

Some applause. Will smiled to himself. "I put that bit in," he whispered to Fiona. She gave him a cheeky thumbs up.

"However I like to think that here with Nirvana Atoll we have taken the next step forward. We have created a new island where once there was just ocean, for the benefit not just of the tourists but of the local wildlife. The new reefs we have built are home to a myriad species of sealife. And our aquarium seeks to protect and preserve rare species in danger of dying out."

He nudged Fiona and she smirked.

"In addition, we provide employment for the wonderful Maldivian people, and a work environment which is future-proofed. Because we have built this island higher than any other, the rising sea levels will not threaten us as they sadly do most other islands in this great country."

Strong applause.

"When my father died so unexpectedly a few years ago I was proud to take over the great company he had founded and built up. But I also wanted to take it in a new direction. I signified this new direction by renaming it The Life Group. Our aim is to reclaim the empty and unused areas of the world. Bringing life to desserts, renovating industrial wasteland, reclaiming land from the sea. But all with the health of the planet in mind, all with ecological benefits. New plant life and trees, new coral reefs for sea life. Uluru was reclaimed from the dessert, this resort from the sea, just the start of an exciting resort building programme to create life where none existed. We have spent decades, centuries even, taking and destroying. Now is the time for giving and rebuilding."

She took off her glasses and walked from behind the lectern to the front of the stage. She looked at every table in turn as she spoke. Either she's committed the last part to memory or she's going off script, thought Will.

"But we need to do more than this."

Off script.

"And we will do more. Humankind can achieve anything we set our hearts on. We can control the planet – but for good not bad. We can improve and help Nature. All thanks to the power of our ever advancing science and technology. The future of the planet is in our hands. Thank you."

Huge applause. And then a standing ovation. Flashes from cameras and iphones.

Will smiled from the back of the room. What a company. What a woman. They loved her.

Penny held up her hands. "Thank you ladies and gentlemen. Now any questions before you enjoy your lunch and a tour of our wonderful resort."

Will saw Bob put up his hand. Penny nodded to him and he stood up.

"First let me say I think what you are doing is magnificent. A truly inspirational vision."

Good old Bob, thought Will.

"But can you tell us what's next? There are rumours that you have acquired land in the Antarctic. Is that the next resort? It seems to fit with your vision of creating life in deserted parts of the globe."

Will had heard the same rumour but the company had told him no comment. He wondered how Penny would answer.

"I can neither confirm nor deny that," she said smiling. "But I can say, ironically since you mention the Antarctic, you're getting quite warm."

Laughter.

A few more straightforward questions followed from guests and media around the room concerning the construction process, the expected number of visitors, the philosophy of the company and so on.

"It's gone well, huh?" said Fiona.

"It's gone great. I'm pleased."

"Are you working at the party this evening?"

"Just a bit of glad-handing. Nothing too strenuous."

"So you'll have time for a drink?"

He grinned at her. "Try and stop me."

Suddenly he was aware of a strange murmur rippling through the audience. He saw a few of the journalists staring at their phones or showing their screens to neighbours.

Penny looked quizzically in Will's direction. He shrugged. Maybe a world leader had died. Maybe another terrorist attack in Europe or the US. He hoped nothing so terrible.

Then Leo, the blogger, stood up.

"Mrs Crawford..."

"Ms Crawford. Or Penny."

"Ms Crawford. Your company has just released some interesting news. A bit surprising as regards the timing I must say. That's what's causing all the excitement."

Will caught Bob's eye. He had an odd look and was mouthing something but Will couldn't quite get it.

"It's about your earnings," Leo said.

Penny shot Will a momentary look of confusion. Then quickly regained her composure and smiled calmly.

What the Hell was this? Will knew he had to put a stop to it, take the questions into a private room. He started towards the journalist. "Thanks Leo, I think we can continue with the Q&A after lunch..."

"I think you're mistaken...Leo is it?" Penny said.

"Oh no," continued Leo holding up his phone. "This is from The Life Group. Official. It says that your latest new resorts, including this one, are predicted to boost your net worth to 9.3 billion dollars. Is that right? Is eco-tourism that profitable?"

Will was horrified. Where on Earth had this come from?

Penny lost none of her composure and confidence. "First, this is not eco-tourism. What we are doing is much more than that. But yes it is profitable. I make no bones about that. It has to be in order to be sustainable. If you make money by doing good then you can do even more good. If you lose money by doing good then the good work soon dries up. Second, as to my personal situation, that is largely thanks to my father. I inherited most of it. And intend to spend it continuing to help our planet and the life upon it. Ok I think I've overrun on questions unfortunately so we'd better crack on with the tour. Thank you again everyone."

Huge smile and final warm applause.

Great response, thought Will. She tackled it beautifully. But God she'd be pissed off someone had leaked her net worth, the big taboo.

As everyone filed out for the tour, Will grabbed Leo.

"What the hell was that Leo? We never send out info about Penny's personal wealth or anything else about her personal life. She's a very private person. Who'd you get this nonsense from?"

Leo looked surprised. "From you, Will."

"What?"

"Look." Leo showed him a press release on his phone.

The sender was Will Sanders, Marketing Manager, The Life Group.

Will's mouth dropped open.

Leo patted him on the shoulder. "Not your best career move, man."

Will caught Penny's eye as she left the stage. It was a look to kill.

Chapter Twelve

H assan had the whole beach to himself.

The launch event had finished and all the VIP guests were now engaged in tours on the other side of the island.

There had been some minor upset during the event - he'd heard from one of the waiters present.

He had been working non-stop during the weeks leading up to today, learning about how to be a receptionist at one of the premier luxury resorts in the world. He was now enjoying a well-deserved afternoon off before restarting tonight in time for the evening's party.

He looked around to check nobody was watching. Then he took off his tight and very hot shoes and socks, and walked down to the cooler wet sand at the water's edge.

Nobody would be around for a couple of hours but he would not take any chances. He'd just take a ten minute stroll along the beach and then head to the staff quarters to chill out.

As he strolled he mused about how lucky he was to have this prestigious job and what a marvel the resort was. And how his friends working at other hotels in the Maldives were envious of him.

He took out his mobile phone and shot a couple of selfies to send to his friends later – one with the ocean, one with the resort.

He was a bit in awe of the resort manager who had hired him. But that guy was a pussycat compared to the brutal looking Scotsman who had flown in to control the marketing. Nobody dared look him in the eye. He was terrifying.

Which was odd, because the brute's boss, Penny Crawford, the Top Lady as they called her, was ten times as powerful and spoken of with awe even by the resort manager – and she had smiled at him so kindly when he had been introduced to her at the staff meeting, and even asked him how he was enjoying his job. This was a very strong person, thought Hassan, but a good person. Quite rare in his, albeit limited, experience.

Hassan glanced at his watch. A couple minutes more and then he'd head back. He'd walk up to the end of the ocean villas jetty and then leave.

The sun was hot and he looked longingly at the sea. The water would be warm but still cooler than the beach. He'd love to take a dip. But that was a firing offence and completely out of the question.

He reached the jetty which connected the luxury over-water villas stretching out to his left with the beach and then a path leading to the hotel, restaurants and swimming pool to his right beyond the exotic trees and bushes.

He decided to duck under the jetty so he could sit in the shade to put his shoes back on.

The jetty was quite high so he didn't need to stoop. Everything at the resort was higher than usual. The sea level was rising a little every year they said and maybe when he was an old man many islands would be under water. But not this one. It made him feel an odd mixture of sadness and pride.

He sat and put on his right shoe.

Then he noticed it.

A dark shape at the water's edge right under the middle of the jetty in the dark.

When he'd seen it from the beach he'd thought it was a rock.

But it was clearly a body.

His heart missed a beat.

He stared at it for a few seconds, gripping his left shoe in his hand.

Then he put down the shoe and walked gingerly towards the object.

His eye was caught by an odd sight to his right tucked against one of the pillars – a tin of something and a T shirt and sandals.

Hassan looked back at the body and drew nearer.

The body was half covered in sand and seaweed and crabs, but the parts that protruded – right arm, right leg, lower back – were covered in wounds.

The poor man had either drowned and been partly eaten, or had been attacked by something, Hassan thought.

He felt sick.

He'd seen dead bodies before on beaches. Oddly for a country of islands, local people didn't always have access to the sea. Many beaches were owned by luxury resorts. So many people never learnt how to swim. Drownings happened. But he'd never seen a body with wounds like this.

He fought back the nausea and looked again.

He was a local man judging by his skin colour. Indian probably rather than Maldivian.

If they belonged to him – which Hassan thought likely - the tin and T shirt suggested he had been a worker at the resort.

Hassan closed his eyes in a moment of prayer for the drowned man.

He turned to get help, but at the last minute thought for some reason he should take a picture of the body. Maybe it would be useful for the police.

John Mackay walked out of the hotel lobby onto the sun terrace. He closed his eyes and lifted his face to feel the warmth and the gentle sea breeze.

He was pleased with himself.

It had gone well.

Penny had been fuming. She hadn't shown it. She rarely lost her self control. She saw that as weakness. Her demeanour had been calm, cool, serene as ever. But he knew from the fire in her eyes and the edge in her voice that she was angry.

He had acted the angry party well himself. What had possessed Sanders to do this? He knew the rules. Why had he not cleared it with Mackay in advance?

"Maybe you were right," she had said to him. "He should go."

"Well I wish I wasn't," he'd said. "I hate that his cackhandedness might have ruined the launch story. I'll have to go and try to rescue things now with the media."

"Yes do that. Thank you John."

He clapped his hands and opened his eyes. What a triumph. Finally Sanders was out and he could get a more obedient dogsbody. And somebody less cosy with his boss.

At that moment one of the local staff rushed past him. The man looked worried.

He was also only wearing one shoe.

"Hey you!" shouted Mackay. "Where do you think you're going like that?" He pointed to the man's bare foot.

The man hesitated. Caught between his mission and the rebuke.

"Sorry sir. Something horrible has happened."

"Yes you're going around with one shoe on looking like an idiot."

The man wilted before the Scotsman's scowl.

"Where do you work?"

"I'm on reception, sir. But I was on the beach…"

"You were on the beach? That's not allowed surely?"

"There's a dead body, sir."

Mackay suddenly lost his interest in torturing the man.

"What? Shhh. Come over here." He motioned Hassan to follow him to the corner of the terrace out of earshot of the lobby.

"There's a dead body on the beach. Under the jetty. I think he drowned not long ago. Not too rotten…"

Mackay made a face of disgust but said nothing.

"From India I think not Maldives. But working here. I found paint pot too which could be his. I think…"

"Ok Sherlock. Enough detective work. Just take me to the body. And…" Mackay grabbed Hassan by his shirt front and pulled him close. Hassan smelt his bad breath. "…Keep your mouth shut, you understand? I'm in charge here and I'll deal with it. We don't want to ruin the launch do we?" The irony of his words after what he'd done to Will were not lost on Mackay.

"No sir. Not even the Manager?"

"No…er…what's your name?"

"Hassan, sir"

"No Hassan. Don't tell anyone. I'll tell them. I'll handle it." Mackay pointed a finger at Hassan's face. "Or else I fire you, no problem, OK?"

"Yes sir."

Hassan led Mackay back the way he'd come, along the wooden pathways lined with foliage, towards the ocean villas jetty. As he walked Mackay called someone on his phone to meet them at the jetty.

Mackay looked up and down the beach. There were a couple of indistinct figures way off in the distance. Too far to see anything and not walking towards them. Nobody on the jetty. Nobody in front of the resort, most of which was screened by shrubbery and palm trees.

He looked at the body, the limbs, the wounds, the crabs, the sea-weed, torn shorts. He kicked it over gently to look at the face and chest. There were more wounds on the front of the torso and part of the face was missing.

"Christ, this is all I need!"

Hassan threw up in the sand.

"For Fuck's sake! Cover that up."

Hassan kicked sand over the vomit.

Then a voice behind them.

"Hey boss."

A huge mountain of a man with ginger hair and a fat freckled face burnt bright pink in the sun, accompanied by a wiry man that looked like a ferret.

Like the spotty IT youth, these were officially company employees – something to do with security – but really in the service of the Scotsman himself.

"Look at this, boys." Mackay directed his henchmen towards the body.

"Oh Fuck. Not good for the hotel, boss," said Ginger.

"No Shit," said Mackay.

"What do you think caused it?" asked Ferret, poking the body with his foot and peering at the wounds. "Sharks?"

"Probably," said Mackay. "Or conger eels. They can be nasty round here too I'm told. Anyway, whatever it was we can't have it spoiling things round here."

Mackay took out his phone and called the resort manager. They chatted for a couple of minutes sociably, and then Mackay asked casually about whether the staff were all happy, but to Hassan's surprise he didn't mention the body.

Mackay ended the call with a smile and put the phone away.

"Nobody's been reported missing. If they had he would have mentioned it. This is one of those illegal workers from India. He'll not have any records and he won't be missed. Get rid of him. Like nothing happened. We can't have this interfering with the launch. Or anything else."

Mackay noticed the look of shock on Hassan's face.

"Remember you. Not a word. Or you're out of here and you'll never work again."

Hassan nodded meekly.

"Here." Mackay shoved a bundle of notes into his hand. "This'll help you keep quiet. Remember, this is for the good of the hotel, of the island, of the whole country, Hassan. If people hear about shark attacks here they won't come and everything will be ruined. Understand?"

"Yes sir."

Mackay turned to the body.

"We can't help him now. It's fine. Nobody will miss him."

As Hassan turned to go Mackay suddenly stopped him.

"Hey, why were you on the beach anyway?"

"I'm sorry, sir. I didn't think it would hurt. I just wanted to have a quick walk near the sea. Cool down a bit. Take some pictures..."

"You took some pictures?"

"Yes. To show my friends."

"Can I see?"

Hassan handed over his phone.

Mackay scrolled through the selfies. He frowned when he got to the picture of the body.

"Did you send these?"

"No sir. Not yet."

"Not ever I think."

Mackay noticed the people at the far end of the beach getting closer. He barked at his henchmen to get rid of the body quickly and before more guests hit the beach. Then he started walking towards the people to head them off.

"Sir, my phone," Hassan called after him.

"I need to keep it for a while. You'll get it back, don't worry."

Hassan wasn't sure he believed him.

Chapter Thirteen

Will had not been able to talk to Penny after the launch incident. She'd left briskly and was now nowhere to be found.

He had immediately questioned his marketing team. They had all been as shocked as he was. Nobody knew how it could have happened.

He logged on to his PC. There it was. Staring back at him. The press release he'd seen on Leo's phone. Facts and figures about the CEO's private wealth and income. Complete with company logo and his own contact details. And sent from his own email address.

How had it happened? Someone must have hacked his computer. But who? And why?

The release was just enough to turn Penny against him but not so much as to damage the company. It would have been somebody who knew that releasing information about her wealth would really piss her off - not an obvious fact. Only someone working in the company marketing department would know that. And he trusted his team. Their shock was genuine.

It had to be Mackay.

He really wanted him out, thought Will.

Well now he didn't want to go. He'd stay not just because he loved the job, but to piss the Scotsman off.

If he hadn't been fired by Penny already.

He had to find her and tell her he'd been hacked. And that Mackay, for all the skills she saw in him – God knows what – was a liability.

Penny had a suite in the opposite corner of the hotel from Mackay. It took Will just a few minutes to get there.

He knocked.

The door was opened by her PA, a plumpish middle-aged English woman. She always looked jolly but Will knew she had a steel core. She had to, working for Penny.

"She's not happy, Will." It was the first time he'd seen her look so serious.

"I know, Margaret. But I can explain it to her."

"I do hope so."

She let him in. "It's Mr Sanders to see you."

The suite was a mirror image of Mackay's. Except the dining room he now walked into had not been turned into an office.

Penny stood behind the large oval table in the centre.

She did not look angry but Will knew she was, which made her a bit scary.

"Penny I know you're upset but it wasn't my fault."

She stared at him.

"The release was sent from my email account but it wasn't written by me or sent by me."

She moved her head slightly but still kept her steel blue eyes fixed on him. Her mouth was a straight horizontal line.

"My computer must have been hacked by someone. I think by someone in the company as only a company guy would know about the sensitivity to you of this information."

She raised her eyebrows a touch.

But still said nothing.

"I'm sure it wasn't one of the marketing team. I know you rate him highly but I think it was John Mackay."

She hardened her stare, if that were possible.

Finally she spoke.

"Really, Will? You think John did this? Why?"

"Because I don't think my team..."

"No. Why would John do it? What has he got to gain?"

"Well. I think he did it to make me look bad. So you'd fire me after all."

"And why would he want you fired?"

"Because he hates me for some reason. I think he sees me as a threat of some kind. God knows why."

"I see."

She moved to the window and looked out. He couldn't see her face. He wondered what she was thinking. There was a long pause while neither of them spoke. Finally, still looking away, she said calmly: "John has gone to smooth things over with the journalists. To refocus them away from writing about my...money...to writing about what really matters. What we're trying to do here. I think you'd be better at that don't you?"

"Well I do get on with..."

She turned to him and smiled. "Good. Off you go then. Thank you."

He was dismissed.

And still in employment it seemed.

He spent the next hour and a half talking to the journalists and influencers – some individually, some in small groups, depending on how he found them. Some by phone back in their head offices.

A couple of them bargained with him – they'd drop the story about Penny's wealth in exchange for a heads up on the Antarctic project.

But they all liked him and respected him, and finally he managed to get all of them to comply. They promised positive write-ups about the launch. The resort was a fantastic story anyway – the wealth stuff was a sideline. Will had no doubt the facts had been filed away and would appear at some stage in the future. It was inevitable. But at least they wouldn't interfere with the Nirvana Atoll story, the most important news event in the company's history.

It was now late afternoon. Time, he remembered, to meet his girlfriend Veronica who was due to arrive by seaplane at the resort along with a honeymoon couple – competition winners who would be joining tonight's VIP party. Not his job, but he'd offered to do it anyway as he had to be there to meet Veronica.

He grabbed a golf buggy and drove down a winding path above the main beach in front of the hotel. The seaplane would dock at the dive jetty which jutted into the sea at the opposite end of the beach from the Ocean Villas jetty.

He thought about what he was going to say to her. Would she still be angry? It would help if she were. It would make it easier to split up. He couldn't handle her if she were teary, or forgiving, or contrite...well, anything other than angry he guessed.

He arrived just in time to see the plane landing, its floats skidding across the water. It taxied to the jetty and an attractive young couple disembarked. A handsome guy of his own age with a mane of fair hair and matching moustache. His arm around the waist of a slim dark haired beauty with rosy cheeks and a winning smile.

"Welcome to Nirvana Atoll," Will said warmly, "My name's Will Sanders. Good flight?"

They shook hands.

"Hi Will. I'm Jojo Tanner. Yes good thanks." The accent was American. "And this is my girlf...I mean wife..."

She gave him a mock punch on the arm and they all laughed.

"What? Have you forgotten you married me already?" Her voice was British through and through. "Hello. I'm Kate. His wife."

He glanced past them at the plane but saw only the pilot and co-pilot get out.

"You expecting more people?" said Jojo.

"Is there another passenger? A girl?"

"No. Just us."

Somehow he was not surprised. He was relieved.

Nice of her to tell me though, he thought. Did she actually not care for him at all? Then realised he hadn't checked his phone for some time.

"Sorry, guys. One second."

There was the message from Veronica.

"Will I not coming. I think it not working for us. You think same maybe. Sorry. I will always love you. V."

"Not bad news I hope?" said Jojo, seeing his expression.

"You Ok?" asked Kate.

"Yes, all good. Come on. Let's get you settled so you can really start enjoying your honeymoon. You'll love it here."

"You're going to tell us about this mystery girl, though," said Jojo, nudging him as they walked to the buggy.

Will looked at them and smiled. He'd only just met this couple but for some reason he already liked them a lot. He looked forward to introducing them to Fiona.

Fiona. Now he could pursue her without a guilty conscience. It felt liberating.

Job saved. New love interest.

"Yep, you'll love it here," he said again.

Chapter Fourteen

Will tried calling Veronica a few times but it went to voicemail. He was sort of relieved, though felt a bit ashamed for being cowardly. But he didn't know what he was going to say to her. "You're right, it isn't working. Never mind, I've found someone else."?

It was now early evening and the launch cocktail party was well under way in the hotel lounge bar. Waiters and waitresses dressed in smart whites were circulating among the guests with fancy canapés arranged on what appeared to be random pieces of flat driftwood but which Will knew had been specially designed by a leading Italian designer brand.

He was acting as one of the hosts of course. Not a role he greatly enjoyed but it came with the territory. He disliked small talk and found it a bit unfulfilling to chat with someone he knew he was unlikely ever to see again. Even talking to journalists socially was not really his thing. He could talk to them forever about any topics that could help tell the company's story, or could help him understand the journalist himself or their publication (it was a two way street). But to him it was business. They weren't his friends. He'd rather be talking to friends, and not about work.

People behaved oddly at these social gatherings too. The VIPs were the worst. He met a fat man with a curly moustache and beard who talked a lot about himself – when Will spoke he only pretended to listen and soon interrupted to continue his life story. He moved on to two tanned and wrinkly ladies bedecked in jewellery who spent ten minutes trying to outdo each other with advice about the latest luxury spa, the trendiest new shoe designer and the simply-must-go-darling Michelin restaurant.

Next was a cluster of bankers. They regarded him like something unpleasant they'd trodden in – continually glancing over his shoulder for something more interesting or useful to them. Then he was latched onto by a young skinny man with pimples and bad glasses who proceeded to ask him a hundred questions about his life and followed him around the room as though attached by an invisible cord.

Finally though he managed to deposit the man with the group of bankers, much to their horror, and found Jojo and Kate. He'd done his bit for the company. Now he deserved to spend some time with some people who were good to talk to and with whom he had an immediate natural chemistry.

At 32 Jojo was the same age as Will. An American living in London. Handsome, fair haired. A lawyer and a ladies' man. Kate was a dark haired English rose. One of those stunningly beautiful women who actually don't think they're stunningly beautiful and therefore act completely naturally, almost innocently – making them even more attractive in some way.

Jojo and Will had both attended the same university and had fun swapping stories about various antics on campus. Fiona joined them and also immediately bonded with the couple, chatting to Kate about art and culture while the guys regressed into their student world.

At times Will and Fiona would exchange glances and the odd light touch on the arm or back. It was like they were already a couple themselves, thought Will.

Fiona loved the way Will and Jojo laughed and joked. Though there was a moment when both fell deadly serious, even sad, before returning to the joshing.

After a while Will broke off reluctantly to glad-hand a few more guests on his way to ordering more drinks at the bar. Where Fiona caught up with him.

She patted his arm and they smiled at each other.

"You got on well with Jojo," she said.

"Yeah turns out we have a lot in common. Same university. And..." He hesitated. "And?" she prompted him.

"Both our fathers died when we were very young."

"Oh I'm sorry."

"No it was a long time ago. But we both have this feeling even now."

"I saw the sadness for a moment."

"Not just sadness. A sort of sense of the injustice of life. The un-fairness." He laughed. "Sounds a bit stupid I know."

"No not at all." She looked at him as though she saw a new deeper side to him.

"I love Kate too. You got on well with her. Not surprising. Two beauties together." He flushed slightly. "Oh God did I just say that?"

She pulled him down towards her. "Oh yes. You did," she said and pecked him on the cheek.

Will suddenly thought of something and looked her in the eye with mock sternness. "Dr Bell. Are you making advances on me knowing I already have a girlfriend?"

She thought for a moment. "No Mr Sanders. I'm making advances on you knowing – because a little birdie told me, don't ask me who – knowing that your girlfriend who was meant to be on today's seaplane wasn't in fact on today's seaplane and has split up with you."

Will laughed, enjoying her cheek. He leaned down and whispered in her ear, at the same time smelling her skin, her hair. "But how can you be sure she's split up with me?"

She stroked his chest playfully. "Well if she hasn't..." There was a flash as Fiona kissed him. He looked to one side and saw she held her phone up with her other hand and had taken a selfie of them. "...She will when I send her this."

"Hey you!" he said playfully and grabbed at the phone, only to find his arm twisted behind his back by some unseen force. "Ow!" he cried.

"Sorry!" she laughed, letting him go. "Force of habit."

He stared at her, rubbing his arm. Did she really have that strength? She was so small. "Where the Hell did that come from?"

She shrugged. "You were talking about you both missing out on your fathers. I get it. Mine gave me a lot. Including Karate lessons."

She really was a box of surprises, he thought and smiled.

"Impressive," he said. "Do you have any other tricks?"

She thought a moment, then beckoned over a waiter.

Will held up his hands. "Now, now, Fi. Be gentle with him."

"Don't worry. I'm not going to touch him. Watch this."

She took his empty canapé board and placed it between two chair seats. In classic movie style she lifted her straightened hand and brought it smartly down on the board, breaking it in two with a loud crack.

The waiter recoiled and two of the nearest guests spilled their drinks.

Will stood shaking his head in amazement.

"I think it's time to leave," he laughed.

Chapter Fifteen

Will rose early the next morning, showered, shaved and in 30 minutes was sitting at his desk sipping coffee and scanning the web.

His mind kept drifting towards the previous night and he kept smiling despite himself. Maybe was there a divine justice after all.

They had soon realised they were beginning to attract attention in the bar and had agreed to say a few goodbyes to various guests – particularly Jojo and Kate (much winking and nudging) – before taking a midnight stroll through the warm scented tropical gardens.

Sex had been uppermost on his mind but he could sense she did not want to move quite so quickly. They talked. They held hands. They kissed. It had been less than he'd wanted but wonderful nevertheless. And he enjoyed the chase, the sense of expectation. It was fun.

As the early morning progressed, the write-ups of the launch started appearing in the online newspapers and blogs. They only added to his happiness. All glowing reports about the resort; no mention of Penny's billions.

Then an internal email from Penny pinged on his PC. "Great job, Will. Well done. Keep it up."

His joyful state of mind was not even shattered in the usual way by Mackay. There were no Well Dones of course or hearty slaps on the back. But there was no digging or attacking either. The Scot seemed to have his mind elsewhere.

He decided to grab a late breakfast and headed to the restaurant. He bumped into Jojo and Kate as they were leaving.

"Hi Will," said Kate cheerily.

"Hey mate," added Jojo, and digged him in the ribs. "Good night?"

"Jojo. Some decorum please!" scolded Kate playfully. "Anyway," she said smiling, "You don't have to ask – you can see how happy he is!"

"Where are you off to?" asked Will.

"We thought we'd go look at the famous aquarium," Kate said, "And then I'm off to do absolutely nothing by the pool while this one goes diving."

"Just snorkelling today darling," corrected Jojo. "Serious deep sea stuff tomorrow."

"If you feel fit enough," said Kate and looked a tad serious.

Will was confused. Jojo was built like an athlete. "He looks pretty fit to me!"

"No he's got a heart condition..."

"It's not a heart condition darling," said Jojo shaking his head. "It's just a little sort of murmur thing. It's nothing. I've been cleared to dive to the deepest depths of the ocean. Don't worry." He kissed her.

"Well..." she began.

"Anyway," he interrupted, wanting to move things along. "Fiona says we must see her exotic rare fishies so let's go!"

"Oh that reminds me of something," said Will. "I'll go with you."

He'd forgotten to ask Fiona about their newly discovered fish species. Somehow they'd other things on their mind.

The four of them met up again and there was five minutes of friendly banter before Will took Fiona aside to ask her if there was any news on the fish. It would make a good follow up story for the resort, thought Will, though with a seed of doubt – the thing was a bit freaky...maybe it would be more scary to tourists than exciting. Anyway, she said nothing had come back yet from the university so she'd press them further.

Will left the three of them to tour the aquarium. Then Kate headed to the pool and Jojo to the dive shop.

The shop was at the other end of the beach from the ocean villas, which Jojo could see way off in the distance, their windows glinting in the morning sun. In front of him was the jetty which he'd disembarked on the day before. A couple of resort's dive boats and pleasure dinghies bobbed gently half way along it.

He asked for mask, snorkel and flippers, and quizzed the dive instructor – an Aussie named Steve - about what sea life to look out for and which were the best spots along the reef. They also discussed the following day's plan to dive with a small group in the deeper ocean. This was what he was really looking forward to.

"You'll get a chance to see the big beasts – turtles, dolphins, manta rays, maybe giant whale sharks if we're lucky," said Steve, handing him his equipment.

"Great. I can't wait, man."

"You might even spot a few dolphins today, mate. If not, no worries – there's plenty of interesting stuff out there. The new reef's a magnet to them."

"Thanks. Anything nasty to watch out for?"

"Nah. You know what to steer clear of. It's common sense, mate. There's a few jellyfish that'll sting a bit. But they're not dangerous. Hey, don't forget this."

The instructor held up a small pot of Vaseline and winked.

Jojo was confused for a moment, then it clicked.

He smeared a little on his moustache to create a water tight seal with the mask. He'd forgotten to do this on a few occasions and it had resulted in his mask filling up as water leaked in between the hairs on his upper lip.

He also applied sunscreen liberally, then waved goodbye to Steve and headed for the jetty.

The jetty was useful for snorkelers to access the reef which ran parallel to the beach about thirty meters out. He strolled along it, bright blue flippers in one hand, mask and snorkel in the other. Reaching the end he stopped for a moment to put on his flippers then jumped in with a splash. Treading water, he then spat in his mask and rubbed the saliva around the glass and silicone edging and rinsed it in the water. This would help prevent the mask fogging up, though nobody had ever explained to him how.

Then he set off out to the reef, propelling himself with long languid kicks. The sea was crystal clear, the sunlight shining through it and lighting up the multicoloured corals and reef fish. He turned 90 degrees sharp right and slowed his pace further to take in the sights as he skimmed along the top of the reef. The variety was amazing. Bright blue and yellow Angel Fish, Butterfly Fish with elegant elongated trailing fins, green and purple spotted Wrasse. He was an experienced snorkeler and recognised many of the species but there were over a thousand different types of fish in The Maldives so he was constantly thrilled to spot ones he'd never or rarely seen before.

He dived down beside the reef and hung for a while in the water. Arms behind his back and minimal leg movements so as not to scare the sealife. He could hear continual little popping sounds in the water as the Parrot Fish nibbled at the coral. And then excreted it in clouds which would in time form a new sandy layer of beach. It was how all the island beaches were made – but not many of the luxury tourists realised they were sunbathing on fish excrement.

He turned and watched a Goat Fish digging in the sand at the bottom. Nearby he noticed the head of a moray eel sticking out of a rocky cave, gaping with its fanged mouth – it looked menacing but Jojo knew it was perfectly safe unless you actually tried to stick your fingers in its mouth.

More dangerous, though they didn't look it, were the Titan Triggerfish. They could attack divers aggressively to defend their nests if you got too close. He steered clear of these.

The instructor had told him to head past the ocean villas to more open water for an opportunity to see cuttlefish, sting rays and maybe dolphins. It was amazing how the sea life around an island could change so much. As though there were invisible barriers between different zones in the water.

He put on some speed, kicking strongly, his flippers providing extra power.

He was past the ocean villas jetty now and the reef had been replaced by deeper darker water.

But there was nothing much here so he swam away from the shore to try his luck further out.

He hung in the water again, this time unable to see the seabed as it was too far beneath him. He looked out into the Indian Ocean.

He noticed he was being watched. To his right had appeared a long torpedo shaped silver fish with a gaping toothy mouth. A barracuda. It was completely static, staring at him with big glassy eyes. A beautifully sleek predator. Though it wouldn't tackle something his size on its own, he knew.

Then suddenly with a flick of its tail it disappeared back into the inky distance.

Something had scared it.

Probably a shark. Black Tip Reef Sharks were common in these waters. But like the barracuda they were pretty harmless to divers.

He looked around hopefully but couldn't see any sharks.

He had now been in the water for about an hour and was beginning to get tired so decided to head back.

He popped his head above the surface and looked around. He was further out to sea than he'd thought, probably taken by the current.

It was no problem though as he was a good swimmer and confident in the water.

He could see the ocean villas way off to his right. He'd swim first to them and if he was too tired he could always climb up one of the ladders there and rest a while. Even walk back along the beach.

He thought about having lunch with Kate by the pool. Then maybe the afternoon in bed...

He headed off, conserving his energy with long steady kicks. Letting the flippers do the work.

It had been a great swim and he'd enjoyed it tremendously. He couldn't wait for tomorrow's deep sea dive.

Then he saw a tangled mat of algae floating on the surface in front of him. Blocking his way. It hadn't been there before.

It was a big mat, extending as far out into the ocean as he could see.

Before he realised it he was caught up in a thick slimy green mess.

He would have to swim to his left, towards the shore, and around the weed. At least it wasn't forcing him further out to sea, he thought.

He disentangled himself from the seaweed and swam hard towards the shore and then right again back on his original course to the ocean villa jetty.

He was fifty metres from the jetty when suddenly he felt something sharp scrape his leg.

He looked down in time to see a massive black fish, maybe two meters long, swimming slowly away.

Was it a shark? No, it was too wide and misshapen. It had a large bulbous head and a long spiny fin running from the middle of its back to a ragged tail. He'd never seen anything like it.

It left a cloud of blood around his right leg. He thought it must have brushed against him with its hard ridged back, scraping his skin off.

His heart was pounding against his ribcage. What the hell was this creature? And how badly was he hurt?

He felt down and touched his leg.

It wasn't just a scratch.

The thing hadn't just bumped into him. It had attacked him. It had punctured his calf. He felt the hole in his flesh.

He didn't feel pain. He felt intense panic. It surged through him.

He tried to swim but his right leg did not respond.

He shouted towards the jetty but couldn't see anyone there.

Now there was quite a cloud of bright red blood around him in the water.

Suddenly he was bumped from behind.

He span round in the water and his hands touched something rough and ridged. The creature's forehead pushed against him. Milky eyes set deep inside jagged sockets stared at him.

Then the forehead moved upwards as the mouth slowly opened and two enormous fangs appeared, so long that he couldn't see the end of them.

He flailed wildly at the creature, then managed to push against its thick arched upper lip, propelling himself backwards for a moment.

It was a chance to escape. He flipped onto his front and burst into a frenetic crawl using only his arms and undamaged leg.

Then piercing excruciating pain as the fangs pierced both his thighs and jolted him back and down.

His screams were cut off as he was jerked under the surface.

He blacked out due to the loss of blood and the shock.

Perhaps sensing the sudden limpness in its prey, the creature opened its mouth, withdrawing the fangs as though unsheathing swords, and released him.

It looked at its victim with unblinking eyes for a moment, then languidly moved its tail and swam off under the algae and out to sea.

Back at the resort pool Jojo's new wife Kate lay on a sun lounger and turned a page of her romantic novel.

Chapter Sixteen

It was early evening and Will was relaxing in his room. He was feeling good. He'd achieved another successful resort launch, despite all the obstacles thrown in his way. Penny was pleased with his work. Mackay had gone quiet. And he had a new love interest in his life.

He knew it was going to be challenging. It had put a strain on his relationship with Veronica, the travel and time apart. He would be back in Germany soon to plan the next launch marketing campaign, perhaps the Antarctic resort if it was true. Then he'd be off again travelling. While Fiona would presumably go back to Plymouth now the aquarium was up and running. He had a wild idea that maybe she could continue to work with the company. They could live together in Germany and travel the world as a couple.

He shook his head. Christ I'm getting a bit ahead of myself, he thought. We've known each other less than a week!

There was a knock at the door and a female voice calling his name.

"Yes, coming," he said and leapt up to open the door.

It was Jojo's wife, alone and looking agitated.

"What's wrong Kate?" He took her in and sat her down.

"Have you been with Jojo today?" she asked.

"No. Not since breakfast. Why?"

He saw the fear in her face. She walked past him into the room, looking around as though searching for something.

"I thought he was with you. I've lost him. I've looked for him all round the resort. I asked in the bars and restaurants...." She turned and he went to put a comforting arm on her. "He went snorkelling and didn't come back for the whole day. I thought he'd gone for a long lunch with you – he said he might – you got on so well together. Oh I'm so stupid – I thought he was with you." She shook her head, suddenly annoyed with herself.

Will thought it was odd she hadn't seen him all day but his mind searched for positive reasons. He also wanted to reassure her. She was beginning to shake. He held her gently by the arms and looked into her eyes.

"Don't worry. We'll find him. Maybe he went for a diving trip instead of snorkelling. Or maybe he went to another island to snorkel there. Did you ask at the dive shop?"

She hit her head with her palm. "God I AM stupid!"

He took her hand. "No you're not. Don't worry. Let's go now."

They left and walked quickly out of the hotel and down the winding path towards the dive shop.

"I'm sure he's Ok," he found himself repeating, though doubts were creeping in.

"I don't know, Will. I knew he shouldn't have gone. Not with his heart problems."

"But he was cleared right? Medically?"

"That's what he kept telling me. I don't know, Will. I'm scared."

"We'll find him."

They got to the dive shop and found it closed. Will knocked on the window and peered in but there was nobody there.

"It's gone six o'clock. Too late to dive. Let's call the instructor."

Will dialled the number while he watched Kate looking blankly out to sea.

An Aussie voice answered. "Yeah, Steve here."

"Hey, Steve. It's Will. Look, I'm with Kate. Jojo Tanner's wife. He went snorkelling this morning and we haven't seen him since."

"Yeah, I gave him his equipment. Nobody's seen him at all, mate?"

"No, not that I know. Well, Kate hasn't and nor have I. I don't know where else he could be. Could he have hired a boat to visit one of the islands?"

"Let me call Mo now. He's my number two here. I left him in charge this afternoon. He'll know what's going on. Call you back in a second."

Will then called the resort manager and asked him to organise an immediate resort-wide search.

"If he's on the island we'll find him," he reassured Kate, "And if he's out there," Will nodded towards the ocean, "He'll be visiting another island or diving late or something and we'll find him too." He felt a twinge of doubt but dismissed it quickly as he didn't want to alarm her.

"He's had an accident, Will. I know it."

"He's an experienced diver and a strong swimmer from what I heard. Don't worry." He wanted to stop telling her not to worry but couldn't help himself. He knew the more times you told someone not to worry the more worry it created.

His phone rang. The dive instructor's voice was urgent.

"Not good, Will. Mo fucked up. He doesn't remember Jojo returning the equipment. The rules are he should have flagged it up immediately when he did his regular check and found it missing. But he thought it had been a mistake and someone had just forgotten to sign their snorkelling gear back in."

"Shit!"

Kate swung round and looked at Will with frightened eyes.

"You sure he's not on the island?"

"I've asked Christoph to notify all staff. We should hear soon."

"Ok. I'm calling the coast guard now."

"Ok."

"I'll also get people together and we can go out and look ourselves before it gets much darker."

"I'll help. Talk soon."

Will rang off and looked at Kate.

"He didn't return his equipment."

She let out a sharp sob. He went to her and hugged her gently.

"All our staff are on the look out for him around the resort so we'll know very soon if he's on land. Steve's notifying the coast guard now. We're also getting a team together ourselves to search the sea around here."

She convulsed in his arms and he smoothed her hair.

"I know. I know," he said soothing her. "We don't know anything yet, Kate. Try not to think about it. Let me call Fi to look after you. I have to go. We need to try to find him."

He called Fiona and told her the news. She met them as Will was helping Kate back up the path. They exchanged knowing looks. She was the rock Will had expected, gently taking Kate from him and leading inside, holding her close and whispering words of comfort.

The resort manager, Christoph – a pleasant, tall and good-looking middle-aged German - grabbed Will as they entered the lobby. They had not been able to find Jojo on land either. He would notify the police. Jojo was now officially missing.

Will watched Fiona lead Kate away to lie down, then sent texts to Penny and Mackay updating them on events. He got no immediate response.

Ten minutes later, three of the resorts dive boats had been manned by resort staff, including the instructor and his now ashen-faced assistant, and had set off to search the coastline of the island, using spotlights as the evening grew darker.

An hour after that the police arrived from Male by seaplane. Will met them with Christoph.

The senior detective was a short slim friendly young man called Kyle – an oddly Western sounding name for a local, Will couldn't help thinking as the introductions took place. He was accompanied by an assistant, an even shorter guy who looked like a 12 year old boy but who was presumably old enough to be a policeman.

After a brief discussion of the facts, and a quick visit to Kate for an update on relevant personal details about Jojo, a second search of the island was conducted, which Will and Christoph joined.

Meanwhile the sea search was enhanced by a helicopter and power boat from the coast guard. Both vehicles were equipped with strong lights which swept across the surface of the dark and tranquil Indian Ocean.

By one in the morning Will had received two calls from journalists – Bob and Leo - and four from other VIP guests asking what the helicopter and boats were searching for. They'd all been woken up by the sound of the engines and a few of them had gone down to the beach to watch. Will had told them the truth – a guest had not returned from a trip snorkelling and they were searching for him. He told them he would not speculate on what had happened but that they would know the facts as soon as he did. Bob had agreed to keep the news quiet until the details were clear. Leo on the other hand was posting an item online, but Will managed to persuade him to stick to a few lines stating a guest had gone missing.

Half an hour later Mackay somehow found him while he was searching one of the garden areas in a remoter part of the island.

"Ah, Mr Sanders. I found you," said the Scot appearing round a corner.

"You heard what's happened."

"Yes."

"I sent you and Penny a message but didn't hear back." Will had thought it odd but had been too busy to follow it up with a call.

"I've just got back from seeing Penny off actually," Mackay said. "She's gone to Shanghai to speak at some conference about saving the planet."

Will knew about it and nodded. "Shame she can't be here – it would have shown the company cares - but it can't be helped. I'll catch you later John." He was anxious to get on with his search for Jojo, even though he knew in his heart it was probably futile.

Mackay blocked the path and scowled. "She's not at all happy with what's going on here, you know. Nor am I. Not good for the resort."

It seemed to Will that the man was back to his old obnoxious self. "Well it's not really my fault that one of our guests has gone missing, John. It's also not my responsibility either – I'm not the resort manager – but I'm trying to help as best I can 'cause it's all hands to the pump in these situations. Plus I liked the guy. I hope he's OK but I'm sort of losing hope."

Mackay stared at him. "It's already on your blogger friend's site – 'New resort in trouble as guest disappears at sea in launch week' – it'll ruin us!"

Will faced him. "He's not my friend, he's a journalist. He couldn't help but notice the helicopter and search boats. I just told him the facts."

Mackay's face reddened. "What? You told him? I don't believe it! I thought he found out for himself."

"I had to tell him a guest had disappeared when he asked me, John," Will said calmly. "The truth is the truth. If he hadn't heard it from me he'd have heard it from the police or coast guard. If I'd denied it the story would have been an even bigger one about a cover-up. My job in these situations is to try to get these guys not to speculate or make stuff up..."

"Your job, " said Mackay pointing at him, " Is to keep stuff like this out of the news."

"If I can, yes. But I can't lie."

"Then you're in the wrong job."

"I don't have time to argue the point, John. I need to..."

But Mackay cursed and stormed off before Will could finish.

Chapter Seventeen

By four in the morning every inch of the island had been searched. No sign of Jojo. The helicopter and boats were still looking out at sea but they too had found nothing so far.

After checking back with the other searchers and the hotel manager, Will went to check on Fiona and Kate. They had spent the night in Kate's room.

Fiona let him in. Kate was lying on the sofa under a blanket. Her face told him she'd been crying all night.

She looked up at him, her cheeks streaked with mascara.

"I'm sorry, Kate," he said shaking his head. "We haven't found him yet."

She looked away in silence.

Fiona took him to one side. "This is terrible, "she whispered. "Is there no sign at all of him? She's in a right state."

"No. Nothing. It's not looking good I'm afraid. If he's not on the island and they can't find him at sea...I'm trying to hope he's alive and well somewhere, but I don't think so."

"I feel..." She left it hanging.

"I know." He held her. "He's such a...nice guy. They're a sweet couple. It's so unfair."

"And their honeymoon, Will. I can't believe it."

She sighed deeply and they held a hug in silence for a few moments.

Then she patted him on the chest and looked over at Kate who had closed her eyes.

"I hope she sleeps a little. Do you want something? A tea?"

"No, thanks."

"Have you had anything tonight?"

"No. I'm fine."

"Have a tea at least."

They crossed to the sideboard and she clicked on the kettle.

"But what do you think happened to him?" she said, rummaging among a colourful selection of packets of tea. "She thinks he had a heart attack and drowned. She keeps talking about his weak heart. English Breakfast?"

"Fine. I just don't know. He seemed strong to me, but I hardly know him. Let's see what the police think."

She took two cups and searched for sugar.

"She called his mother in the States. He doesn't have a father..." She suddenly remembered. "I'm sorry – you know that."

"The mother's coming on her own?"

"No I think she's flying out with her brother. Jojo's uncle."

The kettle boiled and she made them both tea.

They stood together quietly for a moment, looking at the motionless figure on the sofa.

He thought about how things like this made you appreciate the value of life, and its shortness. It was trite, but true. He glanced at the woman next to him and amidst all the sorrow felt a surge of joy at the thought of their relationship. Then a twinge of guilt.

His phone pinged.

Kate sat up and stared.

It was a text from Christoph:

***Strategy meeting in 15 mins with police, coast guard. My
office.***

"Nothing," he said to Kate quickly. "Just a meeting to decide next
steps in the search."

"I gotta go," he said to Fiona.

"Wait," she said as he headed for the door. "I want to come too."
She looked at Kate. "Will you be OK for an hour?"

Kate nodded. "Please," she said, looking at each of them in turn.
"Find him."

Ten minutes later Will and Fiona were sitting at a tightly packed
oval table in the resort manager's office.

The room was already beginning to feel a little stuffy, the aircon
struggling to cope with ten people squashed into a small room. There
was no time to clear the communal hotel rooms of guests and for some
reason Mackay had not offered his spacious suite.

Will looked round the table. To his right the two policemen were
reading a notebook. Kyle, the senior detective, caught his eye and
nodded. Next to them sat Christoph, texting on his phone rapidly.
To his left were three coast guards, all dressed in the same green and
brown combat uniforms, which he thought was odd considering they
mainly worked at sea. Next to them was the dive instructor, Steve. Like
most Aussies Will knew he was usually pretty chipper, but now he sat
in glum silence. Will thought he probably felt responsible for Jojo's
disappearance.

At the far end of the table Mackay sat with his customary scowl. He
looked impatient to get the meeting underway. He tapped the table.
"OK, let's get going shall we. What do we know? Who's first?"

The middle coast guard, a man in his thirties whose firm jaw line
and black moustache gave him the appearance of an army sergeant,

spoke first. "I'm sorry. It's not good news I'm afraid. We have been searching non-stop now for twelve hours. Using as you know both boat and helicopter. We have found no sign of the lost man at all."

"No clues?" said Kyle.

"No clues. Nothing."

Kyle asked the question that was on Will's mind. "Could he still be alive?"

"I think it's unlikely. I mean it's theoretically possible, which is why my men are still out there searching. If he's a good swimmer..."

"Yes, he is," said Will. "According to his wife. And he looks strong, fit."

"If his mental state is good and he was hydrated enough before going into the water, it's possible. But..." he shook his head grimly, "...From my personal experience I have to be honest and say it's unlikely."

Will felt Fiona grip his hand.

"And the longer a person is lost at sea the more difficult he is to find. Ocean currents can take you miles from where you entered the water, making the search area enormous."

"In most cases of drowning that I've come across," said Kyle, "The diver or snorkeler or swimmer has been caught in a strong current and swept out to sea. They haven't had the strength to make it back to land. The currents can be treacherous round here."

"We'll keep looking until we find him," said the coast guard. "But I'm afraid it's likely we're now looking for a body rather than a survivor."

"I have to say also," said Will reluctantly, "He does have a weak heart. His wife told us. She thinks he had a heart attack."

"Yes I know," said Kyle, "It may well be that he had a heart attack while swimming and drowned as a result. We don't know for sure but it seems the most likely scenario."

"So nothing to do with the resort then," Mackay said tactlessly. "We can't be blamed for a guest with a bad heart having a heart attack."

There was a brief exchange of glances among the others in the room. Will was embarrassed. The man really was something else.

Will noticed Fiona looking at Mackay to kill. "Or maybe he was attacked by a shark," she said. Mackay's mouth dropped open. Good for her, thought Will. She carried on. "There are tiger sharks and hammerheads in these waters. I know it's unlikely and very rare but they could attack a swimmer."

"Now hold on…" blurted Mackay, his face reddening, but Steve interrupted.

"It's worth considering, Doctor Bell. But as far as I know there has never been a shark attack anywhere in The Maldives. Never."

She frowned. "Yes but there was never a shark attack in The Seychelles or Sharm El Sheik either…until just a few years ago when, guess what, some people were attacked and killed by sharks. Never say never where sharks are concerned."

"What do you think you're doing?" shouted Mackay angrily, "You work for us – remember? Nobody mentioned sharks here. The guy had a heart attack and drowned. That's the end of it."

"We don't know that yet," said Will. Mackay glared at him.

"No we don't," said Kyle. "You're right, Doctor. We cannot totally dismiss a shark attack. We won't be sure of course until we find the body. If we find it. Are there any other marine creatures that could attack a swimmer around here? I've heard stingrays can be dangerous?"

"Yes, stingrays can be dangerous…" said Fiona.

"Oh great!" said Mackay, throwing his hands in the air.

"And Lion Fish, and Stonefish. But very very rarely. And only if really provoked or stepped on. And an experienced diver would know this. He'd be cautious around these animals. And none of them would just attack out of the blue."

"So we can discount all this can't we?" Said Mackay, standing up. "Surely, detective, a heart attack is the most likely cause of death?"

The policeman sighed. "Maybe a boating accident. Maybe a shark attack. Maybe a freak current. Could be any of these. We just don't know yet. But yes, Mr Mackay. If unfortunately this poor man has drowned, as seems likely, then a heart attack would appear to be the most likely cause. But all is just theory until we find the body, so I suggest we continue to help our coast guard friends in their search."

They all rose and started to leave, but Will saw Fiona remain in her seat lost in thought.

"What is it, Fi?"

"I don't know. I was just thinking."

"What?"

"If it wasn't a heart attack, or a freak current or whatever. If he was attacked by something...We missed out one possibility."

"Really?"

She looked at him.

"That new species we found. What if there are more of them? And much bigger? Adults."

"Is that likely, Fi?"

She screwed up her face. It was quite cute, he thought.

"Nah. It's a bit fantastical, I guess."

"Don't you mean horrific?"

She nodded slowly.

"Yes. It would be. Horrific."

Chapter Eighteen

Will spent the next half hour preparing a brief statement for media and guests informing them of the disappearance of Jojo at sea and assuring them the company was continuing to work with the police and coast guard to find him but that he was feared drowned - a heart attack the most likely cause but it could not be confirmed at this stage.

The statement reassured the public of the safety of the resort and the surrounding seas, stating this was an unfortunate accident.

He also prepared instructions to staff and a polite request to the police and local authorities to stick to the agreed statement and not to speculate if approached by guests. All media enquiries were to be directed to him.

He tried not to dwell on what might have happened to the man but horrible fears kept creeping into his head.

Mackay asked him why he needed to issue a statement and couldn't they just keep it all quiet. But when Will repeated for the second time that day that the story was already out and refusing to comment would make the company look like they had something to hide, his boss relented and approved it.

He tried again to contact Penny in Shanghai but was told she was in back-to-back meetings, so he sent her the statement with an update.

At around midday Fiona dropped by his office.

She looked despondent but attempted a cheery smile.

"Hi you," she said, stroking his arm.

"Hi Fi. You Ok? Kate ok?"

"She's still sleeping. I think the shock has knocked her out. I've asked the maids to keep an eye on her."

"Well done. Thank you."

"Want to get a sandwich?"

"No I'm not that hungry."

"Me neither."

She sat at the empty desk next to his.

"Will, I hate feeling useless. Let's do something."

He loved her verve, her need to act. He felt the same way.

"Yep, me too. But what? I've already searched the island and sorted the staff and media out. What do you have in mind?"

"Let's grab a spare boat if there is one and join the sea search. I know it's a long shot but I can't just sit around here twiddling my thumbs!"

Will smiled at her. Her spirit was infectious.

"You're right," he said.

"Really?" Her face brightened.

"Really." He sprang up. "Let's go do it."

They half walked half ran down to the dive jetty.

He saw at once that all the powerful dive boats had gone - taken by resort staff helping in the search he guessed. There was just one small motor boat left.

"We're going nowhere very fast in that," he said eying the sad little vessel critically. "But it'll have to do I guess!"

"Do we need to check it with Steve?"

"Nah. He's not here anyway. He's out searching. Has been for hours. Poor guy feels it's his fault for not checking Jojo's equipment was missing."

"It's not his fault."

"I know. Come on."

They got in, started up the outboard and puttered out to sea.

The sun frequently dipped behind a fluffy white cloud which gave welcome relief from the midday heat.

A light breeze made the sea slightly choppy and the boat rocked and bobbed a little.

Fiona sat at the bow looking forward and scanning the sea for any signs of Jojo. She was wearing a baseball cap to shade her eyes. Her dark hair was swept back under the cap but Will noticed how the wind would occasionally blow a few strands across her face which she would flick away with her hand. He immediately felt guilty for watching her when he should be looking for Jojo and snapped his gaze back out to sea. Nevertheless he was smiling to himself.

Fiona caught him. "Why are you smiling? This is not quite the right time is it?"

"I'm smiling at this comically underpowered engine," he lied.

They headed out perpendicular to the beach for a ten minutes and then turned right and started running parallel to it. They could make out in the distance the coast guard and other boats who were much further out, having already searched this area. But they both agreed a second search was worth it as it was so easy to miss someone in the water. You usually only had a head to try to spot, which was extremely difficult in a choppy sea where each wavelet looked like it might be someone's head.

It took them an hour to circumnavigate the island. Several times they spotted what could be a person's head or body bobbing amongst the waves in the distance, only to discover upon closer inspection that it was a piece of driftwood, a floating coconut, or a plastic bottle. But no sign of a man, or a body.

Having returned to their start point they decided to head out to sea for ten minutes and then do another circuit.

"Won't you be missed on land?" she asked.

"This is more important," he said, "What else can I do? I can't comment beyond the statement everyone has. I've amazingly got mobile reception so if anyone gets any news we'll hear it. But at the same time I can ignore my boss's pestering waste-of-time texts, and say I was out of coverage."

Only a few minutes after they had once again turned to do their circuit she let out a shout.

"What have you spotted?" he asked, thinking this time from her excitement it might be Jojo. Though at the same time dreading that it might be his dead body.

"Algae!" she said.

"What?"

"An algae bloom. A huge one. Look." She pointed ahead of them.

"Why's that so exciting?"

"It's unusual in this area. It might tell us something."

"Really?" Will was sceptical. They were now plowing into a huge matted tangle of green weed.

He trailed his hand in the slime and pulled a face. "This isn't going to help us find Jojo."

"Well at least I can find out if it killed him."

"How could it kill him?"

"Some algae is toxic you know. Deadly."

"Eeeugh!" He yanked his hand out of the water.

She laughed. "But not this one I think."

"Great. Come on let's get out of here. It's just slime."

"Just slime? This is phytoplankton. Photosynthesizing microscopic organisms. There are 5,000 known species of it. It accounts for half of all photosynthetic activity on Earth. It's perhaps the most important life form in the ocean...."

"Wait. More important than whales? Don't tell me that. I love whales," he joked.

"Well, without this slime you'd have no whales. This feeds krill, krill feed whales. Phytoplankton, krill, whales – that's a very very short food chain don't you think? Amazing."

"Yeah amazing. Now let's...hang on..."

Will stopped as the engine cut out.

"Great. Looks like your phyto-whatnot has clogged our prop."

"Ok," she said and started rummaging in a small storage compartment in the prow of the boat, pulling out a plastic water beaker. She tipped out the water.

"Hey! We might need that! What if we're stuck out here for days?"

"You've got a mobile phone. The coast guard, the police and half the resort staff are just over there. We're hardly going to be stuck here for days." She smiled and pointed to the engine. "You sort that out; I'm going to collect some algae to test."

She pulled off her skirt and top revealing a blue bikini.

Before he knew it she had dived into the water.

She popped up covered in slime and seaweed.

"What the fu..." He shouted. "Couldn't you just stick your hand in the water?"

"I want to get a sample from a deeper level," she said, laughing. And disappeared.

He jumped to the front of the boat and looked down at the green mat.

He saw nothing but slime and weed. His heart began to race. What was she thinking?

The seconds passed painfully slowly.

Ten seconds. No sign of her.

Twenty seconds.

Was she a good swimmer? How long could she hold her breath?

Half a minute.

Will took off his shirt and kicked off his shoes. He was scared of the water but he was even more scared of what might have happened to her.

Forty seconds.

It was his worst nightmare. He steeled himself to dive in.

Fifty seconds.

He was just about to dive when he saw her surface at the stern.

"Christ you scared me," he shouted down at her, half angry half relieved.

She threw the plastic beaker full of weed into the boat.

"There," she said, "I've collected my sample and freed your propeller. What have you been doing?"

He shook his head and laughed.

Suddenly she let out a cry of pain and ducked under the surface.

He jumped in and surfaced to see her head a few feet away. She looked in agony.

"It's OK, it's OK," she said, spluttering a little sea water. "It's just cramp. It's passing now."

He helped her swim to the boat and pushed her up over the side.

He climbed aboard and wiped off the slime from her head and shoulders as she massaged her left calf.

"Thanks Will. I'm fine. It's gone. Just a twinge."

He shook his head again. "Don't scare me like that."

"You hero. You jumped in to save me."

He smiled.

"I was OK though," she said with a cheeky grin.

He kissed her.

She kissed him back, long and full and tender.

"I don't think I've ever met anyone quite like you," he said, starting the engine.

It spluttered to life.

She winked at him, bits of weed still sticking to her body. "I'll take that as a compliment."

Chapter Nineteen

O nce they had landed back at the dive jetty they checked in with Christoph who told them the sea search was still fruitless and the police and coast guard were likely to call it off within the hour, even though no body had been found.

The mood was despondent.

Fiona said she would drop off the algae sample, shower and change quickly and then return to Kate to give her what comfort she could.

Will agreed to meet up later, after he'd checked in with the office to see how the media were reporting the news.

As he walked through the lobby he nodded as usual to the three receptionists. Two of them smiled and nodded back, but the third did not smile – instead he seemed to give Will an odd look. Probably upset by the news about Jojo, as they all were.

He walked down a corridor towards the resort offices and heard light footsteps behind him.

He glanced back to see the receptionist who had not smiled. The man stopped in his tracks and looked uncertain.

"Hello," said Will. "Did you want me?"

The man just looked at him. He was scared. A local guy, small and slim as most of them were. Standing there in his receptionist's orange jacket and trouser uniform. Looking vulnerable.

"Can I help you?" asked Will gently, smiling and stepping towards him.

The man took an instinctive step back and looked even more scared. "No sir. My mistake." He bowed slightly, turned and walked quickly back towards the lobby.

Will shrugged. Very odd, he thought. Then he went to the office and checked in with his team.

Several stories about Jojo's disappearance were beginning to filter through. All were brief, factual and focussed on the human tragedy, mentioning Jojo's heart problems as the likely cause of his drowning.

He sat at his PC to review the post-launch marketing plan. But he had difficulty concentrating. There was something nagging at his subconscious. What? Jojo's death? He barely knew the guy but they'd made a connection and his death was bound to affect him even more than the death of an anonymous guest – a sad occurrence he'd had to deal with several times before. Millions of people went on holiday every year, and every year some of them died on holiday. It was a fact of life.

He couldn't focus so decided to get some air and headed back to the lobby.

As he passed through he looked again at the three receptionists. The one who had followed him did not return his look but kept his head down.

On some instinct Will approached him. This guy had something he wanted to tell him but was too frightened – Will wanted to know what it was. One of the other receptionists asked how he could help Will but he ignored him and looked straight at the bowed head of the guy in the middle. "Sorry I can't remember your name," he said, which forced the man to look up. He faked a smile and answered, "Hassan, sir."

"Hassan, that's right," Will lied, "Hassan, I needed you to help me with that thing, you remember? Come with me a moment and I'll show you." He smiled and casually gestured to the guy to follow him outside. "Won't be a moment," he said to the other two, who nodded back politely.

Hassan had little choice but to follow him outside onto the terrace. There were a few people milling around and chatting but he saw a quiet corner and gestured the receptionist to follow him there.

Out of earshot of the others on the terrace, he stood facing Hassan and said softly and reassuringly, "I think you want to tell me something, or maybe you need my help? Is that right?"

The two of them made an odd sight, standing face to face, a short local man in orange towered over by a giant Westerner in smart blue shorts and crisp white shirt.

Hassan started to tremble which made Will feel both sorry for the guy and slightly uncomfortable at the same time.

"Hey, it's OK. What's wrong? It can't be that bad."

Hassan finally looked up. "You are Mr Sanders."

"Call me Will."

"You work for Mr Mackay."

Oh God what's Mackay done now, thought Will.

"I do."

"He is a very big boss."

"Yeeeeees. He's very senior. Why?"

"You work closely." Another fact rather than a question.

"Yes we do. Why?"

"Nothing. Nothing. There is no problem. I don't need to talk to you. I made a mistake."

The man made to leave but Will held his arm, gently but firmly.

"Hassan. It's OK. You can tell me anything. In secret. If it's about Mr Mackay, or the resort, or whatever. I won't tell anyone without your permission. OK?"

Hassan looked doubtful but slightly hopeful too. "You won't tell anyone?"

"No, not unless you say it's OK. Now what is it? Tell me."

After a moment of hesitation Hassan decided to take the plunge. "I have a terrible confession. I feel really bad. But he made me not tell anyone."

"Who? Mackay?"

"Yes."

"What did you do?"

"I found a body. A dead body."

Will jumped. "Jojo? The guest that..."

"No no. I'm sorry Mr Sanders. Not the guest. This was an Indian man. I think he worked here. A labourer. One of the poor people. He went into the sea and drowned. His body washed up. Under the pier, the ocean villas pier. I found it when I was walking on the beach. I know I shouldn't have been on the beach..."

"No that's OK. So you told Mackay about the body? Anyone else?"

"No just Mr Mackay. And two of his men came and saw it too. One fat with red hair, one with a pointy nose."

"Yeah I know them. So you showed Mackay the body you'd found under the pier and he told you to keep quiet about it, right? He threatened you?"

"He said I would lose my job. And he gave me money." Hassan reached into his pocket and pulled out a wad of notes which he thrust at Will. "I don't want it. This poor man...called Jojo...has gone. Like the poor Indian man. You knew him. I saw you laughing with him at the party. I wanted to tell you. I'm worried the man Jojo has been attacked like the Indian man was."

Will's heat missed a beat. "Attacked? What do you mean?"

The man hesitated. Will softened his voice. "What do you mean, Hassan?"

"The body under the pier had...bite marks. Maybe a shark, or a big eel, or barracuda. People should be careful in the sea here. There is something there."

Will was struck dumb for a few second. This would damage the resort beyond belief – and felt immediately guilty that this was his first thought. What about Jojo? Had he been attacked like the Indian man? He shuddered at the horror of it. Was there a killer shark out there? Or maybe there had been simply two drownings and the dead body had been scavenged after death?

"Where's the body now?" he asked finally.

"I don't know. The two men took it."

"Shit. I need to talk to Mackay about all this."

"Wait! No." said Hassan in a panic. "He will fire me. I need this job."

"He won't fire you, Hassan, He's the one that'll be fired. He can't threaten and bribe you. He can't just cover up a dead body. He's finished. So you'll be fine. And if you're right and there are dangerous sharks we need to warn people right?"

He thought about how he and Fiona had been in the sea only a few hours ago. He shuddered.

"Ok. Yes we need to warn people. And I will keep my job?"

"Yes you'll keep your job."

"And I will get my phone back?"

"Your phone?"

"Mr Mackay took my phone."

"Why?"

"I don't know. I think because it has a picture of the body."

"Aaaaah. Ok. Yes I'll get your phone back. That will be very useful evidence. Speaking of which I think you should immediately go and report this to the police while I go and tackle Mr Mackay."

"The police? I don't..."

"Yes you must. I'll talk to them too but you need to go now. You did wrong by not reporting this immediately. You will be doing good by reporting it now. It's the right thing to do, Hassan."

"Ok. I will go to the police."

"Good. And I'll go and have my little chat with my boss. Thank you Hassan. For telling me. Well done. You did good."

Hassan smiled and bowed and headed off. Will made for Mackay's office.

His boss was indeed psychotic. How else could you explain it? He's completely lost the plot, thought Will. He's got to be stopped.

Chapter Twenty

He found Mackay in his office, sitting behind his desk flicking through a magazine. Busy man, he thought. Mackay looked up and grinned his ugly grin.

"Ah Mr Sanders. Back from your boating trip?"

Will thought he couldn't dislike someone more.

"Back from helping the police and coast guard search for our missing guest, yes."

Mackay grunted. "Find the body?"

Will paused, then said purposefully. "Which body do you mean, John?"

A look of realisation slowly crept over Mackay's face. But he feigned ignorance. "I don't get you."

"We haven't found Jojo's body. Tragic but it is a body we're looking for – we have to presume he's drowned, poor guy."

"I didn't know there was any doubt."

"But we have found another body. Would you believe it?"

Mackay kept a blank face. "You've found another body?"

"Yes. A poor Indian worker must have drowned a few days ago and his body was washed up under the ocean villas pier."

"Oh really? How unfortunate. Where is this body now?"

"I was hoping you could tell me, John."

"Oh, why?"

"Because I think you have hidden it somewhere."

"Hidden it?"

"Yes. I talked to Hassan, one of our receptionists. He told me the whole story. He showed you the body. You hid it somewhere. Where is it, John? And more to the point..." Will raised his voice, "Why the fuck did you do it?"

The Scotsman leapt up and turned on Will angrily, "Now look, Sanders. I don't know what you think you're playing at! But enough's enough! This is a fantasy!"

"Oh really?"

"Oh really! I don't know this receptionist and I don't know anything about some dead Indian. Where's your proof? Where's this body?"

"I don't know John. You do."

"Ah." Mackay sat down again. "But I don't, Will. I know absolutely nothing about it."

"Give me Hassan's phone."

"Why would I have his phone?"

"He says you took it from him. It has a photo of the body on it."

"He's lying."

"Why would he lie? He was scared shitless. You threatened him and bribed him, John."

"Now that's some accusation, Will."

"Why did you do it?"

"Look. You've been hoodwinked by some lying local who is mad or deluded or wants his name in the papers or something. I'm going to get Christoph to check him out. We can't have a madman working here. Now, fuck off and write another resignation letter. Or I'll fire you again, this time for making up false accusations about your boss."

As was happening with increasing regularity, it seemed to Will, they stared at each other in angry silence for a while.

Will finally broke the deadlock. "I'm not resigning, John. I'm going to uncover the truth. Or the police will. Hassan's talking to them now."

"What? Are you mad? We'll look like idiots! Some lunatic receptionist making up stories about shark attacks..."

"I didn't say anything about sharks John."

"Or however this Indian is supposed to have died...it doesn't matter. We already have one missing guest dying of a heart attack at sea. We don't need a mental member of staff making up stories too. What are you trying to do, Will? Kill the resort?"

"No John. I'm trying to save it. From you."

"Hah! You're as mad as your receptionist! I don't have time to discuss this nonsense further Will. You're dismissed."

"I'm going to talk to the police John."

"You're an idiot Will. Goodbye. Close the door behind you."

Once Will had gone Mackay made three short phone calls in quick succession.

The first call was to the lanky young hacker.

"Carl. I have a new job for you. Listen. We have a receptionist working at Nirvana called Hassan something. I presume there's only one Hassan. You can find out his details I'm sure?"

"Yes boss."

"Good. He's causing trouble. I need him to be discredited. I need people to disbelieve the story he's spreading around. You can hack into his personnel files at HQ. Can you do that? Make something up?"

"Of course."

"And see if we can apply pressure to any weak points. Family members maybe."

The second call was to the resort manager.

"Christoph. I'm afraid one of your staff is causing trouble."

"Causing trouble Mr Mackay?"

"Yes. One of your receptionists. He's called Hassan I think."

"Hassan? Really? He's a good guy."

"He's not a good guy Christoph. He's a liar. He's mad I think. Spreading rumours about dead bodies and sharks and all sorts..."

"Sharks?"

"Yes or some such nonsense. The guy's deluded. Check him out please. Then get rid of him. We can't have bad apples spoiling our launch. But wait an hour. I need to think about how to handle things with the media."

"This sounds bad Mr Mackay. I can't believe it. Yes sir I will deal with it immediately."

"Wait an hour."

"Ok sir. Yes."

"Oh and you may get approached by Will Sanders, one of my team. He's been taken in by this man's lies I think. He's a bit...well..unhinged because the guy who drowned, Jojo, was a friend of his. I'm being gentle with him but you should be a bit wary."

The third call was to the chief of police.

After walking out of Mackay's office, ruminating about how he did not believe a word his boss had said and wondering at the sheer evil of the man, Will decided to quickly check on Kate to see how she was doing.

He found Fiona with her. After a few comforting words to Kate he took Fiona to one side and updated her on his conversations with Hassan and Mackay. She was outraged.

"What are you going to do?" she asked him.

"I wanted to check on Kate first but now I'm going to talk to Christoph and then catch the police detective before he leaves. Don't worry. I'm not about to let Mackay get away with this."

"What about Penny? She'll string him up won't she?"

"She will. But she's out of contact at the moment. In China."

"Ok Will. Good luck." She gave him a peck on the cheek and her skin smelled of scented soap.

"Nice to see you without algae all over your face."

"Why thank you. Which reminds me, I have things to do to. I want to test that stuff and also check up with Plymouth."

Chapter Twenty-One

Twenty minutes later Will had crossed the resort to the manager's office and was now sitting at a small meeting table waiting for him. His PA had said he was away on a call and would be back shortly.

A couple of minutes later Christoph walked in. Will stood up to shake his hand as he crossed the room to the table. The tall handsome German matched him for height and good looks, and usually outdid him for the size of his smile.

But he wasn't smiling now. He looked glum, which was unusual, though not surprising given recent events.

"Ah Will. What a time we're having eh? First a guest goes missing, feared dead. Well, according to the police and coast guard very likely dead. A terrible thing. Poor man. And now this business with one of my receptionists."

Will had been expecting to tell Christoph about Hassan finding the body so he was surprised the man already knew something.

"What business? Do you know about the body washed up under the pier?"

"Will, let's sit down." They sat. "Coffee? Tea? Something stronger?"

"No. Thanks. So you've heard? From Hassan?"

"Well not exactly Will. I've been hearing *about* Hassan."

Will looked puzzled.

"I know he's been telling you stories about a dead body, as you say..."

"Stories?"

"Will, I don't think he's to be believed. I think unfortunately he's one of those people that make things up. A compulsive liar, I think they're called."

"No I don't think so Christoph." Will was taken aback. "I don't think he's lying myself. Why do you think that?"

"It's not me, Will. I've been talking to HR in Germany. According to his personnel file he has been caught telling lies twice in the past and is on a final warning. I didn't know. I feel bad. I'm responsible for hiring him."

"What?"

"I need to let him go Will. I'm sorry because he seems so good at his job and is a very nice fellow, but I can't have a liar working here. And anyway I have no choice – HR insist he must be fired. It's protocol. Three strikes and you're out."

Will's mind raced. Had he been completely taken in by this man's story? Was he that gullible? He thought he was a fairly good judge of character and not a complete sucker, but he had to admit he'd completely misjudged two or three people in the past. Hassan seemed so genuine though. He couldn't be that good an actor surely?

"I don't believe it Christoph. I don't believe he's lying. Why would he?"

"Who knows how some people's minds work..."

"And he was so scared. I could see it in his eyes. Mackay threatened him you know."

The German stiffened slightly. "Look Will. I know you and Mr Mackay don't get on well…"

"It's got nothing to do with that."

"And where's the body?"

"Mackay hid it. I don't like to talk about him behind his back but anyway I've said it to his face so… "

"But he says very clearly he knows nothing about this."

It dawned on Will that Mackay had been one step ahead of him. "You've talked to Mackay?"

"Yes. He called me about it. He told me to check with HR too."

"I see."

There was a knock at the door.

Hassan entered.

"Ok!" cried Will, leaping up. "Now we can get some clarity here. Let's see who the liar really is shall we! Come on over Hassan."

But Will's enthusiasm waned upon seeing the receptionist's downcast expression.

"My resignation letter, sir." He handed an envelope to the manager.

"Thank you Hassan," said Christoph. "It's better this way. You'll be able to get a job at another resort if we do it like this."

Will couldn't believe what was happening.

"Come on Hassan," he said, holding the man by the arm, trying to reassure him. "You don't have to resign. I know you didn't make up that story. Did you?"

Hassan looked down at the floor.

Will grabbed him by both arms and squeezed gently. "Come on, man. You don't need to be scared. I can help you."

The receptionist glanced at Will, then at Christoph and back at the floor before mumbling, "I'm sorry, Mr Sanders. I lied."

Will was shocked and let him go. "What?"

"I made it all up. There was no dead body under the jetty."

"Has he said something to you? Mackay? Has he forced you to do this?" asked Will.

The receptionist hesitated, and then summoning up something from deep inside he lifted his head and looked Will straight in the eyes. "No, Mr Sanders. He isn't forcing me. I just lied. I'm sorry." He turned and left before Will had a chance to stop him.

"Well there you are," said Christoph, sighing. "The man's a liar. A fantasist. Who knew?"

"I don't believe it," said Will.

Though he wasn't sure what he believed.

Chapter Twenty-Two

An hour later Will went to greet Jojo's mother and uncle together with Kate's parents who had all travelled together to the resort by seaplane after meeting up in the capital Male.

A handful of other senior resort staff had gone too, including Christoph who went out of his way to avoid talking to Will. Mackay had refused to go, saying he was too busy. Will was not surprised.

The chief of police had already briefed the families as soon as they had landed in the capital but wanted them all to meet with the detective leading the investigation, Kyle, to get a final update on the search and ask any detailed questions.

Everyone seemed to accept that, unless the body was found and an examination proved otherwise, Jojo had most likely drowned accidentally after a heart attack.

Both the mothers shed silent tears throughout the meeting and said little. Kate's father held his daughter's hand and looked resigned.

Jojo's uncle, on the other hand, asked the detective a series of questions in a polite but businesslike manner. A retired American businessman, Harold Tanner was short, maybe in his late 60's thought Will, with a largely bald head and large round glasses. He was clearly amenable and friendly but he didn't let pleasantries get in the way of finding out the facts. The meeting turned into a brief question and answer session between Mr Tanner and Kyle.

"Tell me, detective. Why was Jojo's equipment not reported as missing?"

"The hotel does admit responsibility for that. Human error. The dive instructor's assistant neglected to notice it had not been returned."

"I see. One for our lawyers to pursue I think." Tanner half smiled and fixed the detective with a stare through his thick lenses. "Have all guests been questioned about my nephew's disappearance?"

"Yes sir. And all staff. No further facts were forthcoming."

"Have all areas on land and at sea been thoroughly searched in your opinion?"

"They have, sir. It's been 24 hours. We've searched every inch of the sea out to a distance of 12 miles."

"Ok. Are there strong currents around the island?"

"There are. The coast guard's search took that into account. They computer mapped where a body...I'm sorry sir..."

Tanner waved his hand for the detective to continue.

"....Where someone might have been carried away to. They've done a thorough job in my opinion. I'm only sorry Jojo hasn't been found."

"Detective, is there any dangerous sea life in these waters?"

"No. Not for an experienced diver like your nephew."

Will wanted to interject when the American asked the last question but he stayed quiet. He didn't want to upset Jojo's mother with talk about shark attacks. In any case he now had a seed of doubt about Hassan's whole story. He decided to mention it to Kyle separately. And maybe to Jojo's uncle too.

Kyle finished by assuring the families that while the sea search could not be maintained at its current intensity they would nevertheless continue checking the coastlines of all surrounding islands. They had also alerted local fishermen and other resorts.

The families said they would stay at the resort overnight and decide what to do next tomorrow. Kate's parents had wanted to leave and take her home but respected her wishes to stay at least one day more. Jojo's mother was too shocked still to make any decision.

His uncle said he was staying until Jojo's body was found or until he felt there was nothing more to find out – however long it took.

As the meeting ended and everyone started to leave, Will approached the detective and asked for a quiet word. He was desperate to tell him about Hassan's story about the dead body and get his opinion on whether there was a cover-up going on.

They retreated to a corner of the room.

Before Will had a chance to open his mouth the detective said, "Will, if this is about the receptionist's story about a body washed up on the beach I can't help you."

He was completely taken aback. It was like his conversation with Christoph all over again.

"I heard all about it," Kyle continued, "And I can't get involved. The guy's said to be a serial liar and there's no evidence. Sorry, Will."

"But what if he's not lying? What if it's all a cover up? Can't you at least talk to Mackay? See what you think?" Will pleaded.

"Sorry," shrugged the detective, "Out of my hands. My boss says not to waste time on it. Now I have to go and check back with my men. See you later."

He smiled and walked off.

Will went to the window and looked out but at nothing in particular. He was being foolish. Hassan had taken him in. God knows why. Let it go and move on. Yet...he'd seemed so genuine...

"You look lost."

A deep, kindly American voice behind him.

He turned to find Jojo's uncle holding out his hand.

"Hi. Will, right? I'm Harold Tanner. Jojo's uncle."

"Hi Mr Tanner." They shook hands.

"Harold, please." The American smiled up at him warmly. His eyes were enlarged slightly by his oversized glasses and fixed Will for a few seconds with an unblinking stare.

"You knew my nephew I hear?"

"Not really. Well a little. We just met a couple of times here during the launch events. I never knew him before. We clicked though. He was...is a great guy. And Kate too."

"Yes. He's my only nephew. The only boy. I taught him how to play baseball. I have three daughters you see, and none of them was particularly interested in baseball." He smiled to himself.

"You were close."

"Yes we were. A great boy. It's a tragedy. That word is overused. But it's a tragedy."

The older man seemed on the verge of emotion but something suddenly seemed to click inside him and he changed back to his businesslike tone. Still warm, but businesslike.

"I saw you talking to the local cop. You don't seem happy. Anything I should know?"

"I..." Will hesitated at opening a can of worms.

"Let me put it another way," said Tanner staring at him, "If you think it's got anything remotely to do with my nephew then I want you to tell me."

Will told him. He felt he had every right to know. Everything Hassan had said, and the responses of Mackay, Christoph and Kyle.

The old man didn't take his eyes off Will and didn't interrupt.

When Will had finished Tanner nodded and stood motionless for a while staring into the middle distance with a slight frown.

Then he turned back to Will. "Something smells bad," he said finally. "I think I need to talk to these three guys. I better catch the cop before he leaves. Then tell me how to find the manager and this boss of yours."

He smiled at Will. "You did good, young man."

An hour and a half later the two men reconvened over a coffee in the lobby. Will arrived first and took a seat at a small table in the corner.

He noticed Hassan had been replaced by a young woman behind the reception desk.

A minute later Tanner walked over, grimacing and looking pained.

"You Ok Harold?" asked Will, helping him sit. "Is it Mackay? I told you he's a nasty character."

"The guy's a prize asshole. But I've dealt with his kind before. No, it's my legs. Skiing accident fifteen years ago. Broke them both in quite a few places. Still play up. I can't move around as fast as I used to."

"You're pretty good for....um...."

"An old bird?" said the American grinning.

"Well I was going to say a man in his sixties..."

"Seventies, Will, seventies. Seventy-what I'm not sure though. You tend not to count after you're fifty."

They laughed.

A waiter came over and they ordered two flat whites.

Will was desperate to know how Tanner had got on. "So? How was it?"

"Well....they all told me exactly what they told you. The manager – Christoph right? – the cop, and that charming Scottish gentleman. I laid into all of them. Haven't made any friends. But I gotta know the truth."

"And do you believe them?"

"Of course I don't believe them. Will, I can spot a liar a mile away. I came across hundreds of them in my working life. Only one of them's a bastard though. You know which one right?"

Will laughed.

"But what I don't know is whether this has got anything to do with my nephew disappearing. Why am I gonna waste my time on trying to prove they're all lying about some poor Indian guy drowning if it's got nothing to do with Jojo? Tell me what you think, Will."

Will thought a moment.

"Well. I'm wondering...If they're covering up the Indian...which I think they are...then they may also be covering up something about Jojo. To protect the resort."

"Ok."

"Plus...if something – a shark maybe – attacked the Indian, maybe...I'm sorry, it sounds terrible to say it, but maybe it attacked Jojo too. Maybe it's a danger to more people. Who knows."

"You think my nephew was killed by a shark?" The old man grimaced.

"I'm sorry. This isn't helping."

"No. It is. We gotta look into every possibility. I need to know what happened to Jojo. Maybe it was his heart – he always had problems – but maybe it wasn't. There's something going on at this resort I don't like the smell of."

"There's something else too. It may be totally unconnected. Probably is."

Tanner nodded for him to continue.

"This sounds a bit odd...but a new species of fish has been found in these waters. We had a juvenile in our aquarium here but it died. Fiona – our marine expert – is looking into it."

Tanner looked puzzled.

"It's a gruesome looking thing. And if there are larger versions of it out there they could be dangerous. I don't know. As I say it's unlikely to be related, but who knows."

The old man looked like he was processing what Will had said.

"We gotta get this phone, Will," he said finally. "The one the receptionist took a snap of the body on. We gotta get it from the Scottish guy."

"Mackay. You do think he's got it?"

"He was very very certain he doesn't. So, yeah, I think he does."

"How do we get it?"

The flat whites arrived and they both took a sip while they thought about the answer.

"He's not going to keep it with him," said Will. "So it's very likely to be in his suite somewhere. So...we search the suite. Maybe?"

"Right."

"Which I guess is breaking a law or two. Plus a firing offence. But I've already been fired twice so a third time won't matter."

Tanner grinned. "I like your attitude, kid."

"We need to make sure he's not going to be there though," Will continued. "I'll get Bob – he's one of the journalists – to interview him. He usually hates interviews but if I say it's a profile piece on him – nothing about the issues at the resort - he'll go for it. He has an ego the size of Jupiter."

"It's a plan, Will. Let's do it."

Bob was confused by Will's request for him to interview Mackay. "Why would I want to do that? The guy's a twat." But Will told him that he'd promised Mackay that he'd get him profiled and this would really help him out. Bob liked Will and was finally persuaded to do it as a favour, as long as he didn't necessarily need to publish the final piece. Will said it didn't matter. He'd tell Mackay the article had been postponed, and then he'd forget all about it. It would not be the first time Will had pulled this trick he had to admit to himself.

The interview started an hour later. Mackay had almost spoilt the plan by suggesting it took place in his suite, which doubled as his office – but Will had suggested the restaurant would be more convivial and Mackay had agreed.

Will sat in for the first five minutes. He'd asked Bob to string it out for an hour. Mackay launched immediately into his views on the principles of marketing to today's consumer. Bob shot Will a pained look. He owed him big time.

Will made his excuses and left them to it. He knew where the maids were at this time of day and went in search of one he knew.

"Hey, Sana! Sorry I've lost my card key again. Lend me your master will you. I'll get it back to you in half an hour ok?"

"Ok Mr Sanders. No problem." The maid smiled and handed Will her master key which gained access to all rooms in the hotel. She'd done the same a couple of days ago when he'd locked himself out of his room.

"Thanks Sana!" Will called to her as he hurried off to meet up with Tanner at the stairwell leading to the suites.

Wish me luck, he thought.

Chapter
Twenty-Three

Tanner was waiting at the bottom of the stairwell. "Is our suspect detained?" he asked with a twinkle in his eye.

The old guy's enjoying this, thought Will. He'd expected him to baulk at breaking into someone's suite in a hotel. Far from it.

"Suspect is detained," he said. "Though I feel sorry for poor old Bob."

They climbed the single flight of stairs leading to the suite level on the first floor of the two story main hotel block. The stairwell was empty as Will knew it would be. It was for emergencies only, the guests and staff using stairs located elsewhere.

Will saw an aerosol can in Tanner's hand.

"What's that for, Harold?"

Tanner tapped his head. "Thinking ahead, kid. Thinking ahead. Now help me will you. These stairs are killing me."

He was intrigued but decided to let it go. He took the older man's arm and helped him climb.

They reached the top of the stairs without meeting anyone. Will listened at the door leading to the corridor to check for footsteps or talking, then opened the door and peeked out.

"All clear."

He was about to enter the corridor when Tanner grabbed his arm. "Hang on."

"Why?"

"Do you wanna get caught on camera breaking into your boss's room?"

Will noticed the CCTV security camera for the first time. It was in the corner above and to the left of the doorway they were in, just below the ceiling. A small glass hemisphere with a red light. Every corridor had one. He should have thought of this. "Shit!" he said under his breath.

"Don't worry. I've got it sorted," said Tanner. He reached into his jacket pocket and pulled out a pen.

"Excuse me." He nudged Will out of the way.

"According to my guess-work we're in a blind spot here so they can't see us yet. Their field of vision covers the part of the corridor with the suite doors over there. Now, I'm gonna shine this laser pen at the camera. You take this..." he handed Will the aerosol can, "...And while I'm blinding the camera so it doesn't see you, you go and spray the lens with the shaving foam."

Will looked at the little old guy in amazement.

"It's a little trick I learnt," said Tanner. "Now be quick 'cause I need to keep the beam directed at the lens and I can't keep my arm steady for too long. You need to do the spraying 'cause you're tall. Now go."

Will wondered for a moment quite what Tanner's job used to be but he had little time to think about it as the man was already holding up the laser pen and shining a thin red beam directly at the CCTV camera.

"Go now, Will."

He quickly walked the ten or so paces to the camera, shook the can, and sprayed white foam on the lens. If Tanner was right, nobody would have seen their heads poking out of the stairwell exit and now nobody would be able to see them break into Mackay's room.

"Won't they come running when they see their camera's been blocked?" asked Will as Tanner joined him at the corner of the corridor.

"I'm betting not," said the old man crossing his fingers. "They use these cameras to record mostly – so they can go back and check if a crime's reported. There are too many of these things around the hotel for them to sit and watch every one of them."

"I hope you're right."

"We'd better be quick just in case. Have you got the key?"

Will produced the master key card and they tried it on the middle of the three doors which led to the three suites, only one of which was currently in use. Mackay's.

A red light flashed next to the door handle.

"Damn," said Will.

He tried it again.

This time a green light and the lock clicked.

They opened the solid wooden door and went in.

Will closed the door and called out tentatively, "Hello?"

No answer.

They were in the entrance hall of an enormous suite.

Tanner whistled quietly, "Wow. This guy doesn't like to slum it, huh?"

"Nope. This is one of the best suites."

They took a quick look round. To their right was the dining room Mackay was using as a temporary office and which Will was very familiar with from their eventful meetings over the past few days.

To their left a huge long living room, off which was a kitchenette. Further down the suite was a walk-in wardrobe and then the bedroom. Running along the length of the bedroom and living room was an open air decked terrace with sea view. The décor was modern and stylish throughout, with lots of hardwood and muted colours.

After their quick scout around they headed back to the dining room. It was scattered with files and papers. There were two laptops on the table.

"This is the only room he works in, said Will. "He has no other office here. It's the most likely place he'd hide the phone I think."

They split up and examined every part of the room separately, being careful to replace any papers or objects they moved.

There was a desk with three drawers. Will opened the first two and found nothing but pens, pads and a calculator.

The third drawer was locked.

"Bugger! I bet it's in here Howard."

"Locked?"

"Yep."

"I need paperclips," said Tanner, scanning the desktop. "Doesn't anyone use paperclips anymore? Ah! Here we go."

Tanner picked up two piles of papers from the desk and removed a paperclip from the corner of each.

"You gotta be kidding," said Will, shaking his head.

"Another old trick I know," Tanner said, opening up one of the paperclips and bending it into a long hook. He did what looked to Will like something similar but not exactly the same with the other paperclip. Then he inserted one clip in the drawer lock and held it tight while he pushed the second clip in above it and jiggled it around.

"I thought this only happened in movies," said Will. "Harold, you are full of surprises."

"It's nothing, kid."

After a few seconds the lock clicked and Tanner pulled the drawer open.

They both looked inside. Then they both let out short laughs.

There was a wad of bank notes. And some paperclips.

"Ok, nothing here," said Tanner. "Let's split up and search the other rooms. I'll do the living room, you try the bedroom."

They headed off, Will striding out in front.

Then they heard the door click.

As it opened, they both took the nearest cover. Tanner slipped into the kitchenette and ducked down by the sink. Will dived into the walk-in wardrobe and gently closed the door.

Neither man knew if they'd been heard or spotted by whoever was entering.

Mackay's unmistakable voice called out. "Sanders, You bastard!"

They'd been spotted. Will's mind started racing with excuses for being in his boss's room.

Then Mackay said in a mock posh English accent: "He won't ask you anything about the drowning!" Then in his own Scots voice, moving further away towards the dining room office. "Christ! Where's that bloody press statement?"

Will closed his eyes and sighed to himself quietly.

Then it struck him that Mackay might look in the wardrobe room for some reason. He backed further inside and tried to conceal himself among some jackets which were hanging up. He felt stupid as he knew he'd still be clearly seen if the man walked in. He hoped Tanner was well hidden.

Moments later, presumably having found the press statement for Bob, Mackay hurried from the room, muttering more expletives and slamming the door behind him.

Will pushed the hanging jackets aside and as he did so his knuckles rapped against something hard.

He reached inside the jacket and found a zipped inner pocket. He unzipped it and took out a mobile phone.

"Hey, you in there kid?" came a voice and Tanner opened the door. "That was a close one!"

"Look what I found." Will held up the phone. "Too old a model to be Mackay's I think. Must be Hassan's."

"Bingo!"

"Hang on though," said Will and started searching through all the jacket's pockets.

"What are you looking for?"

"The passcode. Mackay will have needed to get it from Hassan to open the phone and delete the pictures. Otherwise he could have just destroyed the phone, and he hasn't. My guess is he wrote it down. But it's not here. It's probably in his wallet. Which he'll have on him."

"Or it could be anywhere. Or maybe he didn't write it down. Or didn't get it at all. It doesn't matter – the police can open it."

"Do you trust the police after what Kyle said about Hassan?"

"Well we can't stand around gassing, Will. We gotta get outta here."

"Yeah. And there might be another way around this..."

Will rearranged the jackets as he'd found them. Then they left Mackay's suite, first listening at the door to check no-one was outside in the corridor.

As they walked back under the camera Will had a thought.

He took out the aerosol can and sprayed randomly up the wall.

He then called Housekeeping and told them it looked like some drunken guest must have had some fun with their shaving foam and could they clean it up at once.

Chapter Twenty-Four

T hey went straight to Will's room with the phone.

"I have an idea," he said, taking out his own mobile and dialling.

"Who are you calling?"

"A friend of mine. Works for a tech magazine. He might be able to help...."

Danny was an IT journalist he'd worked with closely on several projects in the past. They'd got on well and had enjoyed a few drinking sessions together. It had been two years ago and they hadn't spoken since but he knew such time gaps didn't matter to blokes.

A voice answered: "Hi Will."

"How'd you know it was me, Danny?"

"Ha! I know everything, Will. Hey, how are you man? It's been years! Where are you?"

"I'm in The Maldives..."

"Oh my heart bleeds for you. Another day in Paradise."

"I know, I know. I have a tough job. Sorry it's been so long, mate. We must meet up when I'm next in town, right?"

"That'd be great."

"Look, Danny, I need your help."

"Sure."

"I think I remember you telling me once there's a way you can unlock your phone if you forget your password. Well I've..."

"Yeah, there's a few ways you can do it. If it's Android you can go to your Google account...."

"No, it's not my phone so I can't do that. I just found it and I want to see who it belongs to so I can give it to them."

Will hoped this didn't sound suspicious. However, Danny sounded completely unfazed.

"Oh ok. I get it. In that case....you got the phone there?"

"Yeah. Go ahead."

"What make is it?"

"It's an i-phone."

"Ok. This usually works. Not always. But usually."

"Ok. Let's try it."

"Ok. Now. Hold down the home button at the bottom of the phone until you get that annoying Siri guy."

Will did so. The phone's screen lit up with Siri asking how it could help. "Got Siri."

"Now, ask Siri what time it is."

"What?"

"Ask him what time it is, Will. Go ahead."

Will spoke to the screen. "What time is it?"

The screen displayed a clock.

"I have a clock on the screen, Danny."

"Good. Click on it."

A new screen flicked up.

"I have a new screen with Word Clock, Alarm and stuff..."

"Ok. Click on the Timer icon."

"Done."

"Now select When Timer Ends."

"Done that. Comes up with a list of ringtones."

"Yep. Scroll to the top of the ringtone list and select Buy More Tones."

"The Apple Store has opened up."

"And now if you click the Home button again you'll be able to access the phone."

Will did so and the main phone screen appeared. "Wow. I'm in! You're a genius Danny."

"Yeah I know."

They said their goodbyes.

Tanner clapped his hands in appreciation. "That's impressive! And a bit worrying."

"Yep. Nothing's safe anymore Harold. All you need is two paper-clips and a tech journalist! Now let's look at the photo library." Will flicked through images showing different features of the resort. A few included selfies. "This is Hassan's phone alright."

The last photos showed Hassan walking on the beach. But there was nothing after that.

"Mackay must have already deleted the picture of the body. It's not here."

"Damn!" Tanner said. "All this for nothing."

"Not necessarily, Harold." Something had occurred to Will. There was one chance. "Mackay is no IT expert. He has minions that do it for him. So he may not have..." Will clicked on the Recently Deleted file. A picture appeared of a body on a beach covered in horrific wounds and seaweed. "He deleted this but you need to delete a photo twice to get rid of it. Otherwise you can retrieve it within thirty days. Yes! I knew he wouldn't know that!"

Tanner gave him a thumbs up and a huge smile: "Great work again, Will."

"And now I'm going to show this to the police."

"I thought you didn't trust them?"

"I'm going over Kyle's head. I'm going straight to the police chief himself!"

Chapter Twenty-Five

Will reached the chief of police on the man's home phone after pushing past several attempts to block him. It was late, the chief was off duty, he didn't like to be bothered outside the office....the usual stuff.

After apologising for disturbing him Will told the chief about the picture of the body on Hassan's mobile. The chief said he'd heard about what he called 'the dead Indian story' but was sceptical as nobody had been reported missing. If Will texted him the photo he'd examine it and call back straight away.

Half an hour later he called back. He said it was difficult to see where the body was or what had caused the wounds but he assured Will he would look into the matter first thing in the morning. He asked Will to hand the mobile to Kyle before he left the island the next day so the detective could bring it to him. When Will asked why the chief told him it was standard procedure and the mobile would need to be submitted for forensic examination. Will agreed, reluctantly.

When he suggested the chief might wish to speak with John Mackay about the body's disappearance he was told the police were quite capable of conducting any investigation and that currently their priority as far as Nirvana Resort was concerned was the disappearance of Jojo.

"Maybe they're connected," suggested Will.

"Maybe they are. Maybe they aren't," replied the chief. "We will find the answer, Mr Sanders, don't worry."

Will was far from reassured but the man brought the conversation to an end.

He went to bed early and slept fitfully, his mind troubled by a nagging uncertainty about the honesty or otherwise of the local police. He was thankful though not to suffer his recurring sea nightmare, particularly after the previous day's events.

He woke at sunrise with the light streaming into his room. He showered quickly and skipped breakfast. He was determined that before he handed the mobile to Kyle he wanted to show Fiona the picture to see if she could shed any light on the bite marks herself.

He found her at the aquarium, hard at work despite the early hour.

She was standing at the top of a ladder peering into one of the tanks and twiddling with some gizmo or other at the surface of the water. She wore shorts and polo shirt and had her hair tied up while she worked. Will stood and watched her for a moment. She saw him and smiled. "Hey Will!"

He felt embarrassed for having been staring at her so overcompensated with an enthusiastic "Hi Fi! Great to see you!"

She scooted down the ladder and came over and gave him a quick kiss on the lips.

"Careful," he said raising his eyes, "Cameras everywhere!"

"Oooops! Wouldn't be on would it? Two members of staff kissing. But I won't be a member of staff for long."

"Maybe I won't either."

"Still problems with your boss?"

"Yeah. Maybe the police too."

"The police?"

"They don't seem to believe this is really serious," he said, showing her the photo of the body.

She took the phone. "Poor man. How awful." She used her fingers to zoom in on the body. "Let me look at these wounds a bit closer."

"Is it a shark? Do you think it got Jojo too?"

She screwed up her face as he'd noticed her do whenever she was trying to concentrate on something. "I don't....no I don't think it's a shark. The bite marks don't look like a shark's. They're more like big puncture wounds."

"So they are bite marks? Not coral or a propeller or something?"

"I think so. But it's hard to tell."

"And do you think something attacked him while he was swimming or just took bites out of him after he drowned?"

Fiona shrugged. "Will, I just don't know."

"What about that monster fish you had in the tank? Could it have done this?"

She looked harder at the close up of the wounds. "Not the one we had. These wounds are too deep. But maybe his big brother. He was a juvenile after all. Unlikely though."

"Why?"

"I've been back and forth with the university, my professor there. I didn't have a chance to update you. We do think it could be a new species. But we're unlikely to find another one. It's from the deep deep ocean we think. Which is why nobody's ever seen one before." She handed the phone back. "And why it died in our tank probably. It couldn't survive at the surface for long. Are you going to announce it to the media? It's a huge story. New species of fish discovered."

Will thought for a second. "I'm not sure this is the time are you?"

She nodded slowly. "No you're right. It's nothing compared to poor Jojo. I hope Kate's coping ok."

"She's in good hands."

"I know. Poor girl."

"Maybe we talk about this fish when it's all cleared up."

"Ok. I'll tell the university."

"Meanwhile I guess I'd better give this to Kyle."

They agreed to meet up later for a drink and Will left to find the detective.

Chapter Twenty-Six

The huge red and white tanker ploughed through the sea at a steady 24 knots.

It was 180 meters long – medium sized for a bulk carrier – with a bridge at the stern and five separate cargo holds along its length.

It was a thoroughly international ship - built in South Korea, registered in Panama, Chinese owned, and with an Indian captain, Raj, who now stood in the bridge behind a console of knobs, wheels and buttons, sipping from a mug and surveying the ocean.

He was a very large man with thick arms and neck, and an enormous pendulous belly which strained against an XXXXL white polo shirt and hung over the top of navy blue shorts whose waist size could only be imagined.

He was glad the company didn't go in for uniforms. Collared shirts always choked him and to find a captain's hat big enough for his rotund head had always been a struggle.

He put down his tea and took a bite from a moist brown cake which looked average sized in his podgy paw but could probably have fed a family.

He always ate a lot when he was bored. And he was bored quite often. He'd done this trip several times over the past few months and it was very tedious. 9,400 nautical miles there and back. Down through

the South China Sea and across the Bay Of Bengal into the Indian
Ocean. Do the business and then return and repeat. A circular trip of
16 days.

But it was very very well paid. A lot more than any of his previous
jobs as a merchant captain.

Undoubtedly because it was so hush-hush, he thought.

They had the bare minimum crew. Just 15 men. Barely enough to
operate a vessel of this size. But the greater number of men, the greater
risk of blabbing.

Two crew members had got drunk one night and started talking
about their journey to the Indian Ocean and the odd thing they did
when they got there. The men had suddenly disappeared, no-one
knew where. It had been a sobering lesson to the rest of the crew.
Nobody talked after that. Not even to wives and girlfriends.

Some of the crew would ask him now and then what the purpose
of their secretive missions was. He would always tell them sharply
to mind their own business and keep their traps shut, or face the
consequences.

The truth was he didn't know himself.

Chapter
Twenty-Seven

L ater that morning Will sat in the bar and waited for Fiona to
  meet him at the agreed time. She was late, but she was always
late. It was in her Mediterranean blood, thought Will.

He ordered a flat white. Then, feeling a pang of hunger, a brownie.

"Make that two," came an American voice behind him. It was
Harold Tanner.

He joined Will at the bar. "I need it after the morning I've had."

He told Will how he'd spent the last two hours trying to get answers
out of Mackay, Cristoph and Kyle. None of them would comment on
the stolen phone and its picture of the Indian body. Nor was there any
news about Jojo.

"I've been stonewalled. Completely and utterly. I'm not getting
anywhere. My sister's given up hope and is catching a plane back to
the States tomorrow. But I'm staying on until I get some answers.
Somehow."

The coffees arrived and they sipped at them sombrely.

They were in the middle of discussing a possible course of action
when Fiona joined them.

Will thought she looked like she'd come to a momentous decision of some kind. Tanner must have sensed it too and the two men waited for her to speak. They had stood up when she'd arrived and they now all three stood in a circle.

She looked at them in turn. "I want to take another look around out there. I've been studying the algae we collected. It shouldn't be here in this quantity. And I think it's affecting the marine eco-structure. I want to go diving and see for myself. Oh, can I have a coffee please?"

Will thought she was mad. "Isn't that a bit dangerous considering what's been going on?" He said before turning to call the barman. "One more of these please."

"I want to see if I can find any more deep water species."

He turned back to her. "What? The monster killer fish you mean?"

She smiled. "We don't know they're killer fish. And they're not monsters, they're just fish. And anyway, we don't know if there's any more of this species we found coming to the surface, or if there are any more different types of deep sea species."

Tanner looked confused. "You think there is some connection between the fish and this algae you both saw – Will told me how you'd dived in like, how did you put it, a cross between a mermaid and wonder woman."

Will blushed. "Not quite what I said."

"Exactly what you said." Tanner smiled at him and Fiona laughed.

"I don't know," she said. "But maybe. Phytoplankton – algae – is the life-form at the bottom of the food chain in the oceans. It's where everything starts. It's eaten by zooplankton which in turn is eaten by fish. So yes I think it's worth investigating why at the same time around here we have a huge boom in algae and the appearance of a new species of fish never seen in shallow water."

"Nevertheless, young lady," the American continued, "I agree with Will. You going off on your own looking for sea monsters sounds dangerous."

"Thank you Harold," said Will. He hoped they could both put her off the crazy idea.

"Which is why," continued the old man, "Will should go with you."

Not quite what he'd expected to hear. "What?" he said, spilling Fiona's drink as he handed it to her.

"No it's OK," she said, "Steve's taking me. I asked him just now. He wants to know too." She held Will's hand. "Don't worry. I know you hate the sea."

"You're afraid of the sea, kid?" asked Tanner, his eyes wide behind his glasses.

"Well....I had a bad experience when I was a boy."

"I understand," said the old man, patting his other hand. "These things can traumatise you."

"But of course I'll go with her," Will said. The prospect terrified him but he wasn't going to show it in front of either of them.

"Good-oh," said Fiona and clapped her hands.

Christ, I must have fallen for her, thought Will as they finished their coffees. There's nothing else would get me into the ocean with God Knows What.

They set off within the hour. Will, Fiona and Steve the dive instructor.

Tanner came to see them off and waved to them from the jetty as they sped away in one of the dive boats.

As Will couldn't dive and Fiona wanted to study the surface waters they decided to snorkel.

They were going to circle the island, stopping at several spots to dive for half an hour each time.

Fiona chatted with Steve at the front of the boat while Will sat in silence, his heart thumping and wondering what he was doing there.

It took them just five minutes to reach the first spot.

They all donned mask, snorkel and flippers and plunged into the calm blue waters.

Will spent the first five minutes staring around him and stayed close to the boat. But after a while he forgot his fears and grew accustomed to the new undersea world. He started to enjoy the buoyancy of his body in the warm water and the stunning sights around him.

His attention was drawn by Fiona to a group of blue and yellow Angelfish and he was entranced as he watched them darting about.

Then she pointed to a cluster of anemones and he recognised the orange and white striped Clown Fish – Nemos – ducking in and out.

The second dive spot was further out, in the deeper sea away from the coral reef. Here his fear returned in pangs and he spent a few minutes imagining shapes in the deep blue ocean around him. Again though he was drawn out of it by the marine life. This time a school of small translucent white squid darting around him playfully.

Then, amazingly, a huge Manta Ray, maybe four meters wide from wing tip to wing tip. He watched in wonder as it glided past him and then on until it disappeared into the blue-black distance.

By the third dive spot he forgot to be afraid at all and actually looked forward to getting into the water. This could become my new hobby, he thought.

Here his attention was grabbed by an enormous school of large silver and black fish which swam in unison. He marvelled at how they would change direction together at the same time as though they were really one single great creature.

He was so distracted by watching them that he failed to notice the circling sharks.

There were five of them. No, six. Three at his level, three just below. They were over two meters long with a grey body and a black tip on the dorsal fin. They slid effortlessly through the water with a languid snake-like motion.

He felt a sudden massive surge of adrenalin and panic.

He looked around for Fiona and the instructor but couldn't see them.

The sharks seemed to tighten the circle.

He surfaced and tried to control his fear. Couldn't sharks sense fear? He was sure he'd seen a programme about that.

He looked around for the coloured top of a snorkel. Nothing. Where the hell were they? Surely not attacked and dragged to their deaths...

Then he saw them sitting in the dive boat chatting.

"Hey!" he shouted.

They turned their heads and Fiona called, "Will! Time's up! Come in."

He hated her calmness, and shouted again..."Sharks!"

They both dived in and swam towards him.

He looked down again into the water. To his relief the circle of sharks seemed to be moving away.

Steve reached him first. "No worries, mate," he said in his laid-back Australian accent. "They're just reef sharks. Black Tips. They won't hurt you. They're just curious, mate."

Will started swimming back to the boat with him and met Fiona half way. They bobbed in the water together while the instructor got back into the boat.

"Only reef sharks Will," she said.

"Yeah, so I'm told. But still sharks and still scary."

"You're first time swimming with sharks?"

"And my last I think!"

"They're beautiful creatures."

"I'm not sure that's how I'd desc..." Will stopped as he saw Fiona suddenly dive down.

A few seconds later she resurfaced and called to the boat: "Hey! Steve! Camera! Throw me my camera!"

"What is it?" said Will. But she'd ducked under again.

She surfaced quicker this time. And her eyes looked wide behind her mask. "Back to the boat, Will. Quick."

They swam fast towards the boat. Will tried to keep his mind clear of the spectre trying to break into his consciousness. He knew fear would paralyse him so he focussed on the boat which was now just a few meters away.

He saw Steve leaning over with a boat hook and thought for a moment he was going to push Will under with it. But he was aiming it in the water just to one side and started jabbing.

Against every instinct to clamber aboard Will waited and pushed Fiona into the boat.

Then he felt something graze his leg.

He looked down in time to see a massive bulbous black head and an arched gaping mouth with a row of translucent teeth, the two at the front like javelins.

The instructor dealt the creature a blow in the centre of its head as its mouth was just inches from Will's body.

The giant fish turned sharply down and away, but as it passed it took a side bite at Will's leg, drawing blood which spurted into the water.

Will half jumped and was half tugged into the boat.

He lay on the floor, his right leg a bloody mess.

Fiona looked at him in shock. "Will!" she cried.

"I told you the sea was scary," he said. And blacked out.

Chapter
Twenty-Eight

Will is a little boy again.

He is caught in the strong current off the north Cornish coast, being dragged out to sea.

He tries to swim against the current, tries to make it to the beach, but the sea holds him in its cold iron grip and drags him further, further, and then down and down, into the murky grey depths.

He kicks hard and pulls upwards with his arms, stretching his neck to try to make the surface. It works. He takes a gasp of air.

Something is different now. It is dazzlingly bright sunshine and the sky is blue. The sea is translucent turquoise. He looks to the shore. The rugged grey Cornish cliffs have been replaced by a paradise palm tree sandy beach.

But he is still caught in the current which is pulling him away from the land.

He looks behind and sees a giant cave of a mouth, lined with hundreds of long sharp silver teeth.

The monster is sucking the sea into its mouth, creating the current which Will is caught in.

He kicks again and swims with all his might. Straining to get away. But it's no use.

Now he is half way into the mouth and the jaws snap shut around his body, the teeth piercing his bones.

Will woke with a start and a shout.

He was in bed but not at the resort. Fiona was sitting in a chair next to him. "It's OK Will," she said soothingly, "It was just a bad dream."

He sat up and looked around him. Everything was clean white and stainless steel. Apart from Tanner slumped asleep in an armchair in the corner.

"Where am I?" he asked, feeling like a character in a movie.

"You're in Male hospital. You're all right, don't worry." She stroked his arm tenderly.

He suddenly remembered the creature's attack and looked at his leg under the white sheet, half fearing it not to be there.

"You're OK, Will. Your leg's OK. It just scraped you. Luckily. It didn't fully bite you. There was lots of bleeding which caused you to black out. That and the shock. But we bandaged you up and were lucky enough there was still a coast guard chopper around so they took you to hospital in no time."

"How long have I been out?"

"You were sedated while they cleaned you up and put in a few stitches. About six hours I think."

"What time is it?"

"It's about seven pm."

"And my leg's OK?"

"It's fine. No muscle damage or anything. Doctor says you can be up and about tomorrow. You were lucky."

He lay back down and felt relieved. Then the image of the black scaly head and the gaping mouth with huge fangs came into his head. He shivered involuntarily.

"Fi...What was the thing? It was horrible. A monster. I think I just had a nightmare about it."

"I'm not surprised," said a deep voice from the corner as Tanner stirred and then walked over to Will's bedside. "How are you son?" He held his other arm. Will felt glad to have the two of them there.

"I feel OK. Nothing hurts too much. Just a throbbing in my leg."

Fiona looked a bit ashamed."I'm sorry I suggested the trip. Thanks for helping me into the boat first. That could have been me."

Will smiled. "No, you're too skinny. He was after me – I've got more meat on me. Anyway, it's Steve we need to thank. He was the one who fought the thing off. Good man!"

"And it was Fiona who bandaged your leg and stopped the bleeding," added Tanner proudly.

"Then thank you Fi. You're a life saver. And I feel such a dick for blacking out."

"You didn't see the blood," said Fiona shaking her head, "That and the sight of that monstrous head and teeth would give most people a heart attack I think. Would you like some water?"

She handed him a glass from a bedside table and he drank thirstily.

"Thank you. So what was it? Any ideas?" He asked again, handing back the glass.

Fiona started pacing the room while she spoke, as though walking helped her think.

"Well...I didn't see it very clearly in all the commotion. What with the water foaming and trying to help you into the boat and blood gushing everywhere..."

"I'm sorry about that," said Will.

"Yes how inconsiderate of you spurting all that blood," said Tanner.

The two men laughed but Fiona ignored their joshing.

"...But I saw enough of it to be able to say with a fair amount of certainty that it's the adult version of the species we found in the aquarium. A totally new species. This one I estimate to be about six foot long. Around two meters...."

"Wow, that's some fish!" exclaimed Tanner.

"Yeah, and how can it possibly be a new species at that size? It's huge. How come nobody's seen it before?"

Fiona continued pacing. "The Coelacanth is probably the most famous new fish species discovery. It was previously thought to have been extinct. Only fossils had been found. So the scientific consensus was that the Coelacanth had died out roughly 66 million years ago. Until a living one was caught off South Africa in 1938. They've also been spotted around here in the Indian Ocean too you know. And they're pretty big – around six foot. So a fish as big as a tall man managed to go unnoticed for centuries. Amazing isn't it?"

She stopped and looked at the two men who nodded in agreement.

"But," she continued, raising finger, "That's not the most amazing new discovery. In 1976 a new species of shark was discovered. Never been seen before until then. You know how big that fish is?"

They shook their heads, enjoying the lecture.

"Guess."

"Six foot, like the Coela-watsit?" ventured Tanner.

"Coelacancth," she corrected, smiling, "Nope. Bigger."

"Bigger than this new monster that attacked me?" said Will.

Fiona paused for effect. "Three times bigger."

"What?" exclaimed Will.

"The Megamouth Shark. 18 foot long. Six meters. Three times the size of our monster. And only discovered in 1976!"

"You're kidding me," said Tanner, his eyes bigger than usual behind his round glasses.

"That IS amazing," said Will.

"So if a fish that size can go unnoticed until just forty years ago it makes our creature less surprising doesn't it? And they are also found in the Indian Ocean by the way." said Fiona.

"But how could these things not have been spotted?" asked Will, "With all the diving and sea exploration that goes on."

"The sea's a pretty big place. And also most of the new fish species discovered are from the deep sea. The Megamouth usually swims around 200 meters down or deeper during the day and then comes up to shallow water at night. A lot of marine species do this. They follow the plankton as it migrates up from the depths over night."

"So this shark eats plankton?" asked Tanner.

"Yes. It's like the Whale Shark. It eats plankton and other small creatures including jellyfish."

"But our creature doesn't eat plankton does it?" said Will. "Not with those teeth! It was trying to eat me! Maybe it killed Jojo. And the other guy. Is that possible Fi?"

She nodded slowly. "It's possible."

"And it's a deep sea species too?" asked Tanner.

"We think so," she replied. "It seems to be a cousin of the Anoplogaster Cornuta, commonly called the Fangtooth for obvious reasons. Sometimes called the Ogrefish, again for obvious reasons."

Will winced at the image of the gruesome head which again popped into his mind.

"There's quite a size difference though between these two species. The Fangtooth is only six inches – this one's over ten times bigger."

"And those front teeth, Fi," said Will, wide eyed. "They were massive."

"Yes. Impossibly big. I saw them. Its smaller cousin has the largest teeth of any fish in the ocean proportionate to body size. They are so large it cannot close its mouth completely, despite having sockets on either size of the brain which the fangs fit into."

"If it's not a plankton eater," said Will, "If it's not following the plankton up, why's it coming to the surface? And why's it attacking people?"

Fiona looked at him and raised her eyebrows. "I don't know. The little Fangtooth eats small fish and crustaceans. It's got very poor eyesight so it hunts by chemoreception..."

"Chemoreception?" said Tanner frowning.

"It follows scent trails in the water and then bites whatever it bumps into if it thinks it's edible."

"Like me," said Will.

"There's not much food in the deep ocean so it needs the big mouth and big teeth to be able to attack and hang onto anything it finds. It's very much a matter of 'bite first, ask questions later'. These are not fish that sit around and lure their prey with a light on a stick. They are active predators, aggressive hunters who seek out their food."

"That's scary," said Will. "If there are loads of these giant Fang-tooths swimming around on the surface. That's scary."

"Yes."

"How many of these things are there?" asked Tanner.

"I'm afraid I don't know that either," she said.

Chapter Twenty-Nine

John Mackay was in his office talking on the phone when Christoph burst into the room. He looked at the resort manager to kill and held up a silencing hand while he continued his conversation.

"No you won't say anything to anyone, do you understand?...I don't give a shit what you thought you saw...I need to look into it first myself...Do we have a problem here?...Good...I'll call you later..."

He put the phone down and looked contemptuously at the man hopping from one foot to the other in front of him.

"Mr Mackay...you've heard?" said Christoph.

"Do come in!" said the Scot with a snarl.

"Sorry. I meant to knock. But I'm in a bit of a..."

"Panic?"

The resort manager looked embarrassed.

"You and our dive instructor both. Why don't you sit down," said Mackay gesturing to the chair on the opposite side of his desk, "And tell me what you're panicking about."

The man sat. "But you've heard right?" he said, "About Mr Sanders and Miss Bell being attacked by some creature just off shore? It's terrible. He got his leg bitten and had to be flown to hospital in Male..."

"Oh really?" Mackay studied his finger nails.

"But luckily Miss Bell was not hurt..."

"Luckily."

"And Mr Sanders is OK. They say he'll be up and about by tomorrow."

Mackay gave a rictus grin. "Oh that is good news."

"Mr Tanner, the uncle of the poor boy who drowned, is with them too."

"How nice."

"But what are we going to do? The news is all over the resort. People keep asking me what happened. They think it's a shark attack or something. They're..."

"Panicking too?"

"Well...yes."

"And so you thought you'd start panicking to join in eh?"

Christoph opened and closed his mouth but no words came out.

"Och you look like a damn fish yourself you soft idiot!" Mackay's voice had risen in volume and taken on a hard edge as he leant towards the manager and eye-balled him. "You're meant to be in charge, for God's sake! You're meant to set an example of calmness! Be a leader. Not run around like a headless chicken screaming about sea monsters!"

"I...um...I'm sorry. But I've never been in this position before, Mr Mackay..."

"Yes and you won't be in this position, or any other position in this company again, unless you pull yourself together, man! Now show some backbone. Show some initiative."

"I'm sorry."

Christoph got up to leave.

"Where are you going now?"

"I think I should take some action like you say. We should close the resort..."

Mackay leapt up. "Close the resort? You're off your head! Do you know what that would do to us? What it would cost us? In money and in reputation? Do you? We don't close the resort, you idiot. We..."

But his flow was interrupted by a quick knock at the door and his PA popping her head round.

"No interruptions I said!" he shouted at her.

"I'm sorry, Mr Mackay, but I have the a government minister on the phone saying it's urgent he speak to you."

"Which government?"

She looked puzzled for a moment. "The Maldives Government, sir. The Minister for Fisheries. He's very insistent..."

"Yes OK I'll take it. You wait here a moment," he said, stabbing a finger at Christoph.

"And Plymouth University have called a third time..."

"No I won't speak to them. Time wasters. Tell them to sod...Tell them I'm busy."

"Yes sir."

Christoph looked like he wanted to escape but Mackay motioned for him to sit down again.

"I just need to take this call. Then I'll handle your problems for you as you're clearly unable..."

The phone rang on his desk and he picked it up.

"Ach, Minister. Hello. How are you?....Oh I see. What's the problem?....Yes we have had a couple of people go missing but it's nothing to worry about. These things happen all the time. I know it sounds harsh, but they do....No it won't affect anything. It's business as usual. Leave it to us to smooth things over here. And I'll send you over our agreed position so we can both be singing off the same hymn sheet....What? Yes it means both saying the same thing, telling the same story..." Mackay shook his head and raised his eyes as though he were talking to an imbecile. "No it'll all be fine, don't worry....Of course you can trust us...." He pursed his lips in anger. "Well if you don't trust us, Minister, we can find someone else to do business with. Are you forgetting what's at stake here?...No I'm not being disrespectful to you, Minister. I'm just reminding you of the amount of money you're going to lose if we all start panicking here....Ok then. I'm pleased we understand each other. Have a good day, Minister."

He looked at Christoph as he put the phone down. "Idiot. I'm surrounded by idiots."

Christoph looked at the floor.

"I have to deal with a nosy university, a politician who thinks he's President Of The United States, and a resort manager who's a wet blanket."

Christoph looked up, his face reddening. "Well if you want me to resign..."

Mackay held up his hands. "Hey.Why does everyone want to resign around here? Why does everyone want to shirk their responsibility? We're in a mess and we need to sort it out. You need to sort it out. It's your resort. Or yes I guess you could resign and never work in this industry again."

Christoph took a breath and glowered at Mackay.

"You can look at me like that all day long and it won't change anything," said the Scot plainly, "Now are you going to do what I tell you so we can clear this mess up, or are you off to look for work mending fishing nets or something?"

Christoph lowered his shoulders in defeat and the fire went out of his eyes.

"Right then," continued Mackay, "This is what happens next. You suspend swimming and watersports around the island due to...what was that aquarium bint jabbering about the other day?...algae...yes, algae...You suspend swimming in the sea because we have noticed some algae nearby which scientists think may be a bit harmful...may cause mild sickness – nothing too drastic...happens all the time, all around the world...nothing to worry about but just as a precaution etc etc and will clear up soon... are you writing this down?"

Christoph fumbled in his pockets and took out a pen and note pad.

"For Chrissakes write it down or you'll forget it you idiot!...Right ....algae. Cleared up soon. Quite normal. Nothing to worry about. Use the swimming pools etc etc...Apologies for inconvenience...By way of a thank you for your patience all food and drink free...No, everything free...Food, drink, accommodation...And those on freebies anyway like the journos get a free stay in the future for their families at any of our resorts...As long as they keep their mouths shut..."

The resort manager looked up from his notes and opened his mouth to speak but was silenced by a wave of the hand.

"No I know you can't say that but just make something up for Chrissakes or do I have to do everything for you?...Talk of attacks is nonsense...No sharks or anything else...Just sad case of a guest having a heart attack at sea....Happens all the time etc etc. Nothing to worry about, etc etc...Sanders not attacked by some sea monster...Haha! All in their imagination.... "

"What about Mr Sanders? He..."

"What?...Don't worry, I'll sort them out. Sanders and that aquarium bint. And the dive instructor I guess..."

"And the American..."

"Tanner? No he wasn't there...Ignore him...Got all that? Right. Get on with it!"

With that the resort manager was dismissed. As he left the office Mackay called out to his PA. "Is Carl out there? Ok, tell him to come in."

The lanky IT youth loped in.

"Sit, Carl. Now I have three more thorns in my side which I need you to do something about."

Carl grinned.

Chapter Thirty

W ill stared at a room full of flowers.

He had dozed off and when he'd woken up he thought for a moment was in a florist shop.

"They came while you were asleep," said Fiona, sniffing a huge bunch of lilies. "They're beautiful."

"And there's a lot of them," added Tanner. "Who's your admirer, young man?"

"I don't know," said Will.

Tanner handed him a tiny envelope. "This came with them."

Will took it and opened it.

"Are they from John Mackay?" asked Fiona with a cheeky grin.

"I sincerely hope not," said Will reading the card inside:

Poor thing!

I hope you're feeling OK and have a very speedy recovery, Will.

Warmest wishes, Penny

"They're from Penny," said Will and he repeated the words out loud. "That's so nice of her."

"Nice?" Fiona spat out the word. "She buggers off somewhere, disappears from the face of the Earth, leaving everyone to pick up all this mess at her resort!"

"She hasn't disappeared, Fi," said Will, taken aback by her ferocity. "She's had to go to Shanghai for a conference. She's obviously just been told I've been injured but she doesn't know about this creature we've discovered or about Jojo and the Indian guy."

"Doesn't she?" asked Fiona, raising a sceptical eyebrow.

He didn't understand her attitude and her attack made him feel oddly defensive of Penny. "No of course she doesn't. It's her company for God's sake. Don't you think she'd be back here to sort things out if she knew the full extent of what's been going on?"

"How can she not know, Will?" asked Tanner. "She's the CEO. Like you say – it's her company."

"It's Mackay!" said Will, slapping the bed with the palm of his hand. "He's hiding all this from her. He does that. I've seen it before. He's a lying little cheating...bastard."

They looked at him quizzically.

Tanner shrugged. "Then you need to tell her, Will."

"Yes I agree," said Fiona. "You have to tell her the truth."

"Oh I will, don't worry. I'm going to tell everyone." He made to get out of bed but Fiona pushed him gently back.

"Tomorrow," she said.

"Doctor's orders," said Tanner.

Will considered getting up again but their looks told him he'd have a fight on his hands so he lay back. Tomorrow he would make sure the world and its wife knew what had happened. Tomorrow.

Chapter Thirty-One

It took a lot to shock Professor Kenton. He was a very laid-back man, practically horizontal. But he was shocked now.

He sat staring at a PC screen in his second floor corner office at Plymouth University. In his thirty years of teaching he had never misjudged a colleague as much as he now felt he had misjudged Fiona Bell.

Over the past few days she had got him really quite excited about the discovery of a new marine species. There were plans of writing a scientific paper and a big announcement event for fellow marine biologists and the media. But now that was all a pipe dream.

Dr Fiona Bell seemed to have lost her marbles.

Kenton reached for the packet of cigarettes in his tweed jacket pocket and lit one up. It was against the law of course but this was an emergency. He inhaled deeply, not for a moment taking his eyes off the screen.

Dr Bell's website, previously full of her fascinating reports of a new deep sea fish, now contained her musings about sea serpents, a giant octopus as big as a ship, and a new sighting of the Loch Ness Monster.

The professor's mood went from shock to anger. What a waste of his time. It seemed everything had been an elaborate joke of some kind. Kenton was not amused.

Chapter Thirty-Two

Will was already wide awake and eager to get out of his hospital bed when Fiona walked in that morning with coffee and muffins.

Unusually, thought Will, her hair was tousled and she looked distracted.

"Bad night?" he asked.

"Terrible night," she said, handing him a muffin. "I can't believe it."

Will sat up, concerned for her. "What is it?"

She reached into her bag and pulled out her laptop. She opened it up and placed it on his lap.

He stared at the screen. It looked like an illustrated story of mythical sea monsters. Pictures showed massive tentacles rising from the sea and crushing a ship, a fearsome looking serpent entwining a hapless swimmer, and a giant set of shark jaws. The main header read:

Monsters Of The Indian Ocean: Scary But True!

He was puzzled but gave a short laugh to humour her. "No wonder you can't sleep if you're reading stories like this at night!"

"They're not stories, Will. Look at the home page."

He flicked to it and saw her name and picture. His mouth dropped. "This is your website?"

"It WAS my website. It contained all my research, including my latest reports on my work here, the setting up of the aquarium, the algae study I did...and the new species we discovered. Now it looks like I'm some kind of mad fucking scientist!"

He'd never heard her swear before.

"I'm sorry, Fi. I don't know...hang on...give me my phone could you? It's over there."

She handed it to him. She was about to take a bite from a muffin but thought better of it and put it down gloomily.

He dialled Danny's number and put him on speaker so Fiona could hear.

"Hey Danny. It's Will again."

"Hey Will! Whassup? Found another phone? Or do you just love to hear my voice?" Danny guffawed.

"I love your voice Danny, but it's your mind I'm after..."

"Flatterer. Hey where are you? You sound like you're in a box, man"

"I'm in hospital. With a work colleague. And on speakerphone so she can hear."

"Hey, hold on there! You're in hospital...?"

"It's a long story. I'm OK. I'm leaving today. Just a minor injury..."

"Glad to hear it. But why do you have a beautiful woman visiting you?"

"How do you know she's beautiful?" Will looked at Fiona who smiled and blushed. He was glad the banter was lifting her mood.

"I told you, man. I know everything!"

They laughed.

"I need your help again, Danny. Sorry. Owe you double big time. Several rounds on me."

"No worries, man. What is it?"

Will explained the web page and then waited a few seconds in silence. Finally Danny spoke;

"Yeah I pulled up Dr Bell's site. Quite an imagination!"

"Nothing to do with me, I assure you," Fiona interrupted. "Hello Danny."

"Hi....Dr Bell?"

"Fiona. Thank you for helping. Do you know what happened to my site?"

"Well...Yes...As I guess you've figured out, you've been hacked. Some naughty person has taken over your website remotely without you knowing it. Probably your social media accounts too if you have any. There's a few different ways it could have been done, but it's not that difficult. There's a lot of hackers out there."

"Can you find out who did it?" asked Fiona.

"Mackay I bet," said Will, shaking his head.

They heard a lot of tapping at the other end. "I'm trying but...no I don't think I can."

Will got out of bed and stood gingerly. Then he walked a few paces.

"How do you feel?" whispered Fiona.

Will gave the OK gesture and smiled. He then mimed getting dressed. She nodded and made to leave but stopped when Danny spoke again;

"Uh-oh. Will have you looked at your Facebook and Twitter feeds recently?"

Will frowned. "No, I've been a bit out of action...Oh shit! What?"

"They got you too. Made you look like a complete schizo."

"What?!"

"And a drunk....and a whole load of other nasty stuff...Wow they really went to town on you."

"Nobody will believe it," said Fiona but looked worried.

"You'd be surprised, "said Danny. "People believe a whole load of nonsense they read online. It's like the internet doesn't lie. Someone must really not like you two guys."

"And clearly want people not to trust a word we say," said Fiona.

"Well they're not going to get away with it," said Will, flexing his legs. "Especially now I'm up and about. I need to make Penny face reality and get rid of that little shit Mackay!"

"Good luck with whatever you decide to do, man," came Danny's voice. "And take care. There's someone very nasty and very tricky out there and he's got you in his sights."

"Thanks Danny. See you soon."

He handed the phone back to Fiona as Tanner knocked and walked in.

"Hey Will. You're up and about. Good to see." The old man smiled warmly.

"Yep. And just in time," said Will, walking to and from the bed to test his legs. "I need to go to Shanghai."

"What?" said Fiona.

"In your pyjamas?" said Tanner.

Will laughed. "Fi and I have been hacked and discredited online."

Tanner looked from one to the other with a frown.

"Mackay's behind it, I'm sure," said Will. "He doesn't want people to believe us when we start talking about the scary fish with the nightmare teeth. I don't know why. Might not be good for tourism perhaps?" He smiled wryly.

"I guess so," said Tanner. "But I'd have thought it could actually be used to attract tourists. Well, divers. If handled right."

"Me too," said Fiona.

Tanner shook his head. "This is a heck of a lot of trouble to go to to try to cover up a fish attack…"

"Plus two fatal attacks maybe," said Will, holding up his hand.

"Yeah, I guess," said Tanner.

"Anyway, I need to talk to Penny about it and I can't seem to reach her by phone so I need to fly to China and see her. Whatever Mackay's reasons what he's done is criminal."

"She probably knows already," said Fiona, slumping into a chair.

"I don't think so," said Will.

Tanner nodded. "I agree with Will. She's too professional to allow a criminal in her company. I think you should go, young man. As long as you feel well enough."

"Fighting fit," said Will, and did a quick boxer's jig.

Fiona laughed.

"And I'll cover all expenses," said Tanner, making to leave.

"You don't…" Will started but was halted by the American.

"No arguments. We need to find out what happened to my nephew. And we need to expose this criminal Mackay. I'll go book your flight now."

He disappeared from the room and Fiona stood up and hugged Will.

"I can't believe it. You're going to China. Maybe I should go with you?"

He kissed the top of her head. "I'd love that. But I need you and Harold to keep an eye on the evil Scot."

Chapter Thirty-Three

The local fishermen were not singing as they headed for home later that morning.

They should have been happy. They would be with their families earlier than usual, and their catch of tuna had been magnificent.

But they were in sombre mood. None of the men in the five boats spoke a word. Thirty silent gloomy faces. Just the puttering of five engines and the shriek of the sea birds following them to shore.

The captain of the lead boat looked back at the huge silver blue fish lying in rows on deck. And then on top of them their latest horrific catch.

A man's dead body, now wrapped in sailcloth out of respect.

He shook his head. Such a waste of a young life. And a handsome young man too – he could tell that in spite of all the terrible wounds. A European or Australian, he thought. Fair skinned and fair haired. With a stylish moustache.

Chapter Thirty-Four

Mackay's trouser pocket vibrated and he took out his phone and looked at the screen. The Chief of Police.

He swore under his breath and glanced around. He was walking one of the garden paths to get some air and to escape the guests. Nobody was around. He took the call, swiping the answer button on the screen.

"Mr Police Chief. Hello."

"Mr Mackay. We have a problem."

"Oh good. As if I don't have enough."

"Pardon?"

"Nothing, Chief. Go ahead." Mackay rolled his eyes to Heaven and took an intake of breath.

"Mr Mackay, we have found the body of Mr Tanner I believe..."

"Mr Tanner? The old guy?"

"No, no. The nephew. The young man who disappeared while snorkelling off your island."

"Jojo. Ok. I guess he was bound to turn up sometime." Mackay looked around again quickly to check he was still alone. "Keep it quiet, Chief. Like we agreed."

"Yes but the body, you see...it is covered in the most horrible wounds..."

"Really? I don't see the problem. He had a heart attack at sea because he had a health problem and after he tragically died he was bitten by sharks or eels or something. Whatever. Keep it quiet."

"That will be difficult, Mr Mackay. You see, the bites do not look like those of any known creature in these waters. Big puncture wounds. We believe this to be an attack by the new creature you discovered..."

"We?!" shouted Mackay down the phone and then lowered his voice again. "Who's 'We'? How many people know about this?"

"Well, apart from myself, there's the fishermen who found the body this morning..."

"How many?"

"Around thirty I believe. And now they are with their families so many more will know. As well as my fellow police officers, the coroner..."

"And Uncle Tom Cobley and all...Christ!"

"Uncle?"

"Forget it. Shut them all up. Like we agreed. Or you kill this resort. And our other business venture here. That's a lot of money, Chief. You want that?"

"I don't know, Mr Mackay. It will be difficult....And this creature, it gets people talking."

"I don't care about some sea monster. IF it exists, which I doubt. It makes no difference what ate Jojo Tanner, whether a shark, a conger eel, a barracuda or the Loch Ness Monster...tourists don't like to visit places where there is a chance they might get eaten, regardless what animal is doing the eating! More importantly, it's going to get people snooping into our other business venture." And it will put at risk an even bigger project, he knew. But he couldn't mention that. "Now look...we've made it clear there is to be no swimming at the resort due to a potentially toxic algae bloom – which is partly true. You know the story. Stick to it."

"And how do you expect me to keep all these people from talking?"

"Well, Chief...I find that the combination of a pile of money and a few heavy threats usually does the trick, don't you?"

"I see. I...er...might need some money as an incentive..."

Mackay held out his phone at arm's length for a moment and stared at it. "I'm sorry, Chief. I thought you said you needed some money. But that can't be right as we've already paid you several hundred thousand dollars. I must be going deaf."

"Mr Mackay. That was money for one purpose. This is another purpose. You cannot expect me to use my own money."

He bit his lip to stop himself exploding. He considered for a moment threatening the Chief with something nasty and painful, but decided to give way on this one. He would let the man win this battle but as always the Scot swore to himself that he, Mackay, would win the war.

"Ok Chief. But this is the last payment. How much will it take?"

"Oh...Forty people...At maybe a thousand each...Plus me of course...Add incidentals...Let's say a round hundred thousand dollars."

"Let's say fifty thousand."

"Eighty."

"Seventy."

"Done." I have been, thought Mackay, and made another mental promise to screw the Chief over at some time in the not too distant future. He always enjoyed revenge, but preferred the dish lukewarm not cold. "The money will be in your account this afternoon. And Chief..."

"Yes?"

"If you fuck this up you'll lose more than the money."

"Are you threatening the Chief of Police Mr Mackay?"

"No I wouldn't dream of doing that. Just stating a fact."

The line went dead and Mackay pocketed the phone. It had been an expensive morning. But disaster had been averted. The last thing they needed was to attract unwelcome attention.

Chapter Thirty-Five

The red and white tanker sat motionless in the middle of a dead calm sea. It had reached its Indian Ocean destination on time and without incident. Sitting in his captain's chair on the bridge Raj was content.

"Any sign of anything?" he asked the chief mate, his second in command, who had been scanning the horizon on all sides with large black binoculars.

"Nothing, Captain. No vessels in sight."

"And this is the exact location?"

"Yes. This is the spot."

"Good. Begin the process."

"Aye aye sir."

The chief mate picked up the ship's intercom and began barking orders with a deep voice at odds with his tall skinny frame.

Raj picked up the triple decker club sandwich in front of him and took a hearty bite. Creamy white mayonnaise squirted out onto his podgy left hand and runny yellow egg yolk onto his right hand. He broke off chewing to lick each hand in succession, like a massively overfed grizzly bear licking honey from its paws.

It made the chief mate feel slightly queasy. "Process started, Captain," he said, trying not to look at the egg yolk smear on his boss's chin.

"Gooo," Raj mumbled spitting breadcrumbs onto the console in front of him. The chief mate understood this to mean 'Good' so continued barking orders through the intercom at the ten men scattered on the long deck below them.

The two men on the bridge watched as the five cargo hatches slowly opened and then five metal conveyor belt arms were rotated over the open holds, one over each.

Five of the men had disappeared below decks to attach extensions to these conveyor belts from within the holds. In this way the cargo could be transferred much more quickly than by crane from the holds to the surface.

One of the men on deck gave a thumbs up and the chief mate looked at the captain.

"Take one more look around quickly," Raj ordered. His employer had assured him that what they were about to do was not illegal and did no harm, but because there were pressure groups that didn't approve of it and liked to cause trouble he had to make sure there were no witnesses.

Once the chief mate had scanned the surrounding ocean and given the all clear for the second time, Raj gave the order to proceed to the next stage.

The ship juddered as the five conveyor belts started up, two swung over the port side of the ship and three to starboard.

A minute later the powdered material in the hold was in full flow and the ship exploded with five huge spurts of green into the sea.

The powder hit the flat ocean in five loud continual splashes like dazzling green waterfalls, spreading out on the surface for a few meters before being absorbed.

He knew the dissolved powder would spread out to an enormous area.

Raj watched half nervously in case a vessel suddenly appeared and spotted them but half in wonder at the dazzling green sight.

He didn't know what it was all for, but it was beautiful.

Chapter Thirty-Six

Having double checked with Tanner, Will took the 8 hour overnight flight from Male to Shanghai, landing at Pudong International Airport 9.30am the next morning.

There was only a 3 hour time difference so his body clock was not too messed up as he made his way through the gigantic white steel terminal building, weaving in and out of various groups of new arrivals from all over the world.

Having cleared passport control with minimal queuing needed, he headed for the futuristic Maglev train which would take him directly to the Expo Centre where Penny was attending a conference on Business In The Environment.

The sleek white train with its aerodynamic sloping front arrived and Will took an aisle seat.

He marvelled at the verve and dynamism of the Chinese. The fastest train in the world, the Maglev would take just 8 minutes to travel the 19 miles to the Expo Centre.

He felt a thrill as he watched the speedometer at the end of the carriage racing to 267 mph. He was whizzing along smoothly and silently at over twice the speed of a so-called high-speed train in Britain. He shook his head and smiled at the thought.

The train pulled in at Longyang Road Station and Will walked the 10 minutes to The Shanghai New International Expo Centre, to give it its full name. He was wearing jeans, a polo shirt and a light cotton sweater and shivered as he walked. For some reason he had expected it to be warm but it felt like 10 degrees C, which was 20 degrees lower than he had got used to in the Maldives.

It didn't matter. He wasn't planning on staying – he'd brought no luggage – and the walk from the Maglev to the Expo was the only time he'd be outside.

The Expo was a massive collection of 17 giant rectangular metal halls, like aircraft hangars, arranged in a triangular formation over 300,000 square meters.

They held over 100 exhibitions every year, from the Shanghai Motor Show to the Tennis Masters Cup. And now, the Business In The Environment conference.

On Fiona's advice Will had not told Penny's office he was coming. "Don't give her time to think. Catch her by surprise and look her in the eye," she had said, "That way you'll know if she's telling you the truth or not."

Will had remonstrated with her. He trusted Penny. He also thought he could look like a complete fool sneaking up on his boss and springing a surprise in this way. He had images of himself jumping out from behind a pillar in front of her like some buffoon jack-in-the-box. But he had also grown to trust the pretty young marine biologist, so had relented and agreed to her terms.

There was one problem however. He had no ticket to get into the conference.

Will walked into the Expo entrance hall like he belonged there, striding with purpose and head held high. He'd learned long ago that absolute certainty and supreme confidence could get you into many places you had no ticket for. He'd accessed many a First Class lounge on an economy ticket. Just look the part.

This time when he was stopped at the entrance by a security guard it also took a wave of his Life Group identity card and a few indignant mutterings about having left his exhibitors pass inside, but in less than a minute he was through.

He went over to a wall plan of the exhibition. He studied the triangular layout of the 17 halls. He was at the South Entrance. Directly ahead of him were 5 West halls in a row one after the other, leading to the North Entrance. Diagonally off to his right were 7 East halls leading to the East Entrance. And at the top, joining the North and East entrances were 5 more North halls. The plan was colour coded, each colour representing a different stakeholder exhibiting in different halls, all with some interest in protecting the environment and working with businesses to do it.

The halls coloured purple held the exhibition stands for governments and local authorities. Blue was for indigenous peoples, yellow for trade unions, green for farmers, orange for science and technology, brown for environmental pressure groups and other NGO's, and the one he was looking for – the 4 halls coloured grey for the international corporations, running diagonally right of him from East Hall 1 to East Hall 4. He would find Penny either there at the Life Group exhibit or in North Hall 1 at the top of the triangle which was given over to a conference arena where high profile speakers gave their talks throughout the day.

He decided to start with the Life Group exhibit in East Hall 3 and headed off.

He walked through the first hall along its left hand wall, looking to his right into the exhibition space as much as he could without bumping into people in case he spotted Penny visiting other stands.

The hall seemed to be largely given over to the motor industry. There were futuristic looking concept cars everywhere, presumably all either hybrid or electric thought Will. There was a blue Ford dazzling under spotlights rotating on a podium. Three silver Volvos suspended by steel cables seemingly flying in formation overhead. A stage with a group of Honda robots dancing in unison to some modern pop song Will couldn't identify.

He was about to move into East Hall 2 ahead when his eyes were caught by the sight of an elegant long pair of ladies' legs getting out of large sleek burgundy Bentley. A hulking body guard in black moved in and held out a burly hand to help her. She took it and emerged, a vision of red silk matched by a ruby necklace which glinted in the spotlights.

He couldn't believe his luck. He'd found her already. "Penny!" he called and strode towards her.

A second bodyguard, also dressed in black but even larger, intercepted him and held him back with a big hand on his chest. Will knocked it aside and sidestepped the gorilla but was blocked a second time by the man who'd helped Penny out of the car.

The gorilla now grabbed him from behind, shoving his powerful arms under Will's armpits and then locking his hands behind his neck. Will instinctively stamped as hard as he could on the man's right foot. The gorilla was clearly not expecting resistance. He yelped and loosened his grip enough for Will to pull forward and break free, only to be punched in the jaw by the first bodyguard.

Will saw stars, felt a searing pain rip through his mouth and head, and fell to the floor.

"Stop it! Stop it!" came Penny's commanding voice, "He's with me, you idiots! Help him get up."

The two bodyguards looked confused for a moment. Then the one who'd offered his hand to Penny now did the same to him. Except Will was flat on his arse in the Expo centre not stepping out of a Bentley concept car.

Will ignored the proffered hand above him and got up. He massaged his jaw. He didn't know his boss had such protection around her and wondered why she felt she needed it.

Penny touched his arm and then laid her hand gently on the side of his face. "Will I'm so so sorry. These barbarians will be dealt with, I promise you. Are you all right?"

He remembered Fiona's instruction and looked her in the eyes. It wasn't quite the surprise they had planned but he'd give it a go anyway. She smiled at him, smiled with her mouth and with her beautiful blue eyes, usually piercing but now warm and concerned. His pain seemed to subside and he felt like he was in an otherworldly presence – then immediately felt stupid for such a trite thought.

"Penny, I've been trying to reach you for ages…"

"I know, Will, poor boy. It's completely my fault. I should have got back to you. I've been so tied up. I haven't had a moment." She leant towards him and whispered in his ear. He smelt the rich floral fragrance of her perfume, which he knew to have been made exclusively for her by Caron in Paris. "You know why I was in that Bentley, Will? I wasn't window shopping – it was the nearest private space I could find to take a call from Mutti." Will knew 'Mutti' or 'Mummy' referred to the German Chancellor not her own mother. "And earlier today it was the U.S. President warning us not to trespass on his Antarctic territory. And this afternoon it'll be some other bigwig. So once again,

Will, please forgive me for not taking your call this past week. Oh, and I heard about your injury – poor boy, how's your leg?"

"Fine, I'm fine. Thank you. Look..."

"Good. I was so worried about you. It was a shark or something wasn't it? Terrible. I presume they're handling the situation there OK. I haven't managed to check on it as closely as I'd have liked."

"It wasn't a shark, Penny. That's the point. It was a new kind of fish. A new discovery..."

"Really?"

They were interrupted by a thin young man in a shiny suit who had been impatiently hovering nearby. "Ms. Crawford, I'm sorry to interrupt but we need to move to the next appointment."

"Yes of course," she said, nodding. "I'm sorry Will..."

The shiny suit tried to lead her away but Will nudged him back.

"Hold on," he said to the man, and then to Penny, "I realise how busy you are. But you've got to know what's going on at Nirvana. It's a disaster! People have been attacked and killed. This new fish species we've discovered is a monster. And John Mackay is..."

The shiny suit pushed Will on the shoulder. "You'll have to wait, sir. Ms Crawford has to go..."

Will shrugged him off.

"Wait a second, Nigel," Penny said and shiny suit backed off with a sulky glance at Will. "John Mackay is what exactly? Look I know you two have your issues but..."

"It's nothing to do with that. This is serious. He's trying to cover everything up. He's mad. And he's a criminal. He's bribing the local police..."

Penny held up her hand. She looked shocked in a way Will had never seen his totally self-controlled boss look before. "Ok, ok, Will. This is a lot to take in. And I am late for my speech." She glanced at her Graff watch, encrusted in rubies matching her necklace. "Yes, VERY late. I have to go. Then I have to meet the African delegation on a crucial issue. Look...meet me at The Bund tonight. Seven o'clock."

"But I..."

"You clearly have a lot to tell me. This needs time. I'll cancel my cocktail appointment and meet you instead, all right? The Bund. Seven."

And with that she was gone, sweeping through the hall like a red goddess, her bodyguards and PR minders surrounding her as acolytes.

Chapter Thirty-Seven

Will was sitting at a window table in one of the trendy international bars on The Bund, the famous waterfront strip running along the western bank of the city's Huangpu River.

It was approaching 7 o'clock in the evening, night time, and the view over the river was breathtaking. And quite unlike anywhere else in the world, he thought. Gigantic colourful video advertisements crisscrossed each of the huge modern glass skyscrapers lining the opposite bank of the Huangpo. Like a scene from Bladerunner.

To the left of the skyscrapers he could see Shanghai's iconic landmark, the Oriental Pearl TV Tower, its two giant spheres also pulsating with a colourful LED display.

Will shivered. Despite the chill outside the bar was pumping out gusts of cold air conditioning. The frozen cocktail the bar had convinced him to order wasn't helping. He wished he'd gone for a hot coffee.

A minute after Penny had swept out of the hall leaving him standing bemused with an aching jaw, his phone had rung and Penny's office had given him directions to a luxury hotel that had been booked for him for the night. He'd taken a taxi there immediately, checked in, and in his room – a rather grand suite – he'd found a selection of clothes in his size, a toothbrush and other personal hygiene items, and a card with the bar's details and meeting time.

He'd called Tanner and Fiona to update them on the situation and they'd both agreed it sounded promising and wished him luck. Fiona had blown him kisses. Her affection for him gave him a warm feeling inside. He'd then spent the unexpectedly free afternoon sightseeing around the city like a tourist, which had actually been rather enjoyable, as unexpectedly free time often is. He'd returned to the suite, showered, shaved and dressed in his smart, stylish and no doubt highly expensive new Pal Zileri jacket and trousers,

He now buttoned the jacket for a little extra warmth, pushed the frozen concoction away from him and stared out of the window. On the opposite bank of the river a giant Chinese lady dressed in red and gold silk blew a kiss at him and then disappeared from the side of the skyscraper to be replaced by a car ad.

He thought back over the extraordinary events of the past few days. He'd come to the new Maldives resort hot on the heels of a successful resort launch in Australia which had made him a star within the company and brought praise from the mighty CEO herself. He'd looked forward to similar success at Nirvana. But then Mackay had stuck his ugly great nose in. He'd tried to interfere at Uluru too, Will recalled, but as the Scot hadn't been there in person Will had found it easy to ignore and sidestep him. Nirvana had been different, with Mackay permanently in his face. First scuppering Will's marketing and advertising plans, then framing him for the press leak about Penny's wealth, and finally – most worrying and sinister of all – covering up the deaths of a worker and a guest at the resort using bribery, threats,

IT hacking and god knows what else in his toolkit of trickery and deception.

Two people were dead. There was some gruesome looking and undoubtedly deadly sea creature, or creatures, circling the island. Will and Fiona's reputations had been besmirched online. Will himself had been attacked. The local authorities seemed to be turning a blind eye to everything. How the resort was still operating Will did not know. Perhaps when Penny knew the whole truth she'd cut her losses and close it all down.

What a mess.

In between all this, of course, he'd lost one girlfriend and gained another. An upgrade at that. He pictured Veronica nagging him about his job, his attitude, his habits...and then pictured Fiona laughing at him through a tangled mass of algae. He smiled. At least there was one bright point.

Will looked at his watch. Five past. It was unlike Penny to be late. Maybe bad traffic.

He heard a voice behind him.

"Hello Will."

His heart sank. It wasn't Penny. The voice was deep, Scottish and somehow ugly.

He thought for a moment that the two had come together but this hope was soon dispelled by Mackay as he sat down opposite Will and grinned that sardonic crooked-toothed grin of his.

"Are you looking for your mentor, Mr Sanders? Sorry, it's just me I'm afraid."

"Yes, I was expecting someone more attractive, intelligent and charming than you, John...but I guess a skunk could have fulfilled those criteria."

Mackay leaned towards him across the table, his white pock-marked face reflecting the bright lights of the bar like the crater-ridden side of the moon. "You're a funny man, aren't you?"

Will leaned forward too so their faces were uncomfortably close. The man smelt of something unpleasant, causing Will to wrinkle his nose a little.

"How's this for funny. I know it was you. You hacked my computer, and Fiona's. You covered up two deaths. You lied, you bribed, you cheated. You're a piece of shit, John. And you'll be made to pay."

They eyeballed each other for a moment and then sat back, Mackay first and then Will.

"Oh I don't think so, Will. You're not really in a position to make anyone do anything are you now? You have no support from the police – I can assure you of that. You have no reputation – not that you had much of a reputation before. And you have no job – I know we've been playing the resignation and firing game for days but now there really is no going back...you are now no longer an employee of the Life Group. So you see, Will... " Mackay stroked his bristled head and grinned again, "The joke's on you."

"Does Penny know this? Does she know you're firing me? Does she know about your lies and cover-ups at Nirvana? And the deaths?"

Mackay cocked his head to one side like an ugly mongrel dog. "Penny knows only what I let her know. She's a busy lady. She wanted to come and meet you, Will, but..." he shrugged, "I offered to handle it for her. Very kind of me don't you think?"

Will shook his head. "Sure you know what you're doing, John? I don't think she's going to be happy about all this when she finds out."

"Och, you'd be surprised, William. I think I can make something up. Like you say, cover-ups are my speciality. Anyway, it's not your problem. Your problem is what the fuck are you going to do now?

Nobody believes you, nobody trusts you. The internet says you're a nobody. That means you really are a nobody. You might as well not exist."

He's right, thought Will. His reputation had been muddied and he was now unemployed. He was up against a multi-billion dollar corporation whose Number Two was a ruthless criminal. Tough fight.

He examined the man opposite. "How do you live with yourself, Mackay?"

"Very easily."

"Don't you know when you're doing bad?"

"Bad is a relative term. One man's bad is another man's good."

"Lying is bad, John. Bribery is bad. Ruining reputations is bad. Putting people at danger because you're covering up the truth...that's bad, John. Don't you see that?"

"And if I tell a lie to save a life? If I bribe to protect the innocent?"

"Yeah but you're not are you?"

"You realise how many lives would be ruined if that resort closed down? Let alone the bigger picture which you're oblivious to. Get real, Sanders. You want the truth? I'll tell you the truth. A worker happens to drown at sea because he went swimming where he shouldn't. A man with heart condition goes snorkelling and surprise surprise has a heart attack. And maybe or maybe not some new type of fish pops up that may or may not take bites out of people. The first two were accidents and not our fault. The fish, if it exists, we can guard against – maybe even profit from. Anyway, none of it need hurt the resort or the company. But oh no. You don't agree. You want to go out there – the big important Will Sanders – and blow all this up, get everyone rushing around like headless chickens, and kill the resort. Hah! And you're the PR man! You're meant to be on our side!" Mackay got up. "Actually, Will, you ARE a funny man."

Will stood up too. "Twist it all you like, John. That's what bad guys do to justify their crimes. But they're still crimes."

"Blah, blah. Bye, bye now." Mackay turned to leave, then stopped and took an envelope out of his pocket. He handed it to Will. "Och I nearly forgot, Will. A little something from me."

He walked away as Will opened the envelope.

It was his termination letter.

Chapter Thirty-Eight

Will let Mackay leave the bar and ordered a large beer from the waitress.

He downed it in one go and ordered another.

He stared out the window. The giant Chinese lady in the red and gold silk dress was back and he raised his glass to her. She blew him another kiss.

His phone vibrated. It was Fiona.

"Will, how are you?"

"Well..."

"How's it going with Penny? Sorry, hope I'm not interrupting."

"She didn't show up."

"What?"

"Mackay came instead."

"What? Why?"

"Dunno. He said he'd told her he'd handle it."

"The little shit! I don't believe it!"

Will was impressed with her choice of words.

He took a gulp of his beer. She must have heard it down the phone.

"Will, are you still in the bar?"

"Yep."

"Are you drinking on your own?"

"Yep."

"Have you had a few?"

"Not yet. But I intend to."

"I wish I was there with you."

"So do I."

"I have some news."

"So do I."

"Oh? What is it?"

"I've been fired."

"That's about the fifth time isn't it? Must be some sort of record."

Will laughed. She always managed to make him feel better.

"Will, does Penny know do you think?"

"I really don't know. I hope not. But I don't know."

"She must do surely. She's in total control of everything."

"I'm not sure about that, Fi. Mackay's a devious little shit. Anyway, what's your news?"

"Oh yes. I think they've found Jojo's body..."

"What?"

"Well, nobody is saying anything as usual. Everyone's clammed up. But the local fisherman who brought us the juvenile fish that died in our tank...I bumped into him on my way back to the resort...And he let slip something about them finding a body at sea just off Nirvana...A young man with blond hair and a moustache..."

"Jojo. Oh my God." Will sat up in his seat. A new sadness enveloped him.

"Must be. And he said the body was covered in puncture wounds. Like what could be caused by those javelin teeth on our fish maybe."

"Poor guy, poor guy. The same as happened to the Indian worker I bet. And caused by that monster that went for me, don't you think? We have to get this story out, Fi. We owe it to Jojo at least."

"I know, I know. But how? I'm still trying to persuade my professor I'm not a loony, and you're hardly in a better position. Even the dive instructor's been silenced somehow – won't say a word."

"Mackay can get to anyone."

"Yes. Even the police I bet."

"Police, government, anyone. Don't know how he does it."

"What about the media, Will?"

"That's what I'm thinking."

"I'll back you up in whatever you say. I'm a witness."

"Yep. I'll get onto it now." He pushed his half drunk glass of beer away. "Check back with you soon."

"OK. Good luck."

"Be careful on that island, Fi. Watch your back."

"You too. I love you."

"Love you too."

Will called Bob first, the travel journalist from the international newspaper he'd recently met at the resort. He was sure he'd leap at the story. And once it was out Mackay would have nowhere to hide.

"Hi Bob."

"Will. Well what do you know!"

"How are you?"

"More to the point, how are you? I've been reading some pretty odd stuff about you."

"I know. I was hacked. It's all rubbish."

"Well I have to say you didn't look like a schizo alcoholic when I saw you recently."

"Ha. Not quite. Though I'm working on the alcoholic part."

"Hey, I wrote you up a great story on Nirvana. The Paradise Island, I called it."

"Yes I saw it, Bob. Thank you. It was brilliant. But I have more news for you. Not quite so jolly. Less paradise, more Hell."

"Really?"

Will recounted the events of the past few days while Bob interjected now and then with expletives and exclamations of surprise.

When he had finished Bob begged him not to speak to any other journalists but to hold on for fifteen minutes while he went to find his editor.

Will agreed, put down the phone and finished his beer.

He felt relieved but also excited about finally getting the news out into the world. He imagined the exclusive breaking tomorrow and then a frenzy of interviews as media from around the world picked up on the story. Penny would be furious, but tough shit. She needed a wake-up call.

Why hadn't she stepped in, he wondered. A mystery killer fish at her newest resort could ruin the company's reputation and destroy its business. Surely she must see that.

Or maybe she did see that and it was actually she herself giving the orders to silence him and Fiona.

He shook his head. No. He couldn't believe she'd do that. It had to be Mackay. He was running amok under her nose and for some reason she couldn't see it. Maybe he had some sort of hold over her. A terrible secret of some kind.

Half an hour passed before Bob called back.

Something seemed wrong. His tone had changed. It was more distant.

"Will...I....er...don't think I can help you actually. Sorry."

"Oh? Why? It's a big story, Bob."

"Well, my editor says I should focus on positive travel stories. You know, golden sandy beaches, swaying palm trees, that sort of thing. It's what people like to read."

Will couldn't believe what he was hearing. "That's crap, Bob, and you know it. People love to read about holiday disasters too. Bad news sells. I should know – I've been fighting to keep stories like that out of the papers all my working life!"

"I know, Will, I know. I suggested News might want the story. It's a good story, I agree. But I got nowhere. I'm sorry."

"But can't you…"

"Sorry Will. More than my life's worth to go against my editor. You know that. I need my job."

"Ok Bob Ok. I'll find someone else."

Will was gobsmacked by the conversation he'd just had as he rang off. This was the biggest baddest story going and Bob didn't want it.

Ok. There were plenty of journalists. He scrolled through his phone and dialled again.

But with no more luck. He spoke to seven travel journalist contacts. Some went through the same process as Bob, with the same result. Some just cut him off half way through his story and said they couldn't help.

As a last resort he called Lara from the London PR agency they used. She at least was honest with him. "You've been black-balled, my darling. Nobody wants to touch you. Like toxic waste. It's a tragedy, I know. Such a handsome boy too. And so talented. Never mind, my darling. It'll pass. You'll pull through. Stay in touch. We must do lunch when you're in town. Chin up!"

Will was bemused. And angry. It was all so unjust. Here was Mackay acting like the Devil himself and it was Will whom everyone was rejecting.

Fuck it, he thought. There must be someone who'd listen to him. Then Bob called again.

The line was terrible.

"Bob? I can barely hear you. Where are you?"

"I popped outside, Will. For privacy. It's pissing down and blowing a gale. Can you hear me?"

"Just."

"Ok. Listen. Our news guys are interested but they don't dare do anything. However there's a...fffffffffffff....and he'll....fffffffff... ." The sound of the wind obscured the words.

"Sorry, Bob, can you repeat that?"

"fffffff.....a guy in the Shanghai office....very convenient for you ....ffffffff....."

"What?"

The line went clearer. "Ok I'm in a bus shelter. Hear me now?"

"Yes."

"He's called Chen Yang. He feeds stories all round the world. I'll text you his number. Maybe he can help."

"Thanks, Bob."

"You're welcome. Good luck with it."

Will mentally blessed Bob and ordered a third beer. Rather than befuddling his brain the alcohol seemed to be sharpening his thinking. Anyway, it wasn't hurting.

Bob texted the Shanghai journalist's number and Will dialled.

Chen Yang sounded young and eager. He was excited by Will's story. Will also put him in touch with Fiona so she could back him up. An hour later, and after a fourth beer – which Will had to admit was now making his head spin – the journalist said he was going to contact the resort, the company, the police and the Maldives government for comment and reaction, and would meet Will at noon the next day to touch base.

Will was delighted. And a little pissed.

At last he'd get the story out there.

He returned to his hotel and slept like a log.

Chapter Thirty-Nine

B ack at the Maldives resort Fiona was pleased Will seemed finally to have found a journalist who believed his story. She'd backed him up all the way of course when Chen Yang had called her. He sounded a decent guy, and very interested in what had been going on at Nirvana, including the discovery of a new species – though unlike her the journalist's excitement came not from the discovery itself but the fact it was a suspected man killer.

What Fiona really needed now was for her University to endorse the discovery, rather than back up the online slanders generated by the evil Mackay.

After Will's sacking she wasn't at all sure about her own position so had been avoiding the senior staff at the resort as much as possible. She was now holed up in her room, sitting cross-legged on the bed with a glass of Sauvignon Blanc in one hand and her phone in the other.

She dialled Plymouth University and asked for her professor in the Oceanographic Department.

"Ah Dr Bell," came the plummy BBC and Oxford tones of her Professor, "You've been causing us a little concern."

"Yes I'm sorry, Professor. But I'm not mad, I assure you. I've been hacked."

"Hacked?"

"It's a long story. Just please believe me when I say that nonsense on my website was not written by me."

"I see. I did wonder. Didn't take you as a loon, but you never know do you?"

"There is one true bit, though, Professor. My original report on the new marine species."

"Ah."

"I saw it myself. It attacked my friend."

"Attacked?"

"Yes. It's quite a fearsome looking fish. And big. About two metres. It looks like a Fangooth. Huge teeth which slot into its cranium. But obviously a lot bigger than any Fangtooth we know."

"If this is true it's extraordinary."

"Oh it's true, Professor. Believe me. I think it's a deep sea species which is coming to the surface from its normal deep ocean habitat for the first time in its history...which is why we've never spotted it before..."

"Perhaps...of course as you know other deep water species have been discovered that have been moving freely between the depths and the surface for eons..."

"I know Professor. But this one looks like its habitat is far deeper than a Megamouth or a Coelacanth... It's a real monster..."

"I see."

"Only I don't understand how it can survive at the surface. Deep sea fish are usually killed by the lower pressure and higher temperature at the surface when they're brought up accidentally in fishing nets aren't they?"

"Yes, quite true. But there are some that can withstand the massive changes in pressure and temperature you know. It is possible."

"Ok. Good to know."

"But that's not the mystery. Sea creatures normally come to the surface as they follow the plankton up at night. But this creature you describe..."

"Yes Professor. That's what I can't understand either. It's not a plankton eater. It's a predator. As I say, the teeth are enormous and sharp. And it attacks people."

"Hmmm. That's very odd. Unheard of, actually. A carnivorous deep ocean fish coming to the surface to feed. Unbelievable."

"Unless..."

"You have a theory, Fiona?"

"Well...The other thing I've discovered, but I didn't write about, is a massive algae bloom. Very unusual in these waters."

"Yes indeed."

"Could they in some way be connected, do you think Professor? The deep ocean predator coming to the surface and the algae blooms?"

The Professor did not respond for a moment and Fiona could sense him thinking.

Finally he said, "Dr Bell, you could be on to something. It's just a theory. But it's possible."

Fiona's mind was racing. "The deep sea fish are attracted to the algae in some way?"

"No..."

"The deep sea fish are attracted to smaller fish that are eating the algae?"

"No..."

"I'm sorry, Professor. I should let you speak!"

"The deep sea fish are being forced to the surface to breathe!"

"To breathe?"

"Well, to find oxygen. Look, when algae die and drop to the ocean floor they are eaten by marine bacteria and in this process oxygen is removed from the surrounding water. In normal circumstances this makes little difference. But if huge – and I mean huge – quantities of algae are blooming, then dying, then sinking to the seabed...well, the removal of oxygen this could cause might force fish to shallower waters to survive."

"Wow."

"Wow indeed. But it's just a theory."

"It does tie the two together though – the algae and the creatures."

"Let's beware of jumping to conclusions. Many a scientist has become unstuck by finding non-existent links between facts.

"Ok."

"But it's a start."

"Right."

"It does however raise another question..."

"What's that, Professor?"

"What's causing your massive algae blooms in the first place?"

Chapter Forty

As was the usual procedure, upon completion of the operation Raj called his employer to report.

He ate a quarter of a rather sticky banana cake while he waited for his call to be answered.

"Has everything gone to plan?" came an English voice with a Chinese accent. There was no greeting.

Raj swallowed most of his mouthful of cake and spat out a few remaining crumbs while he spoke. "Yes boss. All to plan."

"No incidents?"

"No boss."

"No curious onlookers?"

"No. All good."

"Good."

Raj eyed another quarter of cake but didn't want to risk it until after the conversation. "Boss, I presume we return and repeat again, right?"

"Yes, Captain. But you will not be alone from now on."

Raj shifted his eyes from the cake to his First Mate and frowned. "Oh?"

"We are stepping up the operation. Five more ships are being prepared to join you. One is already being loaded here and will be ready to sail shortly."

"There's going to be six of us doing this?"

"In your ocean yes."

"In my ocean?"

"Similar fleets operating out of different ports around the world will cover the other oceans."

"Fuck me!"

The line went dead.

"What is it?" asked the First Mate.

But his Captain couldn't answer. He'd needed another quarter of cake to get over the shock.

Chapter Forty-One

Fiona sat with Harold Tanner in a dark corner of the hotel bar nursing large glasses of cognac.

It was midnight and the place was deserted, save for the lone barman.

"We'll be safe here," she said. "Will says Mackay rarely comes to the bar."

"Safe? What are we safe from?" Tanner looked puzzled. He pushed his glasses further up the bridge of his nose.

"If Mackay is the criminal we suspect then I think it's best we keep out of his way, don't you Harold?"

"If I find he's responsible for Jojo's death I'll kill him, Fiona."

He was smiling but Fiona suspected it was true.

"Harold I've been talking to my University professor. He has a theory about the fish."

"Oh yes?"

"He thinks they may be coming to the surface from the deep sea to find oxygen. And the more I think about it the more I agree with him."

"What do you call the deep sea?"

"Anything below two hundred metres where light can't penetrate. Where it's totally dark. And very cold. That's about ninety percent of the entire ocean. A huge area. All sorts of unknown creatures live down there. As deep as five thousand metres."

Tanner raised his eyebrows. "So this thing swam up from there? Because it needed more oxygen?"

"Yes. We think so."

"What took away the oxygen?"

"We think it was the huge amount of algae we've been seeing. When it dies it sinks to the ocean floor and as it decomposes it sucks oxygen from the water."

"Ok." Tanner looked into his brandy glass and pondered a moment. "So why aren't other deep sea fish coming to the surface?"

She looked perplexed. "I don't know. Maybe some others are, but as they're plankton eaters they're not...um..."

"Attacking humans?"

"I'm sorry."

"It's all right." Tanner took a sip and thought some more. "So. Where does all this algae come from?"

She brightened up and clicked her fingers excitedly. "Ha! I was hoping you'd ask me that."

"Oh?"

"That stumped my professor and I've been mulling it over since."

"You think you know?"

"Well...There can be several reasons for large algae blooms. But thinking back over my time here something stuck in my mind."

"I'm intrigued, young lady."

"We get some of our rare fish species for the aquarium from local fishermen. They so sometimes catch them by mistake. I chatted to a few of them. They were always really happy, because they were always catching a lot of tuna. Record amounts in fact."

"Really?"

"Yes. Which made me think...Maybe they're just lucky this algae bloom has come along. Or maybe...someone's creating it."

"Can you do that?"

"Yes. Happens all over the world. You fertilise the water, it encourages algae to grow, and fish feed off the algae."

Tanner's eyes widened. "I guess it's a pretty lucrative business."

"Very."

"Enough to want to defend at all costs."

"That's what I'm wondering, Harold." She grabbed his arm. "Maybe it's not just tourism that would be upset if a killer fish was on the loose. Maybe it's a massive fishing industry too."

"The Life Group involved in fish farming?" Tanner looked doubtful. "A bit of a stretch. Not really their area of expertise."

She was a little deflated. "Yes, I know. It does sound a little odd." She shrugged. "Just a thought."

"And a good one, Fi." He smiled encouragingly. "I'm not dismissing it by any means. Let's mull it over."

Suddenly her face changed as a new thought occurred to her.

"Harold?"

"Yes, young lady."

"Maybe I should join Will in Shanghai. I could help him with his investigation."

He looked surprised and put down his glass. A little cognac splashed onto the table.

"What? Why?"

She chewed her lip, then looked into his eyes.

"Because I've got a feeling the answers are there, not here."

Chapter Forty-Two

Will woke early.

The morning dragged slowly until Noon, the agreed time to meet with Chen Yang again.

After several cups of coffee Will was hyped as the journalist walked into the lobby of his central Shanghai hotel.

He jumped up and strode to greet Chen, smiling.

His smile soon disappeared though when he saw the downcast look on the journalist's face.

"Come and sit down, Chen. I think I know what you're going to say and I need to be sitting I think."

They sat at a side table away from the milling guests.

"I'm sorry, Will," Chen began. "My editor..."

"Don't tell me. Your editor told you to drop it like a stone, right?"

Chen looked shamefaced. "Yes. Sorry."

Will shook his head. "Shit, shit, shit."

"I'm sorry."

Will saw the look in the journalist's face, the look of someone who knows what he's doing is not right but who has no choice. Will softened.

"Aaaah don't be sorry, my friend. I've heard this before. It's not your fault."

"I wanted to look into it, Will, believe me. But they wouldn't let me. They say you're an unreliable source..."

"And Dr Bell?"

"Another unreliable source."

"And the Chief Of Police?"

"Wouldn't take my call. Like the rest of them. Then – after I tried the Maldives Government – I got called into my boss's office real quick. The company lawyer was there too. They tried to investigate The Life Group once before and they got slapped down by the lawyers big time. Plus they threatened to withdraw hundreds of thousands in advertising. They don't want to go through that again."

"So you're saying The Life Group is too big to criticise?"

Chen looked resigned. "I guess so."

"Criminal isn't it? They're bullies."

"Yes. But what can anyone do?"

Will thought for a moment. A waitress came over and asked them if they wanted a drink. Will declined and Chen waved her away.

"I'm not giving up, Chen. The company is up to something – or at least Mackay and his mob are – and I need to find out what it is."

"Be careful. He's not a nice man, I hear."

"You can say that again."

"What are you going to do now?"

"I don't know."

There was a silence, but Will sensed Chen wanted to tell him something.

"What are you thinking, Chen?"

"Well...If you're set on investigating them further..."

"I am."

"I can't get involved..."

"I know."

"Well...When I was asking round about the company I found out something odd...something I shouldn't have been told I think...but one of my contacts let it slip..."

"Oh? Now I'm interested."

"You know The Life Group has several operations in Shanghai..."

"Yes. What of it?"

"Well apparently, under a different name and very hush hush, they're also now running tankers from the port."

"Tankers?" Will sat up straight. "What, like oil tankers?"

"No I think they're cargo ships."

"Interesting."

"Yes. They've been running one for ages. Doing what, we don't know. But now they've contracted five more."

"Five more ships?" Will was puzzled. He'd never heard anything about the company running ships. Not even cruise ships – Penny disliked them, saying they were polluters of the seas.

"I don't know what it means, Will. It could be nothing. But it may be worth a look."

"It certainly may be, Chen. Thank you. Thank you very much."

Chapter Forty-Three

Penny Crawford, CEO of The Life Group, sat at her desk in the study of her home just outside the picturesque town of Berchtesgaden in the Bavarian Alps.

The house was a stone's throw away from the company's headquarters and linked to it by a covered walkway. Penny had had both buildings built to the same architectural design, so her home looked like a smaller version of the headquarters. They were modern and stylish, the only similarity to the pretty traditional cuckoo-clock chalets dotted around the neighbouring hills being the extensive use of local timber. Both buildings were two stories with huge curved roofing out of which grew a variety of Alpine plants and grasses, and massive wood-framed windows.

The buildings sat on the top of a hill overlooking the town which was a fifteen minute drive below along a winding road. Penny rarely went into the town – when she left the buildings it was usually to take her private helicopter to Munich airport for an international flight.

Nearby were the remains of the Berghof, Hitler's Bavarian residence where he spent much of his time during the war – now just a pile of overgrown rubble having been first bombed by the British in 1945 and then demolished by the local government in 1952.

Visitors to the headquarters – Penny rarely invited them to her home – often joked about the proximity of the two centres of power, one past and one present. They never knew how to take it when she told them she neither approved nor disapproved of Hitler but she had to admire the man's taste in geography.

She chose the spot because her late father was Austrian, from nearby Salzburg, and the family had spent a lot of time in the area on holiday when she was a young girl. The holidays had been miserable – some even deeply traumatic – but this had nevertheless paradoxically created a strong bond with the area she found hard to break.

The home was modest for a billionaire but she felt relaxed here – besides which she had several homes scattered around the world including sizeable properties in London, New York, Tokyo, Paris, The Bahamas and Lake Como. She also had the company luxury resorts of course but she preferred not to spend time at these as she valued her privacy.

There was a light tap at the study door and then she heard it being opened. No employee would dare open the door without a word of invitation.

A teenage girl walked in. She was pretty, with light brown hair in a long ponytail and sparkling blue eyes like her mother's. She wore a striped blue and white T shirt and dark blue jeans with fashionable tears and a few sparkly bits here and there.

"Mama, sorry to disturb."

Penny smiled at her and held out her hand.

"That's alright, Munchkin." She stroked the girl's arm. "What a pretty T shirt."

"Well I don't think you approve of the Green Day one."

"No, it makes you look like a low-life, darling."

"It's cool, Mama."

"Yes I'm sure it is. Now what can I do for my favourite daughter?" Penny stroked the girl's hair fondly.

"I'm your only daughter."

"Yes but still my favourite."

It was an old joke but the girl smiled anyway.

Her mother saw through her easily. "You want money don't you, Clara?"

"Oh Mama! Why do you think that? I only came to see how you are after your long flight from Japan."

Penny raised her eyebrows and smiled. "Ah, I see. How sweet. And it was China."

"Oh it's all the same thing. Mama, can I go into town? I need some new jeans. It's Anna's party tomorrow."

"Oh I thought you'd come to spend time with your mother."

"Very funny, Mama. We both know you're busy."

"Never too busy for you, Munchkin."

Penny stood up and looked at her daughter's jeans, pretending to look shocked. "Oh yes. You must go at once. These have got rips in them – they're ruined."

Another old joke between mother and daughter but both were comfortable with it – the old jokes were part of the family bond.

"Mama! They're not ruined, they're..."

"I know – cool. All right, all right." She reached into the brown Birkin crocodile handbag on the desk and pulled out a matching wallet. "Here you are." She handed Clara two 50 Euro notes.

The girl looked disappointed. "But I can't buy anything decent for that, Mama."

"I'm sure you can find something, darling."

"Something cheap."

"And when you're old enough to get a job you'll be able to buy a more expensive pair, won't you my dear? Besides which, you have about twenty pairs of 'cool' jeans in your closet I believe, half of which haven't been worn once...Come to think of it, I don't know why I'm giving you more money to buy another pair..."

"Ok! Thank you Mama!" the girl said quickly. She kissed her mother on the cheek and ran out before the notes could be retrieved.

"Bye, Munchkin. Make sure Hugo drives you."

Penny sighed as she returned the wallet to her handbag and sat down again at the desk.

She felt a pang in her heart which she recognised was love for her daughter. It was a feeling she'd never had for anyone else, ever.

Her father had done things to her a father should never do. If they knew about it the family did nothing – they were a branch of an ancient and previously powerful European dynasty and the sort of people who preferred dirty family secrets to be covered up. However when she was old enough she had made him pay for his misdeeds. He was dead, she had inherited the company, and justice had been done.

Her mother had suffered from some kind of hereditary mental illness which had come and gone throughout her life, but the death of the poor woman's husband tipped her over the edge. Penny felt she had no choice but to put her into an asylum. A very expensive private luxury asylum but an asylum nonetheless. It was all very hush-hush and nobody knew about it. Penny said her mother had retired from public life to a remote Swiss village and preferred to be left alone. When Clara asked whether they could visit her grandmother Penny always found some excuse.

She had not felt the pang of love for any man either. There had been several male suitors in her life, but like some species of female spider she had been wary of all of them. When she had wanted a child she had used a donated super-sperm sample to give her the desired result without the hassle of a husband.

For her it was important not just to get what you want but to get it the way you wanted.

She firmly believed you shaped your own ends. You were in total control of your future. Nothing was impossible in life. You could do anything you want, be anyone you want, as long as you wanted it enough.

Perhaps it was her powerful dynastic ancestry which gave her an enormous sense of entitlement and power over others. Or perhaps she had developed it herself, each action she has taken to control her life leading to success, and each success a building block to greater power.

She often reflected on these building blocks through her life.

Having her father killed – yes she was content to admit it to herself and live with the fact – had not only avenged the childhood abuse but had given her control of a huge global company which she had then made an even greater success.

Creating Clara in the way she had done had given her a beautiful loving daughter without the baggage of a man and the compromise of a domestic partnership.

Then she had turned her attention to the Earth and outdone Mother Nature herself by taming nature and turning wastelands and desserts into vibrant new habitats in the form of her luxury resorts.

And now her latest control challenge. This was the big one. The existence of all humanity was at stake. Nothing less. She had to take it on. Nobody else was strong enough. Only she had the power to succeed. Only she had such a record of successes.

Her phone vibrated.

A text from Clara, presumably in the back of the company limo en route to Berchtesgaden.

Can't wait to shop! Thanks for the money Mama. Love you lots! (five heart emojis)

Penny felt the pang again.

But she was wrong to think it was purely the feeling of love that caused the moment of pain in her heart.

Searching her feelings, Penny realised there was anger too.

It was an unwelcome epiphany.

Yes she loved her daughter. But at the same time she hated the fact. Love was dangerous. It was interference. It clouded judgement, distracted, prompted illogical and sometimes counter-productive actions.

To control people and situations, to win battles, to succeed, you needed to be single-minded, focussed, strong-willed, and clinical of thought. Past experience had taught her this.

Now more than ever she needed to be on her game.

She pursed her lips and tapped her strong red fingernails against the wooden desk top for a few seconds.

Tak-Tak-Tak-Tak

Tak-Tak-Tak-Tak

Tak-Tak-Tak-Tak

She stopped abruptly and smiled.

No. This was her daughter. Her blood. A part of her.

It could never be a bad thing.

The phone on her desk interrupted her thoughts. She picked it up.

"Yes?...I see...Good work...Nevertheless, we need to move fast. Are all the ships underway?...Well get them moving quickly please...Somebody somewhere is going to try to stop us. It's inevitable. It needs to be too late for them. Act first, explain later....Good..."

There was a knock at the door and the PA popped her head round. "Sorry, Ms Crawford. Herr Weber is here."

"Thank you....I have to go. The police chief needs stroking..."

She was about to ring off when a thought crossed her mind. "Oh, one more thing...This fish creature, whatever it is...Yes...It sounds fascinating...Yes I know it's a problem. We don't need the attention. But I want one. Or several of them if you can get them...Well, do your best..."

She hung up and walked to the window. She stared at the snow-capped mountains, lost in thought for a moment.

A new breed of man-killing fish. And a ruthless one by all accounts. It was fascinating.

Later that day, having received urgent instructions, ships very similar to the one which had spewed its contents into the Indian Ocean were heading out of Shanghai and five other key ports around the globe – Rotterdam, The Netherlands; Vancouver, Canada; Tubarao, Brazil; and Colombo, Sri Lanka.

Each ship carried the same green cargo. Each crew was sworn to secrecy.

Behind them in the ports more ships were being loaded and prepared to follow them out.

Between them they had a presence in every ocean in the world.

Chapter Forty-Four

W ill sat in the back of a black Merc taxi and looked out of the window as it passed endless rows of giant rectangular metal box ship containers.

The scene was awesome. 32 million of these containers holding over 700 million tonnes of goods were shipped every year from Shanghai port, making it the biggest and busiest port in the world.

The port faced the East China Sea to the east and Hangzhou Bay to the south and included the confluences of three rivers – the Yangtze, Huangpu and Qiantang.

The taxi driver saw Will's amazement in his rear view mirror and said, "Two thousand ship leave here. Every month."

"Impressive."

But Will was not looking for a container ship. Following Chen's written directions, they were heading for one of the non-container terminals which handled bulk cargo including coal, grain and gravel.

His mind had not stopped racing since Chen had told him about the Life Group ship. What was it being used for? Was this what Mackay was trying to cover up? Was there something going on that was bigger than just the launch of a new resort in The Maldives?

After a further fifteen minutes the scene changed to rows of warehouses and small mountains of black, grey, yellow and red. Beside each mountain were two or three giant cranes scooping up mouthfuls and depositing them into tankers.

"This Longwu Branch Terminal," announced the driver. "We go in?"

"Yes. Drive on in."

Will looked at the security barrier and guard hut and hoped the combination of his Life Group ID, choice of luxury taxi, and sheer chutzpah would work. Otherwise it had been a wasted journey.

The car pulled up at the barrier. A sign in Chinese and underneath it English read:

Shanghai International Port Group
No Unauthorised Entry
All Passes Must Be Shown

One of two armed uniformed guards stepped out of the hut and approached the driver's window.

In the back seat Will picked up his mobile and pretended to have an intense conversation.

The driver wound down his window and the guard said a few words in Chinese.

"He say please show pass," said the driver looking in his mirror at Will.

Will looked annoyed at having his important phone call interrupted by such a triviality. He fished in his pocket, pulled out his company ID card and flashed it angrily at the guard.

The guard stepped to the rear window and Will wound it down.

"For God's sake I'm in a hurry," said Will, indicating his phone.

The guard beckoned for the ID card and Will handed it over.

He looked at it and said something in Chinese which Will knew must mean that this wasn't a pass so wasn't good enough. Before the driver could translate Will headed him off. "Warehouse 15. The Life Group. I need to be there now!"

The guard looked momentarily unsure so Will pressed his advantage quickly. He held out his phone towards the guard. "Or talk to my boss Penny Crawford."

The guard nodded as though Will had mentioned the correct password. The barrier was lifted and they drove in.

Will hadn't been sure if Penny's name would carry weight with port security, but it clearly did. What on Earth was she up to? He intended to find out.

"Drive to Warehouse 15 please," he said to the enquiring eyes in the rear view mirror.

"Yes sir."

It took them just a couple of minutes, passing rows of identical giant grey metal buildings between which he glimpsed the different coloured mounds, the ships, and the river.

The Merc pulled up in-front of a building with Warehouse 15 written on it in the usual two languages. He told the driver to wait and got out.

There were discordant sounds of machinery everywhere – wheels squealing, engines roaring, winches tugging – accompanied by occasional even louder bangs and crashes which Will took to be the dropping of bulky hard materials into the echoing metal holds of cargo ships.

Several workers in blue overalls and hard hats went about their business. Three men stood at the corner of the neighbouring warehouse chatting and smoking cigarettes. One of the group looked at Will and then rejoined his conversation unconcerned. Visitors were not unusual it seemed.

Will walked round the side of Warehouse 15. Ahead of him was the dockside and a massive red and white cargo ship. In front of it two cranes stood motionless. No sign of workers here.

He turned to his left to face the side of the warehouse. There were three large square entrances, all wide open. There was enough light to see clear into the huge high-roofed metal building and the green mounds of material inside.

He looked around. Still nobody.

He went in and heard crunching underfoot as he walked to the nearest green mound. The grey cement floor was covered in green patches where the material had obviously spilled as it was carried from the warehouse to the dockside for loading.

He knelt down for a closer look at the surface of the mound. It glinted slightly. Like a mountain of tiny emeralds. What he'd thought was powder was in fact crystals. Green crystals.

What were they? What did The Life Group need with this sort of stuff? It had nothing to do with the leisure industry as far as he could see. Perhaps it was used in some ecological project. If so, he had never been briefed on it.

He scooped a handful of the crystals and pocketed them.

Maybe he'd show them to a local pharmacist back in town.

Suddenly a voice outside approaching the warehouse: "Mister Sander! Mister Sander!"

It was not the voice of the driver. He'd been rumbled.

He ran behind the mound and ducked down, hoping the noise of the port machinery outside had masked his scrunching footsteps.

"Mister Sander? Are you here Mister Sander? You trespass. You no should be here!"

Then an exchange of words in Chinese. Two voices. One he recognised as the driver. The other was clearly security of some kind.

He didn't move.

An order was barked and he heard one set of footsteps retreating. Maybe the driver had been sent away.

The man who remained started to walk further in.

Will knew that if he walked left round the mound he would see Will immediately, but there was nothing to be done. The floor was a minefield of loud crunchy crystals. If he tried to move now he'd be heard.

Fortunately the man walked right, through the centre of the building.

From there Will was well hidden behind his mound.

Nevertheless he shrank himself into an even tighter ball.

Will heard the man walking further away towards the far end of the warehouse. He called again as he walked: "Mr Sander! Mr Sander!"

I won't reply, thought Will. Anyway, the name's Sanders.

Then a loud expletive in Chinese and he heard the man coming back towards him.

He'd either spotted Will or given up.

The footsteps scrunched past on the other side of Will's mound and went outside.

Will dared a peek over the side of his green crystal hill.

He saw a security guard stride out of the building and bark something at someone else out of view. He was joined by two other guards and all three of them headed in the direction of the ship.

Will took a deep breath and exhaled slowly.

He stood up and walked to the middle entrance.

He peered out tentatively.

To the left he saw the three guards walking to the ship.

He looked right, expecting to see the taxi. It had gone and in its place was a blue security van. The driver smoked a cigarette behind the wheel.

He was trapped for the moment.

He ducked back inside.

The guards were sure to return from the ship to the van past the open warehouse doors so he couldn't just stand there.

Better to hide at the back of the building.

He walked quickly to the back, following the guard's footsteps from before, between more green mounds.

In front of him was a solid metal wall.

He looked right and saw a closed emergency exit door.

He looked left and saw something far more interesting. A small metal box corner office.

Will tried the door. It was not locked.

He opened it and went inside.

The room was tiny. Just enough space for a small desk, chair and filing cabinet.

Perhaps he wouldn't need to test the crystals after all. If he could find the ship's manifest he would see what the cargo was. And its destination.

He tugged at the three filing cabinet drawers. All were locked.

Remembering Tanner's trick he turned his attention to the desk-top.

Bingo! A sheaf of papers held together by paperclips.

He needed two paperclips so picked up the papers to look for more. Nothing.

None in the drawers either.

He put the papers down again and was wondering whether it was possible to pick a lock with just one paperclip when he noticed the English writing in bold at the top of the cover sheet:

Memorandum

From:The Life Group

To:The Ministry Of Fisheries, The Republic Of Maldives

What had the company to do with the Ministry Of Fisheries?

The gruesome image of the sea creature's gaping toothed mouth sprang to mind.

He scanned the memo quickly and two phrases caught his attention:

Vicinity of newly created Nirvana Atoll ideal for fertilisation...

120 tonnes = 10,000 square km plankton = 100,000 tonnes fish...

This was a million miles away from tourism, thought Will. The Life Group was into, what? Fish production? Why?

And why the secrecy? It wasn't arms dealing. It was fish.

Sounds outside the office snapped Will away from his questions.

Crunch. Crunch, Crunch. Crunch.

Footsteps approaching.

There was nowhere in the office to hide and no time to go outside.

Fortunately Will had closed the office door behind him. He now stood behind it and grabbed hold of the door handle tightly.

From the footsteps and lack of talking Will guessed it was just one man. Perhaps doing a final quick check of the building.

The door handle was the straight lever variety which you pushed down to open. Will used both hands and all his weight to hold it up in the closed level position. He knew if the guard tried the handle with even a modicum of force he would feel a slight give and know it wasn't locked. But Will had little choice.

The footsteps stopped and he sensed the guard on the other side of the door.

He pulled as hard as he could against the handle.

He felt a slight downward tap as the guard tried the door.

Had the handle given too much? Surely the guard hadn't been fooled.

But it seemed he had.

The footsteps retreated.

Will let out a deep sigh of relief for the second time in the past twenty minutes.

He waited a few minutes to let the guard get clear, then looked back at the papers.

He flicked through the sheets. All but the top sheet were in Chinese.

He removed the top sheet only, folded it and pocketed it.

Then he made his way to the warehouse entrance.

This time when he looked out he saw no security guards. The van had gone. There were just workers in overalls. A few of them were more curious this time and looked him up and down. He smiled at them and walked back the way he'd been driven in, towards the port entrance.

It was a long walk. He kept a look out for security but saw nobody in a guard's uniform. Only workers.

He knew from the drive in that the port was surrounded by a high chain link fence topped with razor wire. There was only one way in or out.

As he approached the security barrier and guards' hut he lifted his head up, pulled his shoulders back and walked like he owned the place.

He hoped they only checked people coming in not going out.

When he was a few feet in front of the barrier a guard stepped out of the hut and held up his hand to stop him.

Not a good sign, he thought wryly. Never mind, try to blag it out.

"It's OK," he said to the guard smiling. "They found me and I've sorted everything out. It was a misunderstanding. The Life Group will call you."

He walked past the guard who to his surprise did not attempt to hold him back.

He was beginning to think his confidence act could get him anywhere when another man stepped out of the hut and blocked his way.

His heart sank.

It was Mackay.

"Hello Will," he grinned, "Finished snooping have we?"

Will tried to hide his shock and dismay. "John. How nice to see you again."

Mackay indicated a large silver BMW 7 Series, "Offer you a ride?"

"No I'll walk thanks."

A man mountain with ginger hair and podgy freckled face appeared at Will's side.

"I insist," said the Scot.

Will had no choice.

He got into the back of the car.

Chapter Forty-Five

"Nice of you to give me a ride back into town," said Will, staring at the backs of two heads, a fat ginger one driving and Mackay's bristles in the front passenger seat.

They were driving back towards the container port the way Will had come just an hour or so before.

"You're a bit of a trouble-maker aren't you Sanders?" said the Scot, half turning to look back at Will.

"What the Hell is the company up to? Working with the Maldives government to...what?...farm fish?"

Mackay stared straight ahead in silence.

"Is that what's going into the tankers?" continued Will, "Fish food? Odd looking fish food though."

No response.

"And why a company whose business is tourism would get side-tracked into fish farming I don't know....But that's not the real issue..."

Will paused but the two men in the front of the car remained silent.

"The real issue I think is that somehow it all went tits up and we now have massive killer sea monsters swimming around our new island and attacking our guests. Am I right?"

No response.

"And you're trying to cover it up. Penny must have sanctioned this fish farming – or whatever fishy business you're up to with the government – but I'm guessing she doesn't know about the gruesome side-effect? That tourists are being killed? Somehow I think she might be a bit more disturbed about that than you are, right?"

Mackay seemed to flinch and looked out of the side window.

"I guess you've bribed quite a few people out there to keep this quiet," Will went on. "People in the police. People in the government. But you won't be able to bribe all of them. I'm going to find the honest ones. And I'm going to open their eyes about what's going on. You won't get away with it. I'll make sure of that. I'll never give up..."

"I know you won't," interrupted Mackay at last. "I can see that now. Turn here."

The last instruction was to the fat ginger driver.

It was only then that Will noticed they were not headed back into the centre of the city but were on the outskirts heading out.

He leaned forward. "Hey, where are we going? This isn't the way into town."

"We're going to one of our Conglo sites."

Conglo, Will knew, was one of the Life Group's subsidiary companies. It handled much of the research, technology and design for the parent company.

"Why are we going there?"

There was no response. He felt uneasy. The thought crossed his mind to strangle the fat ginger driver in front of him like they did in the movies. But he'd never killed anyone in his life, by strangulation or otherwise. He tried the door – it was locked of course.

"Why are we going there Mackay?" he repeated forcibly.

Mackay snapped a response: "Because Penny wants to see you."

Will felt both relieved and disappointed. No, they were not kidnapping him. Yes, it looked like Penny knew everything. It was sad. The woman he'd admired and looked up to so much was as dirty-handed as her ugly Scottish sidekick.

Mackay saw Will's face. "Poor young Will. You look upset, laddie."

It was Will's turn to be silent.

They arrived at a high concrete wall with a large solid metal entrance gate with a logo on it:

CONGLO

Designing A Better Future

[Part Of The Life Group]

The ginger man wound down his window and typed a code into a keypad to the left of the gate. There was a moment's delay and then the gate slid sideways open to reveal a large courtyard with marked parking spaces in front of an enormous four story glass and metal building.

They parked up and the three men got out.

Theirs was the only car in the courtyard but all the lights were on in the building.

"Is she here already?" asked Will.

"Yes," said Mackay. "Follow me."

They walked to the main glass door and Mackay punched more numbers into a keypad. The door clicked and opened automatically. They went in, Mackay leading the way and the ginger hulk bringing up the rear.

They were in a vast high atrium, rising the entire four stories up to a white metallic ceiling. Four story terraces towered on either side and in front of them, beyond which were glass and chrome rooms of varying sizes.

There was a white semicircular reception desk, but no receptionist. No security guards either. In fact as Will stood in the atrium and looked up to the terraced floors above him he could not see anyone at all.

"Where is everyone?" he asked, almost to himself.

"Public holiday in China today," said Mackay.

Will frowned. It could hardly be a public holiday – he'd seen plenty of people working.

"Where's Penny? I need to see her now."

"Sure. This way." Mackay gestured towards a row of lifts and they walked over. "You haven't been here before have you Will?"

"No." Will thought it was odd the company hadn't inducted him concerning Conglo. It looked a pretty impressive set up.

"As you may know," continued Mackay, taking on the air of a tour guide, "Conglo is a wholly owned subsidiary of The Life Group. It was set up to meet the needs of the company in developing technological solutions to the challenges of building luxury resorts in hostile environments. After you..."

Mackay gestured for Will to enter the lift. They all went in and Mackay pressed a button marked B before continuing his spiel.

"We have tested many new construction designs here at our Shanghai facility, Will. Currently the guys here are working on developing materials to withstand the extremely low temperatures in the Antarctic, as we hope to build a new resort there soon."

Will was about to say he should have been told about this fascinating place as the media would have loved it – but then remembered he no longer worked for the company. And now intended to damage it severely, perhaps even destroy it.

The lift had descended and the doors now opened to reveal a long white corridor. Mackay led them down it.

"The most recent testing however was for Nirvana. We needed to develop all kinds of new underwater construction technology in order to create our paradise island out of nothing but empty ocean. I know how much you love Nirvana, Will, so you'll find this interesting..."

Will was intrigued, but he was puzzled by the sudden tour guide routine and was becoming impatient. "Yes it's all very interesting I'm sure, but I no longer work here remember? I don't really care anymore about this company. If Penny wants to see me one last time, that's fine. I've got plenty I want to tell her. But I couldn't give a shit about Conglo so you can dispense with the tour, John."

Mackay gave a mock expression of being hurt. "Och, Will. But this is the best bit. Just through here." They had arrived at a closed white double door at the end of the corridor. "Just take a look at this and then we'll go and see Penny."

"What? So she's not down here? Fuck this!"

Will was about to turn and head back to the lift when he felt a searing stabbing pain in his back like plastic baseball bats were hitting him 30 times a second. His limbs went stiff and his whole body juddered uncontrollably. He cried out in agony, one long shuddering cry. He saw Mackay in front of him grinning. The excruciating pain seemed to go on forever but in reality lasted 5 seconds.

Eventually it stopped and he fell to his knees.

"Give me that and help him up," Mackay said to the ginger man behind him. Will watched the man hand Mackay a black object with two metal points. A taser. Then he was grabbed under the armpits from behind and lifted sharply to his feet.

He wobbled a little and felt the adrenaline surging through his body. The pain had stopped completely. It was not a pain he would like to experience again however.

"Now, as I was saying," said Mackay opening the double doors with a flourish, "I think you're going to find this interesting."

Will felt himself being pushed by a big fat hand on his back and staggered into a vast white room.

In the centre of the room there seemed to be a second smaller room made out of clear Perspex. It was perhaps fifteen meters wide and six meters high. It was empty.

Metal steps led up the right hand side of the Perspex box and along the far edge.

Mackay nodded towards the box. "I told you, Will. It's impressive isn't it?"

He felt a surge of fear, only enhanced by Mackay's casual manner. First he'd tasered him as though it was an everyday occurrence, and now Will was sure he was going to do something much worse. What? Leave him to starve in this giant plastic box?

Mackay pointed to the steps. "Up we go."

Will didn't move. "Fuck you."

"Yes I thought you'd be difficult." Mackay gave a meaningful look over Will's shoulder.

Will felt something sting his neck. He wheeled round and saw the ginger man holding a syringe in his raised hand. This time he felt no pain at all. His mind went fuzzy, his vision blurred and he felt himself falling.

He blacked out before he hit the ground.

The ginger man replaced the cap on the syringe and put it in his pocket.

Mackay beckoned to him. "Ok, let's get this over with."

Chapter Forty-Six

W ill opened his eyes.

It was an odd and unsettling sight.

The walls of the Perspex box rising above him and at the top left hand edge the ginger man looking down at him.

The ginger man turned away. "Boss, he's coming to."

He was obviously flat on his back at the bottom of the box.

He tried to move but his body did not respond. He couldn't even move his head. Just his eyes.

His heart raced. Maybe he'd been pushed in and had broken his back.

Mackay's head appeared six meters above him. "Ah, you're awake."

Will tried to speak but his mouth wouldn't open.

"Don't worry, William," said Mackay smiling. "It's just temporary paralysis. Caused by the drug we injected you with twenty minutes ago. It's a new one I've discovered. Really great drug. Leaves no trace in the tissues, which is very handy indeed."

Will felt a sudden deep panic. He tried to force his body to respond but it was useless.

"I've been reading a lot about you, Will. You've been causing me a great deal of trouble so I wanted to know what makes you tick."

Will could only stare at him.

"I'm used to dealing with people who are a bit of a nuisance. There's lots of ways to make someone stop. Or if they won't stop, then disappear."

He tried to summon hatred into his eyes hoping Mackay could see it.

"But you, Will...You've caused me sooooo much trouble I can't simply do away with you. You need to pay for it first."

He blinked.

"Reading your personnel files I see you have a particular fear. Caused by a childhood trauma, right? A fear of water? A fear of.... drowning?"

He felt his eyes water and blinked, but he couldn't feel the tear running down his cheek.

"You may be wondering why you're in this strange box. Well it's not a box as such. It's a tank. Where we test out that underwater technology I was telling you about. During my little tour which you liked so much."

He closed his eyes and tried to clear and calm his mind as new waves of panic attacked him.

"Now here's the story. First you broke into our warehouse to try to find something to hold against us because we'd fired you. Having found nothing there – oh we've retrieved our memo from your pocket by the way - you thought you'd try your luck here. Unfortunately, while snooping around here you accidentally fell into our underwater research tank, had a panic attack brought on by your childhood trauma, and drowned. Very tragic."

Will heard a loud rumbling sound at the far end of the tank in front of him.

Then the unmistakable sound of water gushing and splashing against a hard surface.

He opened his eyes and looked down the tank. He saw a plume of water cascading from a pipe near the top of the tank. He couldn't lift his head to see it hit the bottom of the tank but could hear it and feel the vibrations.

He stared up but now there was nobody looking down on him. He looked back towards the water cascade and behind it could just make out through the Perspex wall the shapes of two men descending the metal stairs.

A split second later he felt cold liquid against his ankles, calves, thighs, back, then the back of his head.

He felt the water surge past his bare arms, and heard it gush just under his ears.

This was it.

Mackay had done it.

He was going to drown. The story would never get out. Whatever the company was up to, they'd get away with it.

He thought about Fiona and hoped she was safe.

The water was coming in fast and now there was an inch covering the whole of the bottom of the tank.

He felt the cold liquid against the back of his neck and the bottom of his ears.

He tried again and again to call out but his mouth still would not respond.

He tried to think of a way out.

The water was now half way up his body and pouring into his ears.

What was the way out? What was the way out?

The water began lapping over his face, into his eyes.

It went into his nose and he blew hard and pursed his lips to try to breathe through his mouth.

But the water kept coming in through his nose and started hitting the back of his throat.

He coughed and spluttered.

He knew it. There was no way out.

Suddenly he is ten years old again.

He feels the current of water surging against his body, sweeping him out to sea.

He tries to fight it but can't. He is powerless in the grip of the sea.

Then it drags him down, deeper and deeper. Into the cold dark depths.

He holds his breath as long as he can, until his brain hurts and his lungs explode with pain.

Finally he can hold out no longer.

He spasms and tries to breathe in, only to fill his lungs with water.

He spasms again.

Then all goes black.

Chapter Forty-Seven

The fat man waved his boss goodbye and passed his chubby hand through his ginger hair.

Great! Mackay was buggering off and he was left to clear up the mess.

He was a lazy man who hated physical activity of any kind. Give him a comfy chair, a TV and a bucket of KFC and he was happy any day.

Now he was going to have to retrace their steps and remove all trace of their being there, wiping down surfaces, disinfecting floors, blah blah blah. He sighed at the thought of the effort required as he waddled over to the elevator.

He punched the button and heard a buzzing sound as the doors opened.

Strange. It didn't usually make that sound.

Then he realised it was the front door.

His boss had forgotten something.

He turned and saw a figure standing behind the glass doors. Too petite to be Mackay. A cleaning girl?

As he approached he squinted to make out who it was he'd have to get rid of.

Not a cleaning girl. She was European. And very pretty. Slim, dark hair, well dressed.

She cocked her head to one side a gave him a bewitching smile.

He was intrigued. If she was a hooker she was the prettiest hooker he'd ever seen in his life.

He pulled his stomach in, though it made little appreciable difference, and gave her his winning smile. "What do you want?"

She mouthed something.

"What?"

She mouthed something again, this time gesturing with her hands too.

He couldn't make it out.

The boss had told him not to open the doors to anyone, but what harm could this slip of a thing do?

He clicked the lock and let her in.

"What's pretty little thing like y...."

But he didn't finish the greeting. A blow to the head knocked him out cold.

Will convulsed and spewed out a lungful of water.

Then he took in a sharp breath of air.

He coughed and opened his eyes.

Fiona's smiling face filled his vision.

He must be dead. Could you dream when you were dead?

He felt her left hand on the side of his head and her right hand gripping his wrist.

"Thank God!" he heard her say. "Will, are you OK?"

His chest started to hurt. He wasn't dead.

He lay there breathing. It felt good to breathe. To be alive.

He was suddenly worried. "Ma...Mackay..." he whispered hoarsely. He could speak again.

"It's OK. He's not here."

"Gin...Ginger man..."

"No, don't worry about him either."

He tried to get up. But his limbs still didn't respond.

Fiona saw it and frowned. "You can't move? Wait. Maybe you hurt your back. Let me see."

She started checking him over but he stopped her. "No...My...My neck. Inject....Injected me..."

"Ok, let me look..." She examined the sides of his neck. "Yes I see a puncture wound. They...They must have paralysed you..." He saw a tear come to her eye.

"I'm...Ok...Fi..." he said. He tried to smile. And found he could. "I...can...speak....now...couldn't before..."

Her face brightened. "That's good! That's good! That means it's wearing off, Will!"

It was. The increasing pain throughout his body told him that.

"How...How did you...get here?"

While she spoke she moved his head from side to side and massaged his arms and chest to try speed up his recovery.

"After we spoke on the phone I was worried about you. I also thought I could help you find out what's going on. I've got a theory. Then Harold thought they might turn nasty on you and wanted to come out instead of me. But I told him it needed a younger pair of legs. He didn't like that! He fought me hard but I won. I think he saw the logic of it. I'm quite tough you know. There...any more feeling yet?"

He was too entranced by her to respond, then recovered his wits and found he could move his head and fingers.

"That's good Will. The drug is wearing off. Keep moving what you can. I'll keep rubbing you to get the circulation going."

She started massaging his legs.

"I think...Getting drugged is...not so bad!"

She smiled at him.

"So anyway...I flew out here and tried to call you but your phone was dead. So I called the journalist...Chen...I'd spoken to him before so he knew me...And he told me about the tip-off he'd given you about the cargo ship."

"Uhhh." Will groaned.

"You OK?"

"Yes. I can feel my arms and legs now." He flexed his arms and then lifted his knees up.

"Ok. I think you'll be able to get up in a minute or two. You're recovering quickly now. So...Then I went out to the port to try to find you. But the security wouldn't let me in."

Will pushed himself up into a sitting position. "Really? You were there?"

Fiona rubbed his back. Her hands were surprisingly strong.

"Aaahh that feels good!" he said.

"Yes. Like being at The Four Seasons isn't it? Well, like being in a big plastic box in The Four Seasons."

"What did you do when you couldn't get in?"

"I didn't know what to do. So I parked up down the road and waited a while. I thought you might come out eventually. And you did. But not quite how I'd expected...."

"No, nor me!"

"I watched them escort you into a silver Beamer and drive off."

"And you followed them here. You're so clever."

"Aren't I?"

"And gorgeous."

"I think someone's feeling better aren't they?"

She kissed him full on the lips. "Can you feel that?"

"Oh yes."

They both laughed.

He got gingerly to his feet with a few grunts.

He looked around. The four sides of the Perspex tank towered above them. Through them he could see the room was empty.

She read his mind. "There's nobody here to bother us. I parked up the road from here out of sight and walked. I slipped in when the main gate opened and Mackay drove out. He didn't see me. I had to ring at the door to the building though because it was locked. The fat ginger guy came and opened it..."

"What? W-Why d-did he let you in?"

Will shivered.

"Will we need to get you out of those wet clothes."

"W-will you j-join m-me?"

"Will, I'm serious."

"Ok-k. Ok."

They headed for a chrome ladder attached to the left hand wall, climbed out onto the walkway and then went down the metal stairs and across the main floor of the big white room. Fiona continued her story as they went.

"The fat ginger guy came waddling across the foyer. He could see me standing outside and was grinning at me. I think he recognised me from the resort. Anyway...he opened the door and started to say something sarcastic. I gave him a *Mae Geri* to the head. A front kick. Knocked him out cold. I told you I have a black-belt in Karate didn't I? Fifth Dan. My father insisted I learn it for self defence. I'm glad I did. Oh yes I showed you at the party – remember the canapé board? Anyway...found some tape and tied him up where he lay. Couldn't move him – God he's heavy!"

They left the room and walked down the corridor to the lift. Will was wide-eyed. "Fiona I don't think I know you very well! Remind me to thank your father if we meet one day."

She called the lift.

"Oh you'll meet him. You'll get on well. I know it."

He smiled.

The lift pinged and the doors opened. They went in and Will punched G.

"I've been up and down in this thing a few times today," said Fiona. "It took me ages to find you. Christ, when I saw you lying at the bottom of that tank covered in water I...."

Her eyes started watering. He hugged her. "You were brilliant," he said. "A real life Wonder Woman."

"I knew I had to act quickly. A few more seconds and you'd have...Well I just hit the big red button that said Emergency Stop and it worked. The gushing water cut out and these huge hatches at the bottom of the tank opened and the water in the tank drained out. Then I climbed down and gave you the kiss of life..."

"You did? I'm sorry I missed that!"

"Yeah. Dad insisted on First Aid training too."

"I think I owe your Dad a very very large drink."

The lift doors opened and they walked out into the atrium.

Will was struck by the strange object on the floor in front of the main door. A fat man with red blotchy skin and ginger hair, his limbs bound tightly to his body by black duct tape, wriggling on his side like a giant grub.

The man saw them and let out some muffled noises, whether in pain or anger Will couldn't quite tell.

Will looked at the slight pretty girl next to him with renewed admiration. "*You* did *that*?"

They left the ginger man wriggling and took Fiona's hire car back into town. Will drove, the heating turned up to the max.

He explained what he'd found at the warehouse – the green crystal mounds and the fisheries memo.

He reached into his jacket pocket to show her the crystals he'd scooped up, but they'd gone.

"They must have dissolved in the water," he said.

"Yes that makes sense," she said, cracking her window slightly to let out the gathering steam from Will's clothing. "I think from everything you've said they must be iron sulphate crystals. They dissolve easily."

"Iron sulphate? Is that significant?"

"It's a common fertiliser. Used on gardens. But also used at sea – to encourage algae growth to feed fish. It's common practice around the world. The more algae in the water, the quicker the fish multiply, and the fatter they get. This is the theory I wanted to tell you about. I think the company is dumping iron sulphate in the sea around the Maldives. Probably in a joint venture with the government. To increase local fish stocks."

"The local fishing industry is based around tuna," said Will frowning. "Do tuna eat algae?"

"No. But they do feed on the fish that eat the algae. The crystals produce the algae, which is fed on by bait fish, which in turn feed the tuna. The locals have been talking about record tuna catches for some time now."

"And the bait fish are also attracting our sea monster?"

"No, not quite. It goes after bigger prey. Which is why it's attacking people."

"So this fish farming project is not connected to our monster?"

"Oh I think it is. The prof was right."

"The prof?"

She opened the window wider and waved her hand in front of him. "Do you mind Will? You're really steaming!"

He laughed. "Sorry. I can't wait to change out of these. Anyway..."

"Anyway...I spoke to my professor back in Plymouth. And, once I'd managed to persuade him I wasn't a loon, he proposed a theory linking the algae blooms we saw near the resort to the monster fish. He said he thought it was possible that huge amounts of dead algae is sinking to the bottom of the ocean around the Maldives and sucking oxygen out of the deeper levels as it decomposes. This is forcing our creature up to the shallows, where it never or rarely goes usually, to find oxygen."

"Where it comes across people too..."

"...And attacks us because it thinks we are food, or because we are in their way, or out of curiosity...who knows..."

"Whatever the reason, it's still a danger. A new danger."

Will paled at the thought of Jojo possibly encountering the creature.

"It has to be stopped," he said after a few minutes' sombre silence. "We have to stop this experiment. Or at least have it recognised that it's got this dangerous side-effect and get it moved to uninhabited waters."

"I agree, of course. But why are The Life Group doing this in the first place? Why is a tourism company getting involved in fish farming?"

"Will grimaced. "Why do companies do anything, Fi?" He rubbed his fingers. "Money."

Chapter Forty-Eight

M ackay grinned. He was at the wheel of the silver BMW and happy despite being stuck in traffic in downtown Shanghai.

Sanders was finally out of the way. A bit of a dramatic exit but he'd deserved it for all his interfering. And the police could be relied on not to investigate too thoroughly – he'd made sure of that. Anyway, it had to be done. Nothing could be allowed to get in the way of the big project.

His phone rang on the passenger seat where he'd left it earlier. He looked at the screen and saw a fat ginger face.

He tapped the phone's loud speaker, "Is the item despatched as planned?"

"I'm sorry boss. We have a problem."

Mackay's lips tightened. "What kind of problem? Don't be too specific – we may be overheard."

"Ummm...I sort of got tied up...with an unexpected visitor..."

"What?" He yelled at the phone. The man in the next car looked at him and looked away quickly at Mackay's glare. "Who?"

"A...er...fish girl we know..."

"A what?!"

"Fi..."

"No names, you cretin!" Mackay tried to grasp what had happened. "So there are now two items to....handle?"

"Er...no boss...They...The two items are no longer here..."

"What? How? Fuck! Fuck! Fuck!" Mackay hit the steering wheel hard with the palm of his hand. His face went an angry red colour and his eyes were hard as stone. This threatened to upset everything. It would attract huge unwanted attention. He caught the man in the car watching him again and gave him the finger with a snarl. The man returned the gesture as the traffic moved his car forward from their ten minute standstill.

The phone squawked again: "I'm sorry, boss....There was nothing I could do...I think she broke my nose..."

"I'm gonna break your bloody *head* when I find you, you fucking useless piece of shit! Stay there, I'm coming back."

Mackay barged his way out of his stationary lane and into oncoming traffic going the other way, forcing two cars to swerve violently.

He gunned it back the way he'd come. The look on his face could have melted steel.

Chapter Forty-Nine

A t Warehouse 15 the green crystals Will had hidden behind were now being loaded onto the docked tanker.

There was a new sense of urgency and this part of the port was now buzzing with activity.

The green mounds would shortly be renewed by a stream of lorries bringing fresh supplies.

Four more tankers were waiting their turn in the bay, and one further ship – the one captained by Raj - was expected back in a week. The operation had been increased six-fold, much to the warehouse manager's surprise. From one ship leaving fully loaded every 18 days to one ship every *three* days.

The ships would not be headed for the Indian Ocean. That area was apparently now being handled out of Colombo in Sri Lanka which was much closer. The destination for the tankers from Shanghai was a point in the west Pacific ocean. He'd also heard that the eastern part of the Pacific was to be handled by tankers out of Vancouver. Meanwhile the Atlantic was covered by Rotterdam in the north and a Brazilian port in the south.

The warehouse manager wondered what possible purpose it might serve to dump such vast quantities of iron sulphate in the world's oceans. The last manifest had mentioned the increase in fish stocks. If that was still the purpose then the world's fishermen were going to have a bonanza like they'd never seen before.

However he kept his thoughts to himself. He knew if he talked to anyone outside the warehouse about the operation his life wouldn't be worth living. People who had talked had disappeared. This was a powerful and scary company.

Chapter Fifty

W ill lay in his luxuriously soft hotel bed and sighed contentedly.
He turned his head and looked at Fiona's sleeping face next
to him.

They had called the Shanghai police from the car on the way into
town and reported what had happened. The duty officer had taken
some convincing that Will was neither a lunatic nor a hoaxer, plus the
conversation in stilted English had been tortuous. But eventually the
officer had promised to send a squad car to investigate and had asked
Will to come into the station to file a report. They had agreed a time
later that afternoon as Will wanted first to clean up.

They had gone to his hotel where he'd gladly peeled off his damp
clingy clothing and taken a welcome hot shower.

He'd been half way through drying off when Fiona had walked in
to the bathroom and things had quickly taken a not unexpected turn.
With Will still feeling bruised and battered, their lovemaking had been
cautious at first, but had soon moved up through the gears as the
passion made him oblivious to the pain.

He got up and winced as the movement triggered sharp daggers of pain in various parts of his body.

Fiona stirred awake. "You OK Will?" she said sleepily.

He kissed her head. "I'm fine. In fact I'm feeling great. How could I not be? I've just made love to Wonder Woman!"

She laughed and threw her pillow at him. "Don't call me that. You know I hate it. I don't wear blue knickers over my tights!"

"Hmmm. Now there's a thought..."

She picked up his pillow to throw at him but stopped. "Hey! Aren't we going to be late at the police station?"

"We have thirty minutes. We need to move."

Her phone rang. "Speak of the devil," she said. "I think it's them calling now. Here..."

She handed him the phone. He'd used it to call earlier as his battery had been dead.

He answered it and walked through the door into the living room area as he listened.

A few minutes later she followed him. She found him sitting on the sofa, the conversation clearly over.

The look on his face told her something was wrong.

"What is it?" she said.

"I don't believe it," he said glumly. "That was the same guy we spoke to. He sent a car to the Conglo site but they found nothing. There was a security guard at reception who told them nobody had been into the place all day. No sign of the ginger guy. He even let them look at the tank and it was completely dry – they said it hadn't been used for a while."

"They covered it all up."

"They did. And bloody fast. Unbelievable. He says we should still come in to the station to make a statement but if we have wasted police time there will be consequences."

"What? They're turning it on us?"

Just then a mobile rang. They both looked at Fiona's which was on the sofa next to Will. Then they quickly realised it was coming from the desk on the other side of the room.

"It's yours, Will. You put it to charge."

He leapt up and walked over to pick it up. As he approached he saw the screen was a snow-capped Alpine mountain. "It's Life Group HQ," he said and pressed the green answer disc.

"Hello?" The voice had a slight German accent. "Mr Sanders?"

"Yes."

"I have Penny Crawford for you. Please hold a moment."

Will's eyes widened.

"Hello?" The voice was now Penny's. The tone was soft and warm.

"Hello Penny," said Will with a steel edge in his voice, "How nice of you to contact me finally..."

"Will, Will. I'm so sorry. I tried to call you but your phone was dead. I wanted to apologise for not being able to make our meeting in The Bund. I had an emergency..."

He cut her off angrily. "Yeah, me too Penny! Your henchman almost killed me a few hours ago..."

"My henchman? Tried to kill you?"

"Yes, you got it. Mackay. Tried to drown me in a testing tank at the Conglo facility on the edge of the city..."

He heard her gasp. Was it real shock or was she putting it on? He couldn't tell.

"I don't believe what I'm hearing, Will..."

Fiona had put her ear close to hear their conversation and now spat down the phone, "Bitch! We don't believe you!"

Will nudged her away but she continued shouting, "You're an evil scheming lying bitch!"

"A friend of yours I take it?" said Penny flatly.

"Look, Penny," he said, at the same time motioning Fiona to calm down, "I can't believe you don't know what's going on..."

"Of course she does!" shouted Fiona from the middle of the room, "She's a lying evil witch!"

Will gestured to her again. "You understand we're upset," he said. "I come to Shanghai to find you to tell you about the absolute mayhem at your new resort, to try to save your company from fucking disaster, and what do I get? You stand me up, then you fire me, then you try to have me bumped off. You understand our annoyance, Penny?"

"Will, I promise you..."

"How can I believe you?"

"Don't believe her! She's behind all this!" shouted Fiona.

"Can I speak?" said Penny, still warm, still calm.

"Sure. Go ahead."

"I promise you, Will. I promise you I know nothing of all this. I called to apologise for standing you up, but what you've told me just now...I can't believe it. I gave Mackay no authorisation to fire you. And to have you...what...killed? That's ridiculous. But I shall look into it, Will. There will be a thorough internal independent investigation. And if there's any truth in any of it...which I can't believe...but if there is, then John Mackay will be brought to justice. In the meantime, so you can see I'm serious, he will be suspended. You, of course, are still my employee. If you're happy to be. Will, you know me I think. You trust me. I promise I knew nothing of all this."

He thought she sounded sincere. He'd never heard that tone in her voice before. "I don't know what to think, Penny…"

"I promise on the life of my daughter. You remember Clara? You know what she means to me. This is not a shallow promise."

Will looked at Fiona. She put her hands on her hips defiantly and said loudly, "I can't hear what she's saying but she's a witch, Will. Don't believe her."

As intended, Penny heard it. "I see your friend will take some convincing, Will."

"Me too," he said.

"Ok. I understand. I think it's time to let you see the bigger picture. We have exciting plans for the future, Will…"

"What, like fish farming? We know what you're up to, Penny. Though God knows why you're into fish production…"

"No, Will. It's a lot bigger than that."

He was taken aback. She hadn't seemed surprised when he mentioned fish farming. And something bigger?

"The Antarctic project?"

"Bigger than that too. Much bigger. Come to HQ and find out. It's time you knew. And I could do with your help."

Will was taken aback. "Come to Berchtesgaden?"

Fiona shook her head vigorously.

"Just tell me now, Penny."

"No. You need to see it for yourself. And it will take some explaining. But it's very exciting. You're going to be amazed, Will. And so will your doubting friend. She should come too."

"Well…" At last here was an opportunity to find out the truth. It was what he'd been searching for these past days.

"Good. I'll get a plane sorted immediately. My office will be in touch with the details. I'm glad we've sorted things out, Will. And I look forward to seeing you very soon."

Penny rang off and he looked at Fiona.

"You're not going, Will. I don't trust her. She's tried to kill you."

"Well, Mackay tried to kill me."

"Under her instructions."

"She says not."

"Pah!"

He kissed her and they hugged for a moment.

Then he said, "Actually...we're both invited."

"You're joking. No way am I going."

She folder her arms defiantly and Will smiled at her.

"Fi...." he said, "Mackay must be going behind her back. Why would she act in such a way as to destroy her own resort, even the whole company? It doesn't make sense."

"Because she's a lunatic maybe? I don't know, Will. I just don't trust her. We're not going to Berchtesgaden."

She actually stamped her foot. He thought only cartoon characters did that and he smiled despite himself.

"I mean it, Will," she said, a look of defiance in her eyes which he found quite charming.

She had a point. In his heart of hearts he didn't know if he could trust the extraordinary Crawford woman. But he felt he owed it to Jojo to find the truth . He took her gently by the arms. "I'm going to go, Fi. I have to find out what's going on. I owe it to Jojo. And Harold."

She was about to remonstrate with him but his phone rang again.

Thinking it was Penny again she grabbed it off him and answered it angrily. "Now look..." Then she stopped and made a face. "Oh. Sorry Harold. I thought you were someone else. You'll never guess what's happened…It's a good job I came out. They tried to kill Will. They tried to drown him in one of their research facility tanks….I know…Unfuckingbelievable…No, he's fine…I'll hand you over…

She handed him the phone.

"Harold?"

"Will. Are you all right, young man? I can't believe all this. They tried to drown you?"

"Yes. I can't believe it either. I found their warehouse in the cargo port. They're shipping out tons and tons of iron sulphate. Presumably dumping it at sea to grow algae…"

"Like Fiona thought…"

"Yes. She was right…"

He looked up at her and she nodded to him firmly.

"And the algae boosts fish production, right?" He heard Tanner curse under his breath. "Why? Why? They don't need the money. They don't have expertise in this area. It's ridiculous."

"I know. I have no idea why they're doing it."

"And this is what probably caused the appearance of that…thing that attacked my nephew."

"Sorry, Harold. It could be, yes."

He exchanged a pained look with Fiona. It must be terrible for the old man to be constantly reminded of the gruesome way in which his nephew died.

"So they found you snooping around and tried to kill you. Jesus!"

"Yep. Mackay caught me at the warehouse and sort of kidnapped me. Before I knew it they'd injected me with a drug which paralysed me and dumped me in a tank to drown me."

"Christ!"

"But Fi rescued me like the Wonder Woman she is…" She punched him softly. "…I'll tell you the story when I see you next. You won't believe that bit either!"

"She's quite something isn't she?"

"Sure is."

"You reported this to the police right?"

"Mackay covered it all up. The police found no evidence. They think I'm lying I think."

"Oh for Chrissakes! What is this organisation? The mafia? They've got tentacles everywhere it seems, kid. I'm telling you. I've tried talking to the local government, the US embassy, the police, and even the United Nations. I got nowhere. Everyone stonewalls me. Like they've been got to in advance."

Will knew the feeling. The company seemed to be untouchable. "I had the same thing with the media."

"Looks like we're on our own, kid. Good job I've got the cash and you've got the muscle!"

Will laughed. "Well, I think it's Fiona who's got the muscle…" She punched him again, harder this time. "Ow! She's hitting me now Harold."

"Tell him about Penny's kind invitation," she said.

"I heard that," said Tanner. "What invitation?"

"Fi and I are invited to meet her at HQ. A town in Bavaria. She swears she had nothing to do with Mackay trying to kill me. I think I believe her."

Fiona shook her head.

"Do you want to go, kid?"

"I think so. What do you think?"

There was silence while the American thought about it. "If you're up for it. And you believe her. I say go."

"Great."

"I'll pay for it."

"Thanks, Harold. But she's sending her jet."

"Keep in touch, yes?"

"I will."

"Good luck, young man. And take care, ok?"

"Will do. Bye Harold."

Will rang off and then repeated the conversation to Fiona.

She paced the room for a minute, turning things over in her mind.

Then she stopped and said to him, "I'm going with you."

He was about to protest but she silenced him with a kiss.

Chapter Fifty-One

H aving been briefed by Penny's PA who had called the moment Tanner had hung up, Will and Fiona were whisked to Shanghai airport by limo and took an overnight flight by company jet, landing 12 hours later at Munich airport.

Another company limo, a long black Merc, picked them up outside the terminal building and whisked them the two hours to Berchtesgaden, mostly along Autobahns but then finally picturesque mountain roads.

Munich had been only a few degrees colder than Shanghai, but as they approached the foothills of the Alps at the southern edge of Germany as it bordered Austria the temperature dropped and the scenery turned gradually from green to white.

It was a bright blue sunny sky though and the small picturesque town of Berchtesgaden glinted in freshly fallen snow as they skirted it and climbed even higher to the hilltop HQ of The Life Group.

Will was used to it but Fiona was enchanted by the passing views. Rows of tall snow-covered pine trees looking impossibly Christmassy, smaller leafless trees with tangled glistening frozen branches, a virgin blanket of white over the fields with the odd snaking tracks of skis and sleds, a soft marshmallow layer on the roofs of the quaint wooden chalets. It was all so dreamy.

"It's all so beautiful!" she said to Will. "I know we're on a serious mission here but I can't help loving the scenery."

"Fresh snow makes everything look beautiful," he said. "Though, yes, even without the snow this is a stunning part of the world."

"It's so remote though. Don't the roads get cut off?"

"We're in Germany, Fi, not Britain. The roads are always kept clear. Here snow does not stop you driving, or getting a train, or flying."

"Still, it's a funny place to have a global headquarters isn't it?"

"I guess you can be based anywhere these days. The chopper must be busy but usually it takes no time to fly from here to Munich, and from there you can fly anywhere of course. Also you can achieve a lot on the internet. We're encouraged to use Skype, Google Hangouts and FaceTime as much as possible. Especially to lessen our carbon footprint, don't you know. Which seems odd considering we're a company that encourages people to jet off round the world."

"I hadn't thought of that. This is an eco travel company but travelling is hardly eco friendly."

"Do you know that just one holiday flight you make cancels out all your great effort in recycling your household waste for the whole year?"

"I bet you don't tell the journalists that."

"They're travel journalists. What do they care? They're getting a free luxury all-expenses paid holiday in exchange for writing lots of good stuff about us."

"My, my, William. Sounds like we're getting a bit of a downer on our employer."

"Now why would I be like that?"

They laughed.

"Wow," said Fiona, looking out the car window as they pulled up to the HQ building. "So this is the witch's lair. Impressive."

"Welcome to The Life Group," said Will.

Penny was waiting for them in reception as they entered the impressive curved wood-and-glass building.

She looked stunning as always, seeming to own the room. She was dressed simply but stylishly in a sleek grey trouser suit. The v neck of the jacket revealed simply her tanned skin, amazingly smooth for a woman of her age. No necklace, just a pair of platinum and diamond pendant earrings.

She smiled warmly as she strode towards them with outstretched hand.

"I wanted to meet you personally. I'm so glad you both agreed to come," she said, and led them to her office, enquiring about their journey and pointing out to Fiona interesting facts about the building.

Will noticed how Fiona's hatred and mistrust of the glamorous CEO seemed to be mollified by the charismatic woman's warmth and apparent openness. He'd seen her turn on the act before and had to admire her for it. She was a supreme manipulator of people.

They arrived at a large top-floor glass corner office, sparsely furnished, with stunning views out over the surrounding snowy mountains.

Will knew it well but Fiona was awed by the building and its beautiful setting. "This place is amazing!" she said, then immediately looked guilty at being so effusive.

"Well, if it was good enough for Adolf," said Penny smiling and gesturing for them to sit on one of two long square modern sofas which faced each other in the centre of the room. Will and Fiona sat together and Penny sat opposite them. "Tea?" she asked, and started pouring from a large white china teapot on the low glass table in between them.

"Thank you," said Fiona. "You mean Hitler lived here?"

"For part of the war yes. It was his favourite home. A stone's throw from here. We could have been neighbours. Milk? Sugar?"

"Milk please. No sugar," said Fiona, casting her eyes between Penny and the mountain scenery. "It really is a quite a view."

"Isn't it," said Penny, handing her the cup of tea. "Not bad for a lying bitch, hmmm?"

Fiona coloured. Will smiled despite himself. He'd wondered how long Fiona's grateful guest act was going to go on and was secretly glad she'd been snapped out of it.

"This is not a social visit," he said, looking at Penny. "We've got a lot of serious shit to sort out."

A look of distaste flickered across her face, quickly replaced by a smile less warm than before. "Serious shit?" she said, fixing him with her steely blue eyes. It made his insides go cold. It was like looking into the face of a Gorgon.

But playtime was over. "Yes. Fucking. Serious. Shit," he said, holding her stare.

"All right," she said after a moment, raising her eyebrows but not looking away. "I invited you here to explain things. Tell me what you know and then I'll fill in the gaps."

Will looked at Fiona, who had paused with her cup midway to her mouth. She nodded to him and took a sip.

"Ok," Will said, "So. We know..."

"Biscuit?" interrupted Penny, offering Fiona a plate. Fiona quickly shook her head. "Sorry, Will. Please go on. I'm listening."

"We know you are dumping iron sulphate into the seas around Nirvana resort to increase fish production. I saw the stuff in your secret warehouse in Shanghai. I've also seen...we both have...the algae blooms it's produced. You have an agreement with The Maldives government – I know this for a fact because I got hold of the ship's manifest. So I presume it's a nice little business making both sides a lot of money. A bit off-piste from the travel industry and all very secretive, but I guess money is money, right?"

Penny gave a half smile and took a sip of tea.

"But there's a problem," he continued, "A big problem. Which we've found out and either you don't know about or are choosing to ignore. All this algae which your dumping is producing is dying off, sinking to the bottom and sucking oxygen out of the ocean."

"Yes," said Fiona, "It's caused by microbes feeding on the dead algae. It happens from time to time and causes dead zones in coastal waters where there have been algal blooms. The oxygen is removed and any fish or crabs or shrimp that can't escape die."

"But here it's happening in the deep ocean," Will said, "And instead of killing fish it seems to be forcing them to shallower waters to breathe. Well, one fish in particular. A six foot monster. Which is attacking swimmers. Two people that we know about so far have been killed by this fish, including one guy I knew personally. Both deaths happened at Nirvana. Your resort. And John Mackay has been trying to cover it all up. I originally thought because he was worried about the resort, but I now see there's the fish farming money to protect too."

Will paused to examine Penny's face but he couldn't quite read it. "Did you know about the attacks Penny?"

She got up and went to a desk in the corner of the room near the window. There was a dark wooden box on the desk. She opened it and took out a long slim cigar. Will and Fiona watched in surprise as she used a small metal implement to cut the end of the cigar, then picked up a lighter and proceeded to warm the other end against a blue gas flame.

"Either of you indulge?" she asked. They both shook their heads. "No, I thought not. Tobacco gives you cancer, of course. But cancer

is not some mystical assassin, you know. It's a disease. And like any
diseases it can be defeated." She examined the end of the cigar and
seemed satisfied with the red glow. She took a drag and exhaled a cloud
of aromatic blue smoke. "My scientists tell me we're close to finding
a cure. So I can continue indulging." She leant back against her desk
and looked at them. "I'm a great believer in the power of science, you
see. Nature can be tamed. The Earth belongs to us. We can shape it
however we want to. If we want to enough. We wanted to go to the
Moon and we went to the Moon. We defeated gravity. I wanted to turn
desserts and wastelands and empty ocean into luxury resorts. People
said I couldn't do it. But I did. With science and technology you can
do anything. Even cure cancer. We're quite close I believe."

"What's this got to do with what we're talking about?" asked Will.
He had once been in awe of her vision and drive but with everything
that had happened in past few days it now seemed irrelevant.

"It's got everything to do with it," said Penny, taking another puff
of her cigar in a way which despite his growing dislike of her made her
look surprisingly elegant. "Let me explain. You're right about our deal
with the Maldives government to increase fish production. But that's
just a bonus. I don't give two hoots about fish farming. It's not the real
goal. I'd be adding iron to the ocean to grow algae in any case. I have
what you might call a higher purpose."

He frowned. Was this the bigger picture she and Mackay had mentioned?

He was about to ask but Fiona beat him to it. "I don't understand,"
she said. "Why would you want to grow algae other than as fish food?"

"You're a biologist," said Penny blowing out another aromatic blue
cloud, "Think about it."

Fiona frowned. "Why grow phytoplankton? What do you gain?"

"Search me," said Will. "Apart from causing this mayhem it just floats around on the surface. Clogs up boat engines. I don't know. Why don't you just tell us, Penny?" He didn't want to play guessing games. People had died because of this.

"Fiona can work it out. It's not difficult."

"What does it do?" mused Fiona. "It covers the ocean. It blocks out the sun...No, wait...." A light flickered across her face. "It absorbs sunlight. It photosynthesises. Like plants and trees."

He didn't like the way she seemed to be enjoying the intellectual challenge.

"Yes," said Penny, "I could have planted lots of trees instead – and I do, at my resorts – but there isn't enough space and this is easier and quicker. Go on, Fiona."

Fiona's eyes widened as her mind worked. "Photosynthesis removes carbon from the atmosphere..."

Penny smiled and nodded.

"That's what you're doing."

"What?" said Will. He wasn't following.

Fiona answered Will but was looking at Penny. "She's using the algae to suck carbon out of the atmosphere. When the algae dies it takes the carbon with it to the sea floor where it's trapped."

"Bravo!" Penny said, clapping lightly, causing the ash to fall from the end of her cigar.

"But I don't understand," said Will, "Why are you doing this? Are you getting carbon credits?"

"Sure, I get credits..."

"What are carbon credits?" asked Fiona.

"Companies with high carbon emissions can lower their carbon footprint by paying other companies who are removing carbon from the atmosphere," Penny explained, noticing the ash and treading it into the rug. "Yes I'm making money from the carbon credits like I'm making money from the fisheries. But that's still not the prime goal. What I'm really doing has nothing to do with money at all." She paused to let her words sink in. "What I'm really doing is saving our planet."

She walked to a side cabinet and pulled out three short crystal tumblers.

Will was finding it hard to believe. "You're saying you're not doing this for profit?"

She shot him a cool look. "That's what I said."

She took out an opaque dark green bottle from the cabinet.

"Trading carbon credits makes money. And the fisheries do too. I wasn't going to bother with either though originally. Too much hassle. But then I thought why not make the whole thing near enough cost-neutral? So now I have an initiative that can save the world from global warming without costing the Earth. Forgive the pun. Rum Fiona?" She waved the bottle.

"No thanks."

"Will?"

Will nodded and Penny poured them a couple of Diplomaticos.

He tried to process what she was saying. He knew her passion for ecology was real and deep-seated, but he had not expected there to be a project of pure altruism behind all the terrible things that had happened.

Before he had a chance to speak she continued. "I know it's trite to say it – and it's hard to believe looking out at all this snow...but the Earth is warming up. And it's due to us. Do you realise that 16 of the 17 warmest years ever recorded occurred since 2001?"

She sat and sipped her rum, then took another toke on her cigar.

"Global sea levels rose eight inches in the last hundred years. Eight inches. And it's getting worse. The rate has doubled in the last two decades. Doubled. That's why we had to build Nirvana so high."

He saw her passion. It muddled how he felt about her.

"It is predicted that the Earth's temperature will rise by two more degrees in the next 20 years thanks to humankind. Once four degrees is reached – probably by the end of this century – the polar ice will be gone and the world will be on a slippery slope of no return to self-destruction."

He noticed a flicker of sadness in her eyes he'd never seen before.

She changed the chip. "Hmmm, there are many more expensive rums," she said, swirling her glass, "But I find the sweetness of the Diplomatico complements the Lancero very nicely. Cohiba developed these especially for Castro you know."

Will leaned forward. "Penny, I get it. Global warming and all that. But you can't hope to fight it on your own..."

"Really?" She flashed Will a look of disdain. "And so I should just sit by while the world powers twiddle their thumbs?"

"They're not sitting by," said Fiona, "They are trying to find ways to reduce emissions all the time. There are..."

"No, Miss Bell. You're deluded. I talk to world leaders all the time. It's money that motivates them, keeping their country's economy going and therefore their people happy. Last year when we were launching Uluru I asked the prime minster of Australia about climate change and he spouted on about it being a top priority, but at the same time he believes coal is 'good for humanity' – in recent years Australia has exported more coal than any other country in the world, while the Great Barrier Reef, the largest living organism on the planet, continues to die – in fact half its corals are now dead."

She waved her cigar in the air I front of them as they listened, neither of them inclined to stop the flow. "India's prime minster told me he knows that climate change is altering the monsoon season and causing more flooding and drought in his country, but he is planning to double their coal production by 2019 anyway – because it's vital to the economy. And countries that should show leadership are no better – Obama used to talk about climate change as the greatest threat to future generations, but under his presidency the US became one of the world's largest producers of oil and natural gas. And don't get me started on China!"

She poured more rum for herself and Will but did not draw breath. "So you think when these world leaders and their minions get together anything's really going to happen? For over two decades more than 20,000 delegates from countries around the world have been travelling from conference to conference to negotiate a treaty to save the world from global warming – Kyoto, Copenhagen, Paris – all a complete waste of time. Lots of talk but no real action. So..."

She got up and went to the desk to tap her long cigar ash into a large Cohiba ashtray, "...So, I decided to act unilaterally. I'd got to know a lot of very good scientists from our work developing the new eco-friendly resorts. A few of them had experimented with so-called geoengineering. That's what they call the practice of intervening in the Earth's climatic system to turn round global warming. I got them together and funded them to develop a plan."

She returned and sat opposite them. "There were a few proposals but ocean iron fertilization was eventually chosen as the one most likely to succeed. It's a proven method. It's been tried before with some success. It had been noticed in the past how huge unexpected algae blooms had suddenly sprung up following massive volcanic eruptions.

Mount Pinatubo in the Philippines in 1991, Mount Kasatochi in the Aleutians in 2008, that volcano in Iceland in 2010..."

"Eyjafjallajokull," said Fiona. Penny smiled at her approvingly.

"Well said, Miss Bell. They spew out huge quantities of iron-rich ash into the ocean which causes massive algal blooms over vast areas."

"I did read about this," said Fiona.

"After the Mount Kasatochi eruption there wasn't just a boom in algae though. They also noticed a tremendous increase in the salmon population."

She drained her glass. They let her continue, intrigued.

"Spotting this, a very clever American entrepreneur...in July 2012...spread a hundred tonnes of iron sulphate into the Pacific from a fishing boat off the coast of British Columbia. It produced a growth of...let me see...yes...a hundred million tonnes of plankton..."

Fiona made a sound of amazement between her teeth.

"Yes. That's one hell of a lot of algae."

"Did it work?" asked Will.

"The following year the west coast of North America had the biggest salmon harvest in history. From fifty million to nearly two hundred and thirty million fish. But more importantly...and here's the thing..." She held up a finger for emphasis, "...They removed a million tonnes of carbon dioxide from the atmosphere."

"A million tonnes?" He said slowly, weighing up the enormous figure. It was beginning to sound a compelling argument. And she was beginning to look again more like an evangelist than a devil.

"So I knew this was the way to go. This was how I was going to really make an impact on the level of CO_2 in the atmosphere. Finally reverse global warming."

"I get it," said Will. He looked at Fiona but she had a concerned expression. Whatever was worrying her, though, she sat in silence while Penny went on.

"This also seemed the natural solution too. After all Mother Nature already does this. The oceans already suck ten billion tonnes of carbon out of the atmosphere every year. That's half of all the CO_2 produced from the burning of fossil fuels. It gets sucked out of the air and transferred to the ocean depths where it's locked away forever. Or at least for millennia. My project would just be giving Nature a helping hand. A much-needed helping hand."

She noticed Fiona's look.

"Do you know John Martin, Miss Bell?"

"Of course."

"Who's John Martin?" asked Will.

"He's a famous oceanographer." Fiona said, still looking serious.

"A great visionary too," said Penny. "You know what he said in relation to all this?"

He shook his head.

"He said: 'Give me a half tanker of iron and I will give you an ice age.' A bit of an exaggeration, but you get the point."

She clapped her hands. "So off I went. I resourced the iron sulphate, leased a warehouse and a ship, did the deal with The Maldives to secure the location, and started the project. A few months ago now. Initial tests show it's working. It takes only a few weeks for the algae to bloom once the iron has been added to the sea. The algae sucks out the greenhouse gas CO_2 from the atmosphere, then – as you so rightly say Dr Bell – it dies, sinks quickly down, and takes the trapped carbon to the seabed for ever. Simple. Problem solved."

She sat back and smiled at them. "And now we see it's working so well I've leased twenty-nine more ships and have started up-scaling the project...."

Fiona choked. "What?"

Will's eyes widened in disbelief at the scale.

Penny laughed at their reaction. "Thirty ships in all. Six tankers in each of five ocean zones. North and South Atlantic, East and West Pacific, and of course the Indian Ocean where it all started. Soon the world will be covered in a beautiful green mat sucking CO_2 and saving the planet. " She opened her arms and nodded. "You're welcome."

Chapter Fifty-Two

"Thirty ships?" said Fiona, looking first at Penny and then at Will.

"Yes." Penny examined her perfectly manicured nails. "Impressive isn't it?"

"All dumping iron into the sea?" said Will. He still couldn't believe it.

"All fertilising the oceans, yes." She blew out another plume of aromatic blue smoke. "It won't take long. I've speeded up the process since the...problems in the Maldives. And your attempts to publicise things. I know the authorities – somebody somewhere – will try to stop me, so I have to be quick. Often in life you have to act first and explain yourself afterwards. Otherwise countless objections are thrown in your way and you never get anything done."

Fiona looked agitated. "But you don't know the effect that adding that much iron to the oceans is going to have on the marine life – it could be a global disaster!" said Fiona, shaking her head in disbelief. "You're messing with the world's eco system on a huge scale!"

"No. I'm saving the world's eco system, Miss Bell."

"But you've already created a monster, Penny," added Will. "Or monsters. God knows how many of these things are coming up from the depths. And two people have died already, gruesome deaths."

"That I agree was unforeseen," said Penny. "And unfortunate."

"Unfortunate!" exclaimed Will.

"Will, I'm not an idiot. People dying is not good for my resorts. And more importantly, it's not good for my geo-engineering programme. It gives the authorities an excuse to interfere."

"It's also inhumane," said Will, staring at her.

"Don't patronise me, Will. What's inhumane is standing by while the Earth dies. What's inhumane is to destroy the planet for the future generations. I want my daughter, and her daughter, to live, Will. To inherit a living healthy planet, not a barren Hell. You think I'm going to let a few fish ruin everything? Ha!" She stubbed out her cigar forcefully. "Ach! Now look what you made me do. You should never extinguish a fine cigar in anger. You should let it rest and die naturally."

He watched her as she took the ashtray to the side board and emptied it into a small metal bin underneath. He felt mixed emotions. He couldn't help but admire her single-minded pursuit of what was a truly great cause. But at the same time he hated her insensitivity to the pain and destruction she was creating along the way. Not to mention Fiona's concerns that the great cause might in fact itself be destructive.

"Look, Penny, it's a great sounding plan," he said as she returned to her seat. "But it's flawed. You've got to see that, surely."

"These monster fish could only be the start of it," said Fiona. "God knows what else we're going to see when..."

Penny held up her hand to silence them. "Look. If I stopped and gave up whenever I hit a bump in the road I'd never get anywhere. Whatever you do – my God even I were Mother Teresa – there are people who will find reasons for you not to do it. There are always reasons not to do something. I'm not giving up on this, believe me. Too much is at stake. Which is why I've stepped up my operations before they can be stopped. There's a lot of sea out there. So we get shoals of these strange fish in the middle of the oceans. So what? Who cares?"

"But what about the two people who have died so far?" said Will.

"So you say," Penny said, pointing at him. "But again, even if you're right, it's still just a bump in the road."

He felt a renewed disgust.

"I don't think you'll be allowed to do this," he said, getting up, joined by Fiona. "Someone will stop you. The UN. The US. The EU. Someone."

"No," said Penny, standing too. "Not once they see the Earth's temperature dropping. Not then."

She walked to the window and looked out. Will saw a new thought crossing Fiona's mind. She crossed the room and touched Penny's arm. The CEO recoiled as though touched by a leper.

"Don't do this, Penny. Please. The risks are too great. Or at least involve the proper authorities. Test it further so we can be sure of the impact on the marine environment..."

Penny gave a short smile. "More tests? Really? More time wasting while the planet continues to die?" She looked at Will. "What's wrong with you people? How many times do I need to explain that it's Mankind's prevarication that's making things worse?" She walked to her desk and sat down. "No, Miss Bell. I've done my tests. I'm satisfied it will work. That's good enough."

"But..." Fiona started.

"Forget it, Fi," said Will, cutting her off. "She's made up her mind and nothing you say is going to change it." He knew his boss's stubbornness. He knew she could not be talked out of this. She'd only stop if she was forced to stop.

"OK. We know your plan," he said, putting his hands on her desk and leaning over her. Not a posture he'd have dreamt of striking previously. But he now saw her in a new light. It was like he was meeting her for the first time.

"People didn't listen to us before, thanks to what you did to us online. But they'll listen to us now. So think about it, Penny. Pull back before it's too late."

She stared at him and nobody moved for quite a while. He saw an odd look in her eyes. He'd expected hatred but it was more like disappointment. She feels I've betrayed her, he thought.

She looked away abruptly.

"You can take your hands off my desk now, Will."

He complied without thinking.

She looked up at both of them calmly. "Yes you're right. You could be believed now, I suppose. And I need a bit more time." He saw her reach under the desk. "You've become a little too risky." His heart skipped a beat as he saw the cold steel return to her face.

Two security guards entered the room.

She looked at Will and Fiona and gestured to the men at the door. "You'll need to be my guests for a while."

"What do you mean?" said Will, a hint of apprehension in his voice. "You're going to have us killed like Mackay tried to?"

Fiona looked alarmed and grabbed his arm.

"No, John went a bit too far...He's a bit brutish sometimes....I just need you two to be out of the way until my project becomes too big to stop. I can't have people making waves, you see. Forgive the pun. And I don't think you're bribe-able are you? No I thought not. These men will see you to your quarters."

"Penny!" shouted Will.

But she returned to the window to look out at the mountains while the men gripped Will and Fiona tightly by the arms and half dragged them out.

Chapter Fifty-Three

The fishermen in the Maldives were again unhappy.

First they had found a dead body. Now it was dead tuna. Hundreds of them. Floating belly up in the sea.

They hauled them into their boats. They had no need for their fishing rods. They used boat hooks and nets. Or their bare hands.

They should perhaps have been full of joy and gratitude. Catching fish had never been so easy. And most of the tuna had not yet started to rot.

But instead they were full of foreboding. They had never seen anything like this. Nor had their forefathers. It was an ungodly sight. Like a plague, inflicted by an angry divinity.

Perhaps the tuna would be inedible. Full of some unknown poison. Some of the men blamed the algae. It must be toxic, they said.

Even if they were found to be safe to eat and could be sold in the market, it did not look good for the future. The tuna would soon die out completely at this rate. The fishermen would have gone from a super abundance of fish to nothing – from feast to famine – in a matter of days. It was a terrifying thought.

And it wasn't just the tuna that was dying. All kinds of dead sealife littered the surface of the ocean. The seabirds were manic. For them it was a sudden bonanza.

But for the fishermen it meant disaster.

Chapter Fifty-Four

Tanner listened to the mobile ring eight times and then go to messages.

"Will. Harold again. Starting to worry, kid. Call me if you get this. I'll keep trying. Bye."

He put the phone in his pocket and sighed.

He was standing on the terrace in front of the lobby looking at the glistening sea. He caught sight of the dive instructor running up the path from the beach. He looked up at the old man and shouted to him. "Hey! Mr Tanner!"

Tanner waited for him to arrive panting onto the terrace.

"What is it, Steve? You look in a hurry."

"I don't know what's going on, Mr Tanner. First those giant fang-tooth fish, now this...I just got back from putting the nets up..."

"Nets?"

"The safety nets. I got told to put them up to stop those fish getting to the beaches. But the surface of the sea looked really strange. So I went out further to take a look." He shook his head. "What a sight. Thousands of dead fish. Dolphins and turtles too. A carpet of them...."

"All dead?"

"Just floating in the water out there. Belly up. It's horrible, Mr Tanner."

The American stroked his chin.

"I've never seen anything like it in my life," said the dive instructor. "I don't know what can have happened."

Tanner eyes blinked wide through his glasses. "I think I do."

Chapter Fifty-Five

Will looked around the room. It was simply furnished. Two single beds, a wardrobe, a desk, a two-seater sofa and an armchair. There was a small ensuite bathroom.

Clearly a guest bedroom in Penny's house which was attached to the main HQ building by a covered walkway. They had been dragged here along an empty corridor in the main building, through the walkway and up a flight of stairs in the house, struggling and protesting in vain. Their phones had been taken away and they had been thrown into the room and heard the door locked behind them.

He had tried the door of course. He now tried the window but it would only open a crack. He pushed and pulled it with all his strength, but it was too sturdy.

They were on the upper floor at the rear of the house with views out over the mountains.

He shouted out of the crack in the window but knew in his heart that nobody would hear him from the main building, and no doubt any staff in the house would have been told to ignore them, not that they'd seen anyone on their way.

Fiona was sitting on one of the beds shaking her head.

"She can't keep us locked up here, Will. It's ridiculous!"

"I know."

Will tried the drawers of the desk, looking for anything to help them – perhaps some implement to force the door or window.

Fiona watched him.

"What is she thinking?" she said.

"I don't know."

The drawers were empty. He searched the wardrobe.

"What she's planning is dangerous, Will."

"Yep."

He took out a wire hanger, flattened out the hooked end and jiggled it around in the door lock.

"She has to be...What are you doing?"

"I don't know. I've never tried this before."

The lock refused to give.

He went to the window and tried to use the hanger on various parts of the frame and hinges.

"We've got to stop her, Will."

"Fuck!" The hangar had snapped. Will hit the window hard a few times with the palm of his hand. "Fuck! Fuck! Fuck!" It didn't budge.

He turned to her, frustrated. "What's a few nasty fish and a pile of seaweed anyway? She's saving the planet isn't she?"

"No. She's destroying the planet, Will. These nasty fish as you call them are only the start of it. She's going to upset the entire balance of life in the oceans. Damage the ecosystem forever."

She got up and crossed to the door. She half turned and gave it a mighty kick.

It didn't move.

She tried again.

Still no effect.

"Reinforced," she said calmly. "Any normal door would have broken."

Will looked at her in awe and smiled. "Kicked your way out of many rooms have you? Did they teach you that in Karate class too?" he said.

She smiled too and shrugged. "No. But I thought if I can break a plank of wood I should be able to break this. Oh well. What do we do now?"

"I guess we wait."

Clara waited until she saw the two burly security guards leave her mother's office. They were the same men she'd seen forcibly dragging the tall handsome man and the pretty dark-haired woman into the house earlier. They had not seen her as she watched them from the top of the stairs.

They looked at her now though as they passed her. She smiled at them but they ignored her.

She burst into the office. "Mama!"

Penny was caught unawares. "Clara! You need to knock before you come into my office!"

Clara rarely saw her mother angry and it startled her. "But I only wanted to show you my new jeans, Mama," she lied.

Penny softened. "They're lovely, Munchkin. But I can't talk now, I'm working. I'll see you tonight."

But the girl stepped further into the room.

"Mama? Who are the lady and man I saw in the house?"

"Guests, dear."

"But why are they locked in the upper spare bedroom?"

Penny hesitated for a moment.

"Because they're getting in the way, Clara."

"In the way of what, Mama?"

Penny walked across the room to her daughter and started stroking her hair fondly.

"You remember I told you once I have a plan to save our beautiful planet for my beautiful daughter?"

"The global warming killing the Earth thing?"

"Yes. The global warming killing the Earth thing."

"Yes you told me. Many times. How you have to do something because nobody else is."

"Exactly. You remember."

"Of course I remember, Mama. I'm not a stupid little girl."

"I know you're not, Munchkin. You're a very clever and beautiful one." She kissed her daughter and held her chin, smiling as she looked into her eyes.

"My plan has started, Clara. And it's working. Like I knew it would. But these two people don't like it. They want to stop it. And I can't let them do that, can I?"

The girl pulled away. "But why do they want to stop you if what you're doing is good, Mama? I don't understand."

"Because that's life, dear. As you grow up you'll learn that however right you are and however good, there will always be people who will find some reason to disagree with you, to fight against you. It's human nature. But you can't let these people stop you, Clara. You have to believe in yourself. You can't let anyone get in the way."

"You could try to persuade them maybe. You're good at that. I've seen you."

"No, my darling. It would just result in endless discussion. And no action. One strong-willed person taking action gets things done. Committees of groups of people arguing their different viewpoints get nothing done. To be a good leader you need to not waver when you are being criticised."

"But Mama, that was how Hitler thought. And he was evil."

"It's how Gandhi thought too, Clara. And he was good. Don't you think?"

The girl thought for a moment.

"So what are you going to do with them, Mama?"

"I don't know yet."

Clara saw something behind her mother's eyes she had only seen once before. It scared her.

"Mama, you're not going to hurt them are you?"

Penny smiled. "Clara. People always get hurt in any plan. You can't make an omelette without breaking eggs. If a few people get hurt in order to save the lives of billions, isn't that worth it?"

Penny saw her daughter recoil slightly. She gave a warm laugh. "No, Munchkin. Don't you worry. I'm not going to hurt them."

"Promise?"

"I promise. Now go. I'll see you later, darling."

Clara walked out pensively.

She wasn't sure she believed her mother.

Chapter Fifty-Six

Penny picked up the phone on her desk and punched a speed dial button.

"Yes Penny?" came Mackay's voice.

"I have had to detain our two guests. I don't know how long I can hold them before they are missed."

"Want me to take care of them?"

"What? Like before?"

"I'm sorry Penny. That was a mistake. It won't happen again."

"No. I'm sure it won't. How are things progressing? Are the ships out yet?"

"Yes. All underway."

"Are they dumping?"

"Not yet. They haven't..."

"Well tell them to get a move on please."

"Yes Penny."

"I don't know how long we've got."

"Yes Penny."

"The dead boy's uncle is still on the loose I suppose?"

"Shall I take...Do you want him out of the way too?"

"What's he up to?"

"He's talking to a lot of people. But I've got it covered. No-one's listening. There is one problem on the island though."

"Oh?"

"A whole load of dead fish have turned up. Just floating on the surface of the sea. Not sure why, but maybe connected to our operation."

She frowned, then opened her humidor and took out another long slender cigar. She pressed along its length with her finger and thumb, testing its density.

"Penny? You still there?"

"Yes. I'm thinking." She rolled the cigar under her nose and sniffed it.

"Penny?"

"Be quiet a moment."

She took a cutter and held it to the tip of the cigar but didn't cut it. She looked into the middle distance, lost in thought.

"John."

"Yes Penny."

"I'm not bothered about the fish. Maybe it's not connected. And if it is it shouldn't stop us. But it's another reason to move fast."

"Yes I agree."

She snipped the cigar carefully and examined the end.

"One more thing, John."

"Yes?"

"Get me one of those new species. The type that killed the boy. In case they all start dying too. It'll look good in the aquarium. The killer from the deep. The last of its kind."

She clicked her lighter and a fierce blue flame shot out.

Chapter Fifty-Seven

At the UN's Global Ocean Observing System, or GOOS for short, Brian Schulz stared at his screen. He was looking at a large oval green patch on a blue background.

He called to one of his colleagues.

"Hey, Matt. Take a look at this."

A young man in polo shirt and chinos at a neighbouring desk wheeled over in his chair.

"What's up, Bri?"

"That green patch off the Maldives...what is it do you think?"

The colleague looked at the screen.

"I think it's algae."

"I never saw a patch of algae that big. It's huge, man!"

"Me neither. Better flag it to the WMO."

He picked up a red handset in front of him.

"Hi. This is Brian Schulz at GOOS. We've spotted an anomaly in the Indian Ocean just west of The Maldives. We think it's a massive algal bloom. You may want to monitor it further."

"Thanks for the heads up. Will do."

The man who's answered worked at the World Meteorological Organization, also part of the UN. They monitored changes in the Earth's atmosphere and climate.

The man had 10,000 weather stations, 7,000 ships, 3,000 aircraft and 66 satellites at his disposal.

He started planning which of these massive resources he was going to direct at the Indian Ocean.

Chapter Fifty-Eight

"How long are we going to just sit around? I can't stand it!" Fiona got up and paced the room.

"Let me have another go at this door," said Will. But as he approached it he heard a knock.

They looked at each other, puzzled.

"Do the guards knock here?" asked Fiona.

"Come in," said Will.

The door handle rattled but remained locked.

"I can't," came a girl's voice.

Will put his head next to the door.

"Who is it?"

"I'm Clara. I'm Penny's daughter."

Will looked at Fiona who had also come close to the door to hear.

"The door's locked," said the girl.

"Can you help us?" asked Fiona.

"Yes I think so. Wait."

They heard the sound of footsteps retreating.

Five minutes later the footsteps returned.

They heard a key rattling in the lock and then a click. The door opened and a teenage girl stepped inside quickly and closed it behind her.

"Spare key," she said. "They forgot about it."

"Thank you Clara," said Fiona, holding the girl's arm.

"That's OK. You shouldn't be locked up here. It's not right. And I think..." She looked pained for a moment. "I think my mother might hurt you."

Will puffed out a breath and nodded. He made for the door but Clara stopped him.

"Be careful," said the girl. "There are guards all over the place. But you can get out through the emergency exit at the bottom of the stairs and then walk down to Berchtesgaden. Here." She handed Will a scrap of paper. "I sketched you a map showing you how to get to town. It's an hour walk down through the forest. You can get a taxi there to Salzburg or Munich and get a flight out of here."

He took the map and said, "Won't you get into trouble?"

The girl shook her head. "Don't worry. My mother adores me. I'll be fine. Now go. There isn't much time."

She watched them open the door, peek out and then head off quickly down the corridor.

Chapter Fifty-Nine

Will led Fiona along the corridor and down a flight of steps to a door with a green sign which read *Ausgang*.

Hoping it was not alarmed he pressed the bar to open the door and peeked out.

No alarm sounded.

They were at the back of the building. There was a path leading left and right. In front of them was a patch of level snow with the odd clump of grass sticking up and then the edge of a pine forest.

Will took a quick look at Clara's hand-drawn map, checked again that the coast was clear, then ran to the forest with Fiona following close behind.

They ducked behind a pine tree and looked back. No-one in sight.

Fiona shivered and Will thought that perhaps they should have asked Clara for coats, but then maybe that would have held things up. They were already taking a big gamble that the room would not be checked for at least an hour.

They needed to move fast so that would keep them warm, he hoped.

They picked their way into the forest, moving as quickly as they could while trying not to trip up on tree stumps and fallen branches.

The ground was mostly brown with dead pine needles, cones and twigs, with the odd patch of white where the snow had made it through a gap in the tree canopy overhead. The air was crisp and cold and smelled of pine resin.

After ten minutes hard going they made it to the woodland path Clara had marked on her map. They would make quicker and easier progress from here, thought Will.

They headed right and followed the path as it snaked steeply down-hill in the direction of the town.

The going was easier than the forest but not as easy as Will had hoped, with patches of slippery ice and fallen tree trunks. Twice they had to retrace their steps when the path disappeared beneath deep snow.

After half an hour Fiona motioned to him that she needed to stop to catch her breath. They both stood with hands on hips for a moment, puffing out deep cloudy breaths into the still crisp air.

Suddenly the bark of the tree nearest Fiona exploded and he heard the unmistakable crack of gunshot.

They both crouched to the ground instinctively and Will looked back through the dense trees in the direction of the sound.

"They're shooting at us?" whispered Fiona incredulously.

Then he heard a whizzz fap noise as a bullet flew past his ear and hit the ground behind him like someone hitting a pile of mud with a sledge hammer.

"Shit!" he said, and lurched sideways onto Fiona taking them both sprawling to the ground.

"To the bank!" he whispered to her, nodding to the ridge of snow to their right at the edge of the path. He hoped whoever it was with the gun would not be able to see them there.

She looked at him, her eyes wide with fear, then slid across to the bank. He followed quickly.

He felt his heart beating rapidly in his chest.

He listened for a moment to see if he could hear the sound of footsteps from above them up the slope. There was silence. Not even birds.

He looked behind himself up the path the way they had come. If there was no sound it meant the shooter was either waiting for them to move or he was walking carefully down along the path, in which case he might appear at any moment.

No, surely even if he walked stealthily there would be the odd crunch of snow, the crack of twigs underfoot.

He must be waiting.

He took a chance and peeked above the ridge of snow.

"Can you see him?" Fiona whispered, her eyes wide.

"No. I can't see anyone."

Who was he, Will wondered. One of Penny's henchmen? Was it really her intention to have them shot? He couldn't believe it. But it couldn't be anything else.

He dropped back down and looked ahead along their intended route. The snowy bank continued alongside the path for twenty metres, after which the path itself snaked round to the left out of sight.

He tapped Fiona on the leg and made a sideways snaking sign with his hand then pointed along the bank.

She nodded and they started half-crawling, half-slithering along the ground.

He was relieved they made very little noise on the slippery snow and ice.

They made it to the end of the bank in no time. Will could now see the path falling away to his left even more steeply than before. If the shooter had stayed where he was they would be out of sight down there. And if he was still watching the spot where they had crouched down he wouldn't be able to change his aim to the right quickly enough to catch them as they broke cover from the bank.

At least that was the hope.

Will shook his head.

Who was he to gamble like this with their lives? If he was alone he'd risk it. But this could get Fiona shot, probably killed.

He was a marketing man, for God's sake, not a marine or James Bond.

She saw the conflict in his face. "Will," she said softly. "What's the plan now?"

"My plan was to make a run for it from here down the path. I was hoping he won't know we've moved along here and won't be able to fire at us until we're out of sight down there. But," he grimaced, "I don't know. Maybe I'm wrong. It's risky, Fi."

"What's the alternative?"

"We wait for him to find us. We give up."

"What do you think they'll do to us?"

They looked at each other for a second. They both knew the answer.

"I trust you," she said.

"Ok," he said. "Let's go. On three. One, two...three, go!"

They both launched themselves up and ran, head low and shoulders hunched, to the other side and down the path.

Another crack rang out from above and behind them. But they didn't see where the bullet hit. They careered down the path now, not daring to look back, arms flailing out to balance themselves as they stumbled and slid.

Another crack and a pine branch Will was about to duck under shattered in front of him. He cried out as splinters of bark pricked his face.

He glanced behind and saw a figure careering down the hillside fifty or so meters behind.

"Go!" He shouted to her and pushed her in the small of the back. "Keep going!"

They were zig-zagging down the path but their pursuer was running down in a straight line. At this rate he'd be on them in seconds.

"Down here!" he shouted at her, running past her and grabbing her by the arm. He led them sharply off the path down through thicker snow and fallen branches. They half ran and half jumped through the treacherous terrain.

Suddenly he heard a thud behind him and a yelp.

He looked behind to see the man falling to the ground.

Then they were out of the forest and onto a smooth sloping hillside blanketed in virgin white snow glistening in the sunlight.

Fiona slipped and fell.

"Come on," said Will, pulling her up. He looked again behind him. "Shit, we're exposed here. Keep moving!"

They ran down the hill, trying to keep to the hidden path but sometimes veering off it and getting stuck in deeper snow. He expected at any moment to feel the impact of a bullet smacking into his back.

Half way down the hill Fiona slowed and then stopped. She doubled over, panting in exhaustion.

"Come on, Fi. You...can do it."

"I...can't...breathe..."

"Ok....Catch your breath."

His lungs were heaving too. Running through knee-high snow was tough going.

He looked at the line of trees.

Nobody.

Then a glint of something. A man appeared.

He unslung the rifle from his shoulder and took aim at them.

Then something caught his eye and he looked to one side, lowering the gun.

It was a black car on the road below, driving towards them.

He waved both arms above his head a shouted. "Hey! Hey!"

When he looked back at the forest the man had disappeared.

"Can you walk now?" he said to her.

"Yes. I'm good. Let's go."

She hadn't seen the man and he didn't want to freak her out so he just held her hand and led her down.

Despite further waving and shouting the car drove past without stopping.

"Bastards," she said under her breath.

"Didn't see us. Don't worry. We're almost at the town. We'll be safe here. He won't shoot at us with people around."

They decided to stick to the plan of finding a taxi. They crossed the road quickly and hurried on across another field in the direction of some wooden buildings marking the outskirts of the town, following a raised track where the snow was only ankle deep.

Following the map they made their way through impossibly pretty streets lined with 17th century three-story stone terraced houses painted in different pastel colours.

The streets were full of people drinking steaming mugs of gluhwein and eating Bratwurst served from wooden huts in front of the houses.

"We've hit the Christmas Market," said Will.

"I keep forgetting it's nearly Chistmas."

"Just nine days to go."

"Wish we could stay and enjoy it."

"Me too." He smiled at her.

"Got things to do though, I guess." She smiled back and shrugged.

"Yep. Gotta save the world from a madwoman."

They felt safer amongst the crowd as they weaved through the people, some dressed in traditional lederhosen.

"The taxi rank should be around this corner," said Will, pointing to a round turret building with a conical roof at the end of the street.

They had barely reached the corner when a series of shots rang out.

They dived to the ground in panic.

They had been found. He'd followed them from the forest after all. They were wrong - he wasn't put off by the crowds.

"Can you see him?" said Fiona.

Will raised his head. Everyone else around them was carrying on as though nothing had happened.

Then he saw several people pointing and laughing at them.

A man in lederhosen, a blue wool jacket and dark green hat with a feather rushed towards Fiona and offered his hand to help her up.

"Keine Sorge!," he said smiling. "Iz okay! Iz Weihnachtsschutzen!"

"Danke," Will said to the man and held up his hands smiling, "Ich hatte vergessen! Weihnachtsschutzen!"

"I'd forgotten," he said to Fiona. "They fire guns here to celebrate Christmas."

"What?"

"Up at the shooting clubs above the town. It's a tradition here."

"You're joking!"

"Sorry. Should have warned you."

They laughed as he helped her to her feet.

"You couldn't make this up!" she said, dusting snow off herself.

"Come on, let's find that taxi. I think we've caused enough hilarity."

Chapter Sixty

"Idiot! Tell me...How did they get out exactly?"

The German security guard towered over Penny and could probably have knocked her out with one swipe of his massive paw, but she had an aura of power that would subdue a grizzly bear.

"Gnadige Frau, the door was unlocked from the outside. It was not forced."

"Unlocked? Who by?"

"We do not know."

She pursed her lips. "Who has a key?"

"I do. And I keep it on my person at all times. There must be another key that we did not know about."

She tapped the desk with her nails. "Well I don't have one. Ask around. Start with the housekeeper." She frowned. "You think a member of staff helped them?"

He looked uncomfortable. "Yes. It is the only answer."

She fixed him with an icy stare. "I want them found. Understand?"

He bowed his head. "Yes, Gnadige Frau."

"And then we'll deal with them." She shook her head. "And I thought I could trust everyone here." She smacked the desk. "Oh well. We'll have to make an example of whoever it is I suppose. To teach the rest of them some loyalty."

He nodded.

"Now. To the more pressing matter...."

She was stopped by a knock at the door and a military looking man in green combat jacket and woollen hat stepped into the room. He exchanged a brief look with the security guard and then inclined his head to Penny.

"Ah. Speak of the devil," she said. "The very man. Did you get them?"

He took a breath. "I'm sorry, Ma'am." His voice was that of an English drill sergeant. "They got away. It was a close one. Almost bagged 'em but they made it into town."

She looked from one man to the other and shook her head. "What a pair. I thought you two were the best there is."

The drill sergeant stuck out his chest. "Don't worry, Ma'am. We'll get 'em. We've got eyes on them now."

"You'd better. Do I need to call the chief?"

"No I don't think so, Ma'am. They're not going to the police station. They're trying to find a taxi, which'll take them a while at this time of year. Trying to get to an airport is my guess. In which case there's only one way they can go. Country road. No witnesses."

Chapter Sixty-One

"Bri! Phone call!"

Brian Schulz responded to the shout from the far end of the GOOS office by waving his half eaten doughnut in the air and shrugging.

The man who held the phone waved it back urgently. "It's Head Office, man!"

Schulz swallowed, choked, and stumbled over chairs and fellow workers to get to the phone. Head Office rarely called him.

He took the handset, swallowing again to try to clear his throat of dry pastry. "Hello? Schulz here."

"Henderson here. You the guy that spotted the algal bloom off The Maldives?"

"Yes sir. I notified the WMO immediately."

"I know. They're monitoring it. It's a big one."

"Yeah, I'm still tracking it here. It's huge."

"Good. Keep your guys on it. The more eyes the better. This one's a real son-of-a-bitch."

"Sir?"

"We're getting reports of dead sea life down there."

Schulz's jaw dropped. This was a new one.

"Toxic algae sir?" He'd seen toxic algae in estuaries and near the shore but never out in the ocean.

"Well...We're not sure. The WMO tell me it's not. But there's still one heck of a lot of dead fish to account for. So something's going on. We've had reports too from a couple of guys on the ground. Including one US citizen on one of the islands. Some weird stuff - a new species of fish attacking swimmers. I don't know. We thought it was a load of baloney at first but now...Well, something strange is going on down there. And we need someone to look into it pronto. Someone we can trust. Schulz?"

"Sir?"

"Can you get on a plane today?"

"Er...Yes, sir, I guess..."

"Good man. Top priority. We've been asked to keep the President informed."

Schulz swallowed hard.

Chapter Sixty-Two

Will opened the taxi door for Fiona then followed her in as she slid over.

"Finally!" she said. They had waited forty minutes. The Berchtesgaden taxi drivers seemed to have taken the day off to enjoy the Christmas market.

Will instructed the driver. "Flughafen Salzburg."

He smiled at Fiona who sat with her head back, relaxed at last. "It'll only take half an hour. The airport's just on the other side of the mountains."

"It's nice to sit down," she said, closing her eyes. "I'm shattered."

"Shame there were no public phones in town. We'll call Tanner from the airport. Plan our next move. Meanwhile you just relax."

She sighed and squeezed his hand.

They sat in silence as the car wound its way north through the mountains. The first ten minutes f their journey took them close to Penny's headquarters, the prison they'd only just managed to escape from. Will peered through the window at the snowy slopes and pine forests. He half expected to see the gunman again, standing in the middle of a white field aiming a gun at the car.

As they left the area he began to relax. In a few minutes they would cross the border from Germany to Austria, the half way point of their short journey.

He wondered what they could do next. He had dissuaded Fiona from going to the police in town as he knew Penny was close to the police chief. He'd seen them at events together and thought nothing of it before, but now things were different and he was suspicious of their relationship. She and her henchman Mackay seemed masters at keeping useful people in their pockets.

They needed to get out of the area, away from Penny's sphere of influence. It would be difficult. Her tentacles seemed to be everywhere. But the nearest airport was a good enough place to take stock. And from there they could go anywhere in the world.

He was jolted out of his thoughts by a loud bang which made the driver slam on the brakes and jerk him forward so the seat belt cut into his ribcage. He heard Fiona yelp as she shot forward too, and saw her head snap down sharply.

He watched in slow motion as the driver grappled with the steering wheel and the car skidded off the road into a shallow ditch of snow.

There was a moment of silence as the three of them caught their breath.

"Scheisse!" said the driver. "Reifenpanne!"

"We've had a blowout," Will said. "Flat tyre. You OK?"

She felt the back of her neck. "Slight pain. I'll be fine."

The driver got out to examine the front right hand wheel which was now half buried in the snow bank. The car was tilted at an angle down into a ditch.

"I'll help him, " Will said. "Wait here."

He had to push his door up and heave himself out.

He looked up and down the road and thought it odd there were no other cars in sight. Had everyone in the area gone into town to enjoy the Christmas festivities? Surely not.

He edged down into the ditch to join the driver who was bent over picking at the tyre with his finger.

"What is it?" Will asked in fluent German.

"A hole. Here, see."

Will bent down and saw a hole the size of a fist. The edges were ragged. A blowout.

"Must have run over something," said Will, straightening up. "Can you call us another taxi?"

"Sure. May take some time though."

"I'll help you change this if you like. Could be quicker."

"Thank you. You could be right."

The driver patted him on the arm and smiled. Then he looked back at the wheel and a puzzled look crossed his face. "Very strange."

"What?"

"They're new tyres. And you can see I didn't run over anything as you suggested. The hole's on the side not the tread."

Will heard a tapping on the car window. He saw Fiona gesturing to the road ahead of them. A taxi was approaching.

He ran up the bank and flagged it down. It stopped on the other side of the road and the driver wound down the window. "Need a lift?"

"Can you take us to the airport?"

"Salzburg?"

"Yes."

"Sure. I just came from there."

Will turned to his own driver. "I'm sorry," he said feeling a little guilty. "Do you mind?"

The man smiled and waved him away. "Don't worry, my friend. I've done a hundred of these. I'll have it done in no time. Go get your plane."

Will thanked him and paid him with a generous tip.

He helped Fiona climb out of the car and they crossed the road.

"How lucky," she said. Not only do we find a cab but we get an upgrade."

True enough, thought Will, looking at the huge black Mercedes.

The driver got out and opened the door for her. He was a tall, well-built man with a tough-looking face and a crew cut. But he smiled politely.

"Why, thank you," she said and returned his smile as she got in. "Other side," she called back to Will. "Can't scoot over. Armrest won't move."

Will looked up and down the empty road. "It's so quiet," he said to the man as he walked round the back of the car to get in the other side.

Crew Cut followed him round which he thought odd as this wasn't the driver's side.

He opened the door but something about the situation made him pause. Crew Cut stood close to him and gestured for him to get in: "Please, sir."

"Did you see any cars on your way here?" Will asked.

The man gave a half smile. "No, sir. No cars."

"Why do you think that is?" Will wanted to talk with this man a little. There was something about him he didn't like.

Crew Cut glanced back the way he'd come and shrugged. "Who knows?" He reached to the side of Will to open the door but Will didn't move out of his way.

The man flashed him a hard look.

Will had a bad feeling in the pit of his stomach. Something was definitely not right about this.

"Get out of the car Fi," he said to her, trying to control his voice. He was not going to let this guy drive them anywhere.

Then he saw the gun. Tucked into the man's waste band. Crew Cut noticed, smiled and nodded. "Best if you do as I say."

There was a shout from the other side of the road. "Hey! Is there a problem there?"

It was their old driver. He was walking towards them, clearly wondering what the delay was.

Before Will could answer his eyes were drawn to something moving on the edge of the snow-covered field behind the man. At first he didn't believe what he was seeing. A snowy mound stood up and became a man dressed in camouflage whites.

The white figure walked forward a few paces, lifted a rifle and fired.

Will heard Fiona's gasp of shock inside the car, and watched as their old driver dropped like a stone.

"Get in the car, Will," said the white figure, now climbing up onto the roadside opposite and aiming the rifle at the far side passenger window. "Or your girlfriend's next."

Will could have frozen.

But he didn't.

On some impulse he swung round, grabbed Crew Cut's gun, whipping it from his waistband before the man could react. Crew Cut lunged at him but Will sidestepped and pushed him, the momentum causing him to fall to the ground.

Will aimed the gun at the white figure and fired.

He had fired guns on a range but never in the open. And never at a man.

The shot surprised both of them.

The man in white dropped his rifle and looked down at the red stain expanding over his chest.

Still on the ground, Crew Cut kicked Will's legs from under him and he lost balance.

He fell to the ground and Crew Cut leapt on top of him, punching him in the face.

Will hit him on the side of the head with the butt of the gun he was still gripping in his right hand.

The man took the blow and grabbed the gun with both hands. He tried to pull it from Will's grasp but he held on.

Will fired but the shot whistled past Crew Cut's ear.

Then the man was pummelling his face again. And again.

He thought he heard the car door open and Fiona get out on the far side.

Crew Cut sprang up.

Will got up but he was blinded by the blood in his eyes. He tried frantically to wipe it away.

He heard blows and cries on the other side of the car.

Crew Cut didn't know he was dealing with a black belt, he thought, as his vision cleared a little and he struggled to the front of the car to help her.

Suddenly the door slammed shut and the car skidded backwards at speed.

He looked for Fiona.

She wasn't there.

The car spun and swerved on the road and then hurtled towards him.

He dived to the side.

When he got up the car was disappearing into the distance at speed.

He was alone on the empty road.

Him and two dead men.

Chapter Sixty-Three

Will looked down at the man in white who was lying face up on the roadside. His eyes were still open. He nudged the torso with his foot, wondering if there was a chance he might still be alive after all. Then he knelt beside the body and held his palm over the man's face. Feeling no breath he closed the eyes out of some feeling of respect despite what the man had done.

Then the realisation struck him that he himself had become a killer. He shivered.

He'd shot a man. Murdered him.

He felt a deep anguish surge through his body.

He forced himself to rationalise in order not to panic.

This man had killed the taxi driver. Instantly. Coldly. Without a second thought.

Then he'd threatened to kill Fiona. Will had no doubt he'd have fulfilled that threat.

So he'd acted in self defence. He'd had no choice.

In fact he'd acted fast and decisively.

He nodded to himself at the thought.

He took another look at the man in white. He looked like an army guy. Strong face, chiselled jaw line, muscular build. Was he the shooter from the forest? Maybe. He couldn't be sure.

He had to be working for Penny. Will bit his lip. It was unbelievable. Who was this woman? Was she really capable of all this? And could he have misjudged her so drastically?

It certainly looked that way.

He crossed to the taxi driver who was lying face down. He couldn't bear to turn him over. He'd liked the guy and didn't want to see his dead face. And he didn't need to double check the poor man was dead – the round red bullet entry wound in the back of the head told him that.

He patted the driver's jacket pockets and quickly found what he was looking for.

A mobile.

He dialled 110, the number he knew for the police in Germany.

In the distance he saw a long line of vehicles approaching from the direction of Berchtesgaden, from where the guy who had kidnapped Fiona had been heading.

Behind him there was still empty road.

They must have put road blocks up at either end, he thought. Then the fleeing car must have cleared one of the road blocks in order to escape, letting the built-up traffic through.

"Police." A female German voice on the phone. "What is the location of your emergency?"

"I'm on the 305. Ten or so kilometres north of Berchtesgaden. Two men have been killed. Shot."

"Please confirm. Two fatalities? Caused by shooting?"

"Yes."

The line of traffic was getting closer. At the front was an orange and white ambulance with flashing blue lights.

Odd, he thought. How had got here so fast? And in front of the other cars?

"Is the shooter still in the vicinity?"

He hesitated.

"Sir. Is the shooter still in the vicinity?"

"No. Well. Look, my friend has been kidnapped by a man driving a black Mercedes. I think it's an S-Class but..."

"Sir. Is the shooter..."

"I'm sorry. Have you already sent an ambulance? There's one here."

The ambulance pulled up behind the taxi. The cars behind started winding their way through slowly, the faces of the people inside looking shocked at the sight of two dead bodies and a crashed car.

"Sir. The police are on their way. Can you give me more information about the shooting? Are you..."

He cut her off and crossed to the taxi.

Three men in recognisable yellow and red uniforms got out of the ambulance.

Were they looking at him oddly? Why were they looking at him at all – shouldn't they be rushing to the bodies lying at the side of the road?

He could be being paranoid. But equally they could be more of Penny's assassins in disguise. Just like the taxi driver.

He had nothing to lose.

He jumped into the car, ignoring the shouts from behind him.

Thank God. The keys were in the ignition.

He started the engine and jammed the gear stick into reverse.

The wheels skidded against the snowy bank. He pulled off the gas and lurched forwards a little. Then he tried reverse again and again the wheels span.

The ambulance men were now banging on the roof and windows.

He repeated the forward-backward manoeuvre two more times.

Then finally the wheels gripped on something and the car swerved backwards up out of the ditch, leaving the three men staring up at him.

He threw it into first gear and skidded off down the road a few metres then yanked the car round and headed back to Berchtesgaden.

The people in the line of oncoming traffic now stared in shock at him and his dented, lopsided vehicle, flap-flapping along on its blown-out tyre.

He looked in the rear view mirror. The ambulance was not giving chase.

Then it struck him that at any minute he'd meet the police coming from the town in response to his call. He'd headed this way on instinct because he had to find Fiona. He'd try Penny's place first. But the police would hold him up. And could he trust them?

Catching sight of a side road he jerked the car sharply to the right and gunned it, heading for a line of trees. He glanced nervously several times at the main road he'd left and was relieved not to see flashing blue lights before plunging into the hillside forest.

At the first opportunity he took a turning off the road onto an even narrower track which wound its way deeper into the woods. He didn't know where he was going – he just wanted to get further away and out of sight.

After a few more minutes he pulled off the track and rumbled over rough ground between the trees before coming to a stop where he guessed he'd be difficult to spot from any passing car – though he hadn't seen anyone since he'd entered the forest.

He called Tanner.

The American answered warily.

"Harold. It's Will."

"Hey kid! I didn't recognise the number."

"No, it's someone else's phone. He's dead..."

"What was that?"

"It's a long story. You won't believe it..."

Will updated Tanner on the day's extraordinary events. The old man listened in silence punctuated by exclamations of shock.

"That's quite a story," said the American when Will had finished. "And I thought Shanghai was bad!"

"I know. How many times are they going to try to kill me, right? And now Fi's in trouble too. What do you think I should do, Harold? I can't hang around here too much longer – they're bound to find me soon. Either the police or Penny's thugs. Or both."

"You think she's really in control of the police there?"

"Here, there, everywhere it seems. You better watch yourself too." He had no doubt Mackay would have set his henchmen on trying to silence the old man too.

"Don't worry about me, kid. I've taken precautions. I'm also in hiding. They're gonna want to do away with all of us, Will. You, me and Fiona....we're the only three people outside this Crawford woman's control who can stop her putting her plan into action....I need to tell you something too, kid."

"What is it?"

"The sea around here....it's full of dead fish and other animals. All sorts of sealife. All dead or dying. Floating on the surface. It's got to be caused by this dumping of iron you told me about...."

"Shit! And she's just about to go global with it." So Fiona's fears were right. If the iron dumping went global who knew what devastation it would cause to the world's marine life.

"What I'm going to do now is talk to the UN again. I've already had a few conversations. I think they thought I was pretty loco at first but now they're beginning to come round."

"OK. I'm going to find Fi. She's gotta be at the HQ or the house."

"Be careful, young man. They're not gonna just let you walk in. And they'll be expecting you."

"I think I'll try the daughter. She helped us once – maybe she'll help us again." The idea had been formulating in his mind during the phone conversation. If he could find a way to contact Clara he was sure she'd work with him.

"Good luck, kid."

"You too, Harold."

Chapter Sixty-Four

Penny surveyed the man in front of her. Her head of security had just informed her of the bungled operation and was expecting her to look more angry than she appeared.

"Well. At least we have the marine biologist. She could be very useful. Things have taken a turn."

"Ma'am?"

"Nirvana is shortly to get a visit from the United Nations. They're getting very agitated it seems. I need to tackle them on site before they try to close down the whole global operation. And Dr Bell can help me do that."

The security man looked puzzled so she explained, thinking aloud.

"Yes. Dr Bell can help. She's a marine expert after all. She can tell them everything is OK. Stall them for a while. Give us just enough time to complete our task. But she'll need persuading...You do need to find Sanders. He's our leverage."

The man nodded.

"And don't let me down again."

Chapter Sixty-Five

With the help of a local map he found in the glove compartment, Will forced the car jerkily along a series of country tracks which led to the edge of the forest bordering Penny's estate. The same forest he and Fiona had run through in their escape from the HQ just a few hours earlier.

Progress was painful on three wheels and a bare rim. He was almost glad when the road came to an abrupt end at the tree-line and he was forced to get out and continue on foot.

After half an hour trudging uphill through shin-deep snow, stumbling over hidden rocks and fallen branches, he came across a path which made the going much easier.

He couldn't work out if it was the same path they had used before but it was winding its way uphill so in the right direction. Penny's house and HQ was at the summit.

Every now and then he stopped to listen for footsteps or any other sounds which might indicate he was being followed or intercepted. But he heard only the odd thump when a clump of snow grew too heavy for a tree branch and fell to the ground.

The light was fading. He would be more difficult to spot now. But equally it would be more difficult for him to see anyone else.

After another half hour the path rose up more steeply and he suddenly caught sight of bright lights beyond the forest edge. Buildings.

He dodged from tree to tree until he came to the edge of a flat snow-covered field. He was lucky. He'd come out near where they'd made their escape – at the back of Penny's house – less illuminated than the front of the house or the HQ building.

He looked around, and seeing no sign of guards he ran across the field, slipping and sliding as he went. He used to love the snow. He was less keen on it now.

He headed for the emergency exit door they'd used to escape. His plan was to sneak inside and check the room they'd been incarcerated in that morning, guessing there was a high probability they would use it again to lock up Fiona. Failing that, he'd try to find Clara and beg her to help.

When he got to the door, however, he found it tight shut and with no handle on the outside.

He pushed at it a few times but it didn't budge.

He cursed.

How else was he going to get into the building? He couldn't go anywhere near the front – it would be lit up like a Xmas tree and swarming with people.

Maybe there was a side entrance?

He walked to the corner of the house and peered round.

No doors.

He considered climbing the walls but the sides were too smooth.

At that moment he heard a window open above him.

He backed against the wall and looked up. Had he been spotted?

He expected to see a head pop out and shout down at him, but instead saw a ribbon of grey smoke curl out.

A guard enjoying a cheeky fag.

He guessed it was a first floor corner room. Maybe a store-room or toilet.

There was nothing to do but wait until they'd finished. And hope they didn't look down.

After a few minutes he saw a tiny red glow arc out into the snow as the cigarette butt was flicked away.

Glancing up he caught sight of a small white arm reach out to pull the window closed. It was not the arm of a burly security guard.

Taking a chance, he sprang out and called up..."Clara!"

The window popped open again and Clara's head appeared. She peered into the gloom, then frowned as she caught sight of him.

"Will! What are you doing here? They'll find you!"

"Is Fiona in the house? They took her."

"No. Well she was. But they took her away again. Mother went too..."

He was confused. Penny had taken Fiona somewhere else? Where? Why?

"Will, I've got to go. I can hear someone..."

"Clara, wait!"

"They've gone to The Maldives."

The window slammed shut and she was gone.

Chapter Sixty-Six

F iona heard a throbbing in her ears.

She opened her eyes and found herself looking down the length of a small aeroplane with maybe a dozen grey leather seats.

She tried to move but couldn't.

"Ah, you're awake Dr Bell."

Penny appeared in front of her and sat down in a facing seat opposite.

Fiona opened her mouth to speak but no words came out.

Penny smiled. "You'll be able to talk soon, don't worry. And move. Give it an hour or so. You've been injected by a paralysing drug. I think you've seen its effect before, on our friend William."

Fiona remembered waiting for Will to get into the taxi and wondering what he was talking about to the driver, then getting out and being stabbed in the neck with a needle. Then blackness.

"You're wondering how we managed to abduct you onto my private plane no doubt? We have ways. And connections. It's amazing what money can buy. You can pretty much do anything you want to in this world as long as you have enough money. A bit sad I suppose." Penny accepted a cup of tea from a steward. "Thank you, Michael. Fresh milk?"

"Yes, Ma'am," said the steward.

"I hate that UHT stuff don't you Dr Bell?"

Fiona looked at her to kill.

Penny took a spoon from the saucer and stirred the tea.

"You're also wondering what you're doing on my plane, of course."

Fiona could only glare.

"I need your help. I need you to tell our visitors from the United Nations that there's nothing to worry about at the Nirvana resort. Make something up. Something convincing. To keep them off my back for a while. Maybe send them off on a wild goose chase. I'm sure you can be creative."

Fiona's eyes made her feelings clear.

"Ah. You're thinking, Why should I help you? Well we have your boyfriend, you see. Oh yes. We got him too. If you don't do exactly as I say, he will meet a painful end."

Fiona winced.

"You wouldn't want that would you?"

Penny took a sip of tea.

"Nod if you understand."

She could only blink.

"I'll take that as an affirmative. Good."

She took another sip and looked out of the window at the light blue sky of the upper atmosphere.

"You two have caused me quite a bit of trouble, you know. First you get out of a locked room – who helped you by the way? Never mind – we'll talk later. Then you evade my sharp shooter in the forest. Then another of my men shoots out your tyre so we can...um....retrieve you, and you almost manage to get away even then. But you won't get away again. Until my project is complete. Neither of you."

Fiona searched the cabin with her eyes.

"Oh he's not on the plane. But we do have him safely tucked away somewhere, don't you worry."

Chapter Sixty-Seven

W ill looked out of the porthole window at rows of palm trees and a warm blue sky as his plane taxied slowly towards its stand at Male airport.

He had not slept a wink on the long flight, his mind tortured by thoughts of what they might be doing to Fiona.

The message he'd received 16 hours earlier still burned on his brain.

He'd been on his way back to the half-wrecked car when the phone he'd taken from the dead taxi driver had buzzed with a text:

We have her. Take next flight to Male or she dies. Talk to nobody.

How they knew he had the taxi driver's phone and how they'd got through to it he did not know. But clearly the message was for him.

They had kidnapped her and were using her to lure him in.

But why had Penny taken her to Nirvana? What did they want from her there? And from him?

He didn't know that either. He could only hope that she was still alive. And that there was a chance he could save her. And then some-how stop Penny destroying every ocean of the world. That's all.

He had managed to coax the dying car to Berchtesgaden, caught a genuine taxi to Salzburg and got on a flight that evening to the Maldives via Frankfurt.

He found it hard to believe that it was all happening. That Penny and those around her were capable of this brutality. And that one person could bring about a global catastrophe in the act of trying to save the world.

As the plane arrived on its stand and he joined the rest of the passengers in disembarking down the gangway and into the terminal building he wondered what was waiting for him. Presumably they were going to grab him as he left the terminal and imprison him with Fiona.

How was that going to help her?

His plan was to stay close to other people on the concourse and then see if he could share a taxi with someone else. Then somehow make his escape and try to locate Fiona.

He presumed Tanner was already in New York. He had not dared contact him.

He was through passport control now and headed for the exit doors to the Arrivals area.

He spotted a group of loud young British tourists. Perhaps he could blag a ride with them. He tagged along and started up a conversation with a couple of the guys at the back of the group.

They all passed through the sliding exit doors together.

There were a number of the usual taxi drivers and tour guides lined up holding signs with hotel logos or passenger names.

And there they were. Quite open about it. Two huge gorillas in black suits, smiling at him. One held a sign with his name, ***William Sanders.***

Then their smiles turned to looks of bewilderment as he was suddenly grabbed by the arm by a man even bigger than them and propelled sideways with great force.

He was about to kick the brute when the man growled, "Mr Tanner welcomes you."

Will relaxed a bit and let himself be dragged towards the main doors, glancing behind to see the gorillas entangled in a struggle with two other men.

Before he knew it he was out of the building. There was a brief moment of hot sun on his face and warm moist air in his lungs, then he was thrown into the cold interior of a black people carrier.

The car lurched off at speed, throwing him back against his seat.

Next to him Harold Tanner smiled. "Apologies for the man-handling, Will. Had to be quick or they'd have grabbed you."

"Harold!" said Will, grabbing the old American's arm.

"Long time, kid."

"You got my message. Thanks for picking me up. Where are we going?...." Will was delighted to be with his friend again.

"Hold on, kid. Let's just get somewhere safe first, away from those goons." Tanner turned and peered through the back window. He tapped the driver on the shoulder. "We being followed, you think?"

The driver glanced at his mirrors and shook his head. "No, sir. We got away quick. Nobody following us."

"Good man. You know where we're going right?"

"Yes sir. Will be there in a few minutes."

Will looked at Tanner. "Your guy?"

"Just hired," said the old man. "Like the three man mountains back at the airport. Paid them to tackle the goons Mackay sent to welcome you. Worked OK I think. And this guy here is just gonna drop us at a place we can hide out in for a bit. While we plan what to do."

The car turned sharply into a side street and pulled up at a single story building which looked to Will like a shabby local bar.

Tanner gave the driver a bundle of notes and he drove away. He then led Will into the bar. A wrinkled and tanned old man looked up from behind the counter and nodded.

"This way," said Tanner and they walked down a dark narrow corridor to a back room with a table and four mismatching wooden chairs. There was a bottle of mineral water on the table and a large plate of sandwiches covered in cling-film.

"Hungry?" asked Tanner and sat down at the table.

"Not really," said Will, pouring them a glass of water each.

"Me neither. OK. Here's the thing. While you've been away I've been contacting every international authority I could think of to tell them what's going on here and try to get them to intervene. A lot of blank walls obviously. The Life Group has quite some power and influence, as we know. Disgusting how much corruption there is in this world of ours." He took a sip of water.

"But you said the UN were interested, right?"

"Yeah. They were the only ones who seem to believe what I'm saying. Which is good because they're the guys with the muscle to do something about it. Their global weather department, or whatever they're called, picked up on the algae so they were keen to find out more. I think they're beginning to get freaked, which is good. In fact they're sending a man out to Nirvana. I think that's why Penny has flown out here. To tackle him head on. Buy herself more time."

"Bitch!" Will hit the table with his fist, rattling the glasses.

"You got it!"

"We've got to stop her, Harold. And quick."

"I also overheard Mackay's goons talking about forming a reception committee for you. So I hired some muscle. Too late to help Fiona I'm afraid. But just in time to help you."

"Thank you, Harold."

"Don't mention it, kid."

Tanner peeled off the cling-film and peered at the sandwiches through his round glasses. He decided against taking one.

"So what's the plan?" asked Will.

"That's what we're here to decide," said Tanner. "But we better be quick."

They were interrupted by the ping of an incoming text message. They both reached for their phones.

"It's me," said Tanner, tapping the screen of his phone. "From one of my hired muscle-men." His eyes widened as he read the message. "Says he wants to meet us. Asks where we are."

"Great. We need all the help we can get."

But Tanner looked uneasy. "Smells fishy to me, Will. This was not the plan. These are hired guns, kid. They have no loyalty to me. Only to money. I think someone may have doubled their salary."

Will stood up. "And if they can reach them they can get to your driver too."

"We gotta go, kid."

Chapter Sixty-Eight

P enny sipped an iced tea and surveyed the hotel suite Mackay used as a home office.

The Scot walked in, reading a message on his phone.

"John. How's our girl?"

"Och, a bit feisty. I had to gag her."

"Quite right."

He held up his phone. "Sorry, I'm getting a lot of hassle from our friends at the Ministry."

"Oh?"

"They're losing their heads over the dead fish around here. They also say they're getting heat from the UN about the algae. It's showing up big time on the satellites."

"It was only a matter of time."

"Our friend spilled the beans about the fisheries and the UN are now blathering about upsetting the ecosystem. They've sent someone over called Schulz to talk to us. I've kept him out of the way so far..."

"It's all to be expected. I'll tell them all to chill out. Boosting fish stocks with iron fertilisation is quite legitimate. And the dead fish is just a freak phenomenon. It'll pass." She put down her glass and rose gracefully. "I'll talk to the UN fellow and explain the programme. They can't really object to our bringing an end to global warming can they? And get Dr Bell in here to back me up." She smiled and walked out onto the terrace to look at the sea. "Beautiful view."

Mackay scurried after her. "I'm sorry Penny, we have a problem there."

"Oh?"

"The girl refuses to co-operate. Says she'd rather die than pretend to support you in this."

Penny flashed him an angry look. "The little...Did you tell her what we'd do to her boyfriend if she doesn't play ball?"

"Yep. She says she's sure he'd rather die too than help you get away with this, in her words."

"Well...She may get her wish. Ok. I'll do this without the little bitch. Send in our visitor."

Mackay barked a command on his phone to someone, "Penny will see the UN guy. Send him over." Then he joined her on the terrace. "The minister's also freaking about the deaths at the resort and the rumours of monster fish. Pain in the arse man! As if we don't pay them enough!"

"I'm sure you can handle it, John."

There was a knock at the door and Mackay went to open it.

Moments later he led a young man dressed in beige chinos and a navy polo shirt into the living room where Penny was waiting.

She raised an eyebrow. He looked like a college student. So this was the representative of the United Nations sent to rein her in?

"Mr Schulz I presume?" she said, smiling and offering him her hand.

"That's correct, Ma'am." He looked nervous.

"I'm Penny Crawford, CEO of The Life Group. How may I help you?"

"This is gonna be a difficult conversation I'm afraid, Ma'am."

"Oh really?"

"The Government of the Rep..."

"Do sit down, Mr Schulz." She waved to the couch and he followed her direction.

"Thank you, Ma'am."

"Do call me Penny." She sat in an armchair at his side. Mackay sat next to him on the couch, so close that Schulz edged away slightly.

"The Gov..." he started again but was again interrupted.

"Would you like some refreshments, Mr Schulz?"

"No thank you, Ma'am. Penny." His voice wavered a little.

"Now. Do go on."

"Thank you. The Government of the Republic of Maldives informs me that you are engaged in a programme of marine fertilisation to increase fish stocks via the addition of iron sulphate to the ocean to stimulate algae growth."

She smiled and nodded. "That is correct, Mr Schulz."

"Well, Ma'am, I'm afraid this must cease immediately."

She was taken aback by his bluntness. "Oh really?"

"Also I must inform you that you are liable to be prosecuted for your illegal actions."

Clearly he was not the kitten she'd thought he was.

"I don't understand, Mr Schulz. We have been adding iron to waters around the Maldives with government approval. But in any case that is immaterial as we are about to carry out our programme 12 miles off the coast and therefore outside their territorial waters. Beyond this 12 mile zone nobody has control of the oceans, Mr Schulz, so we can do as we please."

The man's face reddened. She wondered how for he'd go in standing up to her. She always enjoyed a fight. Especially with an opponent she'd underestimated.

"You are mistaken, Miss Crawford. You are in violation of two international resolutions...the UN's convention on biological diversity and the London Convention on the dumping of wastes at sea..."

"Dumping wastes at sea, Mr Schulz? You dare criticise me for dumping wastes at sea?" He flinched. "I'm growing plankton,"

"But you're still dump..."

"What about cruise ships, Mr Schulz? Do you try to stop them? They're the ones getting away with dumping waste at sea."

"Cruise ships, Ma'am?" He looked puzzled.

"Each year a cruise ship will dump 30,000 gallons of untreated sewage and 250,000 gallons of waste water containing harmful chemicals. Overall, that's a billion gallons of sewage dumped into the oceans every year, Mr Schulz. What are your conventions doing to stop them?"

The man's face went a deeper shade of red, but he responded slowly and steadily.

"That's a different issue, Miss Crawford. I'm here to talk to you about what you're doing in the Indian Ocean. You are strictly prohibited from conducting ocean fertilisation programmes..."

"Ah! You're not quite right, are you Mr Schulz?"

"I know international marine law, Miss Crawford...."

"I'm not sure you do. What I'm not allowed to do is make a profit from ocean fertilisation. Well from now on I won't be. I don't give a damn about the fisheries. That's just a sideline. I'm eco-engineering, Mr Schulz. That's my real goal. To combat global warming. In an altruistic, non-profit making way. So you see, I'm not breaking any laws. And you should be supporting me, not trying to stop me."

The man looked confused. Shame, thought Penny. Just when she was beginning to like him.

"You don't care about the fisheries?" he said at last, frowning.

"No."

"The algae is for carbon sequestration?"

She detected a note of admiration in his voice and relaxed back into her chair. "That's right."

"But...Can the Indian Ocean make that much of a difference? I mean..."

"Not on its own no. Which is why we have fleets of ships about to fertilise every ocean of the world..."

Mackay coughed suddenly and stood up. "I think you've had enough of our CEO's time, Mr Schulz..."

The young man from the UN remained seated, staring at Penny. "Fleets of ships in every ocean?"

She realised she'd made a slip-up. It was uncharacteristic and she cursed herself.

"Nice to meet you, Mr Schulz. John's right. I have other appointments..." She stood up.

Schulz rose slowly, ignoring Mackay's attempt to direct him out. "I can't believe this," he said, his voice now firm. "Haven't you seen what it's done to the sealife around here? There's dead fish everywhere! God knows what it will do..."

Mackay took his arm but he shook it off angrily. Penny was surprised. Mackay looked like he wanted to kill him.

"Ok, I'm leaving," he said. "But you have to suspend your activities immediately while we sort out the legalities. You have to call back your ships. You could cause untold damage to the global eco-system."

Penny shrugged. "Ok Mr Schulz. I don't agree with you, and I have no doubt my lawyers will win the argument, but Ok I'll suspend operations."

"Thank you, Ma'am. Also could I respectfully ask that you stay on the island until my superiors arrive? They should get here tomorrow."

"With the lawyers no doubt?"

"I'm guessing so, Ma'am. Maybe also some guys from the US Government."

"Of course. Goodbye Mr Schulz."

Mackay led him out and returned to find Penny looking grim faced.

"Shall I contact the ships?" he asked.

"Yes," she said. "Tell them to speed up operations. We don't have much time."

"Understood."

"And get the sea plane ready," she said, running a hand through her thick blonde hair. "I'm not sticking around to be questioned by these jokers."

"The boat might be better, Penny. Less...conspicuous."

"Yes I agree." She patted his arm as she walked to the door, something she'd never done before. "Good man."

Mackay grinned his ugly grin. He was definitely her favourite now.

Chapter Sixty-Nine

The creature was desperate.

The new paradise had turned into a hell.

The brightness blinded its eyes. The prey it had found on the surface tasted bad. And now it was once again struggling to breathe.

Even the creatures that lived in the new world, creatures it had never encountered in the deep dark, seemed to be struggling. Many were dying. Many were already dead.

It had eaten these at first. Gorged itself on the floating bloated bodies. But now it was not food that was its driving force.

It was so weak it could barely swim. It hung at the surface. It gaped and gaped, drawing in seawater past its long silvery fangs and into its overworked gills.

So much water. So little oxygen.

Chapter Seventy

The boat ploughed through the dark low waves, its bow throwing up a white spray which reflected in the moonlight.

Will stood silent and grim faced in the cabin. Next to him the captain of the hired motor boat, a middle aged man with a dark brown weather-beaten face, rested his right hand on the wheel and puffed on a cigarette hanging from the corner of his mouth. On the other side of the captain stood Tanner. All three men stared ahead through the cabin window at the approaching lights of Nirvana Atoll in the distance.

Doubting the loyalty of Tanner's hired hands, and not knowing who in power locally was in the pocket of The Life Group, they had decided their only option was to try to rescue Fiona themselves, and then the three of them would tell their story to the UN. They knew that if they tried to find the guy from the UN first it could endanger Fiona's life.

They had found the captain in a local bar and Tanner's ready supply of money had swiftly secured him and his boat for the night-time crossing from Male to the resort.

The plan was to land on the East side of the atoll away from the main resort. Tanner and Will would split up and search for Fiona while the boat waited for them off-shore.

Will tried not to think what little chance they had to succeed and wondered if Tanner felt the same. They didn't know her exact location in the resort. The place would also most likely be swarming with security guards.

"Fifteen minutes," said the captain. "I turn off lights now. But there is moon..."

He flicked a switch and all the lights went out on the boat. But the moon still reflected off the wet wooden deck and metal rails.

"Of well," Will said. "Let's hope they're not looking this way."

"And that they're deaf," aid Tanner with a half smile as chugging of the boat's engine seemed even louder in the darkness.

But to their relief and surprise no shouts went up as the boat scrunched gently into the beach and the two men waded ashore and walked up to the path which would lead them to the main buildings.

Will wanted to run but had to hold himself back for the moment and walk at the slow pace of the older man.

"Don't worry, kid. I won't hold you up for long," said Tanner breathing heavily as they climbed up the beach.

"No problem," said Will, giving him his arm, "Without you this rescue would never be happening."

In a few moments they reached the path. The going was much easier here but the American stopped and let out a sharp moan.

"Are you OK Harold?" Will said, holding Tanner's arms to steady him.

Tanner pushed him away gently but firmly. "I'm fine. You go, kid. We don't have much time. I'll catch you up."

Will hesitated.

Tanner looked at him, his eyes large behind his round glasses. "I'm OK, really. Just old age. Go."

The old man looked in pain, but Fiona's life was in danger. Will had little choice.

"OK. But you rest here. Take it easy. I'll come back for you once I've found her. OK?"

Tanner smiled and nodded.

Will turned and ran along the path.

The night air was warm and humid, and sweet with the scent of tropical flowers.

After a few minutes the path turned from earth to hardwood and edged with small solar lights which made him highly visible.

He tried to tread as lightly as possible and strained his ears for the sound of the security guards he knew patrolled this part of the resort.

Then suddenly he heard talking and slipped sideways off the path and behind the wide trunk of a banyan tree.

He waited a moment and then heard slow footsteps and two men talking in what he presumed was Dhivehi, the local language.

Undoubtedly resort security. And thankfully not on high alert it seemed.

Once the guards had passed he continued along the path and in a little while came to a fork in the way.

Right would take him to the hotel. Left wound down to the main beach, jetty and dive shop.

He thought for a moment. Tanner had said that the resort had suspended all diving activities for a while. The dive shop would be closed up and off limits to guests. A good place to hold someone prisoner.

Certainly a good place to start his search.

He headed left and followed the path downhill.

As he emerged from the cover of trees and bushes at the edge of the main beach he could see several figures on the jetty in front of him. But the lights of the jetty were on full and he knew they wouldn't be able to see him as he edged along the vegetation towards the back of the dive shop.

He saw three guards further along the beach too, but they were all looking out to sea.

The back of the dive shop was in dark shadow. There were no windows so Will listened against the wooden wall. He thought he heard the faint sound of shuffling. There was someone inside. He listened again. It sounded like someone struggling to free themselves.

He edged along the wall and peered around the corner.

The guards on the beach were not looking back his way. There were some figures, presumably more guards, at the far end on and around the luxury villas jetty. But they were a long way off. The dive jetty on the other hand was close by, just on the other side of the shop. But the people on it seemed occupied with the boat and various bits of equipment.

He crept around the corner and along the side wall to a small window. He stood on tiptoes to try to look in but the blinds were closed. However he could see there was a light on inside.

He walked quickly around to the front of the building and through the door.

The inside of the dive shop was brightly lit. There were rails with hanging wet suits, racks of gas cylinders and shelves with masks and snorkels.

There was also someone standing in the middle of the room.

Will's heart skipped a beat.

"Hello again, Sanders," said Mackay, smiling. "Do come in."

The Scot was pointing a gun at his chest.

"Och, this little thing? It's my Glock 17. I learnt to use it in the prison service. I'm really quite good with it, you know. Now come in."

Will did as he was told.

"Where's Fiona?" he said, looking Mackay hard in the eyes and trying to ignore the gun.

Mackay moved to the side. "Sit," he said. "Over there." He nodded towards a crate at the back of the shop.

"I'd rather..."

"Sit!" shouted Mackay. "Or I end this here and now."

He moved to the crate and sat as Mackay backed towards the door and then closed it, all the while keeping his gun on Will.

"Where's Fiona?" Will asked again. "If you hurt her I'll..."

"You'll what?" Mackay walked to the middle of the room and stared contemptuously down at him. "What can you do? Nothing, that's what!" The Scot raised the gun and pointed it at Will's head. Will felt a trickle of sweat on his face.

After what seemed like an eternity Mackay lowered the gun to chest height again and grinned crookedly. "You'd be my seventh, Will. Lucky seven. The first man I killed was tough. It got easier after that. The sixth was a cinch. Like swatting a fly."

"You're a fucking monster."

"Careful, Will. Like swatting a fly, remember."

"Where...is...Fiona?" said Will through gritted teeth.

"I don't know what she sees in you. Not our marine biologist. Penny. She always liked you. I hated that. As you know. Though I have to say you're not in her good books any more. She wouldn't give two hoots if I swatted you."

"So why don't you?"

There was a sound of a boat engine starting outside.

"Why do you think I'm aiming a gun at you, William? This is good-bye I'm afraid. We're slipping away by boat while everyone's asleep. But not you. This is where your journey ends, my friend." Mackay grinned as his finger closed around the trigger. "I'd like to say I'll miss you, but I'd be lying. You've been a pain in the arse for far too long. Any last requests?"

Mackay frowned. He had expected his words to have a chilling effect but Will was just staring at him.

Then he understood why.

He felt something sharp stick into his back.

"Drop the gun now!"

Tanner stood behind him holding a spear gun.

Will had seen the door open and the old man come in and take the spear gun from a rack on the side wall. Mackay had not heard it all above the sound of the boat engine. And it had taken all his concentration for Will to keep his eyes fixed on Mackay rather than flicking to his old friend.

Tanner jabbed the spear point a little way into the flesh and Mackay yelped and dropped the gun.

"She's on the boat, Will." Tanner said. "Go get her!"

Will ran out in time to see the boat heading out to sea. Fiona and Penny must have been on board all the time and he hadn't seen them. He cursed himself and ran to the jetty. There were no other boats. He'd have to run back to the other side of the atoll and find the captain. By which time they could be anywhere. And Fiona could be...

Then he saw a small dinghy. It had a tiny engine but it would still be the better option, he thought. He jumped in, started it up and headed off in the direction of the boat.

Chapter
Seventy-One

Brian Schulz paced the room he was staying in at the Nirvana resort while he dialled his boss's number.

He had left the meeting with Penny Crawford convinced of two things: one, she was crazy; and two, she had no intention of stopping her ships. He had emailed his boss immediately with news about her grand plan. The email had been acknowledged but there had been no response.

An hour later and he could take it no longer. He had to find out what the UN intended to do.

After five rings a voice finally answered. "Henderson. That you Schulz?"

He stopped in the middle of the room. "Yes sir. Did you get my message? Did you hear what the Crawford woman is planning, sir?"

"Yes I did, Schulz. I was just picking up the phone to call you now. I need you to keep calm. I've got enough hysteria going on over here. The White House has gone ballistic."

He was relieved. It had gone to the top. Now action would be taken.

"We gotta act, Schulz," his boss continued as though echoing his thoughts. "And we gotta act quick."

"Yes sir. What's the plan sir?" He wondered if the marines were on their way. Maybe with the CIA. Perhaps one of the aircraft carriers was steaming in his direction that very moment.

"Schulz this is nothing short of total global catastrophe. An end to life on our planet. Our top scientists are freakin' out big time. They're saying if this woman goes ahead and simultaneously dumps tonnes of iron into the world's oceans it will suck out the oxygen to such an extent that ninety percent of marine life will die within seven days. And if that happens life on the rest of the planet won't be far behind."

It was even worse than Schulz had feared. "Do you want me to be liaison down here, sir?"

"Liaison?"

"For whoever's gonna sort this out..."

There was a pause.

"Schulz."

"Sir?"

"You're the guy that's gonna sort this out."

He swallowed hard. "I'm what, sir?"

"We don't know where the ships are. Don't ask me how but we don't. But we did manage to capture one of the captains. Big fat Indian guy. Put pressure on him and he squealed. There's an abort code. It's the only way to stop the ships now before they dump. We got maybe one hour he guesses. We tried every obvious word. Family names. Her daughter's. Nothing works. Schulz...Brian...you need to get that code."

He noticed he was sweating and rubbed his forehead. "Ok sir. Who's got the code?"

"Only two people. Crawford and this John Mackay you met."

"Ok sir."

"Only you can get to them on time Schulz. You better get going."

"Yes sir."

"Good luck, son."

He lowered the phone, hesitated a moment, then ran from the room.

Chapter Seventy-Two

Tanner motioned for Mackay to sit on the crate Will had occupied just moments earlier.

The Scot moved the back of the shop and sat down. Tanner kept the spear gun aimed at him all the time.

There was a moment's silence as the two men stared at each other, Mackay with a snarl on his lips, Tanner watching him with owl-like eyes.

"So what do we do now?" said the Scot finally, "Make small talk?"

"We wait for the police to arrive and put you and your boss lady in jail. I called them just before I came in."

Mackay spat out a short laugh. "Pah! You're deluded, old man. The police will do nothing. I can promise you that. You see..." he plucked his trouser pocket, "I have them right here."

"Oh, you thought I meant the local police," said Tanner smiling.

Mackay looked unsettled.

"No. We know you've bribed most of them," continued the American calmly. "Which is why we've contacted the United Nations police. You haven't got to them have you?"

"Who? I don't believe you. There's no such thing. You're bluffing, man." Mackay gave him a dismissive flick of the head but still looked a little unsure.

Tanner was indeed bluffing. But he wanted the man to sweat a little.

"Ah. That means no you haven't got to them. And yes they do exist. My new friend Mr Schulz – I think you know him – contacted them first. For some reason he didn't believe you were going to stop your operations. Don't ask me why."

Mackay narrowed his eyes.

"You think you're clever, old man, but it'll make no difference. We're too big to touch, you see. We can do whatever the hell we like. Here. Pretty much anywhere. We have the power. We know the right people. But most important..." he held up his finger, "...We have the money. Tons of it. And money's what makes the world go round. It's what everybody wants. Even the UN."

"No, Mr Mackay. Nobody is above the law..."

"The law? The law is for the poor. With money you can bend the law. Get people to turn a blind eye...."

"And you have no ethics?"

"No, not that I can think of. I don't see the point."

Tanner shook his head sadly. "You'll regret this one day, believe me."

The Scot snorted and stood up. "Hah!, Oh, let me guess. You're one of those suckers who believes in Karma, right? What goes around comes around? Divine justice? Bad guys get what they deserve in the end? Eh?"

"Yes. I do."

"Nah, that's all bollocks! There is no God. I make my own destiny."
He thumped his chest. "I control my own future. I'm in charge. And
if I need to step on other people to get what I want I do it. Tough shit.
No higher power is going to punish me for that. I know. I've done
plenty of it. And guess what? I'm still here!"

Tanner walked up to Mackay and pressed the spear against his chest,
making him wince.

"What really happened to my nephew? You knew he was killed by
one of those monster fish out there didn't you? And you covered it
up."

Mackay shrugged. "Sure. What was I supposed to do? Close the
resort? Ask Penny to stop saving the world? Get real. Your nephew
was in the wrong place at the wrong time. He got chewed up. Shame.
But he's a nobody in the scheme of things. Like that Bell girl out there
now."

Tanner's lips tightened. Mackay's words cut deep. "You're an evil
creature, aren't you?"

"I've had enough of this," said Mackay and backed away.

"Stay where you are!" Tanner motioned with the spear gun.

"Fuck you, old man! You can't stop any of this. And you're not
going to do anything with that."

He walked towards the spot on the floor where the gun lay. Tanner
cursed himself for not having picked it up or kicked it out of the way.

"Go back and sit down, Mackay," said the American, his voice calm
but the spear gun shaking a little in his hands.

"The police will do nothing. The UN will do nothing." Mackay
bent down and picked up the gun.

"Drop it!" Tanner shouted. "I'm warning you." The old man's
hands were really shaking now.

Mackay ignored him. He turned to the American and pointed the gun at him, grinning. "Nobody gives a shit about you or your dead nephew. Nobody..."

But the Scot had been stopped in his tracks by the spear through his heart. He looked at the shaft sticking out of his chest. Then he looked in shock at Tanner. Then he dropped to the floor, dead.

Tanner blinked his large eyes. "I guess that's Karma," he said.

Chapter Seventy-Three

It was luxurious for a dive boat. Streamlined, white, with two decks.

Penny and Fiona were sitting in the sun at the rear of the upper deck, the former sipping champagne from a flute, the latter bound hand and foot with ropes.

"Oops!" said Penny as the boat lurched and a few drops of the wine splashed onto her billowy white cotton dress. "Bit of a squall coming I think. I hope it doesn't interrupt our intrepid escape."

Fiona stared at her, her eyes a mixture of hatred and fear. "What do you want with me?"

Penny smiled indulgently. "Well. I did want you to help me with our visitor from the United Nations. But you refused. Rather rudely, I think. So now I need to get away from here. And you need to disappear. Lost at sea, I think. As befits your profession." She gave a short laugh, then turned her head and called towards the interior of the boat where one of two large burly men in black polo shirts was steering. "George! How long to Male? I think the weather's turning. We better be quick. I don't want to get caught in a storm out here."

"Yes, Ma'am," came the deep voice of the captain, "We also need to steer clear of all the seaweed and dead fish in case they clog up the prop."

"All right." She contemplated Fiona for a few moments. "Ten more minutes I think. Then we'll pop you overboard."

Fiona shivered.

Chapter Seventy-Four

B rian Schulz could not believe his eyes.

An old man was sitting on a crate at the far end of the dive shop, his head in his hands and a spear gun at his feet. A few feet away lay the motionless body of the man he recognised as John Mackay. A spear was sticking out of his chest.

The old man raised his head as Schulz entered, his eyes red and watery. "I killed him," he said with a croaking voice. "I had to. He was going to shoot me with that gun." Schulz noticed the revolver in the dead man's hand. "And he killed my nephew. I don't regret it."

"You're Harold Tanner, right? I'm Schulz. We spoke on the phone." The old man nodded.

"Ok. This is a police matter. I'm sure everything will get sorted out." He felt for Tanner, and though he'd not witnessed what had happened he was inclined to believe him. But he had something far more urgent on his mind.

"Mr Tanner. This is important. Where's Penny Crawford?"

The old man shook his head. "He deserved it."

Schulz knelt in front of him. "I'm sure you're right, Mr Tanner. But I need to know where Penny Crawford is. It's critical I get to her."

"Penny?"

"I've got urgent instructions from New York. They've found that what she's done here off this island is irreversible. She's killed all the sealife here. Suffocated it. And now she's got ships in every ocean of the world about to do the same thing."

Tanner stared at him.

"If we don't stop them now it'll be too late," said Schulz, trying to break through to the man in front of him who appeared stunned by what he'd done. "It'll reach a tipping point, our scientists are saying. All the oxygen will be sucked out of the oceans and all life will die."

Tanner frowned. "You must stop it."

"We don't know where the ships are right now. And even if we did we couldn't get to them in time. They're on lock down. Only Penny can stop them. There's an abort code. Only she has it. And Mackay..."

They both glanced at the dead body.

Tanner shivered as though ridding himself of his stupor. "She's on a boat. She's headed for the airport at Male."

Schulz took out his phone as he bolted for the door.

Chapter
Seventy-Five

The tankers had all reached their designated locations – two in the Pacific, two in the Atlantic and one in the Indian Ocean.

They had disabled their tracking devices so nobody but the Life Group knew exactly where they were.

In precisely one hour there would be a synchronised outpouring of tons of green iron sulphate crystals in a global operation unparalleled in maritime history.

The captains of all the ships had been instructed to proceed even if attempts were made to stop or interfere with the dumping programme. They were to ignore all external communication.

There was only one code word that could stop the operation. If they received that code they were to cease immediately and return to port.

But only two people within the Life Group knew the code word.

And one of them was now dead.

Chapter Seventy-Six

Fiona strained against the ropes holding her to the bench and looked around in panic. Were they really going to throw her into the sea? How long could she survive? The water would be warm enough so she wouldn't die of hypothermia, but how long could she stay afloat?

The sun disappeared behind a mass of threatening black clouds and the wind started to whip her hair around. The boat's lurching increased.

Then the engines cut out and they drifted to an unsteady stop.

"What is it Hank?" Penny shouted towards the cabin. "Why have we stopped here? This isn't the spot is it?"

The man called Hank appeared on the upper deck, holding the side rail to steady himself as the boat swayed from side to side.

"I thought I saw one of them, Miss Crawford," said Hank. "You said I should tell you if I saw one. There." He pointed over the side of the boat past Penny.

She leant over the rail and peered at the dark choppy water. Fiona was confused. What were they looking for?

Suddenly Penny let out a yelp of delight, uncharacteristic of her. "Yes! I saw it! I saw it! Damn, it's gone again."

She turned to Fiona. "It's one of those fish you found, Dr Bell. I've been dying to see one. Before they all die out."

Then Fiona saw a nasty glint of an idea in her eyes. "Oh, I wonder if we can tempt him up again. They like the taste of human don't they? From what you've told me. Maybe we can...how shall I put it?....kill two birds with one stone." She laughed to herself.

"Take her down," Penny said to Hank.

The man approached Fiona, staggering as the boat jerked around.

He held a large knife I his right hand.

Fiona tried to control her breathing and calm her heartbeat.

He grabbed her arm to steady himself and then cut the ropes around her ankles and wrists.

As soon as she felt the ropes fall away she kneed him sharply in the groin and sprang sideways off the bench.

He yelped in pain and doubled over.

She started towards the cabin.

Suddenly there was a loud bang and the doorframe splintered.

She stopped and turned to see Penny holding a small silver handgun.

"Don't move! I can throw you into the water dead or alive," Penny said calmly. "Your choice. The fish won't mind either way."

The Captain emerged from the cabin pointing a larger black gun at her and she knew she had no chance.

Hank staggered to his feet.

"Grab her, you useless oaf," Penny told him. "Take her below and throw her in."

A rumble of thunder sounded in the distance as the man grabbed Fiona roughly and propelled her downstairs to the main deck.

Penny followed them down.

Fiona was manhandled to a gap in the side rail. She steadied herself against the rail as the boat continued to lurch. Penny leant back against the bulkhead and trained the gun on her.

"Tie her so she doesn't swim too far from the boat," Penny said to the henchman. "You need to be able to net the creature when it goes for her. I want to see the thing up close."

She smiled at Fiona. "I do admire these creatures, don't you Dr Bell? Their own habitat became unsustainable so they moved to a new one and adapted quickly from eating whatever they did in the depths to people at the surface. Real survivors."

"You won't get away with this you evil bitch," Fiona said, trying not to let the fear welling inside her make her voice tremble.

"Oh I think I will," Penny answered calmly. "I always do, my dear."

Hank tied a synthetic blue rope around her waist, then looked at his boss.

Fiona made to slip past him but he caught her by the back of her shirt and tugged her backwards. She felt the rail against her thigh and reached forward to balance. But he gave her a mighty shove in the chest and suddenly she was falling over the side.

She hit the seaweed with a thwack and disappeared under the water.

She surfaced spluttering.

Above her Penny and Hank stared down at her. Penny aimed the gun at her head. Hank held the rope in one hand and picked up a large bundle of fishing net in the other.

Fiona trod water. The sea was choppy and she was lifted up and down violently in the swells. Her nose was filled with the pungent iodine stench of seaweed. It also draped around her hair and face.

"Penny, please!" she called up. "Let me back on!"

"Is it getting too rough for them, do you think?" Penny called down, raising her voice against the wind.

"What?" shouted Fiona, confused and spluttering as her face was continually sprayed with seawater.

"You're the marine biologist. Is this sea too rough for the creatures?"

"Fuck you!" yelled Fiona, spitting out seaweed.

Penny shrugged and then looked up at the ever darkening sky.

Fiona continued to struggle against the waves. Not being able to see through the surface layer of algae and weed made it worse. Her mind filled with images of the sea creature she had seen attacking Will only days before. The long sharp silver needle teeth, the milky staring eyes, the massive scaly head. She tried to clear her head and focus instead on staying calm and keeping afloat.

After five minutes, which seemed to Fiona like an eternity, she felt herself being tugged towards the boat by the rope around her waist.

Then she was banging against the side of the boat and reached up to grab Hank's hands. She was pulled up and into the boat in one swift movement.

She lay on the deck coughing.

A feeling of relief welled up inside her. Penny had changed her mind about killing her. At least for the moment.

However her relief was short-lived.

"We need blood to attract the fish I think," Penny said to Hank. "Cut her. Then throw her back in."

Chapter Seventy-Seven

H ank took out his large knife.

"Cut her arm," said Penny, aiming her gun at Fiona's chest.

"Penny, please," Fiona pleaded.

"Quiet and keep still," said Penny. "Or we'll try it with a dead body."

Hank hesitated. "Shouldn't we head on, Ma'am?" he said, a note of anxiety in his voice. "I'm worried about the storm."

Penny's face hardened. "What did you say to me? Just do your job. Cut the girl."

Hank looked apologetically at Fiona.

"Don't do it!" she said.

He grabbed her arm, pulled it out swiftly and made a small shallow cut.

"Deeper!" shouted Penny in frustration. "We need a lot more blood that that you idiot!"

"Don't. Please," said Fiona, looking him in the eyes, sensing his unwillingness.

Hank looked perplexed.

At that moment the Captain appeared on the deck above them and shouted down, straining his voice to be heard over the howling wind and crashing waves. "Ma'm! Ma'am! We have to head on soon! The storm's getting worse!"

"Cover the girl with your gun," Penny called to him. "Shoot her if she moves." She stared at Hank, who seemed frozen to the spot.

"I can't do it," he said. "She's just a girl. I can't."

"Pathetic man," said Penny with contempt. "Give me the knife."

Hank handed her the knife slowly.

Fiona prepared herself to kick out at Penny when she tried to cut her, and take her chance at getting shot from the Captain above.

But instead of lunging at her with the knife, Penny stuck it deep into Hank's belly.

He gave a yelp of shock and pain.

Hank looked at Penny with wide disbelieving eyes as she withdrew the knife with a fountain of blood and plunged it into his belly a second time.

She pulled it out again and looked admiringly at the two spurts of blood pumping from the man's stomach and splattering onto the deck.

Hank groaned and put his hands over the wounds but couldn't stop the flow.

"There!" said Penny triumphantly. "That should be enough, shouldn't it?"

Then she shoved him with a force surprising for such an elegant lady. He fell backwards and tried to grab the rail but it slipped out of his bloody hands.

There was an almighty splash as the body hit the water. Then the sound of yelling and thrashing around.

Fiona looked at Penny in horror. She was again pointing the gun at her. There were some bright red blood stains on her white cotton dress and bare arms.

Suddenly the yelling from below was replaced with screaming.

"George!" shouted Penny to the Captain. "Get the net. I think we've got one!"

He looked over the side from the upper deck and saw a horrendous sight below in the water. The monster had its huge mouth clamped around Hank's torso. Instead of shaking it side to side like a shark might, the creature seemed to be chomping up and down with its mouth. With each bite more blood spurted from its hapless victim.

"Fuck!" shouted the Captain. "It's a monster!"

He scurried down to the lower deck and picked up the net Hank had been holding earlier.

The girl, still with a blue rope around her waist, was standing back against the bulkhead with a look of shock on her face.

His boss meanwhile steadied herself against the boat's rail, looking serene and composed in her blood-spattered dress, an image of Lady Macbeth.

"Get the fish, George. Quick!" Penny ordered.

But when he looked over the side again he saw the creature diving below the waves and seaweed, still holding Hank's body in its jaws.

"Shit!" he said. "It's gone!"

Penny stamped her foot angrily. "Too slow, George!"

"I'm sorry, Ma'am. It moved too fast."

"Well take care next time."

"Are we not heading on to the airport now?" said the Captain. "Your plane..."

"You too?" said Penny. "You want to join your colleague?"

The Captain shot Penny a look. He was a tougher man than Hank and he towered over Penny. He could have snapped her like a twig. And it looked like the thought was crossing his mind.

But there was something about her that seemed to make her invulnerable. Like a divine force field. She seemed able to wield a hidden power and bend even the strongest to her will.

Penny locked eyes with him. "You have something to say, Captain?"

The wind howled, the boat lurched, the waves and seaweed slapped against the sides.

Fiona saw her opportunity and ran past the Captain towards the prow. If she could find a weapon of some kind, or lock herself in the cabin and make a distress call on the radio...

Suddenly she was jerked backwards from the waist.

The rope. She'd forgotten it. And now she was being reeled in like a fish on a line.

She fought to untie the knot but it was too late. A strong pair of hands grabbed her and a big black pistol was pressed painfully against her head.

The Captain dragged her to the gap in the rail.

Penny glanced over the side. "There's plenty of blood in the water now. And I think I saw some movement down there too under the weed. There's a few of them I think."

Fiona's arms were pinned sharply behind her. She looked down at the churning mass of green water and white spray.

But there was something else too. Moving between the waves. A large dark scaled body with a stubby spiked fin. Then a broad head and indented milky eyes.

It was like they were waiting for her.

"Throw her in!" shouted Penny.

Fiona felt the grip tightening on her arms, and prepared herself to be shoved, to hit the water, and the horror to follow.

Chapter Seventy-Eight

A shout from somewhere behind them made Penny and the captain stop and turn around.

They saw Will in a small dinghy at the stern, trying to get close enough to the violently swaying boat to climb aboard.

"Stop Penny! Stop!" he shouted.

"Ah, the rescuing hero," said Penny. "Or perhaps another piece of bait we can use."

Will grabbed the handrail of the boat and pulled himself aboard.

He started towards Penny but stopped as she pointed her gun at him. Then he saw Fiona, wet and bedraggled, tied with a rope around her waist. It tore his heart to see the scared look in the eyes of such a strong girl. "Fi!" he cried and took an involuntary step forward. He wanted to hold her, comfort her.

"Don't move, Will!" shouted Penny, aiming the gun at his head. "I told you."

"You need to send the abort code, Penny. You've got to stop the ships. If you don't you're going to kill everything in the sea. Everything. The algae remove too much oxygen, Penny. It creates a snowball effect. And it can't be reversed..."

"Says who?" snorted Penny. "You? Your girlfriend here?"

"No. The UN scientists. I spoke to their representative on the way here..."

"Who? That Schulz fellow? He's a pimply youth. What does know?"

"He's just the messenger. Here..." He held up his mobile towards her. "Talk to the scientists yourself if you don't believe me. They're on standby to talk to you. The US President too."

"The President? Ha! What does he care about the planet? He's caused more global warming than anyone else on this Earth!"

"You've got to stop it, Penny. Please! We don't have much time."

She shook her head.

"What the hell are you doing, Penny?" he said, staggering as the boat continued to lurch from side to side. "I don't understand. You built an amazing company. You've achieved so much. You've done so much good. And now you're going to throw it all away. Don't do it, Penny. Please."

"I'm not throwing it away, Will. I'm protecting it. The world is going to hell in a handbasket and nobody's doing anything about it. Oh they're all ready to try to stop me – they can sort themselves out to do that all right – but they won't lift a finger to save the world. And as for you two...well, you're trying to spoil what I'm doing and I can't allow that. You have to go. And if you have to go I might as well get something out of it. Use you to get hold of a couple of these extraordinary beasts down there."

Will shook his head. "You can't do this, Penny. This is murder. You can't just kill us because you think we're getting in the way. And even if you do, the cat's out of the bag. The UN are sending in a police team. You'll be arrested as soon as you reach Male. We can talk this through, Penny. You have some great ideas. You want to save the planet, I know that. That's why I've followed you. I've always looked up to you. Admired you. You're a genius. But you can't do this. You can't kill people. And you can't kill the oceans."

"No Will. My ships are ready to dump their cargo. I've ramped up the operation so the results will be massive enough for the world to take notice. They're not going to stop it. Nobody can stop it now."

"Give me the abort code, Penny," said Will. "Please..."

He took a step towards her.

She jerked the gun at him. "Stop there! Have no doubt I'll shoot you, Will."

He stopped.

"Now get over there with your girlfriend."

She covered him carefully as he walked past her and stood beside Fiona.

"Will, you shouldn't have come," she said, wet and shivering.

He gave her a reassuring smile. "What? And missed all this?"

Penny moved to the handrail and looked over. "There's a few of them down there I think. Get ready to throw them in. Try to catch at least one fish once they start biting."

"You're a monster," said Will, gripping Fiona around the waist.

"Depends on your point of view, doesn't it?" said Penny, studying the water below. "Look at these fish. They're monsters to us because we don't like the look of them and they like the taste of us. But they're just acting naturally. They have no malice. They're surviving. Which is what I'm doing. Ensuring the survival of our planet. Throw them in now!"

Will grabbed the handrail. "What, for a daughter who hates you?"

Penny shot him a look of anger. "Watch your mouth!"

The captain gave him a push but he resisted, holding on tight to the rail.

"She hates you!" he spat out. "Why do you think she helped us escape?"

"Shut up! She wouldn't do that." Penny's eyes flared.

"Really? Who do you think had the spare key to the room?"

She looked pained like he'd never seen her before. "Push him in!" She barked. "Now!"

Suddenly Will headbutted the captain.

Fiona then gave him a sharp kick to the groin.

He groaned and buckled over.

Penny aimed the gun at them.

In the moment she pulled the trigger the boat lurched and she was thrown backwards over the handrail, the shot firing in the air and splintering the cabin above.

Will and Fiona were also thrown off their feet.

Fiona and Penny hit the choppy water at the same time making two splashes.

But Will had grabbed the rail and managed to stay on board.

Initially scared off by the commotion, three or four fish now turned and headed back towards the two women, their scaly backs breaking the surface of the waves.

Will dropped onto his stomach and reached down to Fiona.

He grabbed one of her wrists and tugged her upwards.

He then managed to grab the other arm and hauled her into the boat.

He dropped flat on the deck again to lean over and gesture to Penny with outstretched arms. "Grab my hands!" he shouted at her.

The captain dropped down next to him and reached out too.

Penny tried to swim towards them but was tossed around in the waves like a rag doll. Her hair was now bedraggled with weed. Her make-up was running. But her eyes flared with defiance.

One of the fish suddenly lunged towards her and clamped its enormous mouth around her left arm.

She yelled, half in pain but half in anger. She hit it repeatedly on the head with her free hand.

"We have to help her!" shouted Will, standing up and preparing to dive in.

Fiona grabbed him by the shirt. "Don't Will!"

But a split second later he was gone.

She watched in horror as he swam towards Penny, shouting at the creatures and lashing out at them as he went.

He grabbed her and pulled her to the side of the boat.

Two of the monstrous fish swam after them, their mouths gaping and the light of the boat glinting off their massive fangs.

The captain fired at the creatures' heads, making them flinch and giving Will enough time to grab the ladder hanging over the side of the boat and push Penny up it.

The captain and Fiona grabbed her arms and dragged her on board, her body limp.

Will scrambled up after her and flopped down beside her on deck, panting.

She turned her head towards him. "You...saved me."

He smiled. "Of course I did."

She motioned for him to come closer.

He propped himself up on one elbow and leant over her.

"Tell the ships..." she whispered softly, and lifted her head until her lips touched his ear.

"Munchkin."

Chapter Seventy-Nine

Three hours later Will, Fiona and Harold Tanner were on their third round of stiff drinks in the resort bar.

The drinks were more in bonding than in celebration and the mood was one of sombre relief. Like the three of them had just stopped a runaway train carrying explosives.

Will had immediately radioed Schulz with the abort code "Munchkin". By the time he'd returned to Penny her eyes were closed and her body was motionless. She had lost too much blood.

The captain had not said a word after the incident. He'd simply headed them back to the resort at full speed. Moments after tying up at the jetty he'd disappeared. They didn't care.

Will had not been able to explain his sadness at Penny's death to Fiona. They'd simply held each other tightly in silence during the short trip back.

The UN were now on site and an international investigation was under way.

Without Penny and Mackay the secret alliance among elements of the local police and government officials evaporated. Suddenly there were confessions everywhere as people raced to be the first to 'expose the truth', which meant saving themselves by blaming The Life Group and each other.

The police chief and fisheries minister were under arrest, as were several others who had accepted bribes from Mackay.

Penny's ships had all been stopped at sea, their crew placed in custody and their cargos confiscated. Captain Raj had been dealt with leniently due to the help he'd given.

"You look sad, Will," said Tanner, raising his glass of Bourbon. "We should be celebrating."

"I know," said Will smiling. "I'm sorry."

"What is it?" asked Fiona.

"I can't help thinking about Penny."

"The woman that tried to kill us? The woman that risked destroying the ecosystem of the planet with her hair-brained schemes?" said Fiona gently.

Will laughed. "That's the one yes. But look. I know she was mad. I know she was even evil in many ways. Certainly completely lacking in morals...."

"You can say that again, " said Fiona.

"And I know what she did led to your nephew – our friend's – death, Harold. And I'll never forgive that."

Tanner nodded.

"But even so...she got something half right. She was trying to stop global warming. She went about it the wrong way. But her goal was ....well...a noble one. She did what she did because none of the world leaders would act. They all paid lip service but did nothing. And we're still stuck with global warming as a result."

Tanner nodded again. Fiona shrugged but said nothing.

"And she was a massive presence. A force of nature. And even now she's gone she sort of leaves an impression. You know what I mean?"

"We might agree to disagree on that," said Tanner. "But we can certainly agree on one thing. The three of us deserve a medal. We stopped a juggernaut. Just us. We stopped a potential global disaster. So I propose a toast." He stood and raised his glass. "To us!"

They stood too and all clinked glasses. "To us!" they chorused.

They laughed and sat again. The atmosphere lifted and all three felt suddenly happy.

"I guess I have no right to feel this good," said Tanner reflectively. "I killed a man, after all."

"So did I," said Will glumly.

"But both of you are going to be exonerated right?" Fiona asked, concern in her voice. "There were extreme extenuating circumstances."

"Don't you worry," said Tanner confidently. "I have good lawyers. Your boss was right in that respect. Money can make a lot of things happen."

Chapter Eighty

F iona slipped her hand into Will's as they walked deeper into the Bavarian forest.

Bright rays of summer sunlight broke through the tall green canopy of fir trees and lit up the brown pine needles which coated the path and scrunched under foot.

The air was thick with the sweet aromatic scent of pine resin.

It was June, six months since the events at Nirvana Resort.

They had been highly praised by all and sundry for exposing the truth. The story they had told the media had gone all round the world, and for several weeks they had been celebrities, their faces and voices on TV shows and radio, and in newspapers, magazines and social media.

The Life Group was in the process of being broken up and its parts sold to competitor leisure companies and venture capitalists. Will had picked a job with one of them after several offers. Fiona had decided to take a break. There was talk of a wedding in the Autumn and starting a family. They were blissfully happy.

Harold Tanner's lawyers lived up to expectations and his and Will's pleas of justifiable homicide were accepted. He was not only a free man but was now suing The Life Group for negligence in the death of his nephew. He had also reached out to the family of the local man, Rahul, who had been attacked and was offering free legal advice so they too could claim compensation.

There had been no further sightings of the deep sea creatures and many had been found dead. A massive clean up operation had removed all the algae and dead sea life from the Indian Ocean. Thankfully the tester operation had not permanently damaged the ecosystem.

New international laws against dumping in the open oceans were due to come into force. But no steps had been taken to reduce global carbon emissions.

"Hey!" shouted Fiona suddenly, squeezing Will's hand I excitement. "I can see the lake! Let's go for a swim!"

Will held her back and laughed. "You've got to be joking! I told you - I'm not going anywhere near water ever again!"

But she pushed him away and started throwing off her clothes.

"Sure I can't tempt you?" she said, standing naked in front of him for a moment, then turning and running towards the lake.

He laughed again and started unbuttoning his shirt.

Chapter Eighty-One

Thousands of miles away in a familiar ocean the creature caught the scent of prey in the deep darkness.

It moved its scaly black tail and followed the trail.

The water flowed through its gills. It could breathe again. Here, back in its home world.

The water was thick and progress was slow.

Perhaps one day it would return to the lighter world above. Where the swimming was easy and the prey abundant.

Perhaps one day.

Printed in Great Britain
by Amazon

26694273R00219